INTRODUCING
KATIE MAGUIRE

KATIE MAGUIRE was one of seven sisters born
to a police Inspector in Cork, but the only
sister who decided to follow her father
into An Garda Síochána.

With her bright green eyes and short red
hair, she looks like an Irish pixie, but she is
no soft touch. To the dismay of some of her
male subordinates, she rose quickly through
the ranks, gaining a reputation for catching
Cork's killers, often at great personal cost.

Katie spent seven years in a turbulent
marriage in which she bore, and lost, a son –
an event that continues to haunt her. Despite
facing turmoil at home and prejudice at
work she is one of the most fearless
detectives in Ireland.

THE KATIE MAGUIRE SERIES

White Bones

Broken Angels

Red Light

Taken For Dead

Blood Sisters

Buried

Living Death

Dead Girls Dancing

Graham Masterton was a bestselling horror writer who has now turned his talent to crimewriting. He lived in Cork for five years, an experience that inspired the Katie Maguire series. Visit katiemaguire.co.uk

GRAHAM MASTERTON

DEAD GIRLS DANCING

HEAD
of
ZEUS

First published in the UK in 2017 by Head of Zeus Ltd

9 7 5 3 1 2 4 6 8

A CIP catalogue record for this book is available from the British Library.

ISBN (HB) 9781784976392
ISBN (TPB) 9781784976408
ISBN (E) 9781784976385

Typeset by Ben Cracknell Studios, Norwich.
Printed and bound by CPI Group (UK) Ltd, Croydon, CR0 4YY.

Head of Zeus Ltd
First Floor East
5–8 Hardwick Street
London EC1R 4RG

WWW.HEADOFZEUS.COM

Ná lasadh tine go bhfuil tú féin nach féidir a mhúchadh
(*Do not light a fire that you cannot put out yourself*)
Irish proverb

For Dan and Caroline,
Samuel and Lucy,
with love

One

They had just started dancing to 'Blackthorn Stick' when Catriona stumbled and stopped. She tugged at Brendan's sleeve so that he stopped dancing too. Little Aoife, who was right behind them, almost collided with him.

'What's wrong, girl?' Brendan shouted at her. He had to shout because the pipe and fiddle music was playing so loudly and the fourteen other dancers were rattling their hard shoes on the studio's parquet floor in 6/8 time, which echoed and re-echoed.

'Can you smell something *burning*?' Catriona shouted back.

Brendan and Aoife sniffed two or three times, but then Brendan said, 'Nah, Cat, it's car fumes, that's all it is.'

'*Car* fumes? It doesn't smell like car fumes to me.'

'Sure like, that's what it is! It's that Noonan fellow from the funeral director's next door! He's always leaving that old hearse of his running in case it gives up the ghost before he can drive it to the cemetery! I was almost fecking choked, coming in this morning!'

'Brendan? Catriona? Are you having a problem over there?' called their dance coach, Nicholas. He was standing next to the CD player on the opposite side of the room, one hand perched on his hip, holding up his mobile phone with the other. He was bald, Nicholas, with a neat white goatee beard and single diamond earring.

'No, there's no bother, Nicholas, we're grand altogether!' Brendan called back. He tapped his feet two or three times to catch up with the jig and carried on noisily dancing, and Aoife joined him. After a few steps, though, Aoife stopped again and wrinkled up her nose.

'I think you're right, do you know,' she shouted, leaning close to Catriona's ear. 'There's a funny smell for sure and it doesn't smell like Noonan's hearse to me! I can't see car fumes wafting all the way up the stairs like, either, can you?'

Catriona took in a deep breath, and then another, and then nodded. 'It's getting stronger, too, isn't it? I don't know. It's like that bang you get off of Murphy's Brewery, but a bit more burnt-like.'

She was going to wave to Nicholas, but then she saw that he was down on one knee, busy helping Sinéad to fix a loose buckle on her shoe. He looked as if he were proposing to her – not that he would be, since he was married to his partner Tadhg already. She told Aoife, 'I'll just go and take a sconce like.'

She walked briskly across the studio to the door that led to the stairs, her hard shoes clacking on the floor. She was a tall, skinny girl, pale-faced and freckly, with a mass of curly red hair that she tied up with a ribbon on top of her head, so that she never usually needed a bun wig for dancing. This morning she was wearing a plain emerald-green dance dress and no make-up, but this was only a practice session, after all.

As she approached the door, Nicholas stood up and switched off the CD player. The jig abruptly stopped and so did the castanet clatter of fibreglass toes and heels.

'Your shuffles are *way* out of synch!' Nicholas protested. 'Jesus, you sound like rabbits on a tin roof! That's because some of you aren't swinging your back legs nearly as high as I showed you for the double click. Come on, you know who you are! So – let's start over!'

Now that the studio was quiet, Catriona could hear a strange breathing noise from the other side of the door, with a rustling undertone, like wind blowing dry autumn leaves down a tunnel.

'Cat? Where are you going, girl?' called Nicholas. 'Not giving up on us, are you?'

'There's kind of a smoky smell, Nick,' she told him. 'I was going to see where it was coming from.'

Nicholas sniffed, but then he said, 'No. I can't smell nothing myself. Mind you, I'm still bunged up with a bit of a cold like.'

'I told you,' said Brendan. 'It's Noonan, warming up his hearse. I reckon he wants to spifflicate us all, so he gets more customers.'

Catriona took hold of the doorknob, but instantly plucked her hand away and said, 'Holy Saint Joseph!' because it was hot – hot as a just-boiled kettle.

'When you're *quite* ready, Catriona!' said Nicholas.

Catriona tugged down the long right sleeve of her dance dress so that it covered her hand. She turned the doorknob and pulled the door open wide, but the instant she did so she was buffeted from behind her by a blustering gust of wind, as if an impatient ghost were trying to hurry past her into the stairwell. It made her dress flap and her curls fly up, and it made an uncanny whistling sound, partly doleful and partly triumphant.

Catriona saw that the stairwell was hazy with light grey smoke, but as the air was sucked into it from the studio it exploded with a deafening *boofff!* into a rolling orange inferno. Fire roared in through the door and rushed across the ceiling and Catriona screamed as she was swallowed by flames. All the other dancers screamed and shouted, too, as they were blasted by a scorching gale. Some of them dropped to their knees, others covered their faces with their hands and staggered blindly into each other.

Within seconds, everything flammable in the studio was ablaze and the temperature was climbing so high that the dancers felt as if they were breathing in nothing but suffocating heat. The green nylon curtains were being frizzled up by lascivious orange flames, the padded chairs along the sides of the dance floor were smouldering and pouring out smoke, and even the polish on the parquet was starting to crackle. The wall mirror at the end of the room creaked loudly and then suddenly split diagonally from side to side.

Catriona was on fire from head to foot. She was beating at her face and her chest with jerky, drumstick movements and hopping around and around in a terrible parody of a treble jig. Her red curls had all shrivelled away, except for a few on the crown of her head where her hair was thickest, which were burning like birthday-cake candles. Her freckly white face was already charred into a black demon mask, with deep scarlet fissures across her forehead and around her eyes. Most of her dress had burned into flakes and even her black heavy shoes were on fire.

By now the air in the studio was not only blistering hot but it was quickly filling up with thick, choking smoke. The dancers were milling around in a panic, their shoes clattering on the floor.

'*Stay together!*' shrieked Nicholas. '*Hold hands everybody! Stay together!*'

Even though he was coughing and whining for breath, Brendan tugged off the pale blue cotton sweater that was tied around his waist and held it up in front of him, trying to get close enough to Catriona to wrap it around her and smother the flames. Before he could reach her, though, she pitched sideways on to the floor, knocking her head with a hollow *clonk*. She rolled on to her back and lay there with her clothes smoking and her legs shuddering and her arms crossed in front of her as if she were praying.

Brendan knelt down beside her and tentatively held out his hand towards her, but he could tell from her bloodshot eyes that she couldn't see him and she was too close to death for him to be able to save her. He crossed himself, and coughed, and then stood up. Shielding his face with his sweater, he blundered his way through the smoke and the flying sparks to join the others.

'Up to the attic, everybody!' Nicholas was screaming, his voice hoarse from inhaling smoke. 'We can't get out down the stairs, so we'll have to go up to the attic! Patrick! Help Niamh up, will you? Ciara, this way, love. Come on everybody, *quick*! And *stay together*!'

He was flapping his arms and ushering everybody to the far end of the studio where a small door led up to the attic. Brendan had been up there only once, helping Nicholas to store some old boxes of dance costumes, but he knew it had a dormer window that overlooked the corner of Shandon Street so they would be able to open it and shout for help.

Brendan glanced back at Catriona. By now he could hardly see her through the smoke, but she was still lying on her back,

4

motionless, and she was surrounded by a circle of flames as if she were lying on a funeral pyre.

Young Duncan with the spiky black hair was right beside him, almost bent double and coughing up long strings of phlegm. Brendan caught hold of the back of Duncan's belt in one hand and his shirt sleeve in the other and dragged him jerking and tripping towards the end of the room. The rest of the dancers were crowded together now, jostling each other in panic as Nicholas fumbled with his keyring, trying to find the key that would unlock the attic door. There were some muffled moans, and sobs, but none of the dancers was screaming or crying out. The smoke was too acrid for them to breathe in and most of them had their hands pressed over their faces, as if they were going to speak no evil.

As Nicholas found the right key, the flames in the studio suddenly sank lower, like a pack of mutinous dogs that had been ordered to lie down. The crackling of burning varnish was reduced to a few sporadic pops. There was a breathless tension in the room, interrupted only by the clicking of Nicholas turning the key in the lock.

Holy Blessed Mary, thought Brendan. The fire seemed to have burned itself out and they were going to be saved. With his lungs almost bursting from holding his breath, he lugged Duncan towards the attic door just as Nicholas swung it wide open.

With a gleeful whistle, air rushed down from the attic upstairs and the studio instantly exploded with even more ferocity than before, so that the whole room was filled to the ceiling with roaring flames. Brendan felt a blast of heat on the back of his neck and then his hair caught alight, although he didn't realize it. For a few seconds, Nicholas and his dancers were all swallowed up by a turmoil of orange fire. When they reappeared, they were all blazing from head to foot, screaming and flapping their arms.

They danced a hideous mockery of the 'Blackthorn Stick' with burned flakes of hair and clothing flying around them and their hard shoes clattering on the parquet like a death-rattle. It was like a *feis* held in hell.

One after another, they staggered and collided and dropped to the floor, and lay there burning. The fire appeared to feed on them, but it also seemed to grow hungrier with each dancer it consumed. With a soft roaring sound it passed over them and began to climb the attic stairs, setting the sisal stair carpet alight step by step, as if it could smell somebody else up there and was greedily searching for them.

Two

Katie was running through her quarterly budget figures with Chief Superintendent MacCostagáin when she heard the sirens from the fire station next door.

She thought nothing of it at first and they went on discussing how she could adjust her detectives' rosters in order to save money. She needed to recruit more detectives, too, because Detective Sergeant Lynch and Detective Ó Broin were due to retire in the spring, and she didn't yet have any newly graduated detective gardaí to replace them.

'There's no getting around it, Katie, the ministry's whittled us clean down to the bone,' said Chief Superintendent MacCostagáin. He dragged out a handkerchief and loudly blew his nose. 'All the same, though, we'll have to work out some way of saving the shekels, even if we have to sell all our cars and drive around in steerinahs.' He was referring to children's home-made steering-carts.

'I don't mind that.' Katie smiled. 'My first boyfriend used to pull me around in his steerinah and I loved it. I was four and he was six. Dalaigh, his name was, and he always smelled of toffee. Or maybe it was wee, and I was just being romantic.'

Now they heard another siren, and another, and Chief Superintendent MacCostagáin raised a bushy grey eyebrow at her. 'Sounds like trouble, that.'

He reached across to pick up his phone. but as he did so Katie's mobile played *'Fear a' Bháta'*. She took it out of the inside pocket of her jacket and answered it. It was Detective Sergeant Begley calling her.

'I expect you've heard the fire engines going out, ma'am. There's a major fire at the Toirneach Damhsa dance studio, ma'am. That's down at the bottom of Shandon Street, by Farren's Quay, right next to Jer Noonan's funeral home. The station officer just called me and said that there's people trapped.'

'Did he tell you how many?'

'He didn't know exactly, but it seems like there was a full dance rehearsal going on, so I'd guess there must have been eight at least. They've sent out six appliances already and Assistant Chief Fire Officer Whalen has gone out there, too.'

'Superintendent Pearse is on to it?'

'He is of course. He's sent Inspector Cafferty along there to supervise. The ambulance service has been called out, too, as well as the Red Cross, in case they need any extra white vans.'

Katie covered her iPhone with her hand and said to Chief Superintendent MacCostagáin, 'There's a fire at the bottom of Shandon Street. A dance studio, with people trapped. Maybe as many as eight.' Then she took her hand away and spoke to Detective Sergeant Begley again.

'Did the station officer tell you who raised the alarm?' she asked him.

'Just some passer-by, so he said. They saw flames inside of the windows and smoke pouring out of the roof. Actually, there were seventeen 112 calls altogether, almost simultaneous like. All of their numbers have been recorded, if we need to check them later.'

'All right, Sean, thank you. Are you going over there yourself?'

'I am, sure. I'll be taking O'Donovan and Markey along with me.'

'Keep me up to date, then, okay?'

Katie closed her accounts book and stood up. 'I'd best be getting out there, too. The media will be there in force, for sure, and if the fire brigade are sending out their major incident officer, it would be a good idea if I showed my face as well.'

'Jesus,' said Chief Superintendent MacCostagáin. 'If there's one thing that gives me the heebie-jeebies, it's the idea of being trapped in a burning building. That was the way my Uncle Phelim died. Well, he wasn't trapped, he was conked out, but the result was the same.'

'What happened to him?' asked Katie, as she gathered up her purse and her pen and her notebook.

'He was wrecked as usual. He fell into bed, lit a cigarette and dropped off to sleep. He was a big fellow all right, but my aunt said that when they found him he looked like a little charcoal monkey.'

'I'll see you after so,' said Katie. She walked quickly along to her office and lifted down her crackly yellow high-viz jacket from the coat-stand. The day looked grey and breezy outside, but it wasn't raining yet. Six or seven hooded crows were clustered on the roof of the building opposite, their feathers ruffled by the wind. Katie wasn't superstitious, but she didn't like it when they gathered like that – it always seemed to precede some disaster.

On her way out she stopped at the door of the squad room and called over to Detective Dooley.

'Robert! I'm going across to that fire at Shandon Street! Come with me, will you?'

He reached for his high-viz jacket, but Katie said, 'Don't worry about that. I don't want you looking conspicuous like.'

Detective Dooley was the youngest male detective on her team, with brushed-up hair and jeggings and the fresh-faced look of a college student, although he had just celebrated his twenty-fourth birthday. One of the reasons she wanted him along was because he was good at mingling with crowds of all ages, especially with younger people. When it came to serious fires, the firefighters dealt with the flames, while Katie's detectives concentrated their attention on the people who were watching them. Over three-quarters of arsonists hung around the buildings they had torched because it excited them to see them burn.

Detective Dooley followed Katie to the lifts, half-skipping to keep up with her.

'They're reporting it live on RedFM, the fire,' he told her, as the lift sank down to the ground floor. 'They were also talking on the phone to the fellow who manages the dance troupe – Danny Coffey? He said there were seventeen people in the building at least, sixteen dancers and their instructor. They were holding a last full rehearsal before next week's *feis*.'

'Danny Coffey, yes,' said Katie. 'I've heard of him. He started off with Michael Flatley, didn't he? What's the latest? Have any of the dancers managed to get out of there?'

'Not so far as the reporter could tell, and we've had no update from Inspector Cafferty yet, either.'

They quickly crossed the shiny-floored reception area towards the door that gave out on to the car park. They had nearly reached it when Katie caught the glint of the glass front doors being pushed open, and when she turned her head she saw Conor Ó Máille coming into the station.

Mother of God, she thought. *Not now. And not in front of Dooley.*

Conor caught sight of her at once and walked straight past the sergeant on the front desk. His dark brown beard was freshly trimmed and he was wearing a long olive-green raincoat and polished tan brogues. As he approached, Katie stopped and waited for him, although Detective Dooley took two or three paces back. Like everybody else in Anglesea Street, he knew that something had been going on between Katie and Conor. He had also heard that Conor's wife had come into the station looking for him.

'Katie?' said Conor. He had a complicated look on his face, part pleading and part aggressive. Six-year-old Dalaigh with his steerinah might have smelled of toffee or wee, but Conor smelled of Chanel Bleu aftershave. His eyes were mahogany brown.

'I'm on an urgent call-out, Conor,' said Katie, lifting up both lapels of her high-viz jacket to emphasize the obvious. 'You must have heard the sirens.'

'I have of course. I just needed to talk to you.'

'I need to talk to you, too. About the dog-fighting mainly. But it'll have to wait until I get back. There's people trapped apparently.'

'All right,' said Conor. 'What will you do, ring me?'

'Are you still at the Gabriel guest house?'

'I am, yes, but I'll be going back to Limerick tomorrow.'

'You and Mrs Ó Máille?' said Katie, although she immediately wished that she hadn't.

'Katie—' Conor began, lifting his hand towards her.

'I'll ring you later so,' Katie told him. 'Meanwhile I have to go. There's people trapped in a much more critical situation than you and me.'

* * *

They could see the dark pall of smoke hanging over the river as soon as they turned into Merchants Quay, and when they crossed Patrick's Bridge they could see the blue lights flashing and the six fire appliances clustered on the pedestrian precinct in front of the Toirneach Damhsa dance studio. Jer Noonan, the undertaker, had moved his hearse further up Shandon Street to be out of the firefighters' way and it was parked on the sloping corner of North Abbey Street with a dark oak coffin still inside it, and white roses spelling out DAD. A crowd of at least two or three hundred sightseers had gathered on the opposite side of the Griffith Bridge, and there were more along the North Mall on the same side of the river, but they were being held well back by Garda patrol cars parked diagonally across the road. Four ambulances were already lined up under the trees and Katie could see two more speeding on their way, their blue lights flashing along Bachelor's Quay.

The blue-painted Friary pub on the corner had been evacuated, but one drinker was still standing in the open doorway smoking a cigarette and holding a pint of stout, seemingly oblivious to the crisis all around him.

As Katie climbed out of her car, she was overwhelmed by the noise of diesel engines roaring and firefighters shouting and the blasting of high-pressure hoses. Thick grey smoke blew past her and out across the river, and it carried a pungent smell of burned wood and plastic, and some other smell, too, which reminded her horribly of barbecues. Three ladders had been raised up against the white-painted façade of the dance studio building, two at the front and one in the alley at the side. The firefighters at the front had smashed the studio windows and were spraying the interior with powerful jets of water. The firefighter at the side was wrenching a rusted wire-mesh screen off the window frame so that he could gain access to the first-floor landing.

Smoke was billowing out of the windows and the roof, speckled with orange sparks. Katie could see that some of the rafters must have burned through, because the grey slates had collapsed in the middle, and even as she was looking up at it the dormer window dropped out of sight behind the façade.

Katie watched Detective Dooley cross the road to infiltrate the crowds and then she carefully stepped over the coils of red fire hoses to join Assistant Chief Fire Officer Whalen, who was standing close by with two of his fellow officers. She could see that several reporters were standing on the corner of Farren's Quay watching her – Fionnuala Sweeney from RTÉ, Fergus O'Farrell from RedFM, Jean Mulligan from the *Evening Echo* and a freelance called Jimmy McCracken, who would probably be phoning the story in to the *Examiner*. If Katie had showed up, that confirmed to the media how serious this was.

'What's the story, Matthew?' she asked Assistant Chief Fire Officer Whalen.

Matthew Whalen was a big, stout man whose neck bulged over his collar and whose uniform belt strained around his belly. His cheeks were so scarlet that they looked as if they had been scorched from years of firefighting, and his ginger moustache and ginger eyebrows both bristled as if they had just burst into flame. Although he looked so explosive, Katie had worked with him before on several major incidents, including floods and gas leaks and building collapses, and she knew him to be steady and calm and highly experienced.

'Ah, Katie, how's it hanging? So far as we know like, there are seventeen persons altogether in the first-floor dance studio. That's sixteen dancers and their instructor. We haven't seen a sign of any of them yet. It's unusually intense, this fire, I can tell you, and it's going to take us a few more minutes at least before we can safely gain entry. The trouble is, the stairs have collapsed so we're having to go in through the windows, and of course that's feeding the fire more oxygen.'

Katie could see that flames were still leaping up and down inside the studio, as if they were mischievously taunting the firefighters were who trying to extinguish them.

'Any notion yet what might have started it?'

Matthew Whalen shrugged. 'I'm jumping to no conclusions about that. Once they catch alight, these old buildings have a tendency to heat up fierce quick, do you know, like a Boru stove. They've thick walls on the outside, all right, but inside they're all wormy wood and varnish and ill-fitting doors. But like I say, this fire's unusually intense. Without committing meself, though, let's just say that it wouldn't totally surprise me at all if we find out that it was set deliberate.'

Through the drifting grey smoke, Katie could see that the firefighter at the side of the building had now levered out the window frame and dropped it with a splintering crash into the alley below. Wearing breathing apparatus, and boosted up from behind by another two firefighters, he climbed off the top of his ladder and in through the landing window.

At the front of the building the firefighters were hosing down the last of the flames inside the studio. So much smoke was billowing out of the main windows that at times they completely disappeared from sight.

'I'm holding out very little hope of survivors,' said Matthew Whalen. 'Jim here questioned some of the witnesses as soon as he arrived and none of them saw anybody waving at the windows or any other sign of life.'

Third Officer Phelan nodded. 'Flames, that's all they could see. One of them said that it looked like hell in there. They couldn't hear nobody screaming or shouting for help, neither.'

Inspector Cafferty had been supervising the crowd control, but now he came over and stood beside Katie. He was lean and thin and serious, with a beaky nose and a mole on his chin. 'How are you going on, ma'am? Mother of God, this is desperate, isn't it? I'd say that this is the worst fire I've ever witnessed, bar none. I mean, that blaze last month at the N-Steak House was bad enough, but at least nobody got hurt. I hope to God that some of the poor wretches got out of there somehow, but I don't think there's too much chance of it.'

It was starting to spit with rain, very lightly, so when Katie raised her eyes to the top of the building she shielded her face with her hand. She didn't exactly know why she looked up. Maybe it was the lurching sound of more rafters collapsing and the rattle of slates sliding into the attic. But she was sure she saw something dark bob over the top of the parapet. At first she thought it might have been a pigeon, but it seemed unlikely that a pigeon would settle on top of a burning building. Maybe she had glimpsed nothing more than the end of a fire-charred rafter toppling over, although it had seemed more rounded than that. It could have been a chimney-cowl.

She was about to turn away to see what progress Detective Dooley was making in the crowd when the dark object bobbed up again, and this time it stayed in sight. To Katie's horror, it was the head of a child, a little girl, with a white face and dark eyes and dark, braided hair. Almost everybody else's attention was on the first-floor windows where five firefighters with breathing apparatus were now climbing inside, dragging their hoses in after them. But the little girl continued to stare down at Katie, though she didn't cry out and she didn't wave.

'*Matthew! Look!*' said Katie, seizing Matthew Whalen's sleeve and pointing up at the parapet.

'Jesus Christ Almighty!' said Matthew, as soon as he saw the girl looking down at them. 'Jim! Patrick! There's a kid up there!'

Third Officer Phelan was on to his radio immediately. 'Charlie Two! Charlie Two! Back yourself up to the front of the property and get that aerial platform hoisted up! Make a bust, will you? There's a wain stuck up on the roof!'

The firefighters hurriedly cleared the pavement in front of the studio building. Their Mercedes-Benz aerial platform appliance had been parked further along the quay, but now it started up with a bellow and reversed right up to the front door, in between the two ladders that were already propped against the studio windows. With two firefighters standing in it, the platform was raised with a high hydraulic whine, and within less than two minutes they had reached the parapet. Katie stepped back so that she could see more clearly, but there was still thick smoke blowing out of the studio and every now and then it blotted out her view of the roof completely.

At last, however, she saw one of the firefighters standing on the roof. He lifted the girl out of the gutter behind the parapet where she had been crouching and between them he and his companion carefully lowered her into the platform. As the firefighters brought her down there was clapping and cheering and whistling from the crowds along the quays.

Two paramedics from the Mercy hurried a trolley forward and the girl was helped up on to it. Katie guessed that she was about nine years old. She was very thin and leggy, wearing skinny black tights and a baggy pink cotton top with a sad-faced rabbit appliquéd on the front of it. Her face was smudged with soot and she was coughing, so the paramedics placed an oxygen mask over her face.

Katie leaned over her, taking hold of her hand and giving her a reassuring smile. The girl stared at her with huge brown eyes, although they were reddened from the smoke and her eyelashes were stuck together with tears.

'You're safe now, sweetheart,' Katie told her. 'These nice people will take you to the hospital just to make sure you can breathe all right. I'll come and talk to you later when you're feeling better.'

The girl continued to stare at her and coughed inside her oxygen mask.

'Do you think you can manage one thing for me now?' Katie asked her. 'Do you think you can tell me what your name is?'

One of the paramedics lifted the mask up from the girl's face so that she could speak, but all she did was stare at Katie and then start coughing again. The paramedic put the mask back again.

'That's not a bother,' said Katie. 'Wait till you're well. I'll see you after so.'

The paramedics wheeled the girl away and lifted her into the back of their ambulance. The rest of the ambulances were still parked in line, but although the smoke was gradually beginning to clear it seemed less and less likely that they would be taking any more survivors away to hospital.

'Jesus, she looks about the same age as my own daughter, Orla,' said Inspector Cafferty as the ambulance sped away. 'God alone knows how she got herself out of there.'

'I can't imagine,' said Katie. 'How was she able to climb up on to the roof but nobody else managed it? Maybe they all shut themselves in another room somewhere and they're all unharmed. Well, I hope so, anyway.'

She had hardly said that when Matthew Whalen came over to her, grim-faced, holding up his radio.

'Bad news, I'm afraid, Katie. There's a rake of bodies in the dance studio and as far as they're able to count they reckon there's seventeen of them altogether. It looks like they tried to escape up into the attic but they never made it.'

'Seventeen? That must be practically the whole dance troupe,' said Inspector Cafferty. 'Mother of God, we saw them performing at the Opera House only this summer, the Toirneach Damhsa. They were fantastic.'

'Well, Inspector, I'm afraid they've danced their last jig now,' said Matthew Whalen. He took off his cap and wiped the perspiration from his forehead with the back of his hand. 'The next person they're going to be entertaining is the state pathologist.'

Three

'I'd say that's well alight now, wouldn't you?' said Liam O'Breen. 'It wouldn't surprise me at all if the fire brigade isn't breaking out the sausages.'

Niall Gleeson said nothing, but took a last deep drag on his cigarette butt and then flicked it across the steeply sloping car park.

They were standing in front of the Templegate Tavern on Gurranabraher Road, watching the dark grey smoke rising from Farren's Quay, down in the city far below them. Liam was just twenty-one, pale-faced and podgy. His head was shaved at the sides so that his curly ears stuck out, but he had a mass of wavy brown hair on top, thick with dandruff. He was wearing a green GAA sweatshirt and baggy grey tracksuit trousers from Champion Sports.

Niall was in his mid-thirties, although he looked older because his short-cropped hair was already turning grey. He was dressed in a bottle-green tweed jacket and black waistcoat, and dark grey trousers with turn-ups. He was short, with a thick bullish neck, and his eyes were always narrowed as if he were thinking hard, or focusing on some point miles in the distance.

'Davy should be back soon,' said Liam. It was starting to spit with rain, and he held out his hand and looked up at the clouds.

'Did he say he was coming back?' Niall replied. 'You can never tell for sure with Davy. He's one cute hoor, that fellow.'

'He's okay. He's promised to get me a Glock.'

'What? A fecking Glock? I wouldn't trust you with a scuttering gun full of piss, let alone a fecking Glock.'

'Oh g'way,' grinned Liam, but Niall wasn't smiling.

The smoke from the dance studio fire was now piling up nearly three hundred metres into the air so that it was mingling with the low grey clouds. As Liam and Niall were about to go back into the pub, a white Garda helicopter appeared from the north-east and started to circle with a monotonous clattering drone over the quays.

'You have to give Davy one thing,' said Liam. 'He doesn't do things by halves.'

'He's a fecking header, if you ask me.'

'Maybe he is like, but maybe we need somebody mad for a change, do you know what I mean? And he's *political* mad. Like Bobby was mad all right, but all Bobby cared about was raking in the grade. The politics was just an excuse as far as Bobby was concerned. Not Davy.'

'What the feck do you know about politics, buke? And don't speak ill of the dead. Bobby Quilty was fierce crabbit so he was. You haven't the brains of a dying hen compared to him.'

'I know about the Potato Famine and the Easter Rising and the Tan War. Learned about them in meánscoil.'

'What you need to learn is how to stop making out you're so fecking clever and keep your bake shut.'

They were about to go back into the pub when a silver-grey Mercedes convertible came round the corner from Cathedral Road and parked in front of the Paddy Power bookmaker's next door. A young man in a smart black waterproof jacket climbed out, reaching back inside for a briefcase. Then he came towards them, not smiling or raising his hand in greeting, but when he came close enough he said, 'How's it going on, lads?'

'Oh, grand altogether, Davy, how's yourself?' said Liam. Niall said nothing. He was at least seven years older than Davy and he didn't like being included in 'lads'.

Davy was Black Irish handsome, with tousled hair that curled over his collar and the angular, straight-nosed features of a male magazine model, with fashionable stubble. His eyes were grey, but instead of being seductively twinkling they always seemed to be challenging, even aggressive, bright and hard as two nail-heads. He rarely stayed still – Niall complained that he was always jumping around like a fiddler's elbow – but he carried himself with an air of self-assurance that Niall in particular found more than simply irritating: he found it threatening. From the way Davy walked, he was obviously very fit. He didn't smoke and he didn't spend hours in the tavern with the rest of them, shooting pool and drinking Murphy's with Paddy's chasers and telling filthy stories.

He wasn't a stranger to Cork by any means. He had grown up in Gurra, and Niall had known him when he was a small boy. They had both gone to Scoil Padre Pio. But Davy's family had moved to the North when he was about nine or ten, to the port of Larne, in County Antrim, and he had returned to Cork only seven months ago. All the same, his relatives and friends around Mount Nebo Avenue had welcomed him back as if he had only been away for a two-week holiday.

'So it all went off to plan?' asked Niall.

'What?' said Davy, distractedly, checking his iPhone.

'I said, it all went off to plan like?'

Davy prodded his phone screen and then nodded towards the smoke rising from the city. 'You can see for yourself, can't you, sham?'

'But you had no problems? Nobody lamped you?'

'You're calling me some kind of a fecking amateur, is that it?'

'Go easy, will you? I'm only wanting to know if you had any trouble.'

'If I'd had any trouble I wouldn't be here, would I? It's all dealt with, anyway. There won't be any evidence and we can make a start with planning what we're going to doing next.'

They went inside the pub and sat at the round table in the corner next to the mahogany screen with the stained-glass windows. It was gloomy inside and smelled of stale beer, and although it wasn't particularly crowded it was noisy. Two local boys were playing pool and whooping whenever they potted a ball, and there was loud music playing on the radio from Cork Music Station, Nathan Carter singing 'Don't Know Lonely'.

Two other men were already sitting at the table with half-finished pints in front of them – Murtagh McCourt, a bald, granite-faced character with his four front teeth missing and a tight grey chimp jacket, and Billy Ó Griobhta, who looked like a skeletal Elvis Presley, with sunken-in cheeks and a high pompadour hairstyle combed into a duck's arse at the back.

As tough as he appeared to be, however, Murtagh spoke with a cultured Montenotte accent; and although Billy Ó Griobhta barely spoke at all, he nodded meaningfully whenever Davy or Murtagh or Niall was talking, his quiff bobbing up and down, and it was clear that he could follow what they meant.

'We have a clean slate now, lads,' said Davy. 'All the loose ends have been tied up and all the babbling tongues have been hushed. We have the business side tidy and ticking over like clockwork and the shades off our backs. Now we can start thinking strategy.'

Without being asked, the young barman brought over four fresh pints of Murphy's, but he passed Davy a bottle of apple-and-pear MiWadi, no alcohol and no calories.

'Good man yourself,' said Davy to the barman, but he offered no money and no money was asked for.

'We can start *thinking* about strategy, for sure,' said Niall. 'But for the time being, I think it would make sense for us to keep our heads down like, do you know what I mean? We could gradually build up our funds and our munitions, and you can't say that we couldn't use a few more volunteers. At least a dozen of our fellers in Cork just melted away after Bobby went to higher service, and maybe twice that number in Belfast.'

Davy swigged at his bottle of MiWadi. 'They melted away because they were self-serving sublas, only in it for the money, and not at all political.'

'Davy's right,' said Murtagh, in a dry voice with a slight whistle to it because of his lack of teeth. It sounded like the wind blowing across the sand at Kinsale Beach. 'Scummers like that can't be trusted, especially if the SDU sniffs them out. They never admit it in public like, but the SDU have more than a million euros a year to pay off informants, and what do you think those scummers are going to do if they're offered the choice between a couple of thousand in their bank account or a couple of years in Rathmore Road? They'd rat you out as soon as spit in your drink.'

'I still think we need to stall the beans,' said Niall. 'Whatever we decide to do, we're going to need more fellows with technical expertise, not to mention transport, and communications, and surveillance, and contingency arrangements if things go arseways. Come on, Davy, it's not like it used to be, during the seventies. It's all technomological now. The shades these days can be listening in to your phone calls before you've even decided who you're going to ring.'

'Well, you're right that it's not like the seventies,' said Davy. 'But technology works both ways, sham. We can use it to our advantage just like the shades can use it to theirs. We don't need half the personnel that we used to, back then. We can tell when somebody's tracking us, and we can jam their signals. We can use those untraceable phones. And we can use weapons and chemicals that can't be identified by forensics. We're not farm-boys these days, with shotguns and belted raincoats.'

'I never said we were like,' said Niall. 'I'm just saying that we need to be doggy wide and not go off at half-cock, like the Doyle twins. They were in your class at school, remember, the Doyle twins? Now one of them's dead and the other's been in jail more times than the warden.'

'That's because each of them was thicker than the other. Eddie Doyle thought that thermometers were invented by Freddie Mercury.'

'But what's the urgency? We've been fighting this fight since 1921. A few more months isn't going to make much of a difference.'

Davy swallowed another mouthful of MiWadi and wiped his mouth with the back of his hand. 'You don't get it, do you? When the English voted to leave the European Union, that changed everything. The North voted to stay in the EU, along with us, but now they're going to be forced to leave even though they don't want to. That means the border between us won't just be a line where the road signs change from kilometres to miles, not any more – now it's going to be a real border again, between the EU and Britain, with customs posts and guards. That makes no fecking sense at all, either politically or economically or any other way.'

He leaned forward across the table and stared at Niall as if he were talking to a stupid child. 'Don't you have any fecking notion what an incredible moment in history this is? This is the time for us to say, North and South, we're *all* Irish, and we don't want that kind of a barrier set up between us. This is the time for us to be united, at long last. A chance like this may never come again in centuries, after you and me are long dead and buried. If the Brits can take their country back, then so the feck can we. But we have to strike *now*, while the iron is still red-hot and we have the public opinion back with us.'

'C'm'ere, you have some scheme in mind, don't you, boy?' said Murtagh, tapping his forehead with his nicotine-stained fingertip and grinning with his gappy teeth.

Davy nodded emphatically. 'They said on the news last night that the British defence secretary will be coming over to Dublin next week to discuss how the border's going to be managed from now on, and then he's coming down here to Cork to inspect the naval base at Haulbowline and talk about NATO.'

'So?'

'So I've already spoken to Bobby's old friend Roy McCreesh in Andersonstown. He could send some fellers down that nobody here would recognize.'

'Roy McCreesh?' said Niall, wrinkling up his nose. 'That trick-of-the-loop?'

'You can call him what you like, but he has all the contacts, especially in the PSNI.'

'Are you thinking of trying to do what I think you're thinking of trying to do? You're out of your fecking senses if you are.'

'What else could unite this country in one single stroke? Tell me, go on, and the answer is nothing else at all, not like this. What do you think the boys of the old brigade would say if we pulled this off? What if we managed to do what Liam Lynch couldn't do, nor Mary MacSwiney, nor Éamon de Valera, nor Martin McGuinness nor Gerry Adams, nor any Irish patriot, ever?'

'You're stone-hatchet mad,' Niall told him. 'What do you think the security's going to be like around the British defence secretary? You wouldn't be able to get within a country mile of him. And even if you did, can you imagine what would happen afterwards? The pigs would be tearing the whole country apart looking for us, sod by sod, and they'd probably make sure we got a bullet in the back of the head before they took us to court.'

Davy said, 'There you go again, sham, talking to me like I'm wet behind the ears—'

But Niall was in full flow now, and angry, and he interrupted him. 'No! I don't think you're wet behind the ears! I think you're fecking cracked! I can tell you this here and now, Davy: I know how fierce your feelings are, politically, and I'm not saying that I don't subscribe to them myself. I know your grandfather was standing right next to Liam Lynch on Knockmealdown mountain when your man was shot, and Lynch's blood was spattered on him. You've told me enough fecking times. But this is the twenty-first century, not 1923, and political arguments don't get solved by orders of frightfulness like they did in the past. You can count me out of this, and I'll tell you something else: if I get wind that you and McCreesh are trying to set it up between you, I'll make sure that it's scotched, one way or another. Trust me.'

Davy opened his mouth and raised one finger stiffly, as if he were about to snap back at him. Instead, though, he relaxed and sat back in his chair and said, 'All right, Niall. Fair play to you, sham. If that's the way you feel. I don't want to have an argument with you. Fighting among ourselves, that's not the way we're going to get what we want.'

'We're not going to get what we want by blowing up British politicians, either.'

'Why don't you let me stand you another scoop?' said Davy. He was smiling, but the look in his eyes was even harder than usual.

Niall drained the last of his pint and checked his watch. 'No, I have to drive on. I promised Mairead I'd pick up young Sinead from the nursery school.'

'Ah well, I reckon I'd better be out the gap, too,' said Davy. 'I'll ring you so, and then we can talk about this some more.'

'You won't change my mind, Davy,' said Niall. 'The old days are gone. We have to get what we want with persuasion, not with bullets.'

'Like I say, we can talk about this some other time,' Davy told him. Both he and Niall stood up, while Murtagh signalled to the barman to bring them another three pints of Murphy's.

* * *

It was raining hard when Niall climbed into his navy-blue Ford Mondeo, which was parked right outside the pub entrance. Davy saluted him and then ran over to his Mercedes, with his jacket collar turned up. Niall started his engine and backed into Gurranabraher Road, and then headed north. A few seconds later, Davy started his engine, too, and followed him.

Niall slowed down for the roundabout where Gurranabraher Road ended and carried straight on up Knockfree Avenue. Davy had been keeping fifty or sixty metres behind him, but as he neared the nursery school he flashed his headlights.

At first Niall didn't see him, so he flashed his headlights again. Now Niall drew in to the side of the road and Davy pulled in close behind him. On the left side of the road there was nothing but allotments, and on the right side there was nothing but open parkland. It was raining harder than ever now and both the parkland and the allotments were deserted. The grey clouds were hurrying overhead as if they were late for an urgent appointment.

Davy climbed out of his Mercedes and walked quickly up to Niall's Mondeo, with his shoulders hunched. He rapped on the window and Niall let it down.

'What's wrong?' asked Niall, giving Davy his hard, long-distance look.

'*You*, sham,' said Davy. 'That's what's wrong. You yourself.'

'What the feck are you talking about? I'm late picking up Sinead.'

'Let's put it this way, shall I? Liam Lynch didn't die so that funky fellows like you could let him down.'

'Oh, go feck your granny, will you? I've heard enough about Liam Lynch to bore me into an early grave.'

Davy stood straight and looked up and down the avenue. When he was sure there was nobody in sight, he tugged a black Glock automatic pistol out of his inside pocket, pointed it at Niall's forehead, and fired. It was fitted with a silencer, but the bang was still loud. The bullet hit Niall between his eyebrows and the back of his head exploded so that blood and lumps of brain were splattered all over the passenger-side window.

The long-distance look in Niall's eyes instantly died out and he looked as if he were staring at nothing at all. He slumped sideways in his seat with one hand still caught in the steering wheel.

Davy walked back to his own car, climbed in, and drove off. When he reached Fair Hill, he paused for a moment and looked at his eyes in his rear-view mirror. After what he had done today, he knew there was going to be no going back. Even from here, he could see the smoke rising from the Toirneach Damhsa building.

He drove back to Mount Nebo Avenue, softly whistling 'The Broad Black Brimmer', the song about the IRA uniform still hanging up in his father's room. The only words he whispered from it, though, as he parked outside his Uncle Christy's house, were the last lines of the chorus: *a holster that's been empty for many a day . . . but not for long!*

Four

It was almost midnight before fire officers and structural engineers were able to declare that the burned-out dance studio was safe enough to enter. It was raining harder than ever, which had helped to cool the building, but now the roof was covered with plastic sheeting to shield the bodies inside and to prevent any further forensic evidence from being washed away. The rain falling on the sheeting set up a ghostly rattling sound, as if the dead dancers were still dancing the 'Blackthorn Stick'.

Katie and her team had stayed, taking shelter in the Friary Bar. They sat at a table by the large front window so that they could watch the firefighters, and the landlord brought them cheese and ham baps and mugs of tea.

Shortly after 12.30, Bill Phinner, the chief technical officer, entered the bar, dressed in his rustling white forensic suit, with the hood up. He looked as thin and miserable as ever, but Katie had learned long ago that misery was Bill Phinner's default expression.

'What's the story, Bill?' she asked him.

'Well, it's grim up there, I can tell you. Never seen a fire so bad in my whole career.'

'Any ideas yet how it might have started?'

'Far too early to say, ma'am. It could take us weeks to work out the exact sequence of how it combusted. I can say with a fair degree of confidence, though, that it wasn't accidental. Not faulty wiring – it burned far too fast and far too fierce for that – and so far as we can tell there was nothing stored in the building like propane cylinders or petrol or paint. I would guess that some kind of accelerant was used, and Matt Whalen agrees with me.'

Detective Sergeant Begley pushed his way in, accompanied by the smell of rain and bitter smoke. 'The press are nagging for an update, ma'am. The *Examiner* fellow's complaining that he's missed his deadline for tomorrow morning, and Fionnuala Sweeney asked me if there was anything we were keeping under wraps.'

Katie shook her head. 'That Fionnuala – she could smell a conspiracy in a game of glassy allies. But the press will have to stall up for a while, I'm afraid. I want to see the scene for myself first, before I give out any kind of a statement.'

'Fair play to you, ma'am,' said Bill Phinner. 'We're taking photographs and videos of course, and infrared images, but I think you need to see the victims *in situ*. It'll give you a much clearer picture of what must have happened, and how intense the fire must have been. I'll have Jamie fetch you some Tyvek suits from out of the van. You don't want to be getting your clothes all manky dirty.'

He left the bar, and again Katie could smell that waft of rain and smoke. Meanwhile, Detective Sergeant Begley handed her a clipboard with a printed list of names on it.

'This is all the dancers in Toirneach Damhsa. That's eighteen altogether. So far, though, we've found only seventeen bodies, and we're presuming that one of those is probably their coach, Nicholas O'Grady.'

'Have you contacted all of the next of kin?'

'As many as we've been able to locate so far. There – you can see the ticks beside their names. The families of two of them are away on their holliers and there was nobody at home at one of their addresses. Five of the dancers are living in digs on their own and so we've no way of telling at present which of them was here for the practice and which of them wasn't. We'll know, of course, as soon as their bodies have been identified.'

'Did you find out who that young girl belonged to, and what she was doing there?'

'We're presuming she was a friend or relative of one of the dancers, but none of the families have said that they know her.'

'Well, I'll be going to see her myself in the morning, when she's had time to get over the shock. Hopefully she'll tell me herself who she is.'

A young technician came in with three Tyvek suits over his arm, one for Katie and one each for Detectives O'Donovan and Markey. Katie took off her high-viz jacket and Detective Sergeant Begley helped her to climb into her suit. As she was zipping up the front of it, Detective Dooley came in, soaked and exhausted. His expression reminded her of Barney, her Irish setter, after she had taken him out for a long walk in the rain to the Passage West ferry.

'I don't know,' he told her, running his hand through his dripping-wet hair. 'I mingled with the crowds all right and I did a whole lot of earwigging, but I never saw nobody who looked like they were getting their rocks off from watching the fire, and I never heard nobody say nothing at all incriminating. Everybody knew that there was people trapped inside and the ones who weren't biting their lips was bawling.'

Katie said, 'All right, Robert, that's not a bother. We'll have plenty of video and CCTV anyway. You can start to look through that in the morning and see if you can spot anybody who looks like they're enjoying it. Why don't you knock off now and get some sleep? I'll be tipping off myself after I've taken a sconce at the victims.'

'Jesus. Rather you than me, ma'am. I always have nightmares after I've seen stuff like that. But who in the name of God would want to burn down a dance studio? That's what I'd like to know. Like – a brothel or a crack house, or a bar maybe. Even a church. But what earthly harm could dancers have done to anyone?'

'Maybe it was the people from the floor below,' put in Detective Markey. 'Maybe they were pissed off from all that stamping on the ceiling.'

Katie gave him a sharp look and he said, 'Sorry, ma'am. Not funny.'

* * *

The firefighters had erected a ladder in place of the collapsed staircase. Katie climbed up it with Detective O'Donovan close behind her in case she missed her footing. She was wearing blue Tyvek covers over her shoes, but even though the soles were non-skid the rungs of the ladder were wet and slippery.

The staircase walls were blackened with smoke, like a crematorium chimney. Cascades of water were still clattering down from the upper floors and every now and then there was an echoing clang as scaffolding was brought up to support the ceiling. When she reached the first-floor landing two firefighters reached out their hands to help her step off the ladder.

'I'm grand, thanks,' said Katie, but one of the firefighters said, 'Don't want you falling like, that's all. I think we've had enough fatalities here for one day.'

Katie had never seen firefighters look so serious. Even when they were cutting the victims out of car crashes on the N7, or lifting drowned alcoholics out of the River Lee, they usually kept up a black sense of humour. They had to, for their own sanity – but not tonight.

She lifted her mask over her face before she stepped gingerly over the banisters that had fallen sideways across the floor and made her way into the dance studio. Detective O'Donovan and Detective Markey and Bill Phinner followed close behind her. The studio was brightly illuminated by six LED floodlights that the technicians had set up on tripods all around it, so that it had the appearance of a film set rather than a real-life crime scene.

The varnish on the parquet floor was blistered and bubbled. The curtains were nothing more than drooping grey strings, and all the chairs had been burned into skeletons, with lumps of brown melted foam in their seats. Katie looked up and across the ceiling she could see stormy swirls of soot. The heat had shattered the two chandeliers so that only their wire framework dangled down, like two gigantic spiders.

29

Catriona's body was lying close to the doorway, on her back. She had been cremated so completely that her cheekbones were shining through the black, flaked-off skin of her face, and her finger-bones were showing. Her arms and her legs looked like long sticks of charcoal, and her dance dress had turned to ash.

'We're guessing that this young lady was the first to burn,' said Bill Phinner. 'The forensic evidence will show us for sure, but it seems likely that the fire originated in the stairwell and she was caught in a backdraught when the door was opened.'

Katie looked down at Catriona and crossed herself and whispered, 'Whoever you are, girl, may God hold you in the hollow of His hand.'

Next, she turned to look across the studio at the huddle of sixteen more bodies, all of them clustered around the open door to the attic. They were all charred and tangled together, arms and legs intertwined, so that it was difficult to tell at first sight how many there were. As Katie approached them the technical experts stood aside to let her have a closer look. She saw frizzled clumps of hair and faces distorted in panic and pain. It looked as if somebody had tossed a selection of grotesque carnival masks on to a bonfire.

Although she, too, was bundled up in a Tyvek suit and her face was covered by a mask, Katie recognized the young forensic artist Eithne O'Neill, whose speciality was reconstructing images of badly mutilated faces. She was taking photographs of the dancers from all angles, although she wasn't touching any of them. She looked across at Katie and gave her a quick, grim nod of acknowledgement.

'It's going to take us a fair while to separate all of these bodies,' said Bill Phinner. 'Some of them are almost melted together. After that we can lay them out properly and identify them. The girls are all wearing nothing but dancing dresses and the lads are wearing only shirts and trousers. Almost all of them have left their wallets and purses in the changing room. We'll have quite a job matching them all up.'

Assistant Chief Fire Officer Matthew Whalen came over. 'What a tragedy,' he said, shaking his head. 'They didn't stand a chance in hell of getting out of here alive, none of them.'

'It looks as if they were trying to escape through that door,' said Katie. 'Where does that lead? Up to the attic?'

'That's right. We haven't been able to get up there yet because the roof has all fallen in. I'd say that when they opened that door, though, it had the same effect as when they opened the door to the staircase. It let in a whole rush of oxygen and created another backdraught. They might just as well have poured petrol all over themselves.'

'And – just to repeat – you both think that this fire was set deliberately?'

Bill Phinner and Matthew Whalen looked down at the heap of incinerated corpses and nodded.

'There's no doubt in my mind at all,' said Matthew Whalen. 'I've seen almost exactly the same pattern of combustion so many times. You remember that blaze last October at Reedy's on Oliver Plunkett Street? Only one person was injured then, the fellow who was living in the flat over the shop, but it was the same double-backdraught situation. He tried to get out through the attic but when he opened the trapdoor the whole building went up like a bomb.'

Katie couldn't help noticing the curled-up hand lying on the floor close to her blue Tyvek-covered foot. It was a girl's hand, red-raw like an upturned crab, with a silver engagement ring tarnished by the heat. Katie crossed herself again. Whatever had happened here, whoever had set this building alight, she felt that she had failed these poor dead dancers because no word about a threatened arson attack had reached her team beforehand. There was constant warfare between the drugs gangs and the pimps and the people-smugglers in Cork, but she hadn't heard a whisper about a threat against Toirneach Damhsa, or any other Irish dancing troupe.

'I have to talk to the media now,' she told Bill Phinner and Matthew Whalen. 'I'm not going to tell them yet that we suspect it was arson. First of all, I'd rather have absolute one hundred per cent forensic proof that it was, and not some freakish accident that looks as if it might have been arson. Second, if it *was* arson, I want the perpetrator to think that he or she might have got away with it.'

GRAHAM MASTERTON

'So what are you going to say to the media?' asked Matthew Whalen.

'Nothing that they don't already know. There was a devastating fire and most if not all of the members of the Toirneach Damhsa troupe were tragically killed. The Technical Bureau along with experts from the Cork Fire Brigade are investigating the causes of it.'

'They're not going to be very satisfied with that,' said Bill Phinner.

'Seventeen young people have been burned to death in here, Bill,' said Katie. 'The only satisfaction I'm concerned about is theirs, these dancers – finding out who killed them and having them punished for it. The media – well, they can stall up for a while.'

Five

Katie spent what was left of the night at the River Lee Hotel. She could have slept at the station, but it was always noisy there, with doors slamming and feet hurrying backwards and forwards, and distant phones ringing, and singing drunks being dragged in from the street. Whenever she slept there, too, she always woke up too early and instead of a proper breakfast she would eat a cheese and tomato sandwich or maybe a granola bar, sitting at her desk.

After witnessing the burning down of the Toirneach Damhsa dance studio she wanted to think quietly about who might have done it, and why, and how she was going to set up her investigation. She took a long hot shower to wash off the smell of smoke and then at 3.15 a.m. she went to bed. She lay there for a while listening to the soft swish of traffic along the Western Road and the rain sprinkling against her window.

She had trained herself to switch her mind off and sleep deeply whenever she needed it, but tonight she had a vivid dream – not about the black cremated bodies in the dance studio, but about Conor. It was a sunny afternoon and he was sitting in her back garden, tugging at Barney's ears, with his back to her. He was wearing a brown hat with a floppy brim and a very white short-sleeved shirt so that she could see tattoos on his forearms which she had never seen when they were in bed together. A mermaid with flowing red hair – he had always called her his beautiful merrow.

He kept saying, 'You don't understand, Katie. You have the wrong end of the stick altogether.'

33

Her alarm woke her at six-thirty. Although she had to dress in the same rust-coloured suit and mustard sweater as yesterday, she always carried a clean pair of tights and a thong in her purse. She went downstairs to the terrace at seven o'clock, taking a notepad with her, and chose a table by the window so that she could look out over the river. It was gradually growing light, but although it had stopped raining the morning was relentlessly grey and the river was dull, like a fogged-up mirror. She ordered black pudding and poached eggs on a muffin, and a strawberry and mint lemonade, and a double espresso. Even when she was at home she would start the day with nothing more than muesli and yogurt, but today she had the feeling that she might not have the chance to eat again until very much later.

While she waited for her food to arrive she sipped her lemonade and wrote down a list. Detective Dooley had asked the most important question of all: *Who in the name of God would want to burn down a dance studio?* There were several possible answers to that, but considering that seventeen people had been killed, either deliberately or accidentally, she thought some of the answers seemed highly unlikely. Still, as her father had told her after all his years of experience as a Garda inspector, 'The whole world is highly unlikely, my darling, and after Waterford, Cork is probably the unlikeliest place of all.'

In spite of its gangs, or perhaps because of them, Cork City had one of the lowest crime rates in Ireland, although it had more homicides than anywhere else. Katie put that statistic down to the gangs, too.

But was this fire gang-related? Maybe there had been some long-running dispute over who owned the property. Maybe the arsonist had simply intended to burn down the building and hadn't realized that the dancers would be trapped and have no way of escape.

Maybe, on the other hand, he had borne a grudge against one or all of the dancers, or their coach, Nicholas O'Grady, or Danny Coffey, the troupe's owner and manager. Danny Coffey would be coming back to Cork from Dublin sometime this morning and Katie would have him interviewed and his background thoroughly checked.

Maybe the troupe had been suffering from financial problems and Danny Coffey had arranged for the arson himself in order to collect the insurance.

She knew Nicholas O'Grady to be homosexual because only three or four months ago he had married his male partner in an ostentatious ceremony at the Ambassador Hotel. Maybe some jealous former lover had been out to punish him, or maybe some religious zealot had wanted to express disapproval of same-sex marriage.

Maybe the fire had been set by a member of a rival dance troupe. The regional dance finals were being held at the Cork Opera House on Saturday next week and the competition was fierce, especially among the semi-professional troupes. Winning the championship could bring huge publicity and guarantee bookings both in Ireland and abroad. From what Katie had read about Toirneach Damhsa, they were one of the best step-dance companies in the country. She would send Detective Scanlan to have a word with An Coimisiún Le Rincí Gaelacha, the Irish Dance Commission, to ask if they had heard of any enmity simmering between the competing troupes.

The red-haired waitress brought her plate of black pudding and poached eggs and so she put down her pen. She was tempted to ring Detective Sergeant Begley and ask how the extrication of the bodies from the dance studio was progressing, but she told herself to eat her breakfast first, and stay calm. If there had been any problems, either he or Bill Phinner would have texted her.

It was only when she cut into her black pudding that she realized how much it resembled the charred flesh of the first dancer she had seen, lying on her back by the studio door. She held a lump of it on the end of her fork and told herself not to be so squeamish. She had once seen a woman whose husband had attacked her in the kitchen with a carving knife so that her intestines were hanging out, and that hadn't put her off tripe.

After more than half a minute, though, she realized that she couldn't put it in her mouth. She put down her fork and pushed her plate away. She didn't even feel hungry any more, even for the piece of farl that she had torn off and buttered to go with the black pudding.

The waitress came over and said, 'Is something wrong, ma'am?'

'Yes. No. Not at all. It's not the food. The food is grand. It's me. I've suddenly lost my appetite.'

'Would you like anything else at all? Some whiskey cream porridge, maybe?'

'No, thanks. I'll just finish my coffee. Tell the chef it wasn't his fault. It was my digestion playing up, that's all.'

'Should I fetch you some Alka-Seltzer?'

Katie smiled and shook her head. 'That's sweet of you. But Alka-Seltzer could never settle what my stomach's suffering from.'

* * *

The morning was beginning to brighten, so she walked from the River Lee Hotel to Anglesea Street, going by way of Hanover Street and Sullivan's Quay by the river. Her iPhone pinged six or seven times as she walked, and played '*Fear a' Bháta*' again and again, but she didn't answer it. It would take her only a little over twenty minutes to reach the station and she felt that she needed the fresh air and exercise.

She wanted to think about Conor, too. She wasn't in love with him, but she was passionately fond of him. He was funny, and interesting, and understanding, and he was great in bed. She had found his lovemaking really exciting – and more than that, liberating. With him, she felt she could do whatever she wanted and ask *him* to do whatever she desired, without any embarrassment.

Apart from that, he was one of only a handful of professional pet detectives in Europe, finding missing or stolen dogs and cats, and she found his rapport with animals made him even more appealing.

Katie and Conor had gone together to Tipperary to search for dogs that had been stolen to take part in dog-fights organized by the notorious Guzz Eye McManus. They hadn't yet gathered enough solid evidence to arrest McManus, but they had found out that a major dog-fight was pending and Katie had been hoping that when that took place Conor could help her to prosecute McManus and close down his racket for good. Each dog-fight easily made three times as much money as a drugs shipment or a bank robbery.

But now what was she going to do? Although she found it difficult to admit it to herself, there had been a tiny hope glowing in some dark corner at the back of her mind that their relationship might last longer than just a few weeks, that it might outlive the secretive liaisons they had been enjoying at Conor's hotel while they worked together on the McManus case. That was before a tall, attractive woman had walked into the station and announced herself as Conor's wife. Katie had driven home that evening with tears blurring her eyes and she hadn't spoken to Conor again, not until he had come into the station the previous morning.

Of course, she could pursue her investigation into Guzz Eye's dog-fighting without him, but it would be far more difficult. Conor had built up a comprehensive network of contacts among shady vets and boarding-kennel owners, and other people involved in the stealing and training of dogs for fighting. Without him, too, it would be far more dangerous. Guzz Eye was very influential in the Travelling community and he wasn't the kind of man who tolerated interference in his affairs. The Tipperary gardaí already suspected him of having been involved in the murder of Sean Moody, a dog trainer who had been found dead in a ditch at Saintpatricksrock last October, with his severed genitals stuffed in his mouth, a clear indication that he had been talking to people he shouldn't.

Yes, Kathleen, I deck it, she told herself, as she crossed the stone bridge over the south branch of the river. *I know how totally rash I was to get involved with Conor at all*. But she had been riven with guilt over the death of her erstwhile boyfriend, John, and Conor had given her so much affection and so much strength just when she needed it most. But could she continue to work with him, now that she had found out he was married and had been cheating on his wife with her? She could see all manner of trouble coming, like the bank of charcoal-grey clouds that were rolling over the city close behind her.

As soon as she reached her office and hung up her high-viz jacket, her assistant, Moirin, came bustling in. Moirin was small and chubby, with a heart-shaped face like Snow White, and she looked as if she had only just left school, but in fact she was a single mother of two children and one of the most efficient assistants that Katie had ever employed.

'Superintendent Pearse has been asking for you, ma'am, and so has DI Mulliken. They both said it was pure urgent. Would you care for a cup of tea in your hand?'

Katie sat behind her desk and prodded her iPhone. 'I've been answering nobody this morning,' she said. 'I wanted to give my head a little peace before I came to work.'

'Oh, if only,' said Moirin. 'My two do nothing but scream and shout and beat the living daylights out of each other, morning till night.'

'So, just the same as working here, really?' said Katie. 'Actually, I'll have a cappuccino if you don't mind. And a couple of those Cushendall biscuits if there's any left.'

She called Superintendent Pearse. 'I'll come up,' he told her. 'I could use the exercise.'

Next, she called Detective Inspector Mulliken.

'Moirin told me you wanted to speak to me urgent,' she said.

'I do, yes. There's been a shooting up at Gurra. Niall Gleeson, would you believe.'

'What? *The* Niall Gleeson, Bobby Quilty's *consigliere*? Is he dead?'

'Oh, sure he's dead all right. Shot right between the eyes. We don't know for sure when it happened because he wasn't found until seven-thirty this morning. His car was parked on Knockfree Avenue and a fair few people passed it, but they thought he was only having a kip. It wasn't until some nursery school teacher noticed that there was dried blood on the window.'

'You've alerted the Technical Bureau, and the coroner?'

'I have, sure. The technical experts have gone up to the scene already, but of course the coroner's office doesn't open until nine.'

While he was talking, Katie continued to check her iPhone and saw that she had received texts and voice messages from both Superintendent Pearse and Detective Inspector Mulliken, and from Bill Phinner, too. *Mother of God*, she thought, *I have twenty minutes peace and quiet to myself and while I do the whole world falls apart.*

'Superintendent Pearse is coming up to my office now,' she said. 'I'm assuming that he wants to tell me about Niall Gleeson, too. Why don't you join us?'

'Okay, sure. I'll see you in a minute so.'

Katie listened to Bill Phinner's voice messages. He sounded tired. 'It's going to take us at least another thirty-six hours to remove all the bodies from the dance studio,' he told her in his first message. 'Some of them have their flesh fused together so we have to be extra careful when we're separating them. In the meantime we've taken chemical samples from the walls and the floor and the victims' clothing, too.'

In his second message he said, 'I'm assuming you've been notified about Niall Gleeson. Let's hope for his sake that the devil hasn't heard he's dead. I've sent four technicians up to Gurra to do all the necessary. It looks as if none of us are going to be getting much sleep in the next few days. Niall Gleeson – Holy Saint Joseph. I can't predict who's going to be next, but you can bet your Christmas bonus there's going to be a tit-for-tat killing before we know it.'

Next, Katie rang Detective O'Donovan. He was already in the CCTV room looking through the footage of the crowds that had gathered to watch the fire at the Toirneach Damhsa studio.

'I'm not too hopeful,' he told her. 'There's a whole heap of smoke and because of the wind direction it's blotting out the view altogether most of the time. But I'll keep at it. There's about six hours of it, plus a couple of hours of hand-held videos that the fire brigade took.'

Superintendent Pearse knocked at Katie's door and came in, looking grave. He was a short, stubby man with glittering eyes and tangled eyebrows and a pugnacious lower lip. He was renowned for his temper, but Katie had never worked with anyone who had a clearer head for law-enforcement operations and street policing in particular. He simply couldn't tolerate fools or inefficiency – although it was common knowledge at Anglesea Street that his wife had an even more ferocious temper than he did. Detective Dooley said that she probably sprinkled Semtex on her cereal every morning.

'I'm guessing that it's Niall Gleeson you want to talk about, Michael,' said Katie. 'Actually I've only just found out about him myself.'

'Oh, sorry,' said Superintendent Pearse. 'I thought you would have heard.'

'What's the story? We haven't heard a squeak from the Authentic IRA since Bobby Quilty went to meet his Maker. In fact, I thought they'd pretty much disbanded. Was this a political killing, do you think, or was it personal?'

'Hard to say for certain,' said Superintendent Pearse. 'But Garda Duffy lives on the other side of Fair Green from him, in Bride Valley Park, and he's heard that Gleeson's been having a bit of gonky on the side with some other feller's missus. He's going to be making some discreet enquiries to see if he can find out who it is. So that could be one motive.'

At that moment, Detective Inspector Mulliken came in. He was tall and thin and balding, even though he was only forty-one, with a prominent nose and a straggly brown moustache. He wore a light brown suit that hung on him as if he had bought it when he was five kilos heavier. One of his running briefs was to keep a close watch on the various IRA splinter groups in Cork, such as the Continuity IRA and the New IRA and Óglaigh na hÉireann. The Authentic IRA had been set up by the late Bobby Quilty, financed mainly by his cigarette-smuggling racket, but it had been more of a private army to protect his criminal activities than a genuine republican movement.

Katie said, 'Superintendent Pearse thinks that Gleeson may have been shot by a jealous husband.'

'Well, that's entirely possible,' said Detective Inspector Mulliken. 'Your man was in trouble two or three years ago when he knocked up his pub landlady's daughter. He couldn't keep it in his corduroys, that feller. Myself, I'd say that Niall Gleeson's idea of a united Ireland was him uniting with every woman he ever bumped into.'

'So you don't think it was political?' asked Katie.

'I'm not sure. I get occasional tip-offs from a lad who works part-time at the Templegate Tavern on Gurranabraher Road, and he told me last week that the old Authentic boys seem to have been meeting up there more regular lately, including Gleeson, but also including some new feller that he didn't know.'

'Has he managed to pick up on any conversation, this lad?'

Detective Inspector Mulliken shook his head. 'All he said was, the old Authentic boys seemed to treat this new feller with quite a lot of respect like. And the other thing he said was, the new feller never asks for alcohol, only soft drinks.'

'He's a teetotaller?' said Superintendent Pearse. 'In my books, Jesus, that alone by itself makes him a suspect.'

Katie smiled, but then she said, 'You haven't found any eyewitnesses to the shooting? Or anybody who heard shots and maybe can give us an approximate time when it happened?'

'My lad at the tavern says that Gleeson arrived about two-thirty. There were three of his Authentic pals there, and later on the new feller arrived. This was just before four. They talked for a while and then Gleeson left. The new feller left almost immediately afterwards.

'Gleeson was supposed to be collecting his granddaughter from the crèche up the road but he never showed up, so one of the other mothers took her home. We can probably assume that he was shot round about then and that's why he didn't collect her. His daughter wasn't too worried because apparently he was never too reliable and often forgot to pick up his granddaughter. We're doing the usual door-to-door, of course, but we've found no witnesses so far.'

'Okay,' said Katie. 'As soon as I've heard some more from Bill Phinner, I'll ask Mathew in the press office to put out an appeal to the media for witnesses. Tony, how about you sending somebody out to the Templegate Tavern and having a listen? I don't want us to interview any of those Authentics face to face, not yet. Before we do, I'd rather we got a sense of what they're up to, that's if they're up to anything. Are they still active, do we know, or are they just meeting socially? And I'd like to find out who this new fellow is, this teetotaller they're treating with such respect.'

'Me too,' said Detective Inspector Mulliken. 'I might send out Kyna Ni Nuallán. She has the gift of getting people to talk to her even when they don't really want to.'

'Good idea,' said Katie. 'But tell her since she's going up to Gurra she has only two choices of what she looks like – bag lady or slut. Either no make-up at all and a woolly beanie and a baggy tracksuit, or else heaps of eyeliner and glittery lipstick and a leopard-skin miniskirt. Either of those, and nobody in Gurra will give her a second glance.'

Moirin came in with her cappuccino and a plate of cranberry and almond biscuits. Superintendent Pearse eyed the biscuits hungrily and so Katie said, 'Help yourself, Michael. Isn't Breda feeding you these days?'

'She thinks we ought to be eating more healthy, do you know what I mean, so it's been salads and chicken breasts for the past three weeks. No more pies. No more burgers. No more Chinky takeaways. Myself, I'd rather be full up and dead than fit as a fiddle and starving.'

Katie heard Moirin's phone ring and then a few moments later Moirin came into her office. 'That was Mr Coffey. His first train from Dublin was cancelled but he should be getting into Kent station at about twelve-thirty.'

'Danny Coffey owns and manages the Toirneach Damhsa company,' Katie told Detective Inspector Mulliken. 'At least he *did*, before they were all cremated, God rest their souls. But that's okay, Moirin, if he's going to be late. That means I have time to go

42

to the Mercy and visit that little girl they rescued from the roof. On the way there, though, Tony, I want to see the scene where Gleeson was shot. I'll have Kyna come with me so that she can see the lie of the land. I was going to fetch her along to the Mercy with me anyway.'

Superintendent Pearse said, through a mouthful of biscuit, 'If Gleeson's shooting was political, I'm fierce worried there's going to be some kind of retaliation. The problem is that until we know who did it we won't know who's going to be retaliated against. Who doesn't like the Authentics the most? The New IRA? The Callahan mob?'

'Bill Phinner said the same as you,' Katie told him. 'That's why I think it's a good idea of yours, sending Kyna up to the pub to see what she can pick up.'

'It could have been a gang hit,' said Detective Inspector Mulliken. 'Ever since they heard that Bobby Quilty was out of the picture the Lithuanians have been trying to muscle in on his cigarette trade. It seems like they're not content with stroking charity bags off people's doorsteps before the real collectors have had time to get around.'

Katie said, 'Mother of God, I thought this was going to be a quiet week. I was even thinking of taking a couple of days off and visiting my sister in Youghal. I'll just finish my coffee, Tony, and take a quick look through all my paperwork, and I'll be with you. Can you ask Kyna to get herself ready, too?'

Six

There was another reason why Katie had wanted Detective Sergeant Ni Nuallán to come with her, apart from viewing the crime scene and familiarizing herself with that area of Gurranabraher.

As she stopped at the traffic lights on Merchants Quay, just before crossing Patrick's Bridge, she said, 'Conor came in to the station to see me yesterday morning.'

'What did he have to say for himself?' asked Kyna. She had been fluffing up her short blonde hair in the sun-visor mirror, but now she stopped and snapped the sun visor shut.

'Nothing. There wasn't time. I was on my way to the fire at Toirneach Damhsa.'

'Has he rung you back this morning?'

Katie shook her head. She waited patiently while an old woman crossed in front of her with a walking frame, even though the lights had turned green. Nobody hooted her. In Cork, it seemed to be a ritual that when the lights turned green, drivers would say a short novena before they got around to engaging first gear, and would drive away only at the very moment the lights turned red again.

'So, what are you going to do?' asked Kyna. 'It's not going to be easy to lift McManus and the rest of those dog-fighting scummers without him.'

'I don't know, to be honest with you,' said Katie. 'Why didn't he *tell* me he was married? At least I could have made an informed choice, whether to sleep with him or not.'

'Would you have slept with him, if you'd known? I mean, that's the question, isn't it?'

Katie turned left along Camden Quay. The sky to the west was almost black now and a few spots of rain pattered on to the windscreen. The river looked like burnished lead.

'I don't know. That's the trouble. I like him so much. I was even starting to think that we might have a future together.'

Kyna reached across and gently laid her hand on Katie's arm. 'What can I say to you, except that I know the feeling? But you'll always have me.'

They reached Knockfree Avenue. Niall Gleeson's car had been covered by a blue vinyl tent, and there were three squad cars and two vans from the Technical Bureau parked on either side of it, as well as an ambulance. A small crowd of onlookers were sheltering from the rain under the large tree in front of the Before 5 nursery school and Katie could see Dan Keane from the *Examiner* and Jean Mulligan from the *Echo*. There was no sign yet of the RTÉ outside broadcast van, or Fionnuala Sweeney.

Dan Keane nipped his cigarette between finger and thumb, tucked it behind his ear, and came over to Katie as soon as she climbed out of her car, with Jean Mulligan close behind him.

'How's it going on, DS Maguire?' said Dan Keane. 'I'm hearing rumours that this was a Continuity job.'

'Oh yes?' said Katie, walking briskly towards the tent. 'And where exactly would you have been hearing that?'

'You know as well as I do that I can't reveal my sources.'

'Sure like. And you know as well as I do that I can't comment on unsubstantiated rumours.'

'Has anybody claimed responsibility for it yet?' Jean Mulligan asked her.

'Not so far.'

'Do you think that makes it less likely that it was political? I mean, if the New IRA punish anybody for anything, they usually take the credit for it, don't they, before anybody else can?'

'I haven't even seen the deceased yet, so again, I really can't comment.'

'I've talked to Mrs Gleeson's neighbours,' Jean Mulligan

persisted. 'They all reckon that Niall Gleeson was paying regular visits to a woman along Nash's Boreen while her husband was at work. Maybe the husband found out like.'

'We'll be talking to everybody who might be a likely suspect,' said Katie. A uniformed garda was holding open the tent flap for her, but before she went inside she paused and said, 'The neighbours didn't happen to know this woman's name, did they?'

'No, they didn't,' said Jean Mulligan. 'But her husband drove a green Golf. As soon as the green Golf had turned out of Nash's Boreen in the morning, they'd see Niall Gleeson's car turning into it. Changing of the guard like.'

'Thanks, Jean,' Katie told her. 'That could save us a lot of time.'

She entered the tent and Kyna followed her. It was dazzlingly bright and crowded in there, with four technical experts examining the car for fingerprints and fibres with UV blacklights, a photographer taking pictures from every conceivable angle, and two bored-looking paramedics waiting for them to finish so that they could remove Niall Gleeson's body and take him to the morgue at Cork University Hospital for an autopsy.

Katie peered into the car and she could smell stale alcohol and excrement. She was amazed that passers-by had thought that Niall Gleeson was simply sleeping. Apart from the treacle-coloured spatters of dried blood on the passenger-side window, the hole in his forehead was unmissable, and he was tilted awkwardly sideways at forty-five degrees, his face a dusty whitish-grey, like concrete. His eyes were open and he still had the same thousand-yard stare that he had always had when he was alive, but now he didn't blink.

After two or three minutes Katie pushed aside the tent flap and stepped outside into the rain.

'What are your thoughts?' asked Detective Inspector Mulliken. He wiped a drip of rainwater off the end of his nose and sniffed.

'My immediate thoughts?' said Katie. 'The blood-spatter indicates that he was sitting in the driver's seat when he was shot, so he wasn't shot somewhere else and then placed in the car afterwards. All the indications are that he was driving, and since he didn't arrive at the crèche to pick up his granddaughter at four o'clock, he probably drove here directly from the tavern. But he's parked here, right up against the kerb, as if he's pulled in for some reason. None of the tyres have a puncture, do they, and is the engine still running okay?'

'We tested it, yes, and it turned over fine.'

'Also, his window is down. It had started to rain about that time yesterday, so he wouldn't have been driving around with his window open, would be? My guess is that he stopped for some reason and put down his window to talk to somebody, and that somebody then shot him.'

Kyna said, 'It's likely, too, that it was somebody he knew, or at least somebody he didn't have any cause to be scared of. He wouldn't have parked and put down his window otherwise. He would have put his foot down, wouldn't he, and booted it off up the road?'

'Well, maybe Superintendent Pearse was right,' said Katie. 'Maybe it was the woman's husband from Nash's Boreen who shot him.'

'We'll be talking to him later,' said Detective Inspector Mulliken. 'In a way, I'm praying that it's him. At least that'll be the end of it. If it's political, it's going to be a right cat's malack, I can promise you.'

* * *

Mercy University Hospital was only five minutes away, overlooking the River Lee on Henry Street, but before she took them there Katie drove slowly past the Templegate Tavern. Four or five men were standing outside, smoking and talking, and occasionally pointing up the road towards Knockfree Avenue.

'No prizes for guessing what those fellows are talking about,' said Katie.

'Fair play, it doesn't look a bad pub at all,' said Kyna. 'I've been in a lot worse places undercover. A McDonald's once, in Balbriggan, where one of the staff was selling crack along with the cheeseburgers. Never again. I don't know which was worse, the crack or the cheeseburgers.'

They were met outside the front entrance of the Mercy by Detective Scanlan. She was wearing a creased three-piece suit of ginger linen and clumpy wedge-heeled sandals. She had been awake for most of the previous night and had dark circles around her eyes, and her blonde hair looked as if it needed a wash.

'You can head off home after this, Padragain,' said Katie, as she climbed out of her car.

'Thanks, but I doubt if I'll be able to sleep. I must have drunk twenty cups of coffee since midnight.'

'How's the girl?' Katie asked her. 'Has she told us her name yet?'

'She's not uttered a single word. The nurses are calling her "Adeen" for now, because of course that means "little fire". What's really strange, though, is that nobody has been in touch yet to identify her. Mathew's taken some more pictures and they'll be running them in the *Echo* today and on the *Six-One News* this evening. But nobody's been calling for her so far, and if we don't have any response by Monday they'll have her on *Crimecall*.'

'Maybe the only people who might have missed her were burned up in the fire,' said Kyna.

'Well, that's a possibility,' said Katie. 'How is she physically?'

'She's still suffering the effects of smoke inhalation and she has some fierce nasty scratches on her hands and arms and a burn on her left calf. The doctor wants to keep an eye on her for at least another three to four days, but if there's no sign of any lung infection by then, they should be able discharge her – provided they have somewhere to discharge her to. I've already been in touch with Tusla in case she needs fostering, and Corinne Daley's been in to see her.'

Detective Scanlan led them up to the end of the first-floor corridor, where a uniformed garda was sitting on a small plastic chair, looking as if he was finding it hard to stay awake. The girl they were calling Adeen was lying in a small isolation room with pale green walls and a dark green carpet. It overlooked Millerd

Street at the back of the hospital, but the blind was drawn down and the lights were switched on.

'She acted pure frightened when the nurse tried to put up the blind this morning, as if she was scared that there was somebody out there, so that's why we've left it down.'

'Adeen' was sitting up in bed, propped up with pillows. She looked younger and skinnier than she had when Katie had seen her being lifted down from the roof of the burning dance studio, but that was probably because her bronze-brown plaited hair had been brushed out and washed, and she was wearing a spotted hospital gown that was two sizes too large for her.

Her nose and mouth were covered by an oxygen mask and she was connected to a heart monitor and an IV drip. Her left eye was still bloodshot, but her right eye stared at Katie from over the mask, chocolate brown and appealing, almost like a Disney cartoon character.

The nurse was short and plump with fiery red hair and freckles. She was sitting at the dressing table when Katie and Kyna and Detective Scanlan came in, furiously tapping two-fingered on a laptop.

'Please – give me a minute, will you?' she said. 'The lab has just sent up the latest test results for smoke particles in her lower lungs.'

'And?' asked Katie.

'So far, yes, her airways look reasonably clear. Fortunately for her, she was up on the roof, out in the open air. It might have been a different story altogether if she had been trapped indoors.'

There was a chair on the opposite side of the bed, so Katie walked around and sat down. She took hold of the girl's right hand and gave it a gentle squeeze.

'How are you feeling?' she said, giving her a sympathetic smile. 'My name's Kathleen, but all of my friends call me Katie. My teacher at school used to call me Molly because my surname's Maguire and I was always so bold.'

She turned around to the nurse and said, 'Can she take off the mask for just a moment?'

The nurse came over and eased off the oxygen mask. Although the girl's left cheek was still bruised, Katie could see that she was quite pretty. She had a pale, oval face with a turned-up nose and a very slight underbite. The underbite told Katie immediately that she probably didn't come from a very well-off family, because by this age she should have had her teeth corrected. Either that, or her family were ignorant, or simply neglectful.

'I'll bet you're not half as bold at school as I used to be,' she continued. 'In fact, I'll bet you're teacher's pet.'

Whenever she interviewed children, this question almost always provoked a furious denial, even from pupils who were top of the class and very well behaved. But this girl stayed silent, showing nothing more than – *what was it?* thought Katie, *caution? suspicion?* However she had found herself trapped on the roof of that burning building, she must still be suffering from shock.

'I've told you *my* name, sweetheart. Do you think you can tell me yours? I know they've been calling you Adeen here, but it would help me so much if I knew your real name. You can just whisper it, if you don't want anybody else to know what it is.'

The girl stayed silent. Katie couldn't tell from her expression if she had heard her, or even if she had, if she had understood her.

'They've tested her hearing,' said Detective Scanlan, as if she knew what Katie was thinking.

'Maybe she's an immigrant,' Kyna suggested. 'Maybe she only speaks Romanian, or something like that.'

'They've asked her questions in the ten most common immigrant languages,' said Detective Scanlan. 'She didn't respond to any of them.'

Katie held up the girl's hand. She was wearing a plaited green wristband with a gold-coloured plastic clasp.

'Does this mean anything to anybody?' she asked.

Kyna and Detective Scanlan both shook their heads. The nurse said, 'We don't usually allow patients to wear their own jewellery of any kind, but she became so distressed when we tried to remove that bracelet that we let her keep it on.'

'So it obviously means something to *her*,' said Katie. 'Kyna, would you take a picture of it, please, and Google it, and give the picture to the media, too. You never know. It might have some special significance in whatever country she comes from.'

'All of her clothes were bought locally,' said Detective Scanlan. 'Her sweater and jeans are both from Penney's, and her hoodie came from Dunne's.'

Those brand names reinforced Katie's guess that the girl's family possibly belonged to a lower socioeconomic bracket. She hadn't been dressed in designer clothes from Mischief Makers or Brown Thomas. At Penney's, a pair of jeans for a girl of her age would cost only €18, maybe less.

Katie gave the girl's hand another squeeze and said, 'I'm going now, sweetheart, but my office isn't very far away. If you decide you want to talk to me, ask the nurse and she can call me and I can be here in five minutes. It doesn't matter what you want to talk about. It can be anything you like. You have a TV here, so you can watch your favourite films whenever you want. You like *Frozen*? That's one of my favourites. And *Finding Dory*. Have you seen *Finding Dory*?'

She waited, and kept smiling at the girl, but still she didn't answer. The nurse came over again and said, 'If you don't mind, I have to put the mask back on now.'

Katie let go of the girl's hand and stood up. She had dealt with scores of cases in which the victims of fires or accidents or violent attacks had been so traumatized by what had happened that they were unable to talk about their experiences, but this was the first time she had come across a victim whose shock had been so great that they were unable to speak at all.

As they went down in the lift she said to Kyna, 'You know me. I don't do hunches. But I have the strongest feeling that poor little girl can tell us everything about that fire – who set it, and why. I'll just have to keep on working on her, and see if I can't get her to talk.'

'Well, don't count on it,' said Kyna. 'I had to deal with a fellow in Dublin once who saw his daughter and his grandson open the front door and get shot dead right in front of him.'

'Mother of God,' said Katie.

'Yes. It was a shotgun blast, and it was intended for him, which only made it worse. After that, he couldn't speak. I dropped in to see him nearly every day for a year and a half on my way to the station in the morning but I still couldn't get him to say a single word. In the end he took an overdose of codeine tablets. We had a pretty fair idea of who the shooter was, of course, but the only man who could have identified him in a court of law was struck dumb.'

Katie's iPhone played '*Fear a' Bháta*'. It was Detective Sergeant Begley. He sounded tired, too.

'Danny Coffey's arrived, ma'am, and there's fire coming out of his arse from temper, if you'll forgive me. He's wanting to know why we haven't hauled in anybody for burning down his dance studio yet and already had them tried and convicted and banged up for life. He says he's sure who did it anyway.'

Katie took a deep breath. 'Thank you, Sean. I'll be with you in five. Do me a favour, would you, and ask Moirin to have a cappuccino waiting for me? Thanks a million.'

Seven

Detective Sergeant Begley was right. Danny Coffey was in the filthiest of tempers. He was sitting in the reception area by the front desk, but as soon as Katie and Kyna came through the front doors he sprang to his feet and Katie could see him asking Detective Sergeant Begley, 'Is that her?'

Katie went over to him, holding out her hand.

'Mr Coffey. Thanks for coming. I'm Detective Superintendent Maguire and this is Detective Sergeant Ni Nuallán. I'm sorry to hear you had a spot of trouble with your trains.'

Danny Coffey was a short man in his mid-forties, probably no taller than five foot five inches, with a round face and washed-out green eyes. He was balding, with a comb-over that was stuck down with shiny hair-dressing, and he had no eyebrows, which made him disconcertingly expressionless. He was wearing a beige three-piece suit, so tight that he looked as if he might burst out of it at any second.

'Trouble with my trains?' he retorted, in a hoarse, screechy voice. 'I don't call it trouble. I call it the normal balla malla that you get from Iarnród Éireann. They should rechristen it the Solid Hames Railway, I swear to God.'

'Well, you're here now,' said Katie. 'Why don't you come up to my office? How about a cup of tea in your hand? Or a coffee?'

'I didn't come here for refreshment, Detective Superintendent. I came here because my dancing studio was set on fire and sixteen of my dancers were burned to death, as well as my dance instructor, and I'd like to know why you haven't yet locked up the subla what was responsible.'

53

Katie took hold of Danny Coffey's elbow to steer him towards the lift but he irritably twisted his arm away.

'We haven't yet made an arrest, Mr Coffey, because our investigation is still in its very earliest stages. We don't even know for sure that the fire was started deliberately.'

'Are you codding me?' Danny Coffey protested, as he stepped into the lift. 'I mean – are you *codding* me? What in the name of Saint Jude do you think it was, spontaneous combustification?'

'I very much appreciate your texting us with the names and contact numbers of all of your dancers,' said Katie, trying to calm him down. 'We're hoping that we'll have them all positively identified by the end of the day. There were eighteen in the troupe altogether, is that right?'

'That's right. But Nicholas rang me and said that only sixteen of them had showed up for that final rehearsal. He got cut off before he could tell me who was missing. You don't have to know who they all are, though, do you, before you bring in the fellow who killed them? There's seventeen innocent people dead, no matter who they are.'

'It's like I say, Mr Coffey. We don't have sufficient evidence yet to make an arrest.'

'If I tell you who did it, can you arrest him then?'

'You know who did it?'

They had reached Katie's office now. A cappuccino was waiting on Katie's desk, as well as three files of notes and messages and correspondence. Sometimes Katie felt that she had been promoted to superintendent only because the male officers had wanted a glorified secretary to deal with all their endless paperwork.

The four of them sat down on the oatmeal-coloured couches under the window and Moirin came in to ask if anybody else wanted a drink. Detective Sergeant Begley said that after all the salty rashers he had eaten for his breakfast he was parching for a cup of tea. Kyna asked for a Karmine apple juice. Danny Coffey shook his head and repeated, 'I thought I made that transparent. I didn't come here for refreshment.'

'So then, who do you think's responsible?' Katie asked him.

'It's obvious. Steven Joyce. Who else would have anything to gain?'

'You've lost me there, Mr Coffey. Who's Steven Joyce?'

'He's the owner and manager of Laethanta na Rince – the Days of Dance. He and me were good pals about ten years ago. After I split up with Michael Flatley, me and Steven started Toirneach Damhsa together. When we started getting real successful, though, and making some serious grade, Steven demanded seventy-five per cent of the profits. He reckoned that he was like the creative force behind the company and I was nothing more than the fellow who answered the phone, and arranged the bookings, and drove the bus to the venues.'

'So you fell out?'

'We did, yes, big time. But it was fortunate for me that I had registered the name Toirneach Damhsa myself, so Steven couldn't use it. Much more important than that, though, Nicholas, our dance instructor, stuck with me, and Nicholas is – *was*, anyway – a pure genius when it comes to the choreography. Anyway, Nicholas stuck with me and because of that so did most of our dancers.'

'But Steven went off to start his own dance company, this Laethanta na Rince?'

'That's right. It almost bankrupted him, but he did it. The first time we competed against him in a *feis* was in Killarney, and that was three years ago. His dancers were good, I have to admit, although we beat them in the end. I went to congratulate him after, hoping that we could let bygones be bygones, do you know what I mean?'

'I assume that he wasn't so conciliatory?'

Danny Coffey blinked, and Katie wasn't sure that he understood what she meant by 'conciliatory'. So she said, 'Like, forgiving?'

'Forgiving? He said that he hoped some maniac would come around to my dance studio and cut off all of my dancers' feet with a chainsaw. And then he hoped that he would cut off my mebs and make me eat them in a blaa.'

'I see. Do you have any record of him saying this to you?'

'What do you mean? You don't believe me?'

'I'm not saying that I don't believe you, Mr Coffey. I'm just asking if you have any evidence to substantiate what you're telling me. Anything written or recorded that would stand up in a court.'

'No, I don't. But he said it all right, in the back bar of O'Connor's pub in Killarney High Street, with his mouth half full of steak sandwich.'

'Did anybody else hear him say it?'

'How in the name of all that's holy should I know? There was a woman next to us sounding like ten pigs stuck in a gate. For Christ's sake, isn't it enough that he threatened me? If it's court you're worried about, I'll stand up in front of any judge you like and swear on the Holy Bible that's what he said.'

'All right,' said Katie. 'But can you think of anybody else apart from Steven Joyce who might have wanted to do you harm? Anybody from one of the other dance troupes?'

'We're all of us competitive, and if you come out on top of the *feis* it can make a fierce difference to your bookings. It can even give you the chance of your own show, if the right producers are watching, and then you could end up like Michael Flatley with a twenty-million-euro mansion.'

Danny Coffey paused for a few seconds, his mouth working as if he were chewing on a particularly tough piece of meat. Then he said, 'No . . . there's one or two bastards in the business, but none of them would go so far as murder. Steven Joyce is the only one who holds that fierce a grudge against me. I'll bet you anything you like that he's kicking himself that I wasn't there in the studio, too, and got burned up with the others.'

He paused again, and clenched his hands tightly together, and although his face was so expressionless Katie realized that he had tears in the corners of his eyes. When he spoke, his husky voice was so much softer that she could hardly hear him.

'As it is, he killed Nicholas,' he said. 'He might just as well have killed me, too.'

Katie glanced at Kyna and saw that she had caught that moment of emotion, too. There was more to this case than met the eye, she thought. Maybe Nicholas O'Grady had stayed with Danny Coffey when he and Steven Joyce had parted company out of something more than professional loyalty.

'Has Steven Joyce contacted you at all since the fire?' asked Katie.

Danny Coffey cleared his throat. 'Why would he, except to gloat?'

'Well, we have no evidence so far that it really was him who started the fire, and that's if it wasn't accidental. And if it *wasn't* him, he might have thought to offer you his condolences, no matter that you and he fell out so badly in the past.'

'But it *was* him. I'm telling you. And it was no accident. From what I saw on the news, that building went up like a Halloween bonfire. That wasn't no faulty toaster nor nobody dropping the guts of their smoke.'

'Fair play to you,' said Katie. 'It's going to take a while, but the Technical Bureau and the experts from the fire brigade are working on it. Meanwhile, would you be prepared to go down to the University Hospital and help us to identify some of the victims? We've managed to put a name to most of them because of relatives getting in touch with us, and through photographs, but of course hardly any of them were carrying any ID on them while they were dancing and some of them were very badly burned.'

'I can't say that I relish the idea,' said Danny Coffey. 'If it helps, though, yes. Is Nicholas there? Was he very badly burned?'

Katie turned to Detective Sergeant Begley, who said, 'Yes, Mr Coffey, he was, I'm sorry to say. It looks like he was opening up the door to the attic, trying to find a way to escape the initial blaze, I should imagine. When he did that, though, he must have caught the full force of the backdraught.'

Danny Coffey squeezed his eyes tight shut and wrung his hands even more tightly together. 'Oh, Jesus,' he said.

Katie reached out to touch his arm, but at that moment her iPhone rang. She saw that it was Bill Phinner, presumably calling her from Lower Shandon Street.

'Hey there, Bill, how's she cutting?'

'You'll be needing to fetch yourself over here, ma'am,' he told her, though his tone was just as flat as ever, as if he were telling her about nothing more exciting than a special offer on fabric softener at Dunne's. 'They've just lifted the roof off the studio with the high reach excavator, and would you believe it, underneath all the slates and rafters they've uncovered two more bodies, a man and a woman.'

'Oh, dear God,' said Katie, and crossed herself. 'How are they dressed?'

'Just in normal street clothes, not dancing outfits. They're both charred beyond facial recognition – black, like they've been left on a barbecue. However, your man was carrying his wallet on him and his name on his driving licence is just about legible. Ronan John Barrett, born 16 January 1995.'

'How about the woman?'

'No ID on her, although she's wearing a Pandora charm bracelet which somebody ought to recognize. Failing that, of course, we can always identify her through her dentistry and DNA.'

Katie said, 'Could you stall it a moment, please, Bill? I have Danny Coffey with me here, he's the owner of Toirneach Damhsa.'

She lowered her iPhone and said to Danny Coffey, 'Ronan John Barrett, does that name mean anything to you?'

Danny Coffey stared at her. 'Why?' he asked. 'He's one of our dancers. The second best, if not *the* best. He thinks he's it-and-a-bit like, but there's no doubt at all that he's something incredible, especially when it comes to the *sean-nós* solo dancing.'

'I'm sorry, Mr Coffey, but a man's body has been found in the attic and the likelihood is that it's him. There was a woman with him, too, but she hasn't yet been identified. The only information I have about her so far is that she's wearing one of those Pandora charm bracelets.'

'Holy Mother of God, that's Saoirse MacAuliffe, I'll bet money on it.'

'Is she one of your dancers, too?'

'She is, yes, and she's fantastic, too. Oh, Jesus. She's supposed to be getting married next month. Her fiancé's an architect, I think – anyway he had something to do with the Capitol Cinema development on Pana. But I thought that she and Ronan were coming on a bit flirty with each other lately, do you know what I mean like? What in the name of God were they doing in the attic? They must have been the two that didn't show up for practice.'

Danny Coffey hesitated and looked around at Katie and Kyna and Detective Sergeant Begley as if some momentous truth had just occurred to him.

'That means they're *all* dead and gone,' he said. 'The whole of Toirneach Damhsa. It's gone. It just doesn't exist any more.'

Katie said, 'Me and my colleagues will have to go to the studio now and examine the deceased in person, Mr Coffey. I'm asking you to stay in Cork at least until we've completed the preliminary stages of our investigation. Do we have your address and contact details?'

'You do, sure. I'm living in my late mother's old bungalow in Ard ná Laoí, just off the Middle Glanmire Road.'

'Okay, then. If anything else occurs to you, please call Detective Sergeant Begley directly, won't you, no matter how insignificant you think it is? We'll ring you when we're ready for you to go down to CUH and see if you can put names to your dancers.'

She stood up, and so did Kyna and Detective Sergeant Begley. Before he got to his feet, though, Danny Coffey said to Katie, 'Did anything like this ever happen to you, Detective Superintendent? Did your whole life ever fall to pieces in the space of a single day?'

Katie hesitated. She couldn't help thinking of John. She had loved him so much, even though he had let her down once too often. After he had been kidnapped by Bobby Quilty, and his feet mutilated so that he lost both legs below the knee, she had suffered so much guilt that it had felt like a deep physical ache. After all, he wouldn't have been kidnapped if he hadn't once been her lover and Bobby Quilty hadn't been trying to put pressure on her.

But no matter how great her guilt had been, she had fallen out of love with him and her guilt could never have been a substitute for loving him. He had died trying to win her back, but she still felt remorse, rather than grief.

Even though Danny Coffey's question had put her in mind of her own feelings, it was much more revealing of his. She could see by her one raised eyebrow that Kyna had caught on to that, too. She wouldn't need to ask her to set up some background checks on his personal life.

'Yes, Mr Coffey, I'm afraid that's happened to me more than once,' she said. 'It's part and parcel of being a guard.'

But was *he* feeling guilty, too, she wondered – and if so, *why?*

Eight

When Davy Dorgan walked into the Templegate Tavern the three men at their usual table visibly shrank, like slugs that had been showered with salt.

'What?' said Davy, scraping out a chair and sitting down.

'You must have heard about Niall,' said Murtagh. 'I tried to ring you on your moby but you didn't pick up. It was all on the telly this morning so it was.'

'Of course I heard about him,' said Davy. 'What? Do you think *I* whacked him?'

'I wasn't saying that, for feck's sake. It's just that Niall was as sound as they come. Mouthy, I'll grant you, but he'd never do nothing behind your back when you wasn't looking like.'

'He wasn't to somebody's taste, and that's for sure,' said Billy. 'You don't think it could have been that Dennehy fellow, the one whose missus he was shagging?'

'That's my guess,' said Liam. 'He told me that Dennehy came home early last week because he'd forgotten his piece to take to work. Niall had to climb out the back window and hide in the outside jacks for half an hour.'

'Well, who knows?' said Murtagh. 'There's more than a few people in Niall's past he never talked about. He was in with the O'Flynns when he was younger, I know that for sure. My Breda rang his ex last night – you know, Patty – to give her condolences, but there was no answer. If Patty's any brains in her head at all she'll have changed her name and left the country altogether.'

'It could have been the New IRA,' said Billy. 'They had a couple

61

of cracks at Bobby last year, didn't they, because of him calling us the Authentic IRA, and because he was starting to dabble in drugs.'

'Well, whoever killed him, it's a fierce tragedy,' said Davy. 'He and I didn't always see eye to eye, but he was sound, like you say, and he knew his business.'

'Sure like,' Billy put in. 'Now Bobby's gone and *he's* gone, God rest their souls, how in the name of Jesus are we going to carry on running the fag trade? It was Niall who did all the buying and selling, after all. I don't know shite when it comes to any of that.'

'Not a bother, Billy,' Davy told him. 'I can organize all of that. I have contacts in the customs at Ringaskiddy, and in Larne, too, so we won't have any trouble bringing in the merchandise.'

'What about the street trading?' asked Murtagh. 'We've lost more than half of our street sellers since Bobby copped it. Sure like, we can smuggle in all the duty-free fags in the Western hemisphere but if we don't have nobody to sell them for us, what's the use?'

'Fair play to you, Murtagh, that's going to take some organizing, I'll grant you, but there's a couple of lads I know from Knocka who can soon round up some kids for us. Don't you worry. We'll be back in business before you know it, trust me, full steam ahead, and now we won't be pissing our profits away on fast cars and slutty women, if you'll forgive me for saying so, Bobby, in case you're looking down on us. Or *up*, from wherever you are.'

Murtagh took a swallow of Murphy's and wiped his mouth with the back of his hand. 'So what are we going to do now?'

'I don't understand the question,' said Davy. 'Carry on the way we were, of course, only more so.'

'You don't think that maybe Niall had a point about stalling for a while, just to see how things shape up – you know, politically like?'

'We've a rake of weapons already, Murtagh, and more than enough plastic, no thanks to you-know-who. I was thinking about this last night, though, yes – and I have to admit that Niall was right about a couple of things: we could use some more finance and a few more fellers who know what they're doing when it comes to communications. Every time we've fought against the Brits they've beaten us because they've had better intelligence. This time we have to outsmart them. We don't want the Clonmult massacre all over again.'

'I don't find that very funny,' said Murtagh. 'My great-grandfather was shot at Clonmult, unarmed and with his hands up. And the Tans robbed his Sacred Heart badge off his body, too.'

'I know that, Murtagh, and that's why I said it. I wanted you to remember why we're doing this, and not lose your nerve.'

'There's no way I'm losing my nerve here, Davy. It's just that all of a sudden you seem to be taking charge here, and I don't recall electing you leader.'

'I have the connections, that's all,' said Davy. 'If you think that you can do better, then grand, go ahead. I'll never be deaf to suggestions. But if we're going to take action, we need to strike now, and hard, before everybody forgets what the point of it is. A week's a long time in politics, big man, and you don't want people saying, "What the feck did they go and do that for?" '

'I think—' Liam began, and his voice was half an octave higher than usual, almost like a choirboy who has just smoked his first cigarette. 'I think we ought to hold off altogether for a while.'

Davy turned around in his chair and gave him a stare that was part exaggerated curiosity and part hostility. 'And why do you think that, Liam?'

'Well, we still don't know who shot Niall, do we? They was saying on the telly that the guards don't have any clues yet as to who might have done it. If it was that Dennehy fellow, then okay, we shouldn't have nothing to worry about because none of the rest of us shagged his missus, did we? But if it was the New IRA, or one of the gangs, we could be right in the shite.'

'So you're suggesting we sit on our arses and do nothing?'

'Niall's been *killed*, Davy,' said Liam, his voice even squeakier. 'He's like, *dead*. I don't know about you, or you, Murtagh, or you, Billy, but I don't want to be next. Me and my old doll, we're supposed to be taking our holliers in Santa Ponza next month. I don't want to be lying in St Michael's cementery with a fecking great hole in my head.'

He stood up, tipped back the last of his Murphy's, and said, 'I'm going to drain the main vein and then I'm out the gap.'

Davy Dorgan said nothing as Liam went off in the direction of the toilet.

'What do you think about that, then?' asked Murtagh.

Davy shrugged. 'He's only young. He hasn't seen what we've seen. I'm sure he'll come around if I have a quiet word.' He pushed back his chair and stood up. 'I need to shed a tear for Parnell myself.'

He weaved his way between the tables to the back of the bar and into the gents' toilet. Inside it was gloomy and noisy with the gurgling of a leaking cistern, and it smelled strongly of lemon-scented deodorant blocks. Liam was standing at one of the three urinals, his legs apart and his head tilted back. There was nobody else in there.

Davy came up behind him and tapped him on the shoulder. Liam looked around and said, 'Jesus, Davy. I'm only having a slash here.'

'Good word for it, Liam,' said Davy, very gently. He reached into his jacket pocket, took out a flick knife and clicked the blade open. Then he pushed himself up close behind Liam, so that his chest was pressing up against his back. He reached around him and seized his penis in his left hand, gripping it hard and stretching it out in a spray of warm urine.

'What the *feck*—!' screeched Liam, but then he felt the sharp edge of the flick-knife blade up against the underside of his penis. He stood very still, although he was shuddering and breathing in tiny, contracted sips.

'There's something that appears to have slipped your mind, Liam,' said Davy, so close to his ear that Liam could feel his breath. 'The reason we call ourselves the Authentic IRA is because we're an army, the Irish Republican Army. And since we're an army, we're at war. We're fighting for the Proclamation of 1916. "We declare the right of the people of Ireland to the ownership of Ireland" – and we'll never stop fighting until we get it.'

'Please, Davy, don't hurt me,' Liam whispered.

'But we're at *war*, Liam, that's what I'm reminding you, and when a fellow decides to lay down his arms and walk out on his comrades while the war is still raging, do you know what we call him? We call him a deserter. And deserters are always punished, and punished severely, even if they aren't lined up against a wall and shot.'

He pressed the flick-knife blade harder against Liam's skin. The urine was beginning to dry now and felt sticky.

'Please,' begged Liam.

'Well, you could tell me that you've changed your mind about that little speech you gave out there and that you've decided to stay and support us. Or you could say that you're sticking by what you said and that you're quitting and leaving the struggle to the rest of us. In which case I will slice off your mickey and flush it down the jacks. Which will be less than you deserve for being a deserter, but then I'm known for being merciful.'

'You'll do *what*?' said Liam. He was lost in a haze of fear now and Davy might just as well have been speaking to him in some obscure foreign language.

'Are you deaf, or thick, or both?' hissed Davy. 'If you insist on walking out on us, I'm going to turn you into the soft girl you're behaving like. That's all. And they won't be able to stitch your mickey back on because it'll be halfway on its journey to the Carrigrenan sewage plant by the time the ambulance gets here.'

Liam closed his eyes, although he was still shuddering.

'This isn't a dream, Liam,' said Davy Dorgan. 'This is happening to you now, for real. I'm giving you five seconds and then you can fill in your application form for the LGBT community.'

'All right, Davy,' said Liam, without opening his eyes. 'I'm with you, boy.'

Davy Dorgan twisted his penis in his hand, as if he were wringing out a dishcloth, and gave it sharp upward wrench. 'Good choice, Liam. Now let's go back and have another scoop to celebrate. All men together.'

He released his grip and went over to the basin to wash his hands. While he was holding them under the hot-air dryer he kept his eye on Liam in the mottled glass of the mirror.

Liam stayed where he was until Davy Dorgan had left the toilet and the door had swung shut behind him. Then he looked down at his urine-soaked jeans and he started to weep, his shoulders shaking in humiliation and utter helplessness.

Nine

Bill Phinner was waiting at Farren's Quay when Katie and Kyna and Detective Sergeant Begley arrived. He was standing by the stone wall overlooking the river in his silvery Tyvek suit, like an astronaut who had just landed from a space mission, and he was vaping.

The media were waiting, too, and as Katie ducked under the blue-and-white crime scene tape Fionnuala Sweeney called out, 'DS Maguire! We understand that more bodies have been discovered! Is this true? If it is, how many does that make in total?'

Katie didn't even turn to look at her, and neither did she respond to any of the shouted questions from the other reporters. She usually went out of her way to be helpful to the media, but today she wasn't in the mood. After this, she would have to drive down to the morgue at Cork University Hospital and see how the autopsies on the other sixteen cremated bodies were progressing, and how many of them had been positively identified. She would also have to console their grieving relatives, and that was even harder, because they would always ask her *Why? Why* my *son, why* my *daughter?*

Once all the dead had been named, she would hold a full briefing at Anglesea Street and make another plea for witnesses and information. She would also ask the Very Reverend Eoin Whooley to come in to say a prayer for the victims and the loved ones they had left behind.

'So you've given up the fags, have you, Bill?' asked Detective Sergeant Begley.

'I have, yes. Just like those two we found in the attic, except they won't be vaping any time soon. Or ever.'

Katie wasn't amused. When she was younger her father always used to say that somebody had 'given up the fags' to mean that they had died, in the vain hope that she and her sisters wouldn't understand.

'You won't need to suit up, ma'am,' Bill Phinner told her. 'We've completed all of our blacklight tests and taken all the samples we need. I'll warn you to be wide, though. There's a whole heap of debris and the floor of the attic isn't all that safe.'

He led her into the burned-out studio building. Assistant Chief Fire Officer Whalen was standing inside, talking to two serious-looking investigators from Cumann Imscrúdaitheorí Dóiteán na hÉireann, the Fire Investigation Association. He raised his eyebrows sympathetically when Katie came in. The fire service had to do nothing more than determine how the blaze had started. If it proved to be arson, though, Katie would have to find out who started it, and hunt them down, and bring a successful prosecution against them. On past experience, the chances of her achieving this were less than seven per cent.

They climbed up the shuddering ladder to the first floor. The sour stench of smoke was even stronger than before and when she reached the landing Katie had to take out a tissue and blow her nose to clear the soot she had breathed in.

All of the corpses of the dead dancers had been taken away now, but as she crossed the studio floor she could see the blistered outlines on the parquet where their bodies had been lying. She was reminded of those stories about the atom bomb at Hiroshima, where the blast had been so intense that people's shadows had been permanently burned on to walls, even though the people themselves had been totally vaporized and vanished.

'Tread careful now,' Bill Phinner cautioned as he led Katie up the steep, narrow staircase that led to the attic. The walls of the staircase were streaked with strange curling murals of smoke and the carpet had been reduced to a crunchy black ash.

At the top of the staircase they came out into the open air, with nothing above them but a grey cloudy sky. In the centre of the floor a large blue vinyl sheet covered the two bodies that had been discovered when the high-reach demolition excavator had lifted away the rafters. The sheet made a soft rippling sound in the wind, as if the man and woman underneath it were still stirring.

An entire avalanche of purplish-grey slates was yet to be cleared, as well as scorched tea-chests full of dance costumes and books and assorted junk, like hair-dryers and shoe-stretchers and clothes-hangers and a Raggedy Ann doll with a face burned so black that it looked like a golliwog.

At the far end of the attic, next to the orange brick chimney breast, there was a large pine trunk. It was badly charred on one side but apparently still intact.

'What's in the trunk?' Katie asked Bill Phinner.

'Not much. Some old music scores and accounts books, that's all.'

Kyna came up close behind Katie. 'How that little Adeen survived, I can't imagine. It must have been an inferno in here.'

'About eleven hundred degrees,' said Bill Phinner mournfully. 'Approximately the same as a Boru dry stove when it's going full blast.'

One of Bill Phinner's technical experts was standing beside the blue vinyl sheet, a thin young man in his mid-twenties with circular spectacles and a struggling ginger moustache. His Tyvek suit looked two sizes too big for him.

'Lift off the sheet there, would you, Ruari,' said Bill Phinner, and the young man untied the cord that had been preventing the sheet from flapping away in the wind and folded it back.

The two burned bodies were face to face, embracing each other. It was impossible at first sight to tell that they were a man and woman because they had both been incinerated black, their skin bubbled and their lips drawn back to reveal their teeth in two ghastly grins. In spite of their gruesome appearance, though, Katie found their last embrace deeply moving. They had clung on to each other tightly even as the fire had eaten them alive.

They were lying on a cremated mattress, its kapok stuffing burned and its springs showing.

Kyna took out her notebook and flipped it open. 'You've identified the man already as Ronan John Barrett, but Danny Coffey thinks the girl could be another one of his dancers, Saoirse MacAuliffe. She was engaged to another fellow, but apparently she and Barrett had been flirting with each other recently.'

'So the odds are, they could have come up here for a discreet bit of ping ping,' said Detective Sergeant Begley. 'Talk about choosing the wrong moment.'

'Dooley's taken her bracelet round to the Pandora shop on Winthrop Street to see if they have a record of it,' said Bill Phinner.

Katie nodded. 'Good. There's no way we can ask anybody to identify her until you've separated these two bodies and taken them over to the morgue.'

'I'm not going to try to separate them here,' Bill Phinner told her. 'They're practically welded together. I think it's best to leave that to Dr Kelley.'

'How's it going with the other victims?' Katie asked him.

'We're making good progress with that. We now have dental records for all but three of the members of Toirneach Damhsa, and they've all been X-rayed to show up any historic fractures. Two of my team were down at the morgue this morning. They photographed all of the victims' personal items *in situ* – like watches and bracelets and earrings and so forth – and then removed them all and listed them so that we can show them to the relatives. At least two-thirds of them are burned beyond any facial recognition and some of them have lost sixty per cent of their body mass and several centimetres in height.'

Katie looked around the wreckage of the attic. She tried to imagine what it must have been like for these two when they were suddenly engulfed by fire. She assumed that it must have been sudden because the attic had a skylight, and if there had been time, surely they would have waved or shouted or signalled to people in the street below, or even squeezed out of the skylight and tried to climb over to the building next door, even though it was separated by a two-metre rendered wall.

She went over to the edge of the roof and looked down at Farren's Quay and Lower Shandon Street and the grey River Lee. The traffic continued to crawl up and down the quays and across the bridges as if Cork were Toytown, where nothing tragic ever happened. Kyna came and joined her, her fluffy blonde hair blowing across her forehead in the wind. Kyna the *Aes Sidh*, the faerie.

'What's on your mind?' Kyna asked her.

'I was thinking how lovers always seem to end up getting burned, one way or another.'

Kyna gave her the faintest of smiles. 'Of course they do. That's because love is highly combustible – like whatever accelerant was used to set this building alight.'

Katie couldn't help smiling, too. 'Only a detective sergeant would call love an "accelerant".'

'Well, isn't it? Doesn't your whole life burn quicker and hotter when you're in love?'

'Sure like, of course it does. But everything always seems to end so badly. That's one of the reasons I joined the Garda in the first place.'

She paused for a moment. A squad car was speeding over Patrick's Bridge with its blue light flashing, but silently, with no siren.

'No matter what you do, though, Kyna, everything *does* end badly. Love, happiness. They're preludes to tragedy, that's all. And the more in love you are, the happier you are, the worse it hurts when it's over.'

Kyna said nothing, but stood close to her, looking at her with an expression in her eyes that acknowledged that she couldn't reach her. Not at the moment, anyway.

It was then that Katie's iPhone rang. She had a text from Conor. *What time do you think you'll be free K? I must talk to you.*

Late, she texted back.

I could come to Cobh, as late as you like.

Katie lowered her phone and pressed her hand over her mouth.

'What's wrong?' said Kyna.

'It's Conor. He wants to meet me.'

'Grand. Meet him. Talk to him. Clear the air. If it's over, it's over. At least you'll know for sure.'

Katie turned around, just in time to see Ruari covering up the two blackened bodies.

She hesitated for a moment, and then she texted, *OK, 2300 my house.* She had no idea what she was letting herself in for, but Kyna was right. She and Conor needed to clear the air between them, if only to acknowledge that no matter how passionate they had felt about each other, they should never have become lovers, and it was over.

* * *

It was starting to rain as they drove to Cork University Hospital, not heavily, but enough to speckle the windscreen of Katie's Focus. Before they entered the morgue, they went into the scrubs room to wash their hands and dress up in long blue surgical gowns and cotton caps and latex gloves.

'I'm not looking forward to this at all,' said Kyna. 'I was craw sick the last time I had to attend a post-mortem. I'm glad I had only toast for breakfast.'

Katie took hold of both of her hands. 'Come on, you'll be grand. I'll buy you a drink after.'

They pushed their way into the morgue. Although there was plenty of daylight coming in from the high clerestory windows, all of the overhead lights were switched on, as well as the seven-petal LED lamps over the autopsy table. These were so bright that they had banished even the smallest shadows, so that everything in the room appeared two-dimensional, as if the trolleys and benches and even the lab assistants were all cut out of cardboard. Katie could smell ethanol and charred flesh, which she could only compare with the smell when she cleaned her oven.

She had never seen so many bodies here before, not all at once. Fifteen of the sixteen fire victims were lying on trolleys in four parallel rows, covered by sharply creased green sheets. The sixteenth victim, a skinny girl who looked about seventeen years old, was lying naked on the autopsy table. Along the left-hand wall there were four more trolleys. Katie guessed that three of them were the victims of a head-on crash that had happened yesterday afternoon on the N20 at Killeens – a mother, a seven-year-old boy, and a baby girl.

The fourth would be the body of Niall Gleeson, waiting to have the bullet wound in his head examined.

Dr Mary Kelley, the acting deputy state pathologist, was leaning over the female fire victim, suturing her chest with quick, large stitches. The right side of the girl's body was catastrophically burned, so that her skin was twisted and blistered and knotted and split apart. It was mostly charcoal-black, although where she had been partially shielded by the dancer lying next to her it had turned cherry-red. All the flesh and fingernails of her right hand had dropped off, like a glove, exposing her claw-like finger-bones. The right side of her face had been seared by such intense heat that she looked as if she had been made up for a part in a horror film – one opalescent eye staring, one nostril gaping, and the left side of her mouth curled upwards into a sarcastic snarl.

Dr Kelley finished her stitching with a butterfly knot, tugging at the girl's limp flesh to make sure that it was tight. She lowered her face mask and called out to two young lab assistants, who came over and lifted the girl's body on to a trolley, covering her up with a sheet and wheeling her back to join the other fire victims. Then she approached Katie and Kyna, snapping off the two pairs of forensic gloves she was wearing.

'Well, I have my work cut out for me here and no mistake,' she said. 'I'm going through them as quick as I can, but don't be surprised if I don't send you a preliminary report before the beginning of next week.'

'The cause of death was the same for all of them, though, wasn't it?' said Kyna.

'Oh, much more than likely. But you never know – one of them might have suffered a myocardial infarction before the flames got to him, or her, or died of shock. I have to be thorough and identify the precise cause of death in every case.'

She lifted off her protective glasses. She was a tubby little woman, with double chins, but she had a doll-like prettiness about her. Katie noticed that since she had last seen her she had plucked her mannish eyebrows into two thin, surprised curves.

'I've examined three of them so far,' she said. 'I can't come to any final conclusions yet, but in each of those three victims the cause of death was inhalation of flame. They have burns in the interior of their mouths, nasal passages, larynx and air passages. Their vocal cord epithelium has been destroyed and they have acute oedema of the larynx and the lungs.'

'So it was probably fierce explosive, this fire,' said Katie.

'It certainly looks that way. And it burned at a very high temperature, I'd say. The usual temperature of your average house fire is about six hundred and fifty degrees, compared with a crematorium, say, where the bodies are burned at a thousand degrees for an hour and a half. The effect on these victims was like being blasted with a massive blowtorch. You saw yourself what it did to that girl's skin. It was similar to a chef, you know, scorching the sugar on top of a crème brûlée.'

'Now I'm *really* glad I had only toast,' said Kyna.

Dr Kelley said, 'I've taken samples of every victim's clothing and sealed them in airtight bottles and sent them to the Technical Bureau for analysis. They should tell us if the fire was caused by any kind of chemical and what it was.'

'Have you seen burns like these before?'

'There was an accidental fire last year in a paint factory on the Sandyford estate in Dublin, in which three workers were killed, and their burns were very similar to these. That was caused by powdered iron sulphide, which is pyrophoric – in other words, it can ignite spontaneously when it's exposed to air. But I've never seen anything on this scale, I have to admit.'

'I'm assuming that iron sulphide is used in the making of paint,' said Katie.

'That's right, as a pigment,' said Dr Kelley. 'They use it in hair dye, too.'

'But this fire happened in a dance studio, and so far as we know nobody was making paint there or anything else. There might have been hair dye, but not enough to cause a blaze as fierce as this.'

Dr Kelley nodded, and nodded again. 'Oh, there's little doubt in my mind that this was deliberate, although don't you go quoting me on that. I shall be very interested to hear from the technical experts exactly what chemicals they can identify, and how the fire was set. This doesn't look like a case of some aggrieved individual pouring petrol through a letter box. This was done by somebody with considerable expertise, somebody who knew exactly what they were up to. A trained terrorist is my guess.'

'But it makes no sense at all,' said Kyna. 'Why should a trained terrorist want to burn down a studio full of young dancers?'

Katie looked at the four lines of trolleys and shook her head. 'I have absolutely no idea at the moment. But I'm sure that when we find out why, we'll find out who.'

She went from one trolley to the next, lifting up the sheets so that she could look at the faces of the dead dancers underneath. Some of them were so charred that they looked as if their heads had been roughly sculpted out of lumps of coal. Others were almost completely untouched, including a sweetly pretty young girl with shiny blue eyeshadow who looked simply as if she were sleeping. The only visible evidence of what had happened to her was her blackened nostrils.

When Katie had lowered the sheet on the last burned face, she nodded across the morgue and said, 'I'm guessing that's Mr Gleeson you have over there?'

'It is, yes,' said Dr Kelley. 'I've completed my preliminary examination on him, just to make sure that the gunshot wound to the head was the only trauma he sustained. I'll be writing up my report on him later today, so we should be able to release his body by tomorrow morning at the latest.'

'All right, grand,' said Katie. 'Not that anybody has come forward yet to claim it.'

Dr Kelley raised her thinly plucked eyebrows. 'If there's one thing I've learned in this profession, DS Maguire, it's that not everybody has somebody who loves them.'

* * *

Before they left the hospital, Katie and Kyna went upstairs to the relatives' waiting room. There were seven or eight parents still there, all of them looking glum and exhausted and tearful.

Katie introduced herself and Kyna, and then said, 'I know you're all waiting for final identification of your sons or daughters, and of course you're welcome to stay here if you want. I have to confirm, though, that none of the Toirneach Damhsa dance troupe survived the fire, and that in most cases their injuries were so extensive that it won't be possible for you to view their remains.'

A red-haired woman in the opposite corner of the room let out a funereal keen of anguish, and then bit her knuckles to silence herself. Her husband put his arm around her and hugged her tight, although his eyes were filled with tears, too.

'The state pathologist still has a fair amount of work to do before we can release the remains for burial,' said Katie. 'Our technical experts have a lot of tests to carry out, too. I'm fierce sorry about this delay, but we have to verify the cause of death and make sure that all of the deceased are correctly identified.'

'I brought some pictures of my daughter,' said a middle-aged woman in a drooping grey cardigan. 'Can't you identify her from that?'

'It's possible,' Katie told her. 'But there's no point in my pretending to you that identification is going to be easy. We're relying mostly on the personal possessions that were found on the deceased, like bracelets and watches, and also by dental records and DNA.'

'Holy Mother of God,' said the woman, as the implication of what Katie was telling her began to sink in.

'The Technical Bureau have already started to canvass relatives for samples,' Katie continued. 'In due course they'll be coming to you, too. Apart from that, I'll be holding a meeting at Anglesea Street Garda station either tomorrow or more likely the day after, to which you're all invited. Meanwhile, on behalf of An Garda Síochána, I want to express our deepest sympathy for your very painful loss.'

She went around the room and shook the hands of everybody there, and exchanged some quiet words of condolence. She could sense the feeling of unreality among them. They were gradually recovering from the initial shock of hearing that their sons and daughters had died, but their shock hadn't yet been replaced by acceptance, or by grief. They were all in a state of disbelief, as if this wasn't really happening and tomorrow morning they would go into their children's bedrooms and they would still be lying there, not dead, but asleep.

As they drove back to Anglesea Street, Kyna said, 'You know what my granny always used to say? *Cén fáth go bhfuil bás teacht i gcónaí ró-luath?* That was after my grandpa passed away, and he was eighty-six. "Why does death always come too soon?" '

Ten

It was nearly midnight by the time Katie arrived back home in Carragh View. It was raining hard now, so that her windscreen wipers had been whacking at full speed all the way from Anglesea Street to Cobh. She had been listening to Ludovico Einaudi's soothing *Fairytale* on her car's CD player to calm herself down and try and clear her mind of the grotesque gallery of charred faces that had confronted her in the morgue. In the course of her career she had seen scores of corpses – some shot, some drowned, some crushed, some three weeks dead and swollen up like pale green Michelin men – but the sadness and the apparent pointlessness of those young dancers' deaths made it impossible for her to stop thinking about them.

As Kyna had asked, Who in the name of God would want to kill eighteen young dancers and their dance coach? And why?

When she reached her house she saw that a scarlet Toyota was parked on the kerb outside. She had been so involved with the horror of the Toirneach Damhsa fire that she had almost forgotten about Conor. As she turned into her driveway, the Toyota's door opened and Conor climbed out, turning up his raincoat collar and walking hurriedly towards her.

He opened her car door for her and said, 'Hallo, Katie.'

'Sorry I'm so late,' she told him. 'I expect you've heard about all those young dancers being burned.'

'I have, of course. There was a report about it on the *Six-One News* again, just this evening. I was thinking of you when I saw it.'

Katie lifted her briefcase out of the back seat of her car, locked the doors and then made her way to the house, with Conor following close behind her.

'You're not too tired, are you?' he asked, as she put her key in the front door. 'I'll go, if you want me to, and maybe see you tomorrow.'

'No, you're grand altogether,' she told him. As soon as she opened the door, her Irish setter, Barney, came bustling up to her with his tail slapping against the radiator. Barney saw Conor, too, and snuffled up to him almost as enthusiastically as he had greeted Katie. He and Conor had made friends the last time Conor had come here. Conor and animals seemed to have an almost mystical affinity for each other, which was one of the reasons he had become a pet detective, and one of the reasons why Katie had fallen for him.

Katie was about to say, 'Well, *somebody*'s pleased to see you,' but decided against it. She hung up her coat and then opened the living-room door and switched on all the lamps. After what she had been through today she felt like a drink, but she didn't want to have one with Conor here, and besides she hadn't had any supper and it was far too late to be drinking vodka on an empty stomach.

Conor followed her into the living room and they stood facing each other like characters in a stage play.

'So, what is it you wanted to say to me?' said Katie. She hated it that he was still as handsome as the first moment she had set eyes on him, and still carried that distinctive fragrance of Chanel Bleu. Why couldn't she see now that his nose was too big, or that his beard was too scruffy, and why didn't he reek of BO and disappointment? But she couldn't, and he didn't.

She felt scruffy herself. Her dark red bob needed a trim, and she had dropped mayonnaise on the sleeve of her cream-coloured sweater, and her dark green linen skirt was badly creased from sitting at her desk for most of the day. She didn't want to take off her shoes in case her feet smelled.

'Is this all about Clodagh?' Conor asked her. 'I mean, is Clodagh the reason that you haven't been answering any of my calls or texts?'

'If Clodagh's your wife, then yes.'

'Why didn't you give me the chance to explain?'

'Why didn't you tell me you were married before you took me into your bed? I think that's more to the point, don't you?'

'I am married, yes, Katie, I admit it – but only technically. Clodagh and I separated more than eighteen months ago and we'll be getting divorced. There's been a hold-up over the title to the house, otherwise we would have been divorced already. But when I saw you, I didn't want to wait any longer. What if I'd waited, and you'd gone off with some other fellow, and I'd lost you?'

Katie said, 'Oh, for sure. There's a long queue of horny men outside my office just busting to jump on top of me. I'm a detective superintendent, Conor. Every one of my days is filled from the crack of dawn till midnight with chasing drug-dealers and fraudsters and pimps and other assorted scumbags and sitting in musty courtrooms and going through a heap of paperwork that makes Knockboy mountain look like a molehill by comparison.'

She was trying to sound cross, but she was so relieved by what Conor had told her that by the time she had finished she couldn't help smiling. Barney had heard her from the kitchen and came into the living room licking his lips from a drink of water, and both he and Conor had almost the same expectant expression on their faces, which made her smile even more.

'I should have told you what the situation was with Clodagh, I admit,' said Conor. 'But as far as I'm concerned, our marriage is stone-cold dead, and I know for a fact that she's been seeing somebody else herself, some fellow who works for Coilte, the forestry company.'

He paused, and smiled, and held out both hands. 'Katie, I think you're the liveliest, prettiest, sexiest, most individualistic woman I ever met. Now that I've found you, I couldn't bear to let you go. Not over something as stupid as forgetting to tell you that I'm not quite divorced yet.'

Katie closed her eyes for a moment. Suddenly she felt very, very tired. Her job was so demanding that she forgot sometimes that she needed emotional support as much as she needed her team of dedicated detectives. Kyna was always there to encourage her, and to sympathize with her, and she found Kyna extremely attractive, but she knew that the complications of starting a relationship with Kyna could ultimately wreck one or both of them, not only personally but their careers in the Garda, too.

Barney licked her hand and she opened her eyes again. Conor was still standing there with his arms out. She walked towards him and he held her very close, so that she could breathe him in, not just his aftershave but the smell of his clothes and his body. This was more than emotional support. As tired as she was, she felt that he was holding her up and lifting off her shoulders all the weight of the past few days.

He stroked her hair and she looked up at him. There was such a calm, benign look in his eyes that she pressed her head even closer to his chest and she could hear his heart beating. He didn't have to ask her if he was forgiven. This embrace was more than enough. They stood there holding each other so tight that she could feel him rising inside his trousers.

'I think I need a drink,' she said, at last. 'How about you?'

'A Coke, if you have it, or a tonic water. I don't want to get caught drinking and driving.'

'You don't have to drive. You can stay here for the night.'

He looked down at her acutely. 'You're sure about that?'

'Of course I'm sure. Look – why don't you pour us some drinks while I take a very quick shower? I've been in the morgue today and I'm sure that I still have the smell of death on me.'

'Katie—' Conor began.

'What?' she said, and stood on tiptoes to kiss him. They kissed and kissed and she could hardly bear to stop kissing him. She loved the soft clean bristles of his beard, and the way his tongue tangled with hers and explored her teeth one by one, like a diver exploring an underwater cave.

They didn't have to say any more. Conor went with Barney into the kitchen to fetch some ice for their drinks while Katie went into her bedroom, switched on the lights and undressed.

When she stepped out of her thong she found that it was slippery and when she touched herself she realized just how much kissing Conor had aroused her. She looked at herself in the dressing-table mirror and thought she looked beat out and bedraggled, but she smiled at herself because she was happy and she didn't care what she looked like.

* * *

When she came back into the living room in her thick pink towelling bathrobe she found Conor sitting on the couch stroking Barney's ears, and Barney staring up at him, totally mesmerized.

'I'm sure he has erogenous ears,' said Katie, picking up the vodka-tonic that Conor had made for her and sitting down close to him. 'In fact, I think he's erogenous all over, the way he chases after all the bitches around here. I was wondering if it was too late to have him spayed.'

Conor shook his head. 'If you're going to do it, you should do it when they're young. It reduces the risk of testicular cancer or prostate trouble, and they definitely lose their interest in the ladies. But Irish setters in particular can lose this lovely shiny red coat and develop a "spay coat" instead, which is dry and woolly and not so colourful. So my advice is, leave Barney be. He's glossy, and he's virile, and we wouldn't want to turn him into a sexless hearth rug.'

Katie kissed Conor and snuggled up close to him. She was aware that her bathrobe had opened at the front so that he could see into her cleavage, but she deliberately wanted to arouse him. She knew that she smelled alluring, too, because she had sprayed herself with Daisy Blush.

Every day at the station she always had to be dominant and decisive, even with men who made no secret of the fact that they found her attractive, like Chief Superintendent Denis MacCostagáin and Superintendent Michael Pearse. But Conor made her feel completely submissive, as if she would do anything to please and excite him. It was this shedding of responsibility that she found so arousing.

'Why don't we take these drinks into the bedroom,' she said. 'I love Barney, you know that, but I don't want him dogging.'

'Talking of dogs, I have one more thing to tell you,' said Conor. 'I heard last night from one of my scummy vet contacts that Guzz Eye McManus is holding a special fifty-dog fight up at Ballyknock on Thursday next week, to celebrate his fiftieth birthday. The dogs will be coming in from all over, Cork and Kerry in particular. The bets already placed are astronomical – that's what your man believes, anyway. He's staked five hundred euros of his own money on two pit bulls.'

'That's a fantastic tip-off,' said Katie.

'I was going to tell you, of course, no matter how things were between you and me. I wasn't totally sure, but I guessed your not calling me was all about Clodagh. Your Detective Scanlan told me she'd seen her coming into the station looking for me, and that she and you exchanged a few words.'

'We didn't argue or anything. All I did was tell her where to find you. But I won't pretend that I didn't feel like I'd been hit in the heart with a hammer.'

'Katie—'

Katie smiled and kissed him. 'It's over. Forget it. If I'd been married but separated, the same as you, I probably wouldn't have mentioned it, either. I felt guilty enough having poor John staying with me and all the time him thinking that when he got his prosthetic legs he and I were going to be back the way we were. That – that was more painful than I can tell you. I felt so treacherous. But I fell for you, too, Conor. It's been a long time since I felt such an instant attraction to any man. Don't ask me what it is about you.'

She couldn't help smiling again, and kissing him. 'Maybe it's because you like animals so much. Or you have a bit of the animal in you yourself. Anyway . . . I'll be putting a call in to Inspector Carroll at Tipperary Town first thing tomorrow morning. If McManus is staging such a big event, we should be able to pick up a whole crowd of dog-fighters if we plan it properly, quite apart from him. In fact, it could be the biggest blow against dog-fighting that this country's seen in years.'

'You'll have to keep your operation well under wraps, though,' said Conor. 'McManus has eyes and ears everywhere. That's how he's managed to run these dog-fights for so many years without ever being lifted. Apart from the fact that everybody's scared of him. They say he tied some fellow who cheated him to two SUVs, and drove them off in opposite directions.'

Katie said, 'Unh-hunh, don't let's talk about grisly stuff like that. I've had a bad day as it is. I'm tired and I just want cuddling.'

'You don't mind if I take a quick shower first myself? I've been rushing around today like a pig on PCP.'

'You smell grand to me. But of course.'

Katie made sure that Barney's water bowl was filled for the night and then she took her drink through to the bedroom. She dropped her bathrobe and climbed naked into bed, plumping up the pillows and fluffing up her hair. She had taught herself early in her career to blank out the stresses of the day when it was time for her to sleep, no matter how traumatic they had been. Now, waiting for Conor, she had a similar feeling to finding that emerald earring she thought she had lost for ever, or finishing a novel in which all the characters end up being happy. It was almost smugness, as if she had managed at last to overcome one of life's perpetual disappointments – but it was excitement, too, because Conor would soon have his arms around her.

She took a sip of vodka, listening to the shower pump and the squeak of Conor's bare feet in the shower tray, and she whispered to herself a small prayer that her mother had taught her to say at bedtime.

'I thank you, Lord, for watching me, and seeing what I could not see, that if I opened up my eyes, my life would bring a sweet surprise. That love, and happiness, are always there, if only we believe in prayer. That even in the dead of night, your light, O Lord, will soon shine bright.'

A few minutes later, Conor came into the bedroom, his hair

wet, wearing nothing but a maroon bath towel around his waist.

'Is it okay if I borrow your toothbrush?' he asked her.

Katie didn't answer. She was already asleep. Her lips were slightly parted and her eyelids were flickering as she dreamed some dream that, tomorrow, she wouldn't be able to remember. Conor stood and watched her for a few moments before he went back to the bathroom to hang up the towel and brush his teeth with his finger.

He eased himself into bed next to her and then switched off the bedside lamps. He put his arm around her waist and held her close, his erect penis pressed against her thigh. He didn't feel frustrated, though. He felt the same sense of relief that Katie had felt – that for once in his life fate had been kind to him and brought him that sweet surprise that Katie had prayed for ever since she was a child.

* * *

The digital clock beside the bed read 6:11 when Katie woke up. She blinked and stared at the ceiling. As Detective Ó Doibhilin would say, her mouth felt as dry as Gandhi's flip-flop. But then she felt Conor's warm bare shoulder against hers and heard him steadily breathing, and she turned on to her side and there he was, sleeping like a saint on a sepulchre.

Outside, it was lashing. She could hear the rainwater chuckling to itself in the downpipe outside her bedroom window. But the sound of rain was soothing and reassuring rather than depressing, because here she was snuggled up in bed with Conor.

She stroked his shoulder with her fingertips and he stirred slightly and snuffled, but he didn't wake up. Then she reached under the duvet and ran her fingers into the hair on his chest. He was quite muscular, and he had told her that he still rowed whenever he could with St Michael's Rowing Club on the Shannon. His stomach was slightly rounded, but she liked that.

She kissed his shoulder, twice, three times, and he murmured, 'What? I didn't mean that,' but he still didn't wake up. Katie couldn't help smiling to herself, wondering what it was that he was dreaming.

Now she couldn't resist taking hold of his penis and fondling it, and then slowly rubbing it up and down, with the tip of her index finger circling around the opening. She couldn't tell if he was waking up or not, but he began to stiffen and after only six or seven rubs he was fully erect. She loved his penis. It was so thick and long, with a slight curve to it when it was completely hard. She loved massaging his balls, too, until they were tight and crinkled and as big as two red plums.

'Wufff . . . what?' he said, opening his eyes. Katie kissed his shoulder again and gripped his penis as hard as she could, so that his glans swelled and the opening gaped.

'What's this *wufff*?' she laughed. 'Didn't I say you had the animal in you?'

Conor said, 'Jesus. For a moment there I thought I was dead and gone to heaven.'

'Well, you're not dead, darling, but I hope you're at least halfway to heaven.'

Conor lifted his head from the pillow so that he could kiss her. At the same time he held her breast and started gently to roll her nipple around between finger and thumb. As her nipple stiffened, he tried to raise himself up, with the intention of climbing on top of her, but she sat up and pushed him back down.

'No,' she said. 'This is me, making up for thinking the worst of you.'

'Come on, Katie, it was my fault. I should have told you.'

'All the same.'

She got on to her knees and straddled him, pinning his wrists against the bed.

'This isn't halfway to heaven,' he grinned at her. 'I've arrived. I hope St Peter isn't watching.'

'Well, I'm teaching you a lesson here,' said Katie. 'When somebody's sorry, you should accept their apology with good grace. And this is my apology.'

She leaned forward and kissed him on the forehead, and the eyelids, and the lips, her heavy breasts swinging against his chest hair. Then she reached down between her thighs, grasping his erect penis again and manoeuvring his glans between the smooth waxed lips of her vulva. She was very wet and slippery by now, but she kept a firm grip on him so that he couldn't penetrate her straight away. He tried to hump up his hips because he was so desperate now to push himself inside her, but she held on to him even tighter, relishing the sensation of his glans just inside her vagina, and also the power of keeping him restrained, even though she was acting so whorish.

She squeezed her vaginal muscles rhythmically, at the same time watching Conor's reaction with her eyes suggestively widened and the most provocative smile on her lips.

'God Almighty,' he gasped. 'If you knew what you're making me feel like.'

At last she took her hand away and slowly sank herself down on to his erection, until he was up inside her as far as he could possibly go and she felt as if his wiry pubic hair were hers. He reached up and massaged her breasts, playing with her nipples and pressing her cleavage close together. She leaned forward so that his penis was right on the very edge of slipping out of her, and they kissed again, their tongues fighting together as if they were trying to prove which of them was the more excited. Then she let her hips sink back down on him and the sensation his penis gave her as he slid back up inside her was so intense that she closed her eyes.

Their lovemaking quickly grew more and more frantic. Katie had wanted to keep it slow and measured right until the very moment when they climaxed, but they couldn't help themselves. Conor held the cheeks of her bottom in both hands, with the tip of one finger inserted into her anus, while she rode him and rode him and rode him. He was grunting and she was gasping and then her orgasm rose up between her legs like a huge dark force rising up from the depths of the ocean and she was shaken and shaken until she screamed like she had never screamed before.

Then it was over, and apart from their syncopated panting there was no other sound except the rain.

Katie rolled off him and they lay side by side on the bed, sweating and trying to get their breath back. She looked at the clock and it read 6:31.

'Not even twenty minutes,' she smiled. She could feel his warm semen sliding across her thigh. 'My fault, I was too frustrated.'

'We can always go for a repeat performance,' said Conor, kissing her.

'No. Sadly, I don't have the time. I have to set up a meeting for the Toirneach Damhsa fire, as well as a hundred other things.'

'Oh, well, that's a fierce pity and no mistake,' said Conor. 'But I have to go back to Limerick today myself, like I told you. Clodagh and I have a meeting with our solicitors and there's some business stuff I have to sort out. But I can probably come back tomorrow or the day after.'

'Come and stay here with me,' said Katie.

'You're sure?'

'I still need you to work on this dog-fighting case, Conor, quite apart from needing you to make love to me. And it would save money if the Garda didn't have to pay for your guest house.'

'There,' said Conor. 'You're logical as well as sexy. Those were two things that Clodagh wasn't. And for some reason I could never please her. Probably because she came from Cavan.'

'She's happy now, though, isn't she, with this fellow from Coilte?'

'So she says. They manage most of Ireland's forests, so I suppose he always has wood.'

Katie slapped his arm. 'Mother of God, your sense of humour. You're worse than some of my detectives, you are. You'll be the death of me, Conor Ó Máille.'

* * *

She made them a breakfast of scrambled eggs and grilled tomatoes and wholemeal toast. A little after seven-thirty, Jenny Tierney from next door rang the doorbell to take Barney out for his morning walk. She said, 'Well, good morning,' to Conor when she came into the kitchen in her dripping-wet plastic mac, although she continued to stare at him in a very disapproving way as Katie clipped on Barney's lead.

Conor raised his coffee mug to her and smiled and said, 'Top of the morning to you, too. How's it coming on?'

After they had finished their breakfast, Katie drove Conor back into the city. She took him up Summerhill to the Gabriel guest house where he had been staying since he arrived in Cork to help Katie to track down dog-nappers. They sat in the car with the rain drumming on the roof, and squeezed hands, and kissed.

'I'll text you to tell you when I'm coming back,' Conor told her.

'Text me anyway. Ring me if you like.'

'I think I might be falling in love with you, Kathleen Maguire.'

'Don't say things like that. The Devil may be listening. The luck I've had, do you know, I don't want to risk another disaster. I'll see you when you come back from Limerick so. Take good care of yourself and don't allow the lovely Clodagh to rip you off.'

'Oh, I'm after learning how to take care of meself now, girl,' said Conor, in a strong Northside accent. 'I've spent so much time in Cork, I've turned into a real cute hoor. Cute as the red-arsed bees.'

Katie slapped his shoulder, and then she kissed him, and then it was time for her to go.

She drove back down to the city centre feeling warm and content, and better about herself than she had in a long time. Conor made her feel so attractive, and she was so frustrated that she wouldn't be seeing him again for another twenty-four hours at least. Why did wonderful nights like that always have to be over? Why did happiness fade so quickly but pain nag you for ever?

As she drove over the Brian Boru Bridge, she passed a young mother with an umbrella pushing a buggy and she couldn't help thinking of her own baby, Seamus, and what it had felt like to hold him in her arms and rock him to sleep. She could even remember the smell of him, milk and baby powder, and the feel of his tiny hand clasping her finger. He would be going to bunscoil now if he had lived, and be coming home to show her his crayon drawings. But he had died, like her first husband, Paul, had died, and her lover, John, and like last night there had been no way that she could stop another rainy day from breaking.

When she had parked in Anglesea Street, she had to tug out a tissue and dab her eyes. She checked her make-up in the sun-visor mirror and applied a little more blushed nude lip liner. *Mother of God, Katie*, she thought, pressing her lips tightly together, *you're getting pure morbid in your old age.*

Eleven

She was still walking along the corridor to her office when her iPhone played. It was Dr Kelley calling from the morgue.

'A very good morning to you, DS Maguire. I made an early start this morning on those two last victims they found in the attic. I still haven't separated them yet, because they're literally fused together and it's going to take some very delicate work with the scalpel to cut them apart. I've X-rayed them, though, and you'll never guess what.'

'Surprise me, then,' said Katie. She entered her office and finger-waved to Moirin, who was already sitting in her own small office, hunched in front of her computer. 'What will I never guess what?'

'They've been shot in the head, the both of them.'

'They were *shot*?'

'That's right. The young woman has entry and exit wounds in the left and right sides of her skull, and the young man has an entry wound in his right temple and bullet fragments still inside his skull.'

'Mother of God, I can scarce believe it. None of the other victims have bullet wounds, do they?'

'No, only those two. I thought to myself that there was something unusual about them when their bodies were first brought in here. It would be very unlikely for fire victims to be clinging on to each other like that. Usually if you're alight you're totally concerned with trying to tear off your own burning clothing, and as your tendons tighten up your arms bunch up in that characteristic posture like you're playing a little tin drum. I'd say it's almost certain they were dead before the fire got to them.'

'I'll come over later this morning and take a look for myself,' said Katie. 'I assume that you've advised Bill Phinner.'

'I have, of course. One of his ballistics experts is on his way here so that he can scan their skulls and extract the bullet fragments. They're so badly burned the two of them that it isn't going to be easy to estimate the exact range at which they were shot. As you know, we can usually tell if somebody's been shot point-blank by the powder tattoo on the skin. At a rough guess, though, I'd say from the size of the entry wounds that they were likely shot from less than fifteen centimetres away, if not actually point-blank.'

'That makes sense, sure,' said Katie. 'The space in the attic was very confined, and it's almost certain that they *were* shot in the attic because of the way we found them. I can't imagine that whoever shot them carried their bodies separately up the stairs and then arranged them so that they were holding each other.'

'I'll keep you informed, anyway,' said Dr Kelley. 'Ah, look – here's the ballistics expert now. Jesus, they all seem so young these days, don't they? Sometimes I feel like I'm working with a whole crowd of fierce clever children.'

'I'll talk to you later so,' Katie told her. While she was talking Moirin had come in with a cappuccino for her, as well as a beige folder of letters and other paperwork, and Detective Dooley had appeared in the doorway, waiting for her to finish.

'Robert,' she said, and beckoned him to come in. 'How's it going on?'

He looked refreshed. His hair was brushed up vertically like a startled cartoon character, and he smelled of Lynx body spray. Katie noticed that his forehead was peppered with tiny red spots and hoped that she wasn't overworking him or putting him under too much stress.

'I've identified the girl from the attic,' he told her. 'It *was* Saoirse MacAuliffe, for sure. I took her bracelet to the Pandora shop and they had sales records of all the charms she'd bought. Not only that, she was wearing a pink Lipsy watch and her parents confirmed that they gave it to her for her last birthday, as well as the tackies that she was wearing. The tackies were mostly charred but there was some pink canvas left untouched and they still had the Wedge label inside. The Technical Bureau took DNA samples as well, just to make one hundred and ten per cent certain. We should have the results from those later today.'

'She was engaged, wasn't she?' Katie asked him. 'Did her parents know about any relationship she might have been having with this fellow from the dancing troupe – what was his name?'

'Ronan Barrett. No. She'd told them recent-like that she and Ronan were friendly, and that he'd been helping her with some of the *céilí* dance routines, but she didn't say nothing about any kind of relationship.'

'How about her fiancé? He's an architect, isn't he?'

Detective Dooley took his notebook out of his jacket pocket and flipped it open. 'That's right. Douglas Cleary. He works for Leeside Architects, who submitted some designs for the Capitol Cinema development, although I don't know if they were accepted. He's been away in Manchester for the past two days for some architectural get-together, but he's cut his trip short and he'll be back here in Cork late this evening.'

'So he's been told that Saoirse's dead?'

'Her parents emailed him, but I cautioned them not to tell him that she was found in the attic with Ronan Barrett – and of course even *they* don't yet know that she and Barrett were found hanging on to each other like that. We haven't even told the media about that yet.'

'Well, the plot thickens. Dr Kelley started her autopsy this morning and the first thing she found out was that Saoirse and Ronan had both been shot in the head.'

'You're codding me! Serious? So somebody murdered them and then set fire to the building.'

'Well, let's not jump to conclusions. I think it's safe to assume that they were killed before the fire started, but we don't know for certain who shot them. Maybe it was the arsonist – or arsonists plural. Maybe it was somebody else altogether. Until we hear from

93

the technical experts we can't even be certain if the fire was set deliberately or not.'

'Oh, come on, ma'am, if that was an accident, I swear to God you can call me a two-headed tortoise.'

Katie couldn't help smiling. 'Now you've almost made me wish that it was. But I agree with you, the chances of a fire as devastating as that being accidental are almost nil. Now – was there anything else? How's the CCTV coming along?'

'That was the other reason I came up to see you. I've finished looking through all of the CCTV recordings of the fire, as well as the fire brigade's videos.'

'Did you see anything suspicious?'

'Hard to say for sure like. I've identified four fellers in the crowd in particular and two girls. All of them have a history of convictions or cautions for vandalism or antisocial behaviour of one kind or another. I've emailed you the complete list. When you've taken a sconce at it, maybe we can decide if it's worth my while pulling them in for questioning. There's one of them, though, who was right in the back of the crowd but he jangled a bell the second I realized who he was. Dara Coughlan, from Mayfield. I was involved in hauling him in about three years ago, when I was stationed up there.'

'What's the story about him?' asked Katie. At the same time she switched on her desktop computer and found the list of six names that Detective Dooley had drawn up for her, just to see if she recognized any of them herself.

'Serial arsonist, ma'am, that Dara Coughlan. Total header. He hangs around with that crowd of druggie young gurriers up at Barnavara Crescent. He torched five cars and the excuse he gave in court was that they belonged to fathers who wouldn't allow their daughters to go out on a jag with him. He was only sixteen at the time so they put him on the rehab programme, but that had no effect on him at all like. You might as well have tried to teach table manners to an epileptic monkey. It was only about six or seven months later that he tried to burn down the butcher's shop on the corner of Iona Park, and he said he did it for the same reason. He was sniffing around one of the butcher's daughters and the butcher told him to take a running jump or he'd chop off something important and mince it up for a hamburger patty. So Dara poured petrol through his letter box.'

'So what happened to him then?'

'We hauled him in again and the court sent him off to Trinity House School until he reached seventeen. By the time they let him out I was doing my detective garda training at Templemore, so I never saw him again. Not until I recognized him in that CCTV footage, anyway. He's watching that fire with some slapper and grinning like the epileptic monkey got the nuts.'

'Well, if you have a gut feeling about him, you should bring him in for an interview,' said Katie. 'And think about it – if his motive for arson in the past was always revenge because he'd been told to keep away from somebody's daughter, it would be worth your checking if he'd been making a play for any of the girls who danced for Toirneach Damhsa. Maybe somebody from the dance troupe had warned him off and he took exception. Mind you . . . it doesn't look as if that fire was set off by anything as straightforward as petrol.'

She looked down the list of names on her computer screen. She recognized one of them – Johnny Dunne, a Pavee musician who had been arrested the year before for throwing a flat-screen TV set out of a fourth-floor window of Jurys Inn and seriously injuring a woman who was walking along Anderson's Quay underneath. From what she had heard, though, he had sobered up and got himself a contract with Heresy Records in Dublin.

'None of the others are serial arsonists like Dara,' said Detective Dooley. 'All the same, they've all been had up for serious vandalism, like these two girls. They were caught trying to hobble sweaters from Olivia's Boutique in Oliver Plunkett Street and a given a warning by the owner. They came back a couple of nights later and smashed the front window and threw cans of paint and wood varnish around and set fire to some of the clothes. They caused about thirty-five thousand euros' worth of damage.'

'Well, all six have previous and all six were present at the scene of the Toirneach Damhsa fire, so interview them all. I doubt if any of them were responsible, since we're dealing with a shooting here, as well as arson, but I'd like to be sure. As you know yourself, some offenders' antisocial behaviour escalates as they grow older, especially if they have untreated psychiatric problems.'

Detective Dooley said, 'Those two being shot like . . . that really puts a pure different aspect on this case now, don't you think? It must have been more than just pointless vandalism, or some other dancers trying to mess up Toirneach Damhsa's chances at the *feis* next week.'

'It's impossible to say yet, Robert, and after what Danny Coffey said about his partner Steven Joyce, and the way he threatened him, I wouldn't rule out the possibility of somebody from another dance troupe being responsible. I have to admit that up until now I never knew myself how desperate the competition was between all those rival dancers. *Feis*? Jesus, it's more like Isis.'

'What about Joyce like? Are we pulling him in for an interview?'

'When we have more evidence, yes, we probably will, but not before. I don't want to start making accusations against him based solely on what Danny Coffey told me. We know where Joyce lives, on Connaught Avenue, and what with the *feis* coming up next week he's not likely to be going anywhere – not without it looking fierce suspicious.'

'Okay,' said Detective Dooley. 'I'll make a start with Dara Coughlan. Little psycho. I almost wish it *was* him who did it. I'd love to see him banged up for the rest of his manky life.'

* * *

Katie rang Inspector Carroll at Tipperary Town and told him about the fifty-dog fight that Guzz Eye McManus was planning to celebrate his fiftieth birthday.

'Where did you pick that up from?' asked Inspector Carroll, and then coughed, as if she had caught him in the middle of eating a sandwich. 'We've been hearing rumours, but you know how tight-lipped the Travellers are, especially that shower up at Ballyknock. They wouldn't tell you where your toes were if they were standing on them.'

'I have it on very good authority, Kenny, I promise you,' Katie told him. 'As soon as I hear more details, I'll let you know so. But if McManus really *is* planning a fifty-dog fight, we'll need to set up a major operation, depending on the location. Who knows how many officers and vehicles we'll have to deploy. We'll also be needing some help from the ISPCA. There's going to be a whole rake of fighting dogs that need taking care of, and putting down probably, after we've lifted their owners. I'll be having a word in a minute with Chief Superintendent MacCostagáin. We should start working out a joint contingency plan as soon as possible.'

'That's grand, Katie. I'll talk to Sergeant Kehoe. I'm guessing that Michael Pearse is the man he should be liaising with at your end.'

'To begin with, yes. I'll talk to you after when I know a bit more.'

Katie took her coffee along to Chief Superintendent Mac-Costagáin's office. He was talking on the phone when she knocked at his door but he beckoned her in and gestured that she should sit down. He was in his shirt sleeves and braces as usual, and while he was talking he had been running his hand through his fine white hair, and nodding, and saying, 'Yes, ma'am. Of course, ma'am. That's very welcome news to be sure. No, I'm absolutely delighted.'

She had never heard him speaking to anybody so enthusiastically, and so respectfully, too.

When he had finished on the phone, he perched himself on the corner of his desk and said, 'Well! You'll never guess who *that* was.'

'That's the second time today that somebody has told me that I'll never guess something. I'll bet you can't guess what I couldn't guess the first time.'

'No, you're right, I can't.' He normally looked like somebody's miserable uncle, with his eyes slightly too near together, but this morning he seemed to be in a much more affable mood.

'Those two young people found in the attic after the Toirneach Damhsa fire were not only incinerated, they were both shot in the head.'

97

Chief Superintendent MacCostagáin blinked at her. 'Holy Jesus. That complicates matters.'

Katie told him that a ballistics expert had already gone to Cork University Hospital, and brought him up to date on all the other progress she had made, such as it was. 'There's still no obvious perpetrator, though. Not even a principal suspect, unless you believe Danny Coffey.'

'All right,' said Chief Superintendent MacCostagáin. 'It's early days yet. What about that Niall Gleeson shooting? How's that going?'

'Nowhere at the moment. Again, the ballistics expert will be looking at the bullet, but I'm not too confident that's going to tell us anything much, especially if the NIRA shot him.'

Katie paused, and then she said, 'So who was that on the phone that I can't guess?'

'Commissioner Nóirín O'Sullivan herself. She wanted to tell me that the government have appointed a new Assistant Commissioner for the Southern Region, to replace Jimmy O'Reilly, God rest his poor tortured soul.'

'Well, amen to that,' said Katie, even though Assistant Commissioner O'Reilly had done everything he could to undermine her. He had eventually shot himself after an abortive attempt to involve her in a fake arms deal, which would have ruined her reputation, on top of which he had been deserted by his faithless and sponging boyfriend. Katie couldn't imagine that any new Assistant Commissioner could be worse.

'So do I know him – or her?' she asked.

'You should do. Frank Magorian, the chief superintendent from the Garda College.'

'Oh, I know Frank all right. He was in charge at Templemore when I was taking my senior investigative officer course. He was always very smooth, very unflappable. He'll make a perfect Assistant Commissioner. If the roof fell down on top of his head, he would only say something like, "Oh! Not a bother, let's be thankful it's not raining."'

'He's coming in later, Katie, so I'll give you a call when he's here so that you can reintroduce yourselves. Was that everything? You look like you have something more on your mind.'

'Dogs, sir. It's Guzz Eye McManus rearing his ugly head again.'

She told him about the proposed dog-fight and as she did so his expression grew increasingly morose, like it usually was, and his shoulders sagged.

'Come on, Katie. You know how much over budget we are. So some dogs are going to get killed. Cruel, of course, I'm not saying for a single second that it isn't. Totally inhumane. But under the Control of Dogs Act we would have had to have them put down anyway, if they're the specified breeds and we'd caught them out in public without a leash or a muzzle. I mean, holy Saint Joseph, can you imagine how much an operation like this is going to cost to set up?'

'So what are you saying, sir? You're saying that I should take no action? You know that a proportion at least of those fighting dogs have been stolen from their rightful owners, and that the dog-fighters are guilty of barbaric mistreatment of animals in the ways that they train them. There's also the question of the profits made by dog-fight organizers like McManus. I'm sure the Criminal Assets Bureau would be fierce interested in what *he* rakes in.'

Chief Superintendent MacCostagáin stood up, walked around his desk and opened up a folder of paperwork, as if to indicate that he had more important matters to concern him than dog-fighting. 'All I'm saying is, you can keep your eye on McManus, of course. But this is much more a matter for the ISPCA than it is for us. They have their inspectors, don't they, eight of them at least. They have a sizeable budget. It's their whole mission, to protect dogs from being mistreated for the sake of sport. We can cooperate with them, for sure, and give them backup if they're threatened, but we're not made of money, Katie, and we have a duty to protect human beings before animals.'

'I see. All right. Grand,' said Katie, and stood up, too. 'I'll tell Inspector Carroll. I'm not sure how he's going to take it. There's so much other crime associated with dog-fighting, like theft and extortion, particularly up in Tipp. I think he was quite enthusiastic about hauling in McManus and some of his pals.'

'Well, like I say, if you want to cooperate with Inspector Carroll up at Tipp and go to this dog-fight as an observer, that's fine. If you can get plenty of video evidence, you can present it at Phoenix Park next time we have a major budgetary meeting and make your case for a full-scale anti-dog-fight operation.'

Chief Superintendent MacCostagáin was about to say something when Katie's iPhone played. It was Bill Phinner calling her from the Technical Bureau's laboratory.

'Bill? What's the story?'

'We've run tests on the fire victims' skin and clothing, ma'am. Also on the residue left on the floor and the walls. We haven't come to a final analysis yet, but I think we have a fair idea now of what was used to start the fire and how it was planned.'

'When you say "planned", you're sure now that it was deliberate?'

'Absolutely. No question at all. Whoever burned down that building knew exactly what they were up to. I'd also go so far as to say that they might have done something like this before, and Matthew Whalen has come to the same conclusion. He's going to run through fire brigade records and see if he can find any incidents of arson where there's a similar scenario and where the same pyrophoric agent might have been used.'

'That's grand, Bill. I'm looking forward to your report. How about Niall Gleeson? How's that coming along?'

'Some good news on that, I'm happy to tell you. The bullet went through his head and hit the door pillar of his car, so it was almost totally flattened. All the same, we've looked at it under the microscope and there's still a doonchie bit of rifling on it, so we should be able to make a comparison if you can find the gun that fired it. It's a 9 mm round. Even better than that, though, we were haunted and found the spent casing. It had rolled down the nearest shore into the drain. It's solid brass, a full metal casing made by Magtech.

'We're also examining the bullet and the bullet fragments from the two fire victims. Those are 9 mm, too, but we found no casings in the attic.'

'Just on the off chance, can you compare the bullets from Niall Gleeson with those bullets?'

'You're thinking the same perpetrator might have shot all three of them?'

'I'm not thinking anything at the moment, Bill. But three people were shot in the head within a day of each other and less than two kilometres apart.'

'Fair play to you, ma'am,' said Bill Phinner. 'But when you put it that way, it kind of makes the Northside sound like one of them old John Wayne films, wouldn't you say?'

'Mother of God, Bill. Wasn't it always?'

Twelve

She had only just carried her coffee back to her desk when Detective Inspector Mulliken rang her.

'What's the form, Tony?'

'I have the husband here in the interview room. The fellow whose wife Niall Gleeson was pleasuring while he was at work. He's a bus driver. He's behaving fierce aggressive and I thought you might care to come down and assess him for yourself.'

'Well . . . if you really think I need to.'

'I'm thinking that a woman's touch might calm him down a little, do you know what I mean?' said Detective Inspector Mulliken, and Katie could hear that he was almost pleading. 'I did try to catch DS Ni Nuallán before she went to get herself dolled up for the Templegate Tavern, but she was out the gap already, and Padragain Scanlan is out investigating that jewellery shop robbery in French Church Street.'

'I'm not the only other woman officer in the station, Tony. What about Shelagh Brogan? She doesn't suffer aggressive men gladly.'

'Sure like, I know that, ma'am, but if I let Detective Brogan loose on this feller they'd probably end up the two of them having a bare-knuckle boxing match. You'll see what I mean if you come down to talk to him.'

Katie checked her watch. She had been hoping to drive down to Cork University Hospital to see how young Adeen was recovering, but she supposed she could spare ten minutes to help Inspector Mulliken with his belligerent interviewee. After all, there was a remote possibility that he had shot Niall Gleeson, and that it

102

hadn't been the New IRA or one of Cork's cigarette-smuggling gangs that wanted to make sure that Bobby Quilty's business was finished for good.

She gulped down her cappuccino, although it was tepid now and the foam had turned to white scum. Then she went downstairs to the interview room. Even when she was only halfway along the corridor she could hear a man shouting, and a banging sound, too.

When she opened the door and went inside she found Detective Inspector Mulliken standing with his arms folded, tight-lipped, while Detective Ó Doibhilin was sitting at the interview table next to him, with an expression on his face that was half nervousness and half amusement. A ginger-haired uniformed garda was sitting on the opposite side of the room, red-faced, but it looked more like sunburn from a recent week in Gran Canaria than bottled-up anger.

Sitting opposite Detective Ó Doibhilin was a huge overweight man in a soiled grey tracksuit from JD Sports. He was bald, with enormous fleshy ears, and his face was so distorted with rage that his piggy little eyes had almost disappeared, and his rubbery red lips were wet with spit. He was shouting in a strong Northside accent and thumping the table with his fist to emphasize every word.

'How the *feck* do you think I would have felt about him, if I'd known? I can't tell you how long he and me was friends, but it was a brave number of years anyway. And now you say he was after riding my moth when I was at work! Are you taking the fecking piss like?'

He stopped talking and thumping when Katie came into the room, and wiped his mouth and then his sweating forehead with his sleeve, and loudly sniffed.

'Mr Dennehy, this is Detective Superintendent Maguire,' said Detective Inspector Mulliken. 'This is Mr Bernard Dennehy, ma'am.'

'*Bernie*, for feck's sake,' the man retorted. 'I'm not a fecking dog with a barrel of brandy round its fecking neck. And I don't know why the feck you've pulled me in here, I've done nothing at all like, except now you've told me that my best mucker Niall was riding my Maggie behind my back. So what the feck are you saying like, hunh? That it was me who shot him? I didn't even have an inkling what him and her was up to! And where was I going to get a fecking gun from, even if I did know?'

Katie sat down opposite Bernie Dennehy and gave him a reassuring smile. He smelled strongly of cigarettes and body odour and something else sweetish which she couldn't identify, although she guessed it was diabetic urine.

'You're not under arrest, Bernie, and we haven't charged you with anything. You're free to leave any time you like. It's just that we need you to help us with our investigation into Niall Gleeson's death, and I'm sure you're just as keen to find out who killed him as we are, seeing that he was such an old friend of yours.'

'I don't know nothing at all,' Bernie protested. 'All I know is I went to work and when I come back like, Maggie's bawling her fecking eyes out and telling me that Niall's been found márbh. She never stopped bawling the rest of the fecking day.'

'But you weren't aware that Niall and Maggie were having an affair while you were off driving buses?'

'I just fecking told you, didn't I? So far as I was concerned, the only times those two ever met was when she came to the pub with me, and that was once in a fecking blue moon.'

'So weren't you surprised that she took his death so hard?' Katie asked him.

'What do you mean like?'

'Well, if she'd only met him once or twice, when you took her to the pub, didn't it strike you as strange that she should be so upset?'

Bernie Dennehy stared at Katie hard and it was obvious that he was trying to work out what she was getting at. His eyes were glittery, but the whites were yellow, which indicated that he was suffering from jaundice.

'I don't know,' he said. 'She's always been some sheevra. She wore black for a week when our dog died like.'

'So you're telling me that you had no suspicion at all that Niall and Maggie were getting it on?'

'Haven't I just fecking said so? How many fecking times?'

He looked at his watch and said, 'I need to be starting my shift anyway. You said I wasn't under arrest or nothing.'

'Oh, yes?' said Katie. 'Who do you work for?'

'Bus Éireann, if that makes any odds.'

'So what time does your shift start?'

'Two-thirty. And I can't be late or they'll give me the fecking bullet.'

'Well, okay, we won't hold you up any longer, Bernie. What route are you driving today?'

Bernie Dennehy gave Katie that hard stare again. She could read what he was thinking in his eyes: *What's this fecking woman asking me that for? What fecking difference does it make what route I'm driving?*

'The 245,' he said, suspiciously.

'The 245? That's to Fermoy, isn't it?' said Katie.

'You have it. Cork Bus Station to Duntaheen Junction.'

Katie beckoned to Detective Ó Doibhilin to pass her his notepad and pen. With her hand cupped over the pad so that Bernie Dennehy couldn't see what she was writing, she scribbled down *Call the bus station. Check his story.*

Detective Ó Doibhilin took the notepad and left the interview room.

'Where's he off to?' asked Bernie Dennehy.

'Oh, just routine,' said Katie.

'So can I go now? And how am I supposed to get myself to work?'

Katie was almost tempted to say 'take a bus', but she smiled and said, 'We'll arrange transport for you, Bernie, not a bother. There's just a couple more questions I have to ask you. Like, when was the last time you and Niall got together?'

Bernie thought for a moment, and then he said, 'A couple of nights ago it was, at the pub.'

'Which pub?'

'Niall's regular. The Templegate Tavern.'

'Did Niall give you the impression that he was worried at all? Did he tell you that he was feeling threatened by anybody?'

Bernie Dennehy shook his head so that his jowls wobbled. 'He was complaining about some young gowl who was getting up his honk, but that's all.'

'Did this young gowl have a name?'

'Can't remember. Danny somebody. Danny or Dessy or Davy.'

'But Niall didn't give you any reason to think that somebody might be planning to do him harm?'

'No, not at all. Not a word. So can I go now?'

'Just one more thing, Bernie. Weren't you ever wide to Niall's feelings about Maggie? Didn't you ever suspect that he was seeing her behind your back?'

'No, never. Nothing. And even if I'd found out about it – well, I might have emptied him, but no more than that. I wouldn't have fecking *shot* him like, would I? So *now* can I go? I've been bulling for a piss ever since I got here.'

'Okay, Bernie. If you can hold on just a little longer.'

'What the feck for? I've nothing else to tell you. I didn't shoot Niall and that's an end to it.'

'All right,' said Katie. 'But of course you would say that, wouldn't you, even if you *had* shot him?'

'Oh, come on, you're having a fecking laugh, aren't you?'

The door opened and Detective Ó Doibhilin came back in. He glanced at Inspector Mulliken and raised his eyebrows and then he sat back down next to Katie and passed her the note that she had scribbled for him. On the back he had written, *Bus Éireann let BD go a year ago. Wouldn't say why.*

Katie looked up at Bernie Dennehy and said, 'What if the 245 left at half-past two without you, Bernie?'

'What are you talking about? I'm the fecking driver. It can't leave without me.'

'Sorry, Bernie, but you're not the driver. You don't even work for Bus Éireann any more. It's my guess you're not driving for anybody. I mean, without being personal, look at the state of you la. The benjy off you, Bernie, you can't be driving a bus full of paying passengers smelling like that. Why don't you tell me what's happened? I'm not going to give you a hard time if you tell me the truth.'

'Who the feck told you I was out of a job?' said Bernie. He was trying to sound indignant, but Katie heard him swallowing the sudden weakness in the back of his throat.

'Bus Éireann of course,' she told him. 'They said you haven't been driving buses for them for a year. Come on, Bernie, you might as well take your oil. It doesn't matter if you talk to me or not, I'm a detective and I'm going to find out all about you sooner or later.'

Bernie Dennehy gripped the edge of the table with both black-fingernailed hands, his eyes closed tight. Whatever turmoil was going through his mind, Katie could feel the table actually shaking, as if an earthquake were imminent. A few seconds passed and then he let out a loud blubbery honking noise and opened his eyes, and tears started to stream down his cheeks.

Katie reached across and laid both of her hands on top of his. Behind her she heard Detective Inspector Mulliken murmuring, '*Mother of Divine Christ!*'

'Come on, Bernie, you're grand,' said Katie. 'Just let it all out.'

Bernie Dennehy snuffled, and snorted, and took one hand away to wipe his eyes and his nose with his sleeve.

'It was me and Maggie like. I suppose I was putting on a bit of weight, do you know. And I was having some difficulty downstairs, if you know what I mean. We were hardly ever getting together any more and when we did she just lay there staring at the ceiling like she was praying to Saint Agnes for it to be over.'

He shook his head at the desperate memory of it. 'She said I was so fecking heavy that it was like being under a bus, more than a fecking bus driver. And of course when she said things like that I'd immediately lose the boodawn and that would be the end of it. A few times like that and I could never get it up at all.'

Katie said nothing, but kept holding his hand. After a while he snuffled again and said, 'I took to the drink, which of course made me even fatter, and one afternoon I drove the bus into the back of a parked car on MacCurtain Street, and I was sacked.'

Bernie Dennehy was sobbing so painfully now that he was barely coherent and in between sentences he had to stop and gasp for air.

'So what did you do for money, after you were sacked?' Katie asked him.

'The JB – the fecking jobseeker's benefit. I didn't tell Maggie that I'd been given the push because she would only have fecking gloated. I went off every day like I was going to work, but I spent all day in the pub mostly, making a drink last as long as I could, or sitting on a bench in the Peace Park if it wasn't hooring with rain, or in the Macau club playing the slots when I'd picked up my benefit, to see if I could double it. But I'd been making forty-seven thousand a year on the buses, and now I was only getting a hundred and eighty-eight euros the week. I was broke as a joke, I can tell you. I was fecking desperate.'

'So where does Niall come into this?'

Bernie Dennehy stared down at the table. He inhaled deeply, four or five times, and with his free right hand he crossed himself. When he started speaking again, his voice was much more controlled and level, almost as if he were reading. Katie guessed that he had rehearsed this in his mind, over and over again – if not in preparation for giving a statement to the Garda, then for admitting it to Maggie, his wife, or for confessing it to a priest. For all of his bluster and aggressiveness, she guessed that he was fully aware of the enormity of what he had done.

'I was talking to Niall in the pub one evening about six or seven months ago. He knew that I was in the shite with money. But I'd had a few scoops and I told him about the problem with Maggie, too. You know, the downstairs problem. He knew Maggie better than I told you, because him and her had been doing a line for a while before her and me got together. They'd never been too serious – just on and off like – but I knew that he still fancied her something rotten.'

'Go on,' said Katie.

Bernie Dennehy continued to talk to the table top. 'I asked him if he had the chance, would he be interested in keeping Maggie sweet in the bedroom department, do you know what I mean? He said he'd be delighted. He still fancied her so much that he'd eat chips out of her knickers.'

'You thought that if she was sexually satisfied, you and Maggie would get along better together?'

'Well, yeah, I suppose that might have stopped us having so many ructions,' said Bernie Dennehy, still without raising his head.

'But that wasn't the only reason you asked him, am I right?'

'No. Yes. No. The main reason I asked him was for money. I told him that if I let him have a rattle with her whenever he felt like it, I'd make out that I didn't know what was going on between them, so long as he paid me two hundred yoyos the week.'

'Let me get this clear. Niall Gleeson agreed to pay you two hundred euros a week so that he could have sex with your Maggie as often as he wanted?'

'To be honest with you, I think he would have paid me more, if I'd pushed him. I never wanted to know what business he was in, and I never asked, but he always had plenty of grade on him. And two hundred a week, that's a whole lot cheaper than one of them knocking shops on John Street, they're charging a hundred and twenty yoyos just for one blowjob.'

Inspector Mulliken said, 'You were pimping your wife to your friend so that you could pay off the household bills, is that it? So, without her being wide to it, she was prostituting herself to keep herself in food and clothing and whatever else you couldn't afford to buy her?'

Bernie Dennehy suddenly reared his head up. 'Listen! The fecking TV licence alone, that's a hundred and sixty fecking yoyos! That would have swallowed up most of my whole week's dole money! And Maggie was happy out, I can tell you that for nothing. As soon as Niall started coming around, she was singing and smiling and she even cooked my favourite tripe and drisheen.'

'And Niall?' asked Katie.

'Niall – well, what do you think? Niall was as happy as a dog with four mickies.'

'And you? How did you really feel that another man was having regular sex with your wife?'

'What choice did I have? I couldn't satisfy her myself, but I didn't want to lose her. I love her.'

Katie sat and watched Bernie Dennehy for a while without saying anything, trying to read the look in his eyes and his facial twitches. What he had told her was tragic enough, but she had a strong feeling that there was more to this story than he had admitted.

'What do you think Maggie would have done if she had found out that Niall was paying you to take her to bed?'

'She's never found out.'

'You're sure about that? On the basis of the statement that you've given to me today, I'm going to have to question her, too.'

'Jesus Christ, you're not going to *tell* her, are you? I thought I was letting you know about that in confidence like! For feck's sake! That would mean us marriage down the fecking jacks for good and all!'

'Bernie, if she *has* found out, that could have been a prime motive for her punishing Niall, or for arranging for somebody else to punish him. It's possible, you have to admit. It could be that she's minded to punish *you*, too, so I'd be keeping sketch if I were you, when you're at home, and keep counting the kitchen knives.'

'Oh, stop! You're not saying that *Maggie* could have shot Niall? Maggie wouldn't swat a wazzie even if it stung her. And she'd never lift a finger against me, I can swear to that.'

'I'm only saying that it's a line of enquiry and I'll have to look into it. Unless you want to confess to me that it really *was* you who shot him.'

Bernie Dennehy sat in silence for a long time. At last Katie stood up and said, 'That's all for the time being, Bernie. Like I said, you're not under arrest and you're free to leave. We'll be wanting to question you again when we've made more progress with this case, and we will be bringing your wife in for questioning, too, at some stage. Meanwhile, I have to caution you not to leave Cork and not to discuss what we've said here today with anybody, not even with Maggie. In fact, especially not with Maggie.'

Bernie Dennehy didn't answer but looked up at the clock on the wall, which read 2:31. Katie turned and looked up at it, too. She wondered if he were thinking that the 245 bus would be turning out of Parnell Place now on its way to Fermoy, but he wouldn't be driving it, as he hadn't been driving it for over a year, and never would again.

Thirteen

As Katie was hurrying back along the corridor to collect her coat and her purse, Chief Superintendent MacCostagáin called out to her from his open office door.

'Katie! Frank Magorian just rang me! He'll be here about a quarter to four!'

Katie stopped and went back. 'That's grand. I'm only going to the Wilton Hilton to see that little girl who was rescued from the fire. Mind you, I'm starving. I'll probably drop in to Jackie Lennox's chipper on the way back. You wouldn't want me to fetch you a takeaway, would you?'

'Holy Jesus, I wish! I haven't had a Lennox's since God was a boy. But I have a Masonic dinner tonight at Tuckey Street.'

'Rather you than me, sir. I'll see you after.'

'Stall it a second, though, Katie – I wouldn't say no to you fetching me back a few chips . . . you know, just to keep the wolf from the door.'

'Not a bother, sir. Would you be wanting salt and vinegar on them? Or *au naturel*?'

* * *

It was still raining as Katie drove down to the hospital, but only softly, so that ghosts of drizzle would drift across the road in front of her, like the memories of people who had been run over. Usually she played music in the car to take her mind off work, and she had just bought a new CD by Lisa Hannigan because it was so whispery and romantic. This afternoon, though, she felt like silence, so that she could think about Bernie Dennehy and how he had sold his wife Maggie. How did people's marriages become so shipwrecked, and why did they always choose the most damaging possible way to get themselves off the rocks?

She thought about her own marriage to Paul, and wondered how much her determination to pursue her career in An Garda Síochána had eroded his morale as a husband, and how it had killed him in the end. It had been the same story with John. To begin with she had really adored John, but his involvement with her had destroyed him, too.

In his last days, when John had been suffering so much from having lost his legs, she had turned her back on him. His neediness and his ravaged appearance had been too much for her to take. After his death, though, her guilt about her coldness towards him had grown more and more difficult to bear. She hadn't loved him any more, but she kept asking herself if she should have pretended – or would that have made his suffering even worse?

Sometimes she felt that the motto of An Garda Síochána should be changed from 'Working With Communities To Protect And Serve' to 'Take It From Us – The Truth Is Intolerably Cruel'.

She parked and hurried through the misty rain into the hospital. The uniformed garda who was sitting outside Adeen's room stood up when she appeared, put down his newspaper and said, 'Ma'am?'

'Everything quiet?' she asked him.

'Pretty much like. The big doctor's just been in to see her, and some flowers were delivered.'

'Nothing else?'

'Oh, I had some fellow come by about an hour ago. He asked me if this was where the girl was who was saved from the fire.'

'What did you tell him?'

'I said I was on general security duty and didn't have a notion. He was carrying a clipboard, but he didn't have an ID badge nor one of them stethingscopes round his neck, so I couldn't be sure if he was a staff member or a doctor or not. He might have been a reporter for all I know, which was why I didn't tell him nothing.'

'Did he say anything else?'

'Just "oh, okay, not a bother" and then he went off.'

'Can you describe him?'

The garda frowned. 'He had a thick pair of speckys and one of them buckety tweed hats, do you know? Tallish, but ordinary-looking, maybe mid-thirties. Dark brown suit. He had a touch of an Ulster accent, though, I'd say. Not too strong, but definitely Belfast or Ballymena. My mam's mam came from Newtownabbey so I could hear it clear like.'

'Thanks,' said Katie, with a smile. 'I like a man with well-tuned ears.'

She entered Adeen's room. The blind was still drawn down and the lights were on, although it was so gloomy outside that the lights would have been on anyway. A Taiwanese nurse was sitting in the corner, filling in some charts, but she put them aside as Katie came in.

Adeen herself was sitting up in bed. She was no longer wearing an oxygen mask and her hair was braided into loose Princess Leia loops. She was still waxy pale, and her left eye was still bloodshot, but she was playing a game on a tablet and she looked much more alert than she had when Katie had first seen her. There was a half-finished glass of milky tea on her bedside table, as well as a packet of Kimberley biscuits and two get-well cards – one from Cork Fire Brigade and the other from the Reverend Brian O'Rourke, the rector of St Anne's Church, Shandon, because the dance studio was inside his parish.

Katie drew up a chair and sat close to the side of Adeen's bed.

'Hallo, Adeen. You remember me from yesterday? I'm Katie. I've just come to see how you're getting along.'

Adeen glanced at Katie quickly but then went back to her game.

'You look as if you're feeling a whole lot better now,' said Katie. 'What's that game you're playing?'

Adeen didn't answer, but tilted the tablet sideways. Katie could see three drums on the screen with cartoon versions of Justin Bieber dancing on top of them. Adeen was furiously hitting the drums with drumsticks and occasionally one of the Justin Biebers would turn into a beaver.

Katie watched her play for a while, but then she shook her head and said, 'Sorry – that has me totally puggalized, I have to admit. Still, whatever it is you're doing there, it looks like you're winning.'

She sat there a little longer without saying anything. She didn't want Adeen to feel that she was pressing her. Eventually, though, she laid her hand on the bed and said, 'You know something, sweetheart – it would be a fierce help to us if you could tell us your real name, and where you live. Nobody's come asking after you, and considering your age that's very unusual. We've put out an appeal in the newspapers, and on the television, but we haven't even had a school friend ringing us up to say that they recognize you.'

She waited for Adeen to respond, but Adeen kept on playing the drums and hitting the Justin Biebers.

'Just your first name?' Katie coaxed her. Adeen pursed her lips and drummed and still wouldn't speak.

Katie stood up and went over to the nurse.

'How is she physically?' she asked.

'She's making very good progress, considering,' said the nurse. 'They scanned her lungs again this morning and there's no serious damage from the smoke. Her bloods are good, too. She has some second-degree burns on her buttocks and lower back but I changed the dressings about an hour ago and they are healing very quickly. No sign of infection or any other complications.'

She paused and gave Adeen a little wave. 'If we knew where she lived, we could discharge her tomorrow or the day after. At the moment we're still waiting for Tusla to tell us if they can find anybody to take her in.'

Katie looked around the room. 'The officer outside told me that some flowers were delivered for her, but I don't see any.'

'No. It was a huge bunch of pink roses, with a get-well message. But when Adeen saw the card that went with it, she was pure distressed. She didn't say anything, but she kept flapping her arms and squeaking until we took them away.'

'Where are they now?' Katie asked her.

'I shouldn't think that they'd been binned. Maybe they were taken down to reception. You could ask the duty nurse on the desk.'

Katie went back and stood next to Adeen's bedside. Adeen glanced up at her again but kept on playing her game. She was still wearing the green wristband with the gold plastic clasp, and Katie was reminded to ask Kyna if she had managed to find out where it had come from.

'I have to go now, darling,' she said. 'You can always ask one of the nurses if you want to see me again, though, at any time. And please try to think about telling me your name, and where your home is. All I want to do is take care of you, and make sure that nothing like that fire ever happens to you again.'

Adeen stopped jiggling the tablet for a moment and looked up at Katie with her soulful eyes – one clear, one bloodshot. She opened her mouth as if she were just about to say something, but then she closed it again and turned her attention back to the drums and the dancing Justin Biebers, although she didn't carry on playing. She simply sat there, as if she felt that nothing was worth saying, and that nothing was worth doing, and that she had given up all hope.

Katie was about to leave when suddenly Adeen sat up straight and reached out for the glass of tea on her bedside table. As she did so, though, she let out a high-pitched squeal, and her hand jerked, and she knocked the glass on to the floor.

'*Ah – me scald!*' she panted. She dropped back on to the bed, her eyes squeezed tight shut and her teeth gritted.

Katie pulled the chair away from the bedside and picked up the glass and the nurse hurried around the bed, tearing off two sheets from a roll of paper towels.

Adeen started to weep, letting out a thin mewling sound. Katie laid a hand on her shoulder and said, 'Don't worry, darling, it was an accident, that's all. I'm much worse than you – I'm always knocking my coffee cups over and flooding the place. I'm sure they can fetch you some more.'

'Of course,' said the nurse, down on her knees and dabbing at the carpet. 'If there's one thing we're never short of here, it's tea. Two things this hospital runs on – blood and tea, but mostly tea.'

Katie waited until Adeen had stopped crying. She pulled out a Kleenex and wiped her eyes for her and then she said, 'I'll come and see you again tomorrow. Don't be sad. Everything's going to be all right for you now, I promise.'

Adeen's mouth puckered and it was obvious that she was holding back another sob. But she nodded to show Katie that she understood.

'God bless,' said Katie, and left.

* * *

Before she went downstairs, Katie went along to the duty nurse, who was sitting at her desk chatting to one of the junior doctors.

'Sorry to bother you,' she said. 'But do you happen to know what happened to the roses that were taken out of Adeen's room this afternoon?'

The nurse had those heavy curved eyebrows that always put Katie in mind of crows circling above a field, on the lookout for rabbits. She also had a mole on her chin.

'Oh yes, the roses,' she said. 'The housekeeping services manager took them away. I imagine she's found somewhere to put them. The chapel, probably. That's on the first floor, next to the staff dining room, if you want to go and see them.'

'There was a card with them. Did she take that, too?'

'No, she didn't,' said the nurse. 'I still have it here.'

She reached down to the wastepaper bin beside her desk, but Katie immediately said, '*No!* – please don't touch it!'

She pulled a pair of black forensic gloves out of the pocket of her jacket and tugged them on, finger by finger. Then she took out a small plastic evidence bag. While the nurse watched her in bewilderment, she carefully lifted the card out of the bin and held it up. There was a picture of a sad-looking puppy lying in bed with a bandaged head, and the message *Get Well Soon, Pet!*

Inside, in a back-sloping script, whoever had sent Adeen the flowers had written, *CU Soon C. D. But Zippo. Remember T.*

Katie studied the card carefully, turning it over to see if there were any marks on the back. Its surface was shiny but she knew that Bill Phinner had recently started using a new liquid developed in Australia that could show up fingerprints that had been left on a non-porous surface.

The message was deliberately obscure, but it gave her one or two hints: that Adeen's real name probably began with a C, and that whoever had sent her the card had a name that might begin with a D. 'But Zippo' – what did that mean? Zippo was a brand of cigarette lighter, so maybe it was some kind of reference to how the fire had started. And who was T, who had to be remembered?

'All right, grand, thank you, nurse,' said Katie, and sealed the card into her evidence bag. 'It might be necessary for a technical expert to come here and take a copy of your fingerprints in case there's any confusion about who might have been handling this card, but you won't mind that, will you?'

'If I'd known I shouldn't touch it, I swear to God, I wouldn't have gone nowhere near it,' said the nurse, her eyebrows rising higher than ever.

'Don't worry,' said Katie. 'Even if we do find your fingerprints on it, I don't think you're in any danger of getting yourself lifted for tampering with evidence. Now, I'd better go and find those roses.'

Once she had retrieved the flowers from the chapel, Katie went into the hospital's security control room on the other side of the staff canteen. The duty security officer was sitting in front of his six CCTV screens, cupping a mug of tea in both hands as if it were the holy grail. Katie had met him before: he was a short bulldog of a man with cropped grey hair and was almost military in his efficiency.

'How's it going on, Jerry?' she asked him. 'I hope it's no bother, but I need to see the video from the second-floor lifts, from about an hour and a half ago.'

'No bother at all, DS Maguire,' he told her, and put down his tea to run the footage back. Nurses and doctors and porters all rushed backwards in and out of the lifts, and at last Adeen's visitor appeared, holding up his bunch of roses.

'Freeze it right there, please,' Katie told him.

She leaned forward and peered intently at the screen. The garda on duty outside Adeen's door had been right: he was tall, and wearing a dark brown suit, but his face was almost completely obscured by his bucket hat, pulled down low over his forehead, and his heavy-rimmed glasses.

'If you could take a screenshot of that and send it to me at Anglesea Street,' said Katie.

Jerry the security officer peered closely at the image, too.

'He might as well have a shopping bag over his head, like them Rubber Bandits,' he said. 'I doubt if his own ma would reck him, do you?'

* * *

As she drove back to Anglesea Street, Katie stopped outside Jackie Lennox's chipper on the Bandon Road, but after visiting Adeen she had lost her appetite for a full fish and chip lunch. All the same, she went in and bought a large takeaway portion of chips for Denis MacCostagáin, and before she put them in the boot of her car she ate two or three of them, blowing on them to cool them down.

On the way back to the station her iPhone pinged several times, so as soon as she returned to her office she put down the bunch of pink roses that she had taken from the hospital, and the box of chips, and checked to see who had texted her. The first message had been sent by Bill Phinner, asking her to drop in to the Technical Bureau laboratory as soon as she could. The next had come from Kyna saying that she was all ready to go undercover to the Templegate Tavern in Gurranabraher. She had attached a selfie showing her posing in front of her bedroom mirror in a denim jacket clustered with brooches and buttons and a very short red dress and red wedge sandals. Her blonde hair was gelled and brushed up vertically and her lips were painted scarlet to match her dress.

'Gurra brasser!' she had written. Katie couldn't help smiling. No matter what Kyna wore, Katie thought she always looked sexy. She had such a fashion model's figure: small high breasts and lovely long legs, and she always walked with such a confident loping stride, as if she were showing off the new season's creations at a fashion show.

Moirin came in and said, 'You had a phone call from Corinne Daley at Tusla, ma'am. She's left her number. She says they've found a really nice couple who can take in that girl from the fire at Toirneach Damhsa, when she's ready.'

'Well, that's a relief. Sure look – can you do me favour and take these roses down to the Technical Bureau, as well as this card? I need the card and the cellophane wrapper around the roses checked for fingerprints, and maybe it's worth checking the roses themselves for any traces of DNA, in case somebody's pricked their finger on the thorns. I have to go and see Chief Superintendent MacCostagáin before these chips go cold.

'Here, help yourself—' she said, opening the white polystyrene box. She offered a chip to Moirin and took two more herself. 'We don't want him getting as fat as a fool, now, do we? Have another.'

When she entered Chief Superintendent MacCostagáin's office, carrying the box of chips, she found that Frank Magorian was already there, sitting on the couch under the window. He stood up as soon as Katie came in, holding out his hand and smiling. Katie put the chips down on Chief Superintendent MacCostagáin's desk, pushing aside a report on drug abuse to make room for it.

'Fresh from Lennox's, sir,' she told him. 'You should eat them while they're hot.'

Chief Superintendent MacCostagáin gave her an uneasy look, as if to tell her that he wasn't going to start stuffing his face with chips while he was discussing law enforcement strategy with the new Assistant Commissioner. Katie was beginning to feel hungry again and she wished now that she'd eaten them all.

Assistant Commissioner Frank Magorian came up close and shook her hand. Although he was tall, at least six foot three inches, Katie had always thought that his head was disproportionately large for his body, like a statue of himself. She had known him when he was a superintendent at the Garda College, but this morning she had checked his recent career details online. He was fifty-two now, but to be fair, she thought he looked younger. He was handsome in a George Clooney-ish way that she personally found a little too smooth, with black, slicked-back hair that was greying at the edges, and a long face with a long straight nose and a heavy jaw. His eyes were deep-set, but they were bright and intelligent, and she knew that he had a formidable list of degrees in both criminology and business management, including the executive leadership programme for chiefs of police worldwide that was run by the FBI.

If there was anybody qualified to be a possible successor to Nóirín O'Sullivan as Garda Commissioner, it was Frank Magorian.

'How's it going, DS Maguire?' he asked her. 'It's been a long time, hasn't it?'

'Please, sir. You can call me Katie. And it's ten years next seventeenth of October, which also happens to be the feast day of St John the Dwarf.'

'St John the Dwarf? What was he known for?'

'Obedience, sir. He was told to water a piece of wood every day, and he did it for three years without complaint, even though the water was twelve miles away. After three years, it grew into a tree, and that tree's still standing today. I always tell that story to my new detectives, in case they ever wonder why I'm making them do the same boring thing over and over.'

'Well, Katie, you never cease to surprise me,' Frank Magorian told her, shaking his head. 'I'll tell you something for nothing, Denis. This young woman was the star of Templemore when she was training there. Top marks in everything, and you could never catch her out. When it came to debates on points of law, they used to say, "Look out, everybody, Maguire's on fire!" '

Katie felt herself blushing. *Mother of God, fancy him remembering that.*

'Here, come and sit down,' Frank Magorian invited her. 'I've just been asking Denis about this fire at the dance studio, and how that's coming along.'

All three of them sat by the window. The rain was still pattering on the glass and the pale grey shadows of raindrops trickled down their faces as they talked.

'I'm arranging a conference at three o'clock tomorrow afternoon, sir,' said Katie. 'We've put names to all of the sixteen victims who died in the studio. Some of their bodies were very badly charred, but they were identified by dental X-rays and personal possessions and sometimes by areas of their bodies that were shielded from the flames by other bodies. Dr Kelley hasn't officially finalized the cause of death of each and every one of them, but they all have severe laryngeal oedema, so I think it's fairly safe to assume that they all died from inhalation of superheated air.

'The two bodies we found in the attic were also charred beyond facial recognition, but of course those two had been shot in the head. Dr Kelley has told me that their lungs were not as seriously damaged as the other victims, so in their case I think we can assume that they had already stopped breathing before they were burned.'

Frank Magorian nodded, and then he said, 'The thing of it is, Katie, this case is still making headline news every day. There was a comment in the *Times* this morning which asked how eighteen people could have been killed in such a spectacular way, in daylight, right in the middle of the city, and yet the police still don't seem to have the first clue who might have done it. Like – *do* we have a clue who might have done it?'

He didn't sound censorious, but Katie could understand that the media would question him very intensively about the Toirneach Damhsa fire tomorrow, and he would need to be up to speed on all of the latest developments.

'We have a number of leads we're following up,' she told him. 'It's fierce competitive, step-dancing, and as you may know there's a major *feis* scheduled in Cork for next week, so we've had to consider the possibility that somebody from a rival troupe might be responsible. On the other hand, we're still trying to work out why two of the dancers were shot before the fire was started, and what that little girl was doing in the attic.'

Katie explained that she had just come back from seeing Adeen but had not yet been able to find out who she was. She also told him that Danny Coffey had accused his former partner, Steven Joyce, of being the arsonist, but that she was waiting for more forensic evidence before she interviewed him.

'I did pick up another undertone, though, when I was questioning Danny Coffey. He gave me the distinct impression that there might have been something going on between him and the Toirneach Damhsa dance instructor, Nicholas O'Grady.'

'In what way? A homosexual relationship, you mean?'

'I'm not sure. It could have been that he was simply shocked and upset, do you know what I mean, but he did seem unusually weepy. We know for sure that Nicholas O'Grady was gay. He was married to a young musician called Tadhg Brennan, so if there was anything going on between him and Danny Coffey it was—'

She paused and turned to Chief Superintendent MacCostagáin. 'I don't know, what do you call it when a married gay has a gay affair outside his marriage? Do you call that adultery?'

'You can call it whatever you like, Katie,' said Chief Superintendent MacCostagáin. 'The same laws apply as they do between men and women. If you want to be divorced, as you well know, you have to be separated for four out of the five preceding years, and there has to be no hope at all of reconciliation, whoever you've been messing around with – man or woman or donkey.'

'Well, keep me up to date with any developments, Katie,' said Frank Magorian, checking his watch. 'Denis and I are having a bit of a natter about budgets and Garda station closures, and then I have to whizz back to Dublin. The Commissioner's making her public announcement about my appointment first thing tomorrow morning and I'll be doing a few TV and radio interviews of course. But hopefully I can be back here in time for your conference.'

Katie stood up and smiled. 'It's grand to see you again, sir. Let's hope this is something of a new era for the Southern Region.'

'I'll drop in to say goodbye before I leave,' said Frank.

Katie was tempted to take the box of chips from Chief Superintendent MacCostagáin's desk but decided against it. They were probably stone cold by now, anyway.

Fourteen

When she went down to the Technical Bureau laboratory Katie found Bill Phinner leaning out of the open window of his cluttered little office, vaping out into the rain.

'I hate to say it, Bill, but almost every time I see you these days you seem to be puffing away.'

Bill Phinner took a last drag on his e-cig, blew out the vapour, and then closed the window. Katie could smell vanilla.

'It's the stress, ma'am. I freely admit it. What with this fire, and the Niall Gleeson shooting, and all that groundwater up at Watergrasshill being contaminated, we're pure overwhelmed at the moment. I have two technicians off sick and one on his holliers. I think people forget that inside of our Tyvek suits we're real human beings, and some of the stuff we have to deal with would make you craw sick.'

'I'm sorry, Bill,' said Katie. 'This fire has put a whole lot of pressure on all of us. We have more suspects than we know what to do with but we seem to be going nowhere at all – not even round in circles. It's any real motive that's missing.'

'Maybe there wasn't a motive. Most arsonists burn down buildings just for the thrill of it.'

'I've considered that, of course. But since two of the victims were shot it doesn't seem likely that it was only done for kicks. It could have been that somebody had a personal grudge against a member of Toirneach Damhsa, or maybe it was somebody who didn't want them to score well at next week's *feis*.'

'On the other hand, maybe it was nothing to do with dancing at all,' said Bill Phinner.

'Well, you could be right. Maybe Danny Coffey's been having financial troubles and he burned the studio down himself to collect the insurance. I mean, compo, that's probably the third most profitable industry in Cork, after drugs and prostitution.'

Katie kept a straight face but Bill Phinner couldn't help grinning. 'I'll tell you something, ma'am, you always brighten my day, you do. Look – come on through to the lab and I can show you what we've found out about the way the fire was started.'

Katie followed him through to the laboratory. Eithne O'Neill was sitting in front of a computer, creating 3-D images of some of the worst-burnt victims from the fire. She was rebuilding their faces to confirm their identity, and also to give their relatives a post-mortem picture of them that wasn't a black charred skull with its teeth snarling at them.

Partlan Murphy was there, too, grey-haired and lean and round-shouldered, like a stork. He was a fingerprint expert and one of Bill Phinner's longest-serving technicians. Lying on the bench beside him were the cellophane-wrapped pink roses that Katie had brought back from the hospital, ready for him to process, and he was peering through a binocular microscope at the back of the get-well card.

'How's it going on, Part?' Bill Phinner asked him, laying a hand on his shoulder.

Taking his eyes away from the microscope, Partlan Murphy said, 'Better than I expected, sir. In fact, amazing. I've applied the MOF liquid and at least seven clear fingerprints are showing up.'

'That's the new Australian technique I mentioned to you the other day,' Bill Phinner told Katie. 'There's metallic crystals in the liquid which bind to the residue left behind in a fingerprint – you know, like fatty acids, peptides, proteins and salts. The crystals create an ultra-thin coating that's an exact replica of the fingerprint, and that makes a glowing image which we can photograph, in any colour we choose.'

'Well, that's mint,' said Katie. 'If only it was just as easy finding whose fingers they match.'

'I hate to say it, ma'am, but that's your problem, I'm afraid.'

They reached the end of the laboratory where an angular young man in a long white lab coat was consulting graphs on his computer screen. He had very short red hair and bright red ears. He swivelled around his chair when he caught sight of Katie and Bill Phinner approaching, and took off his heavy-rimmed glasses.

'This is Detective Sergeant Bryan Noone from the Ballistics Section in Dublin,' said Bill Phinner. 'I asked him to come down yesterday morning so that he could take a sconce at the floor and wall and ceiling samples that we took from the dance studio.'

He picked up a charred section of parquet flooring that was lying on the bench, tagged and numbered, and showed Katie how its varnish had been bubbled and striated by the heat.

'You see this? Didn't I tell you that the fire was probably started by some kind of pyrophoric chemical? DS Noone here is the undisputed expert on pyrotechnics in Ireland, if not the entire civilized world, so I thought it would be a good idea if he came down to give us his invaluable opinion. DS Noone, this is Detective Superintendent Maguire.'

Detective Sergeant Noone, to Katie's surprise, stood up and bowed. 'I'm honoured to meet you, ma'am,' he said, in a very Dublin 4 accent. 'I've heard some very complimentary things about you, you'll be happy to know.'

'That makes a change,' said Katie. 'Especially up at Phoenix Park.'

'Oh, the wind is changing, ma'am, now that Commissioner O'Sullivan has taken over, and the smoke will soon be blowing the other way. I'm a bit of an expert on political pyrophorics, as well as chemical ones.'

'Well, let's stick to the chemical ones for now,' said Katie. 'Do you know now what started that fire at Toirneach Damhsa?'

'I have a very good idea, ma'am. It was almost certainly a TPA, which means a thickened pyrophoric agent. In this case, the residue found on the stairs and the floorboards and the wall plaster was triethylaluminium thickened with polyisobutylene. TPA is usually used in thermobaric incendiary weapons, like M74 rockets. It's an alternative to napalm, which the Americans used to burn down villages in Vietnam when they thought Viet Cong soldiers might be sheltering there. It's also used in the manufacture of semiconductors and some plastics.'

'But how was it used to burn down the dance studio?' asked Katie. 'It wasn't dropped in a bomb or fired in a rocket, was it?'

'Oh, no, sure, of course not. But whoever applied it was even more of an expert in pyrotechnics than I am. When TPA is used for incendiary weapons, the thickener is usually six per cent or thereabouts. But you can make it much safer by adding other diluents, like n-hexane, right down to one per cent. What your arsonist appears to have done is spread the TPA over the staircase and also the attic. I can't be sure yet what percentage of diluents was used, or what exactly the diluents were, but for a limited time they would have rendered the TPA non-pyrophoric. That's until they evaporated – at which moment, *whoomph!* You would have had yourself a huge combined fireball of TPA and hexane vapours, or whatever else you might have used.'

'I have you,' said Katie. 'He mixed it in such a way that it gave him time to leave the building before it exploded? Or *she* did, of course.'

'Exactly that. I've known some TPAs take ten minutes or more to self-ignite – again, depending on what diluents are used.'

Bill Phinner said, 'The FIAI investigators believe that there was an initial explosive fire on the first-floor landing. That was so fierce that it consumed nearly all of the oxygen in the stairwell, and so for a while after that it died right down. It was only when one of the dancers opened the practice-room door that it burst into life again. And I mean *burst*. All of the evidence tells us that it was like an incendiary bomb going off. The girl who must have opened the door was cremated on the spot.

'The remaining dancers tried to escape by going up into the attic, but an exactly similar scenario had been set up there. A TPA fire had self-combusted, but it had quickly been suppressed by lack of oxygen. The dancers would have stood more of a chance if they had tried to jump out of the studio windows. But they opened the attic door and fed the fire with a great rush of oxygen, and that was the end of them. One breath of superheated air and they were barbecued from the inside out.'

Katie examined the piece of flooring. If the fire had done this much damage to varnished wood, she could only imagine what it had done to the victims' lungs.

'In your experience, Bryan, who might have the expertise or the experience to use TPA in the way that this was used? Are we talking about soldiers? Or demolition experts? Or maybe somebody involved with special effects for the film business? What about terrorists? Have you ever seen any kind of TPA used in this way before – by the Provos, say, or the Real UFF?'

'Not here in the South, anyway,' said Detective Sergeant Noone. 'I've heard reports of some incidents of arson north of the border that may have been chemically started, but I'll have to have a word with my friend in Forensic Science Northern Ireland to find out if any of them used the same or a similar formula to this one. I should be able to get more details for you in a day or two.'

'You said that they use it for making semiconductors and some plastics. Are there any companies in Cork where the arsonist might have got hold of it?'

Bill Phinner said, 'There's Troy Microsystems in Bishopstown, they use it, and Lee Plastics on Little Island. I don't know of anybody else.'

'I'll have Dooley check them out to see if they're missing any,' said Katie. Then she turned to Detective Sergeant Noone. 'Thanks, Bryan. I'll look forward to seeing your final results.'

'Oh, you're more than welcome. This case has been interesting, to say the least. I spend most of my time firing bullets into tanks of water.'

'Talking of that, Bill,' said Katie, 'how's it going with the Niall Gleeson shooting?'

'I'm having the bullet and the bullet fragments from both Niall Gleeson and the two dancers scrutinized even as we speak. We may even have a result for you later today so. That's if my comparison macroscope isn't banjaxed.'

'Okay, Bill, thanks a million. You've given me a lot to be thinking about, I can tell you.'

'Well, it's not my place to supply you with anything more than forensic evidence, ma'am, but I'll be pure surprised if this fire turns out to have had anything at all to do with dancing.'

'I'm keeping an open mind,' Katie told him. 'You know what Abdul-Baha said – "This universe contains many worlds of which we know nothing." The world of dancing could be one of those worlds.'

'Abdul-Baha?' said Bill Phinner. 'Can't say I ever came across the fellow. Where does he drink?'

* * *

Katie had been back in her office for less than ten minutes before Frank Magorian rapped at her open door.

'Come in, sir,' she said. 'Are you leaving for Dublin now?'

'I am, yes. I'm being driven back there now, but I'll be coming down by chopper tomorrow, so I should be here in plenty of time for your conference.'

'Oh, by chopper! It's all right for some. But I'm pure pleased by your promotion, sir. I hope we can find a little time tomorrow to talk over some operational matters. The drug problem in particular. We've managed to close down one major supplier, but when you do that, of course, five others spring up in their place.'

Frank Magorian looked around. The door to Moirin's office was open, too, and Moirin was tapping away at her keyboard.

'Do you mind if I say a word or two to you in private?' he asked her.

'No, of course not,' said Katie. She got up from her desk and closed the door, and then she went over and sat on one of the couches under the window. Frank Magorian came and sat next to her – not too close, but close enough for Katie to see that his blue tie had a combined pattern not only of forget-me-nots but of the square and compass of the Irish Freemasons.

'You've really built yourself quite a reputation here in Cork,' he told her. 'I was talking about you only a couple of weeks ago to Michael Twomey, the Deputy Commissioner. Perhaps you don't always go by the book, and perhaps you've rubbed one or two people up the wrong way, but there's no arguing that you've managed to chalk up some fierce impressive prosecutions. Getting that pimp Michael Gerrety sent down – now that was a coup. Almost as good as nailing Martin "The Beast" Morgan, if only we could ever find something to nail *him* for.'

He suddenly stopped talking and turned to look out of the rain-dribbled window for a few moments, as if he wasn't quite sure what he was going to say next. Although he had started off by seeming so genial, Katie could now sense some tension in him. He had laced his fingers together and was squeezing them hard. She had seen businessmen do the same when she had questioned them about fraud – or paedophiles, when she asked them why they were loitering around playgrounds.

'Is something wrong, sir?' she asked him.

'Wrong? Well, let me tell you this, Katie. I've always told the outright truth, no matter what. I don't believe in hypocrisy or deceit, even if they might grease the wheels and make life a little easier. I've told you what I've thought about your record here and I mean it, every word of it.'

'Yes, and I really appreciated what you said,' Katie told him. 'There's nothing like an occasional pat on the back like. Sometimes it seems like the higher up the ladder you go in the Garda, the less recognition you get for what you've achieved.'

'There's another side to it, though,' said Frank Magorian. 'I always make a point of telling the truth, and I never forget a favour. But I never forget a *dis*favour, either.'

'Fair play to you,' said Katie. 'I'm just praying that I haven't done you any terrible wrong that I've totally forgotten about but you haven't.'

She was starting to smile, because she hadn't come into contact with Frank Magorian since he was a chief superintendent at Templemore and she couldn't imagine that she had upset him in any way in the intervening years. But when he turned away from the window the bleak look in his eyes told her that he didn't find this amusing at all.

'What?' she said.

'Oh! You never wronged me personal-like. Not me myself. But I was close friends with Jimmy O'Reilly, and you wronged *him* all right. You persecuted him until he had nothing to live for: no reputation, no job, and no lover. No wonder he blew his brains out. You might just as well have pulled the trigger yourself.'

Katie stared back at Frank Magorian in disbelief. 'Jimmy O'Reilly? Stop the lights! *Me* persecute *him*? Didn't anybody tell you what he did? Didn't you hear how he set up a phony gun-smuggling racket that never was, so that I'd get the sack for mounting a full-scale armed raid on a children's birthday party? Apart from that, he was constantly cnaveshawling about me to Denis MacCostagáin, and to anybody else who would listen. As for his reputation, he'd been turning a blind eye for years to Bobby Quilty's cigarette-smuggling business because Quilty was lending him money to pay off his boyfriend's gambling debts.'

'Jimmy rang me only about ten minutes before he took his own life, Katie,' said Frank Magorian. 'He said that *you* set up that arms-smuggling fiasco with the Callahan gang, just to implicate him, and that it was you who broke up his relationship with his partner.'

Katie emphatically shook her head. 'I'm sorry, sir. None of that was true. Jimmy O'Reilly was obviously under fierce intolerable stress, but every bit of it was all his own making.'

For the past few months she had successfully blanked out the mental picture of Assistant Commissioner O'Reilly standing right in front of her in her office and shooting himself in the face, but now it came back to her as vivid and as gruesome as if it had just happened. Her stomach tightened and bile rose up in the back of her throat, which she had to swallow.

'I'm not going to argue about this, Katie,' said Frank Magorian, uncrossing his legs and standing up. 'All I'm going to say to you is that I never once knew Jimmy O'Reilly to tell a lie.'

132

'So what *are* you trying to say to me?' Katie asked him, doing her best to sound defiant.

'Listen, I've openly acknowledged the success that you've achieved. You haven't done bad at all, considering you're a woman, and everybody believes that I'm going to support you and encourage you. But I'm the Assistant Commissioner now, Katie, and I want to see the Southern Region run with discipline and efficiency. I want to know that all of my officers are loyal and trustworthy, and that none of them are undermining each other or stabbing each other in the back – not like you did with Jimmy O'Reilly.'

'Sir, Jimmy O'Reilly went out of his way—' Katie began, but Frank Magorian raised his hand to silence her.

'Let me just finish by telling you this. You're very attractive, but I can see that your looks have blinded some of your colleagues to the maverick way that you conduct yourself, and the irresponsible way that you run your cases. Just because you're a woman, Katie, you can't rely on that to keep your job. I don't give a tinker's whatsit about the Garda's drive for equal opportunity. If you carry on the way you are, behaving like a diva with permanent PMT, I'm going to find a way to pay you back for what you did to Jimmy O'Reilly, and pay you back in spades.'

Katie was so shocked by what he had said that she had to take several quick breaths before she could speak. When she did, she said, 'Would you repeat that, sir? I want to turn on my phone, so that I can record it.'

'What kind of a fool do you take me for?' said Frank Magorian. 'Those words were for you, and you alone, but don't you forget them. Be wide from now on, Katie, and I'm not joking. In the meantime – in public, and in the media – I'm going to be giving you my full and unwavering backing. I'll see you tomorrow so.'

With that, he opened the door and left the office. Katie stayed where she was for a few moments, still stunned. In the back of her mind, though, a tiny bright seed had already been germinated. As a woman in An Garda Síochána she had always found it necessary to be highly self-protective, and that meant anticipating every attack that might be made on her, either physically or career-wise, and being well prepared to take evasive action at a moment's notice.

Her father had lost his job as a Garda inspector because of Jimmy O'Reilly and he had always told her, 'Always keep sketch for the people who heap the most praise on you, Katie. They're the ones who can't hide how jealous they are, and they're the ones who will tear you down first and fastest, and step-dance on you when you're down.'

Step-dance! thought Katie. *How appropriate that I should remember that now.*

It was then that her iPhone pinged, and it was a text from Conor. *Back late tomorrow. House all sorted. Clodagh mollified. Cant wait till hold you.*

Katie sat back, still feeling numb. Was that really how they saw her, those men who weren't attracted to her, a diva with permanent PMT? *Please God let Conor not be blinded, too.*

Fifteen

It was early yet, but when Kyna walked into the Templegate Tavern there were ten or eleven men in there already drinking, as well as one elderly woman who was staring at a half-finished glass of Guinness as if she couldn't remember what it was, and a younger woman with plump tattooed arms who was jiggling an equally plump toddler on her lap.

All of them turned around and stared as Kyna came in, and the three men sitting at the table next to the stained-glass screen gave each other a nod and a wink.

She gave them a challenging look in return and walked up to the bar. A bald middle-aged man in a short-sleeved shirt was polishing glasses with a tea towel and breathing on them to bring them up to a shine.

'Well, now,' he said, laying down the tea towel and giving her a grin with teeth the colour of peanut brittle. 'What takes your fancy and I'm hoping it's me.'

Kyna perched herself on one of the bar stools, crossing her legs and hitching up her skirt. 'I was wondering actually if you had any bar jobs going.'

'Sure like, there might very well be,' said the barman. 'To tell you the truth I believe that there is. But I'm not the manager so I couldn't tell you for certain and I wouldn't myself be in a position to hire you, even though I would if I was. In fact, I'd hire you like a shot.'

'Is the manager here?'

'Not at the moment, love. He's gone over to Lidl to stock up one or two bits and pieces like Taytos and nuts and stuff. And superglue, because the handle fell off of one of the beer pumps. But he'll be back in maybe half an hour or so. Do you want to wait for him? You can have a drink while you're waiting. On the house.'

'Thanks a million,' smiled Kyna. 'And what's your name?'

'Patrick, and I know exactly what's going through your mind. That's a fierce unusual name, Patrick – what in the name of God were his parents thinking about when they christened him that?'

'Patrick, you're right . . . it *is* unusual,' said Kyna. 'It has a certain ring to it, though, do you know what I mean? I'll have a Pinot Grigio, please, Patrick.' She made a point of pronouncing it *pee-not griggio.*

Patrick opened a mini-bottle of Pinot for her and poured it out. As he did so, Murtagh McCourt came up to the bar, carrying three empty pint glasses.

'How's it going on, then, darling?' he asked her.

'She's here for a job,' said Patrick. 'She's just waiting for Roy to come back from Lidl.'

'Was I asking you?' Murtagh retorted, and Patrick visibly flinched. But then Murtagh turned back to Kyna and said, 'If he doesn't give you the job, tell him to come and speak to me, and I'll sort him. Why don't you come and join us while you're waiting?'

'Okay, that's very friendly of you,' said Kyna. 'I'll need to get to know all of the customers, won't I, if I'm going to be working here. I think the personal touch is fierce important, don't you?'

'The personal touch?' said Murtagh, looking at Patrick as Kyna slid herself long-legged off her bar stool. 'With you, darling, I'd say that was practically mandatory.'

She approached the table where Billy Ó Griobhta and Liam O'Breen were sitting, and Murtagh introduced her. 'This is Billy and this is Liam and I'm Murtagh. We're the hardcore regulars, do you know what I mean, but there's others coming later so. We'll be having a bit of a get-together this evening.'

Liam dragged over another chair and Kyna sat down. 'I hope I get the job anyway,' she said, looking around. 'This is a real nice pub now, isn't it?'

She had noticed that all three men were wearing black armbands, although Liam's was only a thin length of black hair ribbon knotted round his upper arm.

'What's the armbands for?' she asked them, as Murtagh brought over three fresh pints.

Liam couldn't take his eyes off her and he fumbled with his pint as Murtagh handed it to him and almost spilled it. ''Twas a good friend of ours, Niall Gleeson. Maybe you heard about it on the telly like. He was going to pick up his granddaughter from the nursery up the road here and somebody stopped his car and shot him.'

'What, like *dead* like?' asked Kyna.

'Well, of course. We wouldn't be wearing the armbands if he wasn't dead. His funeral's tomorrow, which is why we're having a bit of a get-together this evening. What you might call a dry run for the wake, although it won't be very dry.'

'Holy Jesus, that's terrible. Do you know who shot him?'

'There's all kinds of theories, but the shades haven't picked up anyone yet.'

'I still reckon it was that Bernie Dennehy,' said Billy, who had been leaning back in his chair and combing his Elvis Presley quiff. 'I reckon he found out about Niall riding his missus. And you have to admit his missus isn't a bad-looking knock, is she? You'd give her a poke if your telly was broke.'

'I still reckon it was Óglaigh na hÉireann,' said Liam. 'The New IRA. They knew that he'd be taking over from Bobby and they wanted to stop him before he could even get started.'

Murtagh jerked his head towards Kyna and frowned at Liam as if to tell him to keep his bake shut about business. But Kyna was sipping her wine and looking around the pub as if she wasn't listening to them any more.

'They have music here, do they?' she asked.

'That's right. In the pool bar,' said Murtagh. 'They had a fantastic guitarist here last week and there's some singer coming on later.'

'It's fierce sad when somebody dies,' said Kyna. 'My gran died on Easter Sunday. Do you think we all go to heaven when we die?'

'Not Niall,' said Billy.

'He wasn't a bad man, was he?' Kyna asked him.

'Niall? Let's say he'd done a few things in his life Saint Peter wouldn't have approved of.'

'Well, that's for sure,' said Murtagh. 'I don't think *anybody* who worked for Bobby will ever get past the pearly gates, not without an apostolic pardon, anyway.'

'Who's Bobby?' said Kyna.

'Bobby Quilty his name was, and if I was you, darling, I'd thank your lucky stars that you never came across him. He would have gone for a beour like you like a hippopotamus on heat. No, don't you worry about the Big Feller. He's gone wherever big fellers like him get sent to when there's no more room in hell.'

Kyna nodded as if she was only half listening. She *had* encountered Bobby Quilty, and the memory of it still made her feel sick. She had been undercover, trying to infiltrate his hugely profitable cigarette-smuggling business. He had attempted to rape her, and when he had failed to do that, he had forced her into the shower and relieved himself all over her. She could only agree with Murtagh that if hell had an overflow, that was where Bobby Quilty was now, burning for all eternity from head to foot.

The conversation between the three men turned to the senior hurling championships, and how Midleton had beaten Sarsfield. Throughout their talk about rooters and mullockers and tidy players and Sarsfield being windy, Kyna stayed smiling and patient, trying to look interested, and she made a point of catching Liam's eye whenever she could. She could see that he was really taken with her, and that could be very useful. She had been careful not to push her questioning about Bobby Quilty too far, in case Murtagh in particular started to suspect her of being more than just a flirty Gurranabraher bird, but if she managed to gain Liam's confidence she might be able to find out much more than Murtagh was prepared to tell her.

Billy was just starting to talk about the gearbox trouble he had been having with his new Kia when a dark-haired young man walked into the pub, wearing a black suit that Kyna guessed was probably Armani and must have cost him at least seven hundred euros. He was good-looking in a way that she found disturbing for some reason, with emphatic black eyebrows and a straight nose and lips that were slightly too voluptuous for a man. Maybe it was his eyes that unsettled her. He was smiling, but if she had seen the expression in his eyes in isolation, like looking through a letter box, she would have been sure that he was angry about something.

Liam immediately stood up so that the young man could take his seat, and went over to the next table to fetch another chair for himself.

'How's it hanging, Davy?' said Murtagh. 'Want a MiWadi?'

Davy ignored him and stared straight at Kyna. 'Who's this, then?'

'She's the new barmaid . . . or she will be when Roy gets back and hires her.'

'So what's she doing sitting here chatting to you clowns?'

'Chatting, that's all, what do you think?'

'Oh, yes? And what about?'

'Blowing up Collins Barracks,' said Billy. 'What the feck do you think we were chatting about?'

Without warning, Davy took hold of Billy's left ear and twisted it around so hard that it crackled. Billy let out a girlish shriek of pain.

'You looper! You think that's a laugh, do you, Billy?' said Davy, still holding on to his ear and pulling his head down sideways towards the table top. 'How many times do I have to tell you to watch your whist? Christ almighty, you don't have a titter of wit, do you?'

His accent when he had first started talking had sounded local, but now that he was annoyed Kyna could hear an underlying Belfast lilt to it, and no Norrie would say 'titter of wit'.

'Ow, I'm sorry!' said Billy. 'Let go of me fecking ear, will you! I'm sorry! We was only talking about the hurling!'

Davy let him go and he sat up straight, rubbing the side of his head. 'Jesus, you nearly pulled me fecking wiggy off. I could have been half-deafened for life.'

'I'll pull the both of them off if you don't stop running your mouth off, you clampit!' snapped Davy. Then he turned back to Kyna and said, 'What's your name, doll? Where are you from?'

'And what if I don't want to tell you?' Kyna retorted. 'What are you going to do, pull *my* ear too? I'd like to see you fecking try.'

'I don't have to pull your ear, doll. All I have to do is tell the landlord that you won't be working in this pub, ever. And on top of that he'll bar you for life.'

'All right, boy, relax the cacks,' said Kyna. 'There's no need to throw a rabie. My name's Roisin MacColgan, and I'm from Fair Hill. Happy now?'

'What street in Fair Hill?'

'Jesus, the gardaí wouldn't ask me that! Liam Healy Road, if you must know, number thirty. Do you want to know the colour of my toilet suite? Avocado, with gold handles!'

'And what are you doing right now, Roisin?'

'I'm sitting here answering all of your nosy-parker questions.'

'I mean what kind of work do you do?'

'No fecking work at all, or I wouldn't have come in here looking for some, would I?'

Kyna could see Liam with a smirk half hidden behind his hand, and Murtagh's tangled grey eyebrows had bunched together in an anxious frown. It was obvious that neither of them usually dared to answer Davy back. For all his TV-actor looks, she could tell that he was both demanding and ruthless, although she also sensed that he trusted nobody. It was classic criminal psychology that she had learned at the Garda College. He dealt with his own fear by making everybody around him feel afraid.

'Fair play to you, girl,' said Davy. 'But now you can chase yourself off and finish your drink by the bar. I have to talk to these boys in private.'

'Whatever,' said Kyna. She unwound her legs again, stood up, and went back to perch on the bar stool. 'I'll just have to come and talk to you,' she told Patrick. 'Mr Antisocial there doesn't seem too fond of female company.'

'Spot on, girl,' said Patrick. 'Are you ready for another glass of wine?'

'Yes, thanks a million, if it's still on the house,' said Kyna.

Patrick opened another mini-bottle of Pinot and poured it into a freshly breathed-on glass for her. As he passed it across the bar she jerked her head in Davy's direction. 'Are you saying that he doesn't like women?'

Patrick made sure that Davy wasn't looking and leaned forward confidentially. 'A pal of mine has lamped him in the Ruby Lounge quite a few times now. You know, dancing and drinking and sizing up the eye candy.'

'The Ruby Lounge? On Washington Street?'

'That's the one.'

'But that's where all the crafty butchers go, isn't it?'

'That's what I'm telling you like,' said Patrick.

'Jesus, it shows you can't tell just by looking, can you?' said Kyna.

In fact, she had suspected that Davy might be gay from the moment he had first walked in. Straight men almost always eyed her up and down and spoke to her flirtatiously. Occasionally they acted aggressively and tried to bring her down, but that was only a kind of reverse seduction by men who weren't too sure of themselves. They were rarely as consistently hostile as Davy had been – except if she was arresting them.

What few men realized when they first met her was that Kyna herself was gay. She knew the Ruby Lounge well because it was Cork's most popular gay nightclub. She had been there several times herself on Thursday nights, which was lesbian night.

'He's not a friend of your manager, Roy, is he?' she asked Patrick. 'He said that if I upset him, he'd make sure that Roy wouldn't give me a job.'

'You're codding me, aren't you? Roy's allergic to that subla, and so am I. He's a right piece of work.'

'So why don't you find some excuse and bar him? It doesn't look like the fellows he's drinking with are enjoying his company much, either. Your man with the quiff, he almost screwed his ear off because he said something that got up his nose.'

Patrick glanced over again to make sure that Davy wasn't watching him. Then he said, 'Let's say that we'd be asking for big trouble if we barred him. They accused him of walking out of Hennessy's the newsagent up the road here without paying for an *Echo* and the next thing we knew the shop was burned right out. As it is, he never pays for his drinks. But for the love of Jesus and all his disciples, don't tell him that I told you.'

'So him and those other fellows, they're kind of a gang, are they?'

'You're fierce ins-quisitive, girl. If I was you, I'd mind my own beeswax. What you don't know can't harm you, especially when it comes to that crew.'

'It's only if I'm going to be working here, I'd like to know who I'm serving, you know, just in case I say something that accidentally vexes them. I mean, that Davy – he might be gay but he's fierce humpy, isn't he? He's like a bulldog sucking piss off a nettle.'

Liam came up to the bar and asked Patrick for two packets of dry-roasted peanuts. He stood close to Kyna and gave her a shy, nervous smile.

'What's the craic, then, Liam?' Kyna asked him.

'Oh, something and nothing. I was wondering if you fancied going down the Bodega tomorrow night. Ross Curley's on the decks and he's the best.'

'I might,' said Kyna. 'It depends if I get a job here or not.'

'We don't have to go down till late. They charge admission after eleven-thirty but I'm not short of grade.'

'I didn't say you looked like a poverty-stricken pauper, did I?'

Liam's cheeks flushed cherry-red. 'You're pure pretty, Roisin, did anyone ever tell you that?'

'Oh, sure, I've been told that I'm pretty often enough,' said Kyna, batting her eyelashes at him. 'I'm not so sure about the pure, though.'

Liam flushed even redder. 'I'll catch you tomorrow night so,' he said, and went back to join Davy and Murtagh and Bobby. As soon as he sat down, though, Davy laid a hand on his shoulder and at the same time turned around and gave Kyna a hostile stare. Kyna was sitting close enough to be able to catch some of what he said.

'What were you two talking about?'

'Nothing,' said Liam.

'Well, it was something, wee lad, because she was smiling at you like she was ready to drop her drawers at the blink of an eye.'

'It was nothing at all, Davy, I swear.'

'Didn't you and me have a bit of a word about loyalty?'

'Davy, it was just like "how's yourself?" Nothing else.'

Davy seized Liam's right wrist and pressed his hand flat on the table top, palm down. Then he reached into his jacket pocket and took out his flick knife. He clicked out the blade and said, 'Spread your fingers.'

'What?'

'You heard: Spread your fingers. You've asked *me* to trust *you*. Now let's see how much *you* trust *me*.'

'Davy—'

'Spread your fecking fingers, wee lad!'

Liam spread his fingers as wide apart as he could. Davy then stabbed the point of his knife in between them, one after the other, into the table top. He started off slowly at first, but then he stabbed faster and faster, until Liam closed his eyes because he couldn't bear to watch.

'So what did you really talk about?' Davy demanded, as he stabbed from one side of Liam's hand to the other and back again, so fast now that the knife blade was a blur.

'I told you, Davy,' Liam squeaked at him. 'I said "what's the craic?" and she said "what's the craic?" and that was all. Please, Davy – Jesus Christ Almighty.'

'One more chance, Liam. Did you say anything about me? What did you say about me?'

Kyna was tempted to go over and tell Davy that Liam had asked her to go to the Bodega with him and that he should stop being so paranoid. On the other hand, she didn't want to antagonize him any more than she had already – not until she knew a lot more about him, and about Murtagh and Billy and Liam, too. If they had been working for Bobby Quilty, then they must have been cigarette-smuggling, and she guessed that they still were, even if they weren't operating on the same county-wide scale as Bobby Quilty.

'Come on, wee lad!' said Davy, as he kept up the furious stabbing between Liam's fingers. 'What did you tell her?' He was making no attempt to lower his voice and Kyna could see that Liam's terror was making him increasingly excited.

She looked around the pub and she could see that none of the other customers was showing any inclination to intervene, either – not even Patrick, although Davy was stabbing the point of his knife into the varnished mahogany table top. They were all keeping their faces turned away and pretending to continue with their conversations as if nothing untoward was happening at all. The young woman with the plump baby started bouncing him up and down on her knee and singing 'I am the Wee Falorie Man'.

'*I have a sister, Mary Ann – she washes her face in the frying pan – and she goes out to hunt for a man – I have a sister Mary Ann.*'

Kyna thought that they might have a good reason for keeping their distance. Bobby Quilty had not only been involved in cigarette-smuggling, he had formed a dissident IRA splinter group which he called the Authentic IRA – Arm Barántúla na hÉireann. Over the past two years the AIRA had claimed responsibility for several grisly murders and mutilations, including the shooting of five rival cigarette-smugglers and two senior members of the New IRA. Kyna wasn't sure if they were still active, but if they were, nobody was going to risk confronting them. There had never been sufficient evidence for the Garda to make any arrests and no witnesses had ever had the courage to come forward.

Davy's manic stabbing continued for a few more seconds and Liam continued to keep his eyes squeezed tightly shut. Then Davy stopped, although he kept his knife lifted up and didn't release his grip on Liam's wrist.

Liam opened his eyes. Murtagh and Billy had been watching with undisguised apprehension, but now they both sat back in their chairs and Murtagh lifted up his pint of Murphy's in salute.

'That's some party trick, Davy, I'll give you that, boy. You ought to go on *Ireland's Got Talent*.'

'Oh, this is no trick, Murtagh,' said Davy, still holding the knife upraised. 'This is what happens when I give somebody the opportunity to be straight with me, but they throw the opportunity right back in my face.'

With that, he slammed the knife blade right into the middle of Liam's hand, between his second and third fingers, pinning it to the table. Liam let out a shout of pain and surprise, and tried to pull his hand free, but Davy kept pressing the knife down hard.

Patrick said, 'Jesus.' He bent down behind the bar and reappeared holding up a baseball bat, but without even looking over at him Davy called out, 'Paddy – don't you be thinking about interfering, big lad.'

If she hadn't been undercover, Kyna would have tipped Davy out of his chair and pinned him to the floor. She would have responded if Davy had been threatening Liam's life, but instead she had to stay on her bar stool and watch as Davy dragged the knife towards him, little by little, slicing through the flesh in between Liam's finger-bones. Blood ran across the table top and dripped quickly on to the floor.

'Holy cack,' said Billy.

Davy lifted the knife away but he didn't loosen his grip on Liam's wrist until he had wiped the blade on the sleeve of the younger man's denim jacket. Liam said nothing, but clutched his bloody right hand in his left hand, squeezing his fingers together to try and stop the bleeding, and staring in shock and disbelief at what Davy had done to him.

Davy folded the knife and put it back in his pocket, but still nobody said a word to him. The young woman with the baby had stopped singing and was holding the baby close to her.

'What are you all looking at?' Davy demanded. 'You never

saw a drop of blood before? Paddy – bring over one of them bar towels, would you, big lad?'

Patrick lifted up the flap at the end of the bar and came out with a stained white bar towel.

'Hold your hand up high,' he told Liam. 'Now take your other hand away, so that I can take a sconce at it.'

Davy's knife had cut through the cephalic vein in the back of Liam's hand and blood was pouring down his wrist and into his sleeve. Patrick bound the bar towel around his hand and knotted it, and then folded his sleeve down as far as his elbow.

'Is it hurting at all?' he asked, but Liam shook his head, still in shock. His cheeks had flushed when he had spoken to Kyna, but now his face was as chalky white as a clown.

'Keep your hand up in the air,' Patrick told him. 'Murtagh – he'll have to be having stitches for this. One of you needs to take him to the Mercy.'

Billy said, 'It's all right, I'll take him. This was going to be my last scoop anyway, until this evening.'

He stood up, drained the last of his pint, and then helped Liam to stand up, too.

Davy said, 'You'll be okay, wee lad. Only a flesh wound. Tell the doctors you were sawing off a table leg and your hand slipped.'

Liam stared at him with a mixture of bewilderment and sheer hatred, but Billy steered him out of the pub door before he could say anything in reply. Patrick went back to the bar and returned with a wet dishrag to wipe the blood off the table. The atmosphere in the pub was so tense that when he had finished mopping up he switched the radio on to RedFM to break the silence. They were halfway through playing Kyna's favourite song, 'Nothing Compares 2 U', by Sinead O'Connor.

My God, thought Kyna. *How totally fitting is that, a song about pain.*

Murtagh and Davy sat together without speaking for nearly a minute. Then Davy called out, 'I'll have a MiWadi when you're ready, Paddy. Blackcurrant this time, big lad.'

'Well – I doubt that Liam will be giving you any more bother, Davy,' said Murtagh, as Patrick brought over a bottle of MiWadi and a glass. From the look in his eyes, though, Kyna thought that he was thinking something quite different – like *You shouldn't have hurt him like that, you prickly hypersensitive bastard.*

'I warned him before and he took no notice,' said Davy. Kyna couldn't hear what he said next, but then he swallowed a mouthful of blackcurrant juice and added, 'Sure like, you're probably right. I'd say that he's learned his lesson.'

Another ten minutes went by. Kyna was about to ask Patrick how much longer she was going to have to wait for the landlord when the door opened and a short, fat, grey-haired man in a maroon tracksuit came in carrying a large cardboard box of Tayto cheese-and-onion crisps.

'Here's Roy now,' said Patrick.

Kyna could see Roy's face scrunch up in distaste as soon as he caught sight of Davy. *If a look could make a man drop down stony cold dead on the spot.* But then her attention turned from Roy to the dark-haired girl who was following close behind him.

She wasn't often stunned, but this girl stunned her. She was wearing a long white boat-neck sweater and tight black jeans and black leather boots, and her wrists jingled with at least a dozen bracelets. She was carrying an acoustic guitar slung across her back, so that the diagonal strap divided her very large breasts. Her face was a perfect oval, with huge onyx-coloured eyes and sulkily pouting pink lips, and her hair was scraped back from her face and tied in a long shiny ponytail.

'This is Sorcha,' Roy told Patrick, hefting the box of Taytos on to the counter. 'She's our live singer for this evening. She lives in Ballyvolane, so I reckoned I'd kill two birds and give her a lift.'

'Well, this is Roisin,' said Patrick. 'She's looking for bar work so.'

Roy looked Kyna up and down and said, 'Have you worked behind a bar before, girl?'

'The Fob and Gill in Mayfield for six months. It was Martin trained me up.'

'The Rob and Kill? If you worked there for six months I reckon you could work anywhere at all. A good pal of mine had half of his nose bitten off in the Fob and Gill.'

Kyna smiled, although she was only half-listening. She was finding it hard to take her eyes off Sorcha, and Sorcha was staring back at her – as if each of them had found someone they had been looking for all their lives but thought they would never actually meet.

Sixteen

It was almost 8.30 by the time Katie arrived back home at Carrig View. The rain had stopped and the sky had cleared so she could see two misty white moons, one suspended over the harbour, the other reflected in the harbour.

She parked in her driveway, but when she opened the door of her Focus she could hear the distant sound of the carillon of bells from St Colman's Cathedral, high on top of the hill in the centre of Cobh. She hesitated for a moment, listening. The bells pealed on and on, and she felt almost as if they were calling her.

She expected that Barney had heard her car coming back and would be eagerly waiting for her behind the front door with his tail wagging. But Jenny Tierney would have fed him and taken him for a walk and it wouldn't hurt him to wait for another half-hour. She had been planning to attend Mass on Saturday evening, but hearing the bells she felt the strongest urge to go to the cathedral now. She knew that it normally closed at six, but if they were practising the carillon there must be somebody there who could let her in.

She backed out of the driveway and drove into the town, which was less than five minutes away. Cobh had rows of multicoloured shops and pubs, yellow and blue and pink, and the statue of a weeping angel in Casement Square to commemorate the sinking of the *Lusitania*. The carillon was ringing so loudly as she drove up the steep hill to Cathedral Place that she could hear it inside the car.

She parked and climbed out and stood on the cathedral steps for a while, listening and looking up. The cathedral was built in Gothic style, with a spire that was ninety metres high, like a slender rocket ship fashioned out of limestone. Its foundations had been laid in 1868 but it had taken over half a century before it was completed and consecrated. Katie came here as often as she could. Her mother's funeral service had been held here, and so had the funeral services for her baby, Seamus, and her husband, Paul.

The main doors were closed and locked, but she found that the side door was open. Inside it was chilly and the lights were dimmed. The votive candles that had been lit to commemorate the dead were flickering in an alcove behind the pillars. As she walked between the pews towards the altar the bells boomed and reverberated and drowned out the clicking of her footsteps on the mosaic floor. There were forty-nine bells, in four octaves, and the largest weighed over three tons.

She sat down in a pew close to the altar and crossed herself. She wanted so much to pray, but she felt that in the past few months she had almost completely lost touch with God. Dealing with drug gangs and pimps and murderers was partly to blame, because there was no chance of outwitting them unless she behaved as ruthlessly as they did. She had killed a dog-napper with a kick to the heart and she had shot a serial killer who had been murdering sex-traffickers. On top of that, she had driven Assistant Commissioner Jimmy O'Reilly to suicide, and she still felt guilty about it even though he had been doing everything he could to undermine her.

It was the way she had treated John, though, that really made her feel that she forgotten God. John had needed her love and support so badly, but she had turned her back on him to start her relationship with Conor. John was dead now, so it was too late to ask for his forgiveness. But would God forgive her?

Without her expecting it, her eyes filled with tears and she felt a *tocht* in her throat. Even if she had felt able to pray, she would have found it difficult to say the words out loud. She took out a tissue, wiped her eyes and blew her nose. Just as she was doing so, two clergy appeared from one of the side doors, their heads tilted towards each other so that they could hear themselves talking over the booming of the bells.

One of them she recognized: the Reverend Peter O'Farley, who had officiated at Seamus's funeral. He was a broad-faced, handsome man with a high wave of black hair turning grey at the sides. The other was thin and beaky-nosed, with a tangle of gingery hair and rimless spectacles.

'Well, well! Kathleen!' called out Father O'Farley as soon as he caught sight of her. 'It's been a while now, hasn't it? How are you going on?'

'Oh, I'm grand altogether, thanks!' Katie told him, raising her voice so that he could hear her. 'I have to start so early these days I hardly ever have the chance to come to Mass at ten in the morning! I hope I'm not trespassing!'

'Oh, for goodness' sake, Kathleen, nobody trespasses in the house of God! It's pure gratifying to see you here! This is Bryan Hannigan, by the way. He's visiting us from St Malachy's Church in Belfast. Kind of a cultural exchange, as it were. It's a beautiful church, St Malachy's, fantastic. Bryan – I want you to meet Detective Superintendent Kathleen Maguire – one of Cobh's most outstanding citizens and the strong arm of the law in the city of Cork.'

Father Hannigan came up and shook Katie's hand. 'Pleasure to meet you, Kathleen!' he smiled. But then he looked at her more keenly and took off his spectacles.

'I hope I'm not intruding,' he said. He leaned closer so that he wouldn't have to raise his voice so loudly over the bells, and she could smell Fisherman's Friends on his breath. 'But it looks to me like something's upsetting you.'

'I, ah—' Katie began, but then tears filled her eyes again. *Oh, Jesus, the very last thing I want now is sympathy.*

'I'm sorry,' said Father Hannigan. 'You can tell me to mind my own damned business if you like.'

Katie had to press her hand over her mouth for a few seconds to stop herself from sobbing. All she could do was look at Father Hannigan and try to convey to him the hurt and guilt she was feeling through the expression of her eyes alone.

Father O'Farley came up to her, too, and said, 'Kathleen . . .

Kathleen, what's wrong? You've come here for a reason, haven't you?'

Katie nodded and wiped her eyes again. 'I've lost Him. I've lost God. It was my fault. Now I don't know how to pray to Him any more, or if He'll listen even if I do.'

The carillon of bells suddenly fell silent, leaving only a metallic resonance in the air, like the fading hum of a tuning fork. Father O'Farley laid his hand on Katie's shoulder, and now he could speak to her much more quietly.

'Kathleen – you may think that you've lost contact with God, but I promise you that God has never lost sight of you. He knows how difficult your life is, and how hard you have to struggle to keep the peace and protect those around you. You're one of His most precious children.'

Katie swallowed hard. 'It's not so much the job, Father, although that's been desperate enough. I let somebody down very badly, somebody who needed me. I let them down because of my own selfish feelings, and I can't get it out of my mind.'

'Would you like to confess what you did? Would that help?'

Katie thought for a moment and then said, 'Yes.' She hadn't expected to find a priest here to take confession, but she realized that admitting her guilt in front of God was the main reason why she had come here.

'Why don't you make your confession to Stephen here?' said Father O'Farley. 'Sometimes it's easier if you tell your troubles to somebody you don't know so well.'

Father Hannigan smiled at her and Katie said, 'All right. I will. I don't know how else I'm going to get over this. I'll tell you, though, I can't imagine what kind of a penance is going to make up for what I did.'

'Kathleen, the very fact that you've come here at all is a sign that you're already beginning to make amends,' said Father O'Farley.

'Where would you like to talk to me?' Father Hannigan asked her. 'In one of the confessionals? Or we can simply go into the Pietà chapel if you prefer. Or even right here.'

'I think – I think here,' said Katie, looking up at the high vaulted roof and the shining organ pipes and the great rose windows. 'I feel like God's here, even if I haven't been able to talk to Him.'

'Well, He'd hear you in here all right,' said Father O'Farley. Then he said, 'Listen . . . I've a couple of phone calls to make, so I'll leave you two together. Call me when you've finished.'

Katie sat down again and Father Hannigan sat in the pew right behind her so that she could speak to him without having to look at him directly. She crossed herself again and said, 'In the name of the Father, and of the Son, and of the Holy Spirit. My last confession was on St Stephen's Day.'

Father Hannigan spoke very precisely in his soft Belfast accent. 'Jesus said, "Come to me, all you who labour and are heavy laden, and I will give you rest. Take my yoke upon you, and learn from me, for I am gentle and lowly in heart, and you will find rest for your souls. For my yoke is easy, and my burden is light."'

'What I'm feeling, Father, it's more than a burden,' said Katie. 'It's like a never-ending migraine. I just don't know how I'm ever going to get over it.'

Haltingly, she told him how John had been kidnapped by Bobby Quilty to deter her from investigating his cigarette-smuggling racket. She explained how Bobby Quilty had bolted John's feet to a bed when he tried to escape, and how his lower legs had become septic and had to be amputated. Out of guilt and pity, she had agreed to look after him during his convalescence, but his physical condition was so wretched and he had become so emotionally demanding that she had made it clear to him that their relationship was over.

He had tried to win back her love by going undercover and trying to find evidence against one of Cork's biggest drug-dealers, but he had been caught out and murdered.

Katie was making no effort now to wipe away the tears that were running down her cheeks and dripping from her chin. 'I might as well have killed him myself,' she said. 'I could have shot him in his sleep. At least he would have died thinking that I still loved him.'

Father Hannigan said, 'Very often, Kathleen, it is harder to tell a painful truth than it is to hear it. There are times when a white lie is kinder . . . when somebody who is terminally ill says to me, "I'm not about to die, am I?" '

'I could have been so much gentler on John, though. And I didn't have to rub his nose in it by bringing Conor home with me.'

'Kathleen, you are feeling genuine remorse and showing a strong desire to renew your closeness to God.'

'That's all I want, Father,' Katie told him. 'I just need you to tell me how I can.'

Father Hannigan laid his hand on top of hers. 'God is the father of mercies, and through the death and resurrection of His Son, He has reconciled the world to Himself and sent the Holy Spirit among us for the forgiveness of sins. Through the ministry of the Church, may God give you pardon and peace. And I absolve you from your sins in the name of the Father, and of the Son, and of the Holy Spirit.'

'Aren't you going to give me a penance?'

'Your penance is to light a candle in memory of John, and to say a prayer for his soul, in any words you choose, but which you sincerely mean. And I want you to express your gratitude to God, for He has never abandoned you, and He is patiently waiting for you to speak to Him again.'

Katie wiped her eyes. Father Hannigan was right. However much she had hurt John, she would only have hurt him even more if she had deceived him, and nothing could bring him back now.

'Give thanks to the Lord, for He is good,' Father Hannigan coaxed her.

Katie crossed herself and whispered, 'For His mercy endures for ever.'

She stood up and went over to the alcove where the votive candles were burning in their red glass jars. She took a fresh candle and Father Hannigan picked up the box of matches and handed it to her.

'Careful,' he cautioned her, as she struck a match and the wick flared up. 'You don't want to add a scald to your penance.'

She turned to stare at him, with the match still alight. He took hold of her wrist and blew it out for her. *Scald*, that was what the Northern Irish called a burn, but *scald* was what Corkonians called a cup of tea. Adeen had spilled her tea and when she had said 'my scald!' that was what Katie had thought she was talking about, her cup of tea. But perhaps she had meant the burn on her back.

It could be that Adeen came from Ulster and that was why nobody had been in touch to say that she was missing and no school had reported that she hadn't turned up for class.

'What?' said Father Hannigan, taking off his spectacles again. From the look in his pale green eyes Katie was sure that he could read her mind. She had come across priests who understood her spiritual needs, but never one so sensitive to what she was feeling.

'I don't know,' she said. 'I may be totally mistaken. But maybe you were the reason I came here, or maybe I was sent here to meet you by God.'

'I'm not sure I understand.'

'No, Father. I'm not sure that I do, either. But I'll soon find out. And thank you for hearing my confession. You've taken away a lot of my pain so.'

Father Hannigan smiled, although he was obviously still baffled by what she had said. 'Now why don't you say a prayer for your John, and you'll feel better still.'

Seventeen

Detective Dooley and Detective O'Mara stopped outside the tall maroon-painted building on North Main Street and a patrol car with two uniformed gardaí in it drew up close behind them.

It was 3.25 in the morning. Both detectives were tired. Detective Dooley's hair, usually brushed up, was flat on one side where he had slept on it for half an hour on the vinyl-covered squad room couch, and Detective O'Mara, who was broad-shouldered and red-haired and usually red-faced, too, was looking as pallid as pastry.

As they climbed out of the car they could hear a cat yowling somewhere and the muffled sound of a man and a woman arguing, but apart from that the street was quiet. The uniformed gardaí came up to join them, one of them swinging a red Enforcer battering-ram. The other followed him, yawning with his mouth wide open.

'This is where Coughlan's been dossing down lately with his bit of sly lack,' said Detective Dooley. 'He has another girlfriend up in Mayfield, but from what I hear her ma got fed up with him staying overnight and never flushing the toilet, and his own ma won't have him in the house.'

One of the gardaí looked up at the building and said, 'Third floor front, you said?'

'That's right. The one with the droopy curtains. I doubt if he'll give us much bother, like. Even his pals told me that most nights he's either stoned or langered, and usually both.'

'Okay. Ready?' asked the garda with the Enforcer.

'Bang away, boy,' Detective Dooley told him.

The garda went up to the front door and positioned himself on the step with his feet well apart. The door was old, with peeling brown varnish, and Detective Dooley could see that there were two locks on it, a Yale and a Chubb, and it wouldn't have surprised him if there were bolts on the inside, top and bottom. That wouldn't be a problem: the Enforcer could break down doors much sturdier than this and with stronger locks. It was solid steel and weighed 16 kilos, and it was commonly known as the Big Red Key.

The garda swung the Enforcer and it slammed the door off its hinges with a single splintering blow so that it fell down flat in the hallway. It brought down with it a tall mahogany coat-stand and a wide rectangular mirror, which smashed.

'Seven years bad luck there, Sean,' said his partner.

Detective Dooley and Detective O'Mara stepped over the door and crunched over the broken glass. They made their way along to the narrow staircase at the end of the hallway, both of them switching on their flashlights. The building smelled strongly of drains and damp, as well as disinfectant and burned sausages. They climbed the stairs as quickly and quietly as they could, although the cheap brown carpet was worn right through to the string and some of the stairs squeaked like pigs.

They had only just reached the first-floor landing when a door was opened on the third floor up above them and light shone down the stairwell. A thick, clogged-up voice said, 'Who the feck is that down there? What's all that fecking crashing and banging? We're trying to get some fecking sleep here!'

Only a split-second later, though, the detectives heard a woman's voice screeching, 'Dara! *Dara!* There's only a fecking two-bulb outside!'

'Shite,' said Detective Dooley. He hurried along to the end of the landing, but the foot of the second flight of stairs was obstructed by a folded baby buggy and a large green plastic rubbish bin. Before the two detectives could lift them out of the way and start to climb up to the second floor, the door above them had been slammed shut and the stairwell was in darkness once again.

'That's your man Coughlan all right,' said one of the two uniformed gardaí as he came along the landing to join them. 'At least we didn't bash down the door for nothing.'

Detective Dooley reached the second-floor landing. Close behind him, Detective O'Mara was beginning to pant with the effort.

'Jesus,' he said. 'I wish I hadn't ate that vindaloo last night. It was mad hot. I'm going to puke my heart and soul up any second now.'

He paused halfway along the landing, holding on to the banister rail and bending over to catch his breath, while Detective Dooley started to mount the third flight of stairs. His flashlight showed up pale brown wallpaper with blackened spots of mould on it, and a brown fringed lampshade suspended from the ceiling like a giant spider.

He had climbed only three or four stairs when he heard the door open again, although this time the stairwell remained in darkness.

'*Dara!* What the *feck* do you think you're playing at?' the woman screeched out.

Dara Coughlan didn't answer her, but suddenly he appeared at the top of the stairs and Detective Dooley shone his flashlight on him. He was big, and blubbery, with a shaven head and a swollen face. He was wearing a stained white sleeveless vest and Detective Dooley could see his bulging tattooed neck and arms tattooed with snakes and naked women and GAA badges. His vast red nylon running shorts reached down to his knees, but exposed his tattooed calves.

In his right hand he was carrying a black plastic jerrycan with its yellow lid dangling open.

Detective Dooley stopped on the seventh stair. 'How's it hanging, Dara?' he said, trying to sound friendly and briefly shining his flashlight on to his own face to show Dara Coughlan what he looked like. 'I'm Detective Garda Dooley from Anglesea Street. I need you to come in to the station with me now to answer some questions.'

'Get away to feck,' Dara Coughlan growled back at him.

'Listen, sham, I don't want to have to arrest you. It would be better all round if you came in voluntarily-like, do you know what I mean? But I need to talk with you about the fire at the Toirneach Damhsa dance studio. It won't take more than an hour or two, and if you can prove that you had no involvement in it at all then we'll have you back here and tucked up in bed again before you know it.'

'Are you *deaf* like, or what? I said get away to feck.'

'Dara, I have two guards here with me, as well as Detective Garda O'Mara, and we can take you in by force if we have to.'

'What's going on, Dara?' the woman's voice screamed. 'What do they want? What in the name of God have you done now, you stupid gowl?'

'Shut your bake, Millie!' Dara Coughlan shouted back at her. Then, to Detective Dooley, 'Go on, piss off. I've done nothing wrong like, and I'm not going nowhere, not with you nor with nobody else.'

Detective Dooley took two more steps up the staircase towards him and Dara Coughlan lifted up the jerrycan in both hands.

'Come on, Dara, don't be an eejit,' said Detective Dooley. By now Detective O'Mara was standing close behind him, and behind him the two uniformed gardaí.

'I'm warning you,' said Dara Coughlan. 'You come up one step closer, boy, and I'll fecking fry you, and don't think I won't!'

'Spoken like a true arsonist,' said Detective Dooley. 'Now why don't you put down that can and go back inside and put your runners on? Then we can all go to the station together and have a nice friendly chat about who's been burning down what, and why. It's only to eliminate you, Dara, for Christ's sake, but you have to admit that you've set light to more buildings per capita than almost anybody else in Cork, so you can understand why we need to talk to you.'

Detective Dooley took another step up and it was then that Dara Coughlan swung the jerrycan upside-down and splashed petrol all over him. Detective Dooley was blinded and half- choked, and fell to his knees on the stairs, dropping his flashlight. Dara Coughlan carried on violently shaking the jerrycan until it was almost empty.

Detective O'Mara tried to push his way past Detective Dooley and the two gardaí started to heave themselves up the stairs, too. But Dara Coughlan dropped the jerrycan on to the floor so that it bounced back across the landing, still spraying out petrol, and tugged a book of matches out of the pocket of his shorts.

Just as Detective O'Mara managed to climb over Detective Dooley and make a grab for his arm, Dara Coughlan bent the matches over and struck the whole book at once. As they flared up, he dropped them and Detective Dooley exploded into flame.

He screamed, and tried to stand up, waving his arms. For the first few seconds he appeared to be made out of nothing but fire, like a wicker man, but as he grasped the banister rail and struggled to his feet his head appeared out of a collar of flames, with his hair already shrivelled and his cheeks sooty and his lips turning to crackling. His eyes were staring and bloody and already fried.

Some of the petrol had splashed on to Detective O'Mara's clothes and flames were licking at his jacket and his trouser leg. The carpet on the third-floor landing was alight, too, where the jerrycan had tumbled across the floor, and Dara Coughlan's bare feet were scorched scarlet. He let out an elephantine bellow, stamping his feet in pain, and then staggered back towards his open door, colliding first with the banisters and then with the wall.

All of Detective Dooley's muscles were flexed by the heat of the fire that was engulfing him and he pitched over backwards. The two gardaí tried to hold on to him, but only the garda who had been swinging the battering-ram was wearing gloves, and Detective Dooley was burning too fiercely. He tumbled and thumped all the way down to the bottom of the stairs and lay there, twisted into a swastika shape, with orange flames still rippling out of the charred black flakes that were all that remained of his suit.

Both gardaí wrenched off their high-viz jackets and piled them on top of him. They managed to suppress the flames, but he was quaking and shuddering and going into neurogenic shock. One of them switched on his radio and called for an ambulance and backup.

'And as fast as you like, girl, he's one of ours!'

The stairwell was filled with billows of smoke that smelled of petrol and burned flesh. Detective O'Mara had managed to smack out the flames that had scorched his clothes, and even though both his hands were badly blistered and his left leg was so sore that he had to limp, he crossed the landing and approached the dark open doorway into which Dara Coughlan had disappeared.

'*Dara!*' he shouted, his voice hoarse from the smoke. 'Dara, this is Detective Garda O'Mara! You have to come out of there, boy!'

He kept his back to the wall and stayed clear of the fatal funnel, the triangular area where anyone who ventured into a room was most in danger of being shot. Just because Dara Coughlan was a serial arsonist, that didn't mean his only weapon was petrol. He could easily have a pistol or a shotgun. He might rush out with a knife, or a machete, or an axe.

'I'm giving you five to come out!' Detective O'Mara told him, trying not to cough. 'There's more guards on the way, and they'll be armed! You've no chance at all of getting away, Dara! You don't have a hope in hell!'

He heard Dara saying something and then the woman's voice again. 'You're stone mad you are! What did you think you were doing? You could have burned down the whole fecking house! You're fecking botched in the head! Jesus!'

'Shut up, will you, woman, for two fecking minutes!'

'Well, what are you going to do now? You've just set fire to a guard, you lunatic! You think they're going to tell you, "oh, it's no bother at all, boy, think nothing of it," and let you go?'

'Shut up, will you! You're wrecking my fecking head!'

One of the gardaí had come upstairs now to see what Detective O'Mara was doing. Detective O'Mara asked, 'How's Dooley?'

The garda shook his head. 'Bad. I don't know if he's going to make it. The white van'll be here in a minute, though, and they're sending the RSU.'

Dara Coughlan and his girlfriend were still arguing inside the flat, and Detective O'Mara put his finger to his lips. 'From what they've been saying, it doesn't sound like he's armed. In fact, it sounds like he's totally mithered.'

'I heard you shouting for him to come out like. Did he answer at all?'

Detective O'Mara shook his head. 'I think we could risk going in after him. There's no other way out of this flat. It's more of a bedsit like. The fire escape's back there, next to the jacks – and, look, that's padlocked.'

They heard the brief whoop of an ambulance siren in the distance. The garda went across to the banister rail and looked down to where Detective Dooley was lying, with his partner kneeling next to him.

'He's still with us, just,' his partner called up.

The garda came back to join Detective O'Mara. 'Okay,' he said, 'let's scoop the bastard.'

'Dara!' shouted Detective O'Mara. 'You're running out of time now, boy! Three – four – five! Are you coming out now or what?'

Dara Coughlan didn't reply, but his girlfriend screamed, '*Dara!*' at him. 'Dara – what are you doing? Dara, will you get down from there!'

Detective O'Mara and the garda didn't even have to look at each other. They jostled their way into the flat, their flashlights criss-crossing in the darkness. Detective O'Mara shouted, 'Dara! Stay right where you are! Freeze! And put your hands up over your head!'

Dara Coughlan's girlfriend switched on the single overhead light. Detective O'Mara had been right: it was a bedsit, with a messy double bed, a frayed basketwork chair, and a chipboard kitchen counter with a small stainless-steel basin and a microwave oven. The walls were papered with maroon and gold stripes and over the bed hung a large print of Jesus surrounded by children and puppies and kittens.

The room reeked of stale weed and body odour and Estée Lauder White Linen.

Dara Coughlan's girlfriend was standing behind the kitchen counter, her left hand clasping her right elbow, looking more defeated than angry. She had a wild mess of bleached-blonde curls and a face that must have been babyish when she was younger but was puffy now, like a white marshmallow, with eyes blotched with mascara. She was wearing a black see-through negligée, and she, too, had tattoos all the way up her arms, including a Virgin Mary on her shoulder who looked so grumpy she could have been mistaken for Martin McGuinness.

When she first switched on the light, Detective O'Mara couldn't immediately see where Dara had disappeared to. But his girlfriend nodded towards the heavy brown wool curtains and he realized that they were bulging inwards.

'All right, Dara, you can come down off the window sill,' said Detective O'Mara. He was trying to sound calm and authoritative, but he was beginning to feel the shock of being burned, and of seeing Detective Dooley set on fire, and wasn't finding it easy to keep his voice steady. 'You have to understand that I'm arresting you now for assaulting a police officer.'

'Away to feck,' said a muffled voice behind the curtains.

'Come on, Dara, don't be an eejit. There's nowhere for you to go.'

They heard the window being opened and felt a draught.

'Dara! What are you going to do, you headbanger?' the girlfriend screamed out. 'Jump out the fecking windie? Well, why don't you, that's the first and only time you'll ever fly!'

'Whisht up, will you, girl?' the garda told her.

Detective O'Mara said, 'Don't worry about it. It's a good ten metres to the ground. He's not going to jump.'

He started to walk across to the window, but as he did so there was a shuffling sound and the curtains were sucked inwards and then blown outwards again. He heard a sharp crunch and a reverberating clang and then a cry like nothing else he had ever heard in his life. If it reminded him of anything at all, it was the cry of helplessness and bewilderment that his baby son had let out as soon as he was born.

He yanked back the curtains. The window was wide open and Dara Coughlan had thrown himself out of it. Instead of landing on the pavement, though, which might have given him a chance of survival, he had impaled himself on the metal pole of a No Parking sign. He was suspended horizontally two metres in the air, his tattooed arms and legs slowly waving as if he were swimming.

Dara Coughlan's girlfriend rushed to the window, and when she saw him she collapsed on to the floor without saying a word. The garda peered out of the window and said, 'Christ on a crutch.'

At that moment the ambulance turned out of Adelaide Street and came speeding down North Main Street, silently, but with its lights flashing. Detective O'Mara said, 'I think you'd best be calling for the fire brigade, too. I don't know how the hell we're going to get him off that post.'

While the garda called for fire and rescue, Detective O'Mara managed to force his hands into the girlfriend's plump and sweaty armpits and drag her on to the bed. She could only murmur and mumble, but her eyelids were flickering and she was still breathing. All the same, he would have to ask the paramedics to check her out. From the way she and Dara Coughlan had been behaving, it was likely that they had been taking heroin and N-bombs or fluorofentanyl, or all three.

'Right, let's go down and see the fecking harpooned whale,' he said, although his voice was shaking.

As they came down the stairs they saw that a paramedic had arrived and was kneeling down next to Detective Dooley and opening up her medical kitbag. She had short black hair and put Detective O'Mara in mind of one of the Nolans.

'My God,' she said. 'Him outside there, did he leap out the window?'

'High as a kite, more than likely,' said Detective O'Mara. 'He did this – threw petrol all over him. We've called for more backup and the fire brigade.'

At that moment, a grey-haired male paramedic came stamping up the stairs, followed by two armed gardaí from the regional support unit, both wearing body armour.

The male paramedic looked down at Detective Dooley and then he said, 'Your man on the post downstairs, he's gone to meet his maker.' He said it in a flat, matter-of-fact way, as if he saw overweight tattooed men impaled on parking signs every night of the week. Then he hunkered down beside Detective Dooley and said, 'How is he?'

'What's the form?' one of the armed gardaí asked Detective O'Mara. 'Did your man jump out the window or what? Who is he?'

'Dara Coughlan his name is. He's a record as long as your arm for arson. We came here to bring him in for questioning about that fire at the dance studio.'

'And what? He chucked petrol at you?'

'Dooley got the worst of it.'

The armed garda leaned over and looked at Detective Dooley's blackened face. 'Mother of God, is that Bobby Dooley? I went to the Pres with him! Oh, Jesus!'

'Is there anybody else here we need to deal with?' asked the second armed garda, grimly. He was carrying a Heckler & Koch MP7 sub-machine gun, with his finger pressed flat against the trigger-guard.

'Only Coughlan's girlfriend. She's upstairs out of her brain on 4-FBF or something similar. God knows.'

The stairwell was lit up with bright flashing blue lights which showed that the fire and rescue team had arrived. Detective O'Mara said, 'I'd better get myself down there and see what's slicing. I'll have to ring DS Begley and wake him up. He's going to be delighted, not. We'll need some pictures taken, too, and some forensics, so I'd better ring Bill Phinner.'

The second armed garda frowned at him. 'Are you all right, sir?'

'What? Yes. No. I'm grand altogether.'

He looked down at the two paramedics still bent over Detective Dooley and asked, 'How's he coming on?'

The female paramedic stood up and pushed back her hair. 'I'm sorry,' she told him. 'He's passed. There wasn't anything that we could do for him. The shock, mostly.'

Detective O'Mara nodded and crossed himself. He didn't want to look at Detective Dooley again because he wanted to remember him as he was, grinning and young and spotty, not as some ghastly incinerated mask.

He went downstairs. Outside, two fire and rescue vehicles were parked by the kerb and six or seven firefighters were standing in a circle around the parking sign on which Dara Coughlan had impaled himself. Although it was only four in the morning a crowd of onlookers was gathering on the corner of Kyle Street and upstairs windows across the street were all lit up, with people in their nightclothes staring out to see what was happening and taking videos with their mobile phones.

Detective O'Mara went up to the signpost and looked up at Dara Coughlan. His arms and legs were hanging down now, as if he had drowned and was floating. His eyes were still open and staring blindly at the pavement, and a thin string of bloody mucus was hanging from his lips. The metal post had punctured his belly just below his breastbone, but the red-and-white No Parking discs on either side of the post had bent sideways like two large ears and were preventing him from sliding down any further.

All Detective O'Mara could think was, *You deserved this, you piece of shite. I hope you stay like this for all eternity, like a human kebab, and I hope that you burn for ever like all the people you burned and all the people you tried to burn. Amen.*

One of the rescue team came up to him and said, 'Detective? If it's all right with you, what we're planning to do is cut down the post with an angle-grinder. It'll be a whole lot easier than trying to lift him off of it, do you know what I mean? When you look at the size of him like, and he's jammed on there solid.'

Detective O'Mara raised his hand to acknowledge that he

understood, but then he said, 'Stall the beans for a moment there would you? I'll be with you in a tick.'

He turned and walked stiff-legged around the corner into the shadowy courtyard of St Peter's Church. Holding on to the railings, he regurgitated three tan-coloured torrents of curry, which splattered down the side of the limestone wall and over his shoes.

Eighteen

Katie was dreaming that she was shopping in the English Market but that she had lost sight of John. At last, she saw him standing behind the fountain, and he seemed to be looking around for her.

He's walking! He can't have lost his legs after all! Thank God for that! I don't have to feel guilty now!

She called out to him, but her shopping bag was impossibly heavy and the strap was tangled around her wrist and by the time she had managed to lug it to the fountain he had disappeared. She was crossing over to Tom Durcan's the butcher's to ask if they had seen him when her iPhone playing '*Fear a' Bháta*' woke her up.

She sat up, still unsure if she was asleep or awake. It was dark outside and when she looked at her bedside clock it read 5:01.

'Who's this?' she said. Her tongue felt as if it were coated with fine sand.

'DS Begley, ma'am. Sorry to wake you. I have some fierce bad news, I'm afraid.'

She switched on her bedside lamp. She could see herself in the mirrored door of her wardrobe; her hair was sticking up like a cockerel's.

'What is it, Sean?'

'Young Robert Dooley's dead,' said Detective Sergeant Begley, and then stopped, as if he had to swallow.

'*What?* Jesus – how?'

'He was burned to death. He was trying to bring that fire-raiser fellow in for questioning, that Dara Coughlan, and Coughlan threw petrol all over him and set him alight.'

Katie's insides felt as if she had dropped down three floors in a lift.

'Oh, my God,' she said. 'Did he suffer much?'

'O'Mara told me he died almost at once. The shock of it, that's what he said.'

Katie threw back her duvet and sat up. 'How about Bryan O'Mara? Is he all right? And they took a couple of uniforms with them, didn't they? Did either of them get hurt?'

'O'Mara suffered some slight burns, ma'am, but nothing serious like. As far as I know, the two officers backing them up weren't injured at all.'

'Poor Robert. I can't believe it. What a terrible way to go. And he had such a future ahead of him. And he has a fiancée, too, doesn't he? Some girl from Macroom he was going to marry?'

'That's right. But the thing of it is, Dara Coughlan's dead, too.'

'Mother of God, Sean, this gets worse. How did *he* die?'

'O'Mara went after him and he threw himself out of the third-floor window. He and his girlfriend were out of their brains on drugs, so it seems. He fell right on top of a No Parking sign and got himself skewered.'

'You're codding me.'

'I wish I was. The fire and rescue had to cut the sign down and take him off to the mortuary with half of it still sticking out of him.'

'Where was this? Robert told me that he'd located Coughlan somewhere on North Main Street.'

'Sure like, that's where it was, North Main Street. Next door to St Peter's almost, opposite Kyle Street. He was staying with some brasser in her bedsit. She's been taken to the Mercy suffering from a suspected overdose.'

'All right, Sean. I'll get myself dressed and into the station as quick as I can. I should be there by six.'

'You'll have a rake of problems to deal with, ma'am, I can tell you. Mathew McElvey's just been on to me from the press office. The papers and the TV know all about it, and worse than that, there are videos on the interweb already of Coughlan stuck on top of the No Parking sign. They're going viral, apparently.'

'Oh, fantastic. And I have my press conference set up for this afternoon, too, about the Toirneach Damhsa fire.'

'I'll meet you at the station, ma'am. I'll be passing the news on to Chief Superintendent MacCostagáin and Superintendent Pearse. God rest poor Robert Dooley.'

'Amen to that,' said Katie, and put down the phone.

* * *

As soon as she arrived at Anglesea Street she called in Mathew McElvey and his assistant, Siobhán, to prepare an interim press release. Mathew had pulled on a white Aran sweater and a pair of jeans to come in to the station early and he hadn't yet shaved. Siobhán was wearing a tight sparkly black top and a short red taffeta skirt, and she explained that she had been clubbing at the Voodoo Rooms and hadn't even gone to bed yet.

'You'll be relieved to know that Facebook have taken down the videos of Coughlan stuck on the No Parking sign,' said Mathew. 'The TV and papers have the pictures of him of course, but I've already asked them not to use them because they amount to evidence and could compromise any prosecution if they do. Apart from that, I don't think they'll be running them purely as a matter of taste. It's not really what you want to see when you're eating your bacon and eggs, a big fat dead feller stuck on the top of a pole.'

He opened his laptop, prodded at the keyboard, and then handed it over so that Katie could see one of the videos of Dara Coughlan that had briefly appeared on the internet.

'*Urgh,*' she said. 'I see what you mean. I'm glad I haven't had any breakfast yet myself.'

'The Technical Bureau took a load of pictures and of course they'll be far more detailed. I'm sure they've sent them up to you already.'

'In that case, I think I'll stick to coffee,' said Katie, handing back the laptop.

'So what do we say to the media?' asked Mathew, taking out his notepad.

'Only the barest facts, for the moment, but I want to make it clear that we were after questioning Coughlan because he was a serial arsonist and therefore a possible suspect in the Toirneach Damhsa fire. We still haven't exhausted all of our enquiries into his background and whether he might have had some connection with one of the dancers. No, don't tell them that – just say that we haven't exhausted all of our enquiries.'

She paused and thought for a moment, then she said, 'You can say that what happened was a pure tragedy and we're grieving the loss of one our most promising young detectives. He was dedicated and skilled and always willing to take a risk. Our condolences go to his family and friends, and to everybody who enjoyed his wit and charm.'

'Is that all for the moment?' asked Mathew, scribbling notes.

'For the time being, yes. You can tell them that I will be giving out more details at the press conference for the Toirneach Damhsa fire this afternoon, since it was all part of the same investigation. With any luck, I should have much more information by then.'

Just as Mathew and Siobhán stood up to go, Detective Sergeant Begley knocked at the door. Katie had never seen him looking so grim.

'How's the form, Sean?' she asked him.

'Good morning to you, ma'am. I just came up to tell you that O'Mara's been treated for his burns at the Mercy. He says they're only superficial, but he's gone home to change and have a bit of a rest to get over the shock.'

'Has he told you what happened?'

'He phoned in a report while he was waiting at the hospital, and it's recorded of course. I also have the notes of the two officers who went with them. Bryan says if you have any questions at all, he'll be happy to answer them at home.'

'That's grand, Sean. I'll have a listen right now.'

'I've informed Chief Superintendent MacCostagáin about Dooley, and Inspector Murphy, too. Superintendent Pearse is away today. He's attending his father's funeral in Carrigaline.'

The day of the dead, thought Katie. But all she said was, 'I see. Okay. Thanks a million.'

'One more thing,' said Detective Sergeant Begley. 'MacCostagáin asked me to ask you if you'd come along to his office at nine o'clock. He's having some kind of a pow-wow with the new Assistant Commissioner and a superintendent from Special Branch.'

'Oh, okay, sure. Special Branch? I don't think I have to be a genius to guess what *that's* going to be about.'

Katie prised open the lid of her cappuccino. If the Special Detective Unit were involved, they were bound to be discussing the security measures for the visit to Ireland next week by Ian Bowthorpe, the British defence secretary. He would be arriving in Dublin first to hold talks about border security after Brexit, and then he was coming to Cork to discuss the future cooperation of the Irish Naval Service with Britain's navy and the UN.

Normally the Garda would have been given much earlier notice of a visit like this. Katie's detectives would then have had plenty of time to buy a few drinks for their informers and assess if any of the IRA splinter groups in Cork were either interested in or capable of mounting a serious threat to Ian Bowthorpe's life. But the visit had been arranged at very short notice, mainly because of the intense pressure from Sinn Féin for a referendum on Irish unification. Even the Taoiseach had suggested that a popular vote might not be out of the question, so Ian Bowthorpe was coming to reassure the Dáil that there would be no return to the army checkpoints and watchtowers that had separated the border during the Troubles, and that the navies of Britain and Ireland would continue to cooperate closely for their mutual security.

At 7.30 Moirin appeared. Katie had rung her and asked her to come in early because she would have to be fielding questions all morning about Detective Dooley's death and she also needed to prepare for the afternoon's conference. All of the relatives of the dead dancers would be attending, as well as the media and representatives from the fire brigade and the Fire Investigation Association. Katie needed the latest pathology reports from Dr Kelley, and from Bill Phinner she needed not only an up-to-date forensic report on the cause of the studio fire but also a report on Dara Coughlan's death.

Moirin looked shaken. 'I can't believe that young Robert Dooley's gone. He'd bring me a chocolate doughnut more often than not. Such a sweet boy he was.'

'I know,' said Katie. She still felt numb about his death herself, and she found it almost impossible to imagine that he wouldn't be walking into her office at any moment to tell her that he had brought in Dara Coughlan and had him ready for questioning in the interview room downstairs.

He was always joking. She remembered him telling her how his father had been stopped by a guard for driving in the wrong direction along Cornmarket Street. When the garda had asked him where he thought he was going, he had said, 'To work. I didn't realize that this was a one-way street. I thought I was late and everybody else was driving home.'

She smiled sadly, but her eyes stayed dry. She had done enough crying lately.

As the morning progressed, the station's business continued as usual. Phones warbled, footsteps hurried up and down the corridor outside Katie's office. All the same, she was aware that conversation was muted, and throughout the building there was a palpable sense of shock and loss.

At 8.15 Kyna came in wearing a red headscarf and a very short red knitted dress and thigh-boots.

'God, I feel terrible,' she said. 'I feel like I ought to be wearing black.'

'Oh, stop,' said Katie gently. 'Robert would have understood.'

'I saw it on the news when I woke up,' Kyna told her. 'They didn't give his name but I guessed who it was when they said it had happened on North Main Street. It's so tragic. Have his parents been told yet?'

'They're in Portugal on their holidays, but they'll be flying back tonight.'

Kyna sat down. 'Jesus, I can't believe it. And is it true that the fellow he was trying to bring in for questioning jumped out the window and got himself stuck on a No Parking sign?'

'I have the picture on my PC if you want to see it.'

'No thanks, there are some things that once you've seen them you can't un-see. Like last night at the Templegate Tavern. This fellow Davy Dorgan only pinned this other fellow Liam's hand to the table. Like, I mean, right through the back of his hand, with a flick knife. And he did it because Liam was chatting me up but he wouldn't tell him what we were saying.'

'Mother of God. Didn't the landlord throw him out?'

'Nobody said a word. They're all scared to death of this Davy. Later on he had some kind of a get-together in a room at the back. About fifteen more fellows showed up and they were a hardy bunch of snipes, I can tell you. I don't know what they talked about in there, but they came out after about half an hour and drank about fifteen pints each, except for Davy, who doesn't drink. This girl sang "The Lament of the Three Marys" for Niall Gleeson and they all sang along. Talk about a chorus of tortured badgers.'

Katie sat back and said, 'So what do you think? This Davy's taken over from Bobby Quilty? Not just the cigarette-smuggling, but the Authentic IRA? Is that who you think these fellows are?'

'When he first came in, Davy asked these two fellows what they were talking to me about and one of them, Billy, he made a joke that we were planning to blow up Collins Barracks. Davy did ninety and almost twisted his ear off.'

'I'm worried because this British defence secretary is visiting Cork next week. I don't want any stray republican splinter groups having a crack at him, that's all.'

'Well, I've been employed at the Templegate now. The landlord's taken a shine to me and I'll be going back this evening. Most important, though, this young fellow Liam who had his hand stabbed, he's taken more than a shine to me. I think he's in love.'

Katie couldn't help shaking her head. 'If only he knew.'

'That's not the point,' said Kyna. 'The point is that I think I can wangle out of him what Davy and the rest of those fellows are up to. I mean, it may be something and nothing at all. Maybe they're all Freemasons and that's their local lodge meeting. But I never saw a Freemason pin a fellow's hand to a table before, not even with a trowel.'

'All right, then, good luck,' said Katie. 'But for the love of God be wide – especially of that Davy Dorgan.'

'That's one of the reasons I've come in to the station this morning,' said Kyna. 'I think he comes from Cork originally but he's spent most of his life in Ulster. You can tell it by his accent when he loses his temper and the way he says "thon" instead of "that". I'm going to ask the PSNI if they can run a background check on him for me.'

'Okay. Keep me in touch. And don't you go falling in love with that Liam.'

The two of them looked at each other across Katie's desk. If Katie hadn't been a detective superintendent and Kyna hadn't been a detective sergeant, and if they hadn't agreed to suppress any feelings that they might have for each other, they would have stood up and embraced, and kissed. But Kyna said, 'Not a chance. He's about five years younger than me and he has blackheads.'

Nineteen

Before she went into her meeting with Chief Superintendent MacCostagáin and Assistant Commissioner Magorian and the superintendent from the SDU, Katie called for Detective O'Donovan. He looked sober and upset, like everybody else she had seen that morning.

'I'll be making a statement about Robert this afternoon, at the press conference,' she told him. 'Meanwhile, he had two suspects connected to the Toirneach Damhsa fire down for questioning and I'd like you to bring them in later today, after the conference is over.'

'That's no problem at all,' said Detective O'Donovan. 'I'll be downloading all of Dooley's notes anyway to see what progress he'd made with this case.'

Katie looked at her own PC. 'There's Douglas Cleary – he was engaged to the girl who was found shot dead in the attic. Then there's Steven Joyce, who used to manage Toirneach Damhsa in conjunction with Danny Coffey. It seems like there was some fierce bad blood between them after they split up. In fact, Danny Coffey is convinced that Steven Joyce was the one who started the fire, although he doesn't seem to have any real evidence for it.'

'What about Cleary?'

'He was in Manchester when the fire was started, but then again he could have arranged for somebody else to start it for him. It looked as if his fiancée might have been having a fling with one of the dancers, Ronan Barrett, so that would have given him a motive. To be honest with you, I don't think it's very likely that he was responsible, but so far we have absolutely no idea at all who the arsonist was, so I'm not leaving anybody out.'

'Of course,' said Detective O'Donovan. 'Anything else?'

'Bill Phinner told me that the chemical that started the fire is sometimes used by the military. It's like a substitute for napalm, you know? Except that it's self-combusting – as soon as the air gets at it, *whoomph*, up it goes. So it's worth checking if any of the suspects on Robert's list had some connection to one of the defence forces.'

'Sure, I can do that all right,' said Detective O'Donovan. 'I have a great contact up at the barracks – Barry Brady his name is, Dara-Leifteanant Barry Brady. We used to live in the same street and play long slogs together. He's in the First Ordnance Group so if there was any of that stuff gone missing he'll be your man to know about it.'

'Well, that's a stroke of luck. But Bill also said they use the same chemical for making semiconductors and plastics. There's a couple of companies in Cork who produce those, one in Bishopstown and another on Little Island. You'll find their names in Robert's notes.'

'Hard to believe he's gone,' said Detective O'Donovan. 'We were going to watch the hurling together on Saturday, Fermoy versus Kilworth.'

Katie didn't respond to that. Just at the moment, the last thing she wanted to do was start thinking again about sadness and bereavement.

'There's one other avenue you might explore,' she said. 'Danny Coffey was fierce upset about the dance instructor Nicholas O'Grady losing his life. I mean, more upset than you would expect your average straight man to be, even about a fellow he'd known for years. I may have totally misread his reaction, do you know what I mean, but maybe you could have a word with O'Grady's husband, and some of his friends, too, and see if there wasn't more to Coffey's relationship with him than met the eye.'

'I reckon I'll get Scanlan on to that one,' said Detective O'Donovan. 'She's fantastic when it comes to cigires. They'll tell her anything.'

* * *

Katie went into her toilet to fix her make-up and brush her hair. She wasn't happy with the last cut that her hairdresser, Marty, had given her. He had stepped up her bob too high at the back of her neck and his layering had been choppy and uneven. Maybe she would try Kyna's hairdresser, D'Arcy's on Paul Street.

After she had applied her lipstick and mascara she stared at herself in the mirror over the washbasin to see if she could tell how she was really feeling. She found it unsettling that her face gave away so much about her state of mind. She had seen photographs of herself in the *Examiner* and the *Echo*, and recordings of her television interviews on RTÉ news. She always tried to give the impression to the media that she was feeling confident and assertive, and at the time she almost believed her own assurances. But when she studied the pictures afterwards, she was able to see from the lack of focus in her eyes that she was far from sure of her ability to solve whichever crime she was talking about. She had seen that same look in photographs of herself and John, especially near the end of their relationship, when she hadn't been able to decide if she should stay with him or not.

She gave her hair a quick burst of hairspray and as she did so her iPhone pinged. It was a text message from Conor.

Heard from my vet contact. The big McManus birthday dog-fight is definitely on. Next Thurs 1500 approx in a clearing in woods off Cappamurra Bridge btw Goolds Cross and Dundrum. I should be back by 9. Been missing you KM.

Katie quickly answered: *Ring me l8er. Missed you too dog detective.*

She told Moirin to hold any calls for her and then went along the corridor to Chief Superintendent MacCostagáin's office.

Assistant Commissioner Frank Magorian was already there, sitting by the window. It was now ten past nine and he looked at his watch as Katie came in, but said nothing. Chief Superintendent MacCostagáin was sitting behind his desk with a cup of tea and a half-eaten slice of barmbrack in front of him, looking even glummer than usual.

Detective Inspector Mulliken was there, too, on the opposite end of the couch from Frank Magorian, hunched forward and prodding at his mobile phone.

Standing by the bookcase was a short stocky man with prickly grey hair. He was wearing a navy-blue double-breasted suit and had his arms tightly folded, as if he rarely made any concessions to anybody. His chin was receding, but his lower lip was sticking out pugnaciously, which made Katie think that he was in a thick mood about something.

'This is Superintendent Griffin from Special Branch,' said Chief Superintendent MacCostagáin. 'Terence, this is Detective Superintendent Kathleen Maguire.'

Superintendent Griffin came forward and held out his hand. 'We've met before, briefly, DS Maguire, about two years ago at Phoenix Park. That's if you remember me. You were taking part in a panel discussion on women in senior positions in the Garda.'

'I remember you, of course,' Katie told him. 'How could I forget? You made some comment about women being psychologically unsuitable for senior rank because they tended to be too forgiving towards violent men.'

'In your case, I withdraw that remark,' said Superintendent Griffin, without smiling. 'I've seen your record and it seems like you've been as hard as nails with every man you've ever had to deal with – your fellow officers as well as offenders.'

'I just try to be efficient,' said Katie, trying to give the impression from her tone of voice that she didn't want to talk about this any more.

'We've been discussing the visit next week by Ian Bowthorpe, the UK's defence secretary,' put in Detective Inspector Mulliken, sensing Katie's impatience. 'We've been gathering intelligence from several of our sources in the various IRA splinter groups. So far, though, we've no indication that any of them have plans to do him any mischief. In fact, some of them seem to regard Brexit as giving them a good opportunity to unite Ireland without the shedding of any more blood.'

'We'll be providing Mr Bowthorpe with five close protection officers,' said Superintendent Griffin. 'I've brought his itinerary with me. He'll be received by the mayor at City Hall first of all and then he'll be driven out to Haulbowline to inspect the naval fleet there. Then he'll be brought back to the city and he'll attend the step-dancing *feis* in the evening at the Opera House. I believe it's a way of trying to show that the Brits are interested in Irish culture.'

'Three and a half hours of watching pubescent girls jumping up and down with their arms pinned to their sides – of course the Brits are interested,' said Frank Magorian. 'Why do you think they had Operation Yewtree?'

Superintendent Griffin gave him a quick, hard look, as if he wasn't amused at being interrupted, especially with so flippant a remark. 'Within the next two days we'll be supplying you with a detailed itinerary so that you can give Mr Bowthorpe all the added security that he's going to require during his time in Cork.'

'I've already sketched out a provisional plan,' said Detective Inspector Mulliken. 'Apart from close protection, all the vantage points along his route will be sealed off – the tops of the buildings all along Patrick's Street, for example. That's in case of snipers.'

'What about the Opera House?' asked Katie.

'That's not going to be easy, because of course there'll be a capacity crowd. But we'll have armed officers posted at strategic points outside and inside the theatre, and everybody who enters will have to show their ticket and submit to a search.'

Superintendent Griffin said, 'I can't emphasize strongly enough how important it is that Mr Bowthorpe's visit is entirely without any breaches of security whatsoever. It's politically important and it's also important to the reputation of the SDU.'

'Understood,' said Katie. 'As soon as we receive your itinerary we'll work out the finer details for you, and in the meantime of course we'll be keeping our ears to the ground.'

'Thank you,' said Superintendent Griffin. He shook them

all by the hand, Katie last of all. He said nothing, but the look he gave her made her feel that he was challenging her to show him that she was up to the job. She was tempted to say that she wouldn't let him down, but then she thought, *Why should I? I don't have to prove myself to him or anybody else.*

Once he had left, Chief Superintendent MacCostagáin brushed the barmbrack crumbs from his trousers and said, 'That's that sorted. Care for a cup of tea in your hand?'

Katie shook her head. 'Just had a coffee, thank you, sir. And I'm fierce pressed for time.'

'Well, this needn't take long,' said Frank Magorian. 'What I mainly wanted to discuss with you both is how we're going to present our investigation into the Toirneach Damhsa fire to the media, and Detective Dooley's sad demise in particular.'

'We can only say that we're continuing to make enquiries and that Dooley's death was a tragedy,' said Katie. 'It's always a tragedy when an officer dies in the course of duty, especially a young and promising officer like he was.'

'Sit yourself down for a moment,' Frank Magorian told her, pointing to the other end of the couch that he was sitting on. Katie hesitated and then sat, crossing her legs and tugging down the hem of her grey tweed skirt.

'I've been going through the latest figures supplied by the Garda Inspectorate for detection rates in Cork,' said Frank Magorian, holding up a PDF printout. 'In the last year detection rates were down to sixty-three per cent, and in reality they may be a whole lot worse than that because it seems like a rake of low-level crimes have gone unrecorded.'

'Well, sir, yes, I admit we could be doing better,' said Katie.

'With thirty-seven per cent of crimes going undetected? You're not codding, are you?'

'We're desperately short of money,' Katie told him. 'Most of the time I don't have the finance to pay for my team to work overtime, or to pay my office staff. I could easily take on five more detective gardaí if I had the budget, but I don't.'

'Maybe you could run your existing team more efficiently,' said Frank Magorian. 'Like not sending them out to question people who are obviously not capable of committing the crimes that you're investigating.'

'You mean Detective Dooley going to interview Dara Coughlan?'

'That would be a prime example, yes. That fire was started by somebody with a high level of technical expertise, as well you know, not by some overweight drugged-up psycho.'

'Maybe it was, but we have to check out everybody who might have had some involvement in that fire, no matter how remotely. My team are all painstaking and dedicated, and considering their workload I think their achievements are fantastic.'

'The statistics don't agree with you, Katie, do they? Sixty-three per cent.'

'We're already stretched to breaking point,' Katie retorted. 'One of our biggest problems is that our equipment is so out of date – again, because we can't afford the new crime-solving technology like Throwbots and drones and DNA phenology, which really would have been a boon with the Toirneach Damhsa fire. We have an urgent need for up-to-date computers and software, and there are still too many places around Cork where our radios don't get a decent signal. The service in Kilworth and Araglin is patchy to say the least, and Doneraile has no signal at all.'

'There was a robbery last year up in Ballyvolane,' put in Chief Superintendent MacCostagáin, with his mouth full of barmbrack. 'Tens of thousands of euros' worth of farm equipment taken. Kathleen was the first detective to point out that in the Republic we don't have a national database for tool marks or shoe prints.'

'That's all well and good,' said Frank Magorian. 'But what I'm seeing here in Anglesea Street is inefficient investigative processes and poor supervision. It doesn't matter how advanced your computers are if your management is out of date.'

'Again, I'll admit that some of our procedures are time-wasting,' said Katie. 'Most of all, we could improve our working relationship with the courts. But it's six of one and half a dozen of the other:

the courts could equally improve their responses to what *we* need.'

'But what about all the crimes that don't get recorded?' Frank Magorian retorted. 'Are you quietly forgetting to report them because you can't be bothered to solve them, or because you don't believe you *could* solve them, even if you tried? Or are you simply massaging your statistics to make yourself look cuter and more competent than you really are?'

Katie was growing impatient now. She knew that Frank Magorian was deliberately needling her, but she wasn't going to rise to the bait and behave like a premenstrual prima donna.

'Sir – I've introduced a zero-tolerance policy when it comes to minor crimes. I expect every misdemeanour to be reported, even if it's only a vandal keying a car or a drunk making threatening remarks in a pub. We're using laptops now instead of notebooks, so that makes it much easier and less time-consuming.'

Frank Magorian pressed his fingertips to his forehead as if he could feel a headache coming on. 'What I'm trying to say to you, Katie, is that unlike most detective superintendents you involve yourself personally in your investigations. What you should be doing is sitting here in the station making sure that the whole investigative process runs smoothly. Instead of that, you still behave as if you're a front-line officer. You're a loose cannon, Katie. That doesn't make for crime-solving that's either efficient or effective.'

'With respect, sir, I couldn't disagree with you more,' said Katie. She was trying hard to keep her voice as steady as she could. 'I know that I involve myself more actively in some investigations than other superintendents. But in doing that I can see for myself first-hand how we need to improve and modernize the way we catch criminals.'

'So how close are you now to finding out who burned down the Toirneach Damhsa studio and killed eighteen innocent dancers?'

'We're following a considerable number of possible leads, as you must be aware.'

'But are you any nearer to finding out who might have done it?'

'We may be.'

'You may be, but even if you are, you don't know it? Is that what you're telling me?'

Katie stood up and turned to Chief Superintendent MacCostagáin. 'If that's all, sir, I have a whole heap of work to catch up with.'

Frank Magorian said, 'This afternoon when I'm briefing the media I'm going to put a very positive spin on this investigation, Katie. I just hope for your sake that you can match the positive spin with positive police work. That's all I'm telling you.'

Katie had been wondering if she ought to bring up the subject of Guzz Eye McManus's fiftieth birthday dog-fight, to see if she could get Frank Magorian's approval for a full-scale Garda operation. But after the way in which he had been demeaning her performance she decided not to, at least not for now. She knew what he would say: that she should leave dog-fighting to the ISPCA and concentrate instead on catching people who killed human beings.

He raised one provocative eyebrow, challenging her to answer him back, but she wouldn't be drawn and said nothing. She turned again to Chief Superintendent MacCostagáin, to see how he had reacted to what Frank Magorian had said, but he was too busy brushing more barmbrack crumbs off his trousers.

Twenty

Davy Dorgan was sitting in the Templegate Tavern with Murtagh and Billy when three hard-looking men came in, still breathing out smoke from the cigarettes they had tossed away outside. There were only seven other customers in the pub, four middle-aged men and three women, but when these three appeared they suddenly stopped talking.

Kyna was behind the bar, taking pint glasses out of the dishwasher and polishing them with a tea towel. Without looking at the three men, she said to Patrick, out of the corner of her mouth, 'Gluc the gilmosh them shams, Pat.'

'Be wide of them, Roisin, I tell you,' said Patrick. 'They're serious wackers, them three.'

'They were here last night, weren't they? I reck the feller with the squashed-flat bake. And that dartboard feller, too.'

One of the men pulled over an extra chair and then the three of them sat down at the table with Davy. The biggest of them was bald, with a face like a pug dog and a studded black leather jacket and tattoos all over his hands. One of the others was wearing a shiny grey suit and a thin red tie and looked like a disreputable accountant. The third was short, but bulky, with a thick neck and close-shaven ginger hair and freckles all over his face, which was why Kyna had compared him to a dartboard. He was wearing a tight lime-green sweater and navy tracksuit trousers and had heavy silver rings on all of his fingers.

Billy came up to the bar and asked for three pints of Murphy's and a double Paddy's whiskey for a chaser.

'I'll fetch them over for you,' said Kyna.

Billy leaned over the bar and grinned at her with gappy teeth. 'I'll tell you something for nothing, girl. If this pub totally ran dry of drink, not a drop of nothing in the whole place, I'd still come in here, just to lamp you.'

Kyna gave him an exaggerated pout and blew him a kiss. Today she was wearing a clinging beige woollen dress that was almost indecently short and her heels were so high that she tottered when she walked. She had brushed up her blonde hair and wore a cheap sparkly tiara made of Swarovski crystals. As she carried over the drinks on a tray, the men broke off in mid-conversation to stare at her – all except for Davy Dorgan.

The man in the black leather jacket waited until she had set down their glasses and then he said, 'We could be in the shite like. It's Dennehy's moth, Maggie.'

'What about her?' asked Davy.

'She came around last night and she was talking to my Sive. She's fierce upset about Niall. She knows that he was in with us like, and she knows that you and him had a bit of shemozzle about this and that.'

Davy stared at him hard. 'So what?' he demanded.

'Well, she knows for a fact that it wasn't her Bernie that killed him, because Niall told her right from the start that he was paying Bernie to give her a regular belt of the relic, although she never told Bernie that she knew. She didn't mind at all because Bernie could never give her what she wanted in the flange department, and the grade was welcome.'

'All right. So what are you saying?'

'I'm saying that out of all the people who might have had a reason to shoot him, Maggie reckons the only feller who had the motive and the means to do it was you.'

'Ah, that's some *raiméis* she's talking. Why would I want to do Niall any harm, of all people? He was building up the business again after Bobby went to hell and he was building it up fantastic. Granted, he and me saw things a bit different as far as politics was concerned, but I liked the man. He was sound.'

'Listen, don't blame me,' said the man in the black leather jacket. 'I'm only telling you what she told Sive, that's all.' He took a swallow of his beer, wiped his mouth with the back of his hand, and let out a crackling burp.

Davy said, 'Whatever she told your Sive there's nothing she can do about it, is there? She doesn't have any proof that it was me, because it wasn't me.'

'I believe you, but she's ripping about it and she told Sive that she was going down to Anglesea Street to talk to the shades. Even if it wasn't you, they're going to come sniffing around asking you questions, aren't they? Like, where were you when Niall got shot, things like that.'

'I was in here, that's where I was. Murtagh here and Billy can vouch for that, can't you, boys?'

Both Murtagh and Billy pulled faces that confirmed that they would. Neither of them was going to dare to say that when Niall had left the pub and driven away, Davy's Mercedes had been right behind him and heading in the same direction.

'There's that CSI stuff they can do now,' put in the dartboard man. 'I seen them on the telly. Like they can prove ninety-nine per cent certain that it wasn't you, by the NDA, and they can do tests on the bullet like, shooting it into a tank of water, to show that it didn't come out of your gun.'

'Well, that'll be easy to prove because I don't have a gun that it didn't come out of. And it's DNA, not NDA. NDA's a fecking toyshop.'

'Maggie's still going to go and talk to the shades,' said the man in the black leather jacket. 'Sive said she'll be doing it first thing tomorrow morning, when she goes into town to get the messages.'

'Where does she live, this Maggie?'

'Nash's Boreen, up by Fair Green. I don't know the number, but it's the first house after you've passed the halting site.'

Davy didn't answer that. He sat silent for a while, obviously thinking. The other five men at the table exchanged questioning glances, but none of them spoke, either.

At last, Davy picked up his glass of lemon MiWadi, drained it, and put it back on the table very quietly and precisely. Then he stood up and said, 'Right, let's go.'

'Go where?' asked Murtagh.

'Where do you think? Nash's Boreen. I think we have to have a discouraging word with this Maggie.'

'What, you mean *now*?' asked Billy.

'Now's as good a time as any.'

The other four men looked at each other, and then they all lifted their pints of Murphy's and swallowed them down as quickly as they could.

Kyna watched them from behind the bar as they all stood up from the table and made their way to the door. She had been trying to listen in to their conversation, but the man in the black leather jacket had spoken very quickly and indistinctly with a strong Mayfield accent and she had only picked up the gist of what they were saying.

Just before they reached the door it opened and Liam came in. His navy-blue nylon windcheater was slung over his shoulders because his right hand was bandaged and his arm was supported by a sling. He saw Kyna and gave her a thumbs-up sign with his left hand, but Davy said something to him and he had to turn around and go out again, with Davy and Murtagh and Billy and the other three men following.

As the door closed behind them, Patrick came up behind Kyna and said, 'Somebody's in for it.'

'What do you mean?'

'When that bunch of scummers all go out together, they're on their way to soften somebody's cough, believe me.'

'I heard them talking about some woman called Maggie.'

Patrick stuck out his lower lip and shook his head. 'Sure like, I know a couple of Maggies but I wouldn't be able to tell you which one they meant. Whoever she is, I think we should be saying a lorica for her. She's going to need it.'

* * *

Davy's silver Mercedes drew up outside the first in a row of white-painted houses on Nash's Boreen. It was followed a few seconds later by a dusty black Kia Sorento driven by the dartboard man.

Nash's Boreen was a narrow lane that ran westwards along the brow of the hill from Fair Green and eventually dwindled out into a cul-de-sac. To the north there were usually views of fields and farms and distant green hills, but this afternoon the clouds were dark grey and hanging low. Over towards Blarney rain was beginning to drift in, like a procession of very tall ghosts, so it was hard to see any further than Blackstone Bridge.

Davy and Murtagh and Billy and Liam climbed out of the Mercedes and the three other men jumped down from the Kia. The man in the black leather jacket was smoking, but he flicked his cigarette into the hedge.

In the front window of the house next door a curtain was tugged to one side and an elderly woman in curlers stared out at them. She looked like an inquisitive rhesus monkey. As soon as Davy stared back at her, however, she promptly vanished and the curtain was tugged back. In the Dennehy house, though, the front room was in darkness and there was no outward sign that anybody was at home.

'Maybe your one's not in,' said Billy, with a sniff.

'Well, we'll have to see, won't we?' said Davy. 'Give her a knock, will you?'

'Who me?'

'No, you gobdaw, your long-dead grannie.'

Billy went up to the green-painted front door and said, 'There's a bell.'

'Then ring the fecking bell, for the love of God.'

Billy pressed the bell and they could faintly hear it chiming inside. They waited, but there was no answer.

'She better not have gone to the pigsty already, I tell you,' said Davy. 'Give it another go.'

Billy pressed the bell again and this time they heard a door slamming and a woman's voice calling out, 'All right, all right! I'm coming! Stall the ball, will you?'

The door opened and there was Maggie Dennehy, looking flustered. She was a small woman, about forty-five years old, with short dark hair in a messy fringe and long dangling earrings. She was wearing no make-up but she had large brown eyes and high cheekbones and a squarish jaw, and as Billy had said, she was quite a fair knock for her age.

She was wearing a loose ginger sweater and black leggings and fluffy white slippers.

As soon as she saw Davy, she tried to slam the door shut, but Billy stuck his foot in it and pushed it back open.

'What are you after?' she demanded, although it was obvious that she was frightened.

'Just come to have a bit of a chat, that's all,' said Davy.

'I have nothing to say to you, Davy Dorgan.'

'Maybe not, Maggie, but I have one or two things that I need to say to you. Like, for instance, what a load of conna you're thinking of telling to the shades.'

'Who told you that?'

'Never you mind who told me. Let's go inside and talk it over, shall we?'

Again Maggie wrestled to shut the door, but Billy wouldn't let her even though she slammed it against his foot five or six times.

Davy came right up to the door and said very calmly, and with a strong hint of an Ulster accent, 'Come on, wee doll. Cool your jets. You know that if you don't let us in we'll only be after breaking down the door.'

'Away to feck with you,' said Maggie, gritting her teeth and trying to slam the door shut yet again.

'Kevan,' said Davy. The dartboard man came forward and while Billy leaned back to give him some space he pressed his shoulder against the door and his weight alone was enough to force it wide open.

Maggie was pushed backwards into the hallway, but she immediately turned around and stumbled into the front living room, slamming the door behind her.

Kevan didn't need telling again. He stepped into the hallway, rested his back against the wall opposite the living-room door, and gave it a kick that burst the lock and swung it wide open.

Davy walked into the living room, dry-washing his hands together and smiling. The rest of the men followed him, although Liam stayed close by the door with his back to the wall.

Maggie was crouching in the corner behind the large brown corduroy couch, as if by curling herself up small enough she could make herself invisible.

'What do you want?' she said, although she didn't look up at them and her voice was little more than a whisper, so that it didn't sound like a question at all.

'I want to know what you were thinking of telling the shades, wee doll. That's what I want.'

Maggie squeezed her eyes tight shut. 'I wasn't thinking of telling them nothing.'

'Oh yes, you fecking were,' said Davy. He turned to the dartboard man again and said, 'Kevan,' and nodded towards the large flat-screen TV standing on a table at the end of living room. The dartboard man went up to it, lifted it over his head and threw it against the wall, so that the screen broke diagonally in half with a sharp crack like a pistol shot. Maggie let out a little whimper.

'There's no use in you spoofing,' said Davy. 'You were going to rat on me to the shades even though you had no reason to. You really think I killed Niall? Jesus – you've a wee want if that's what you believe! I know one thing, though. You do it for the money. You're no better than any dockside brasser, are you?'

Maggie kept her eyes tight shut, but she began to sob.

'I'll tell you what, wee doll,' said Davy. 'You can pay me back for what you were thinking of doing, the same way you paid Niall back for his money. Billy – Kevan – Alroy – Darragh—'

Billy and the man in the black leather jacket and the man in the shiny grey suit all made their way around the couch. Billy and Alroy gripped Maggie by the arms and pulled her upright. She opened her eyes and screamed and kicked, but between them they heaved her around to the front of the couch and forced her to lie down on it.

'*Get off me!*' she screeched. '*Let me go! Get your hands off me you bastards! Get off me!*'

Davy looked around and saw that the curtains were held open by wide pink cotton tie-backs. He yanked one of them free and handed it to Darragh. 'Here, big man. Shut her bake for me, would you?'

Kevan and Alroy were keeping Maggie flat on her back on the couch, while Murtagh and Billy were holding her ankles to stop her from kicking. Darragh pushed the tie-back into her mouth and then gripped her hair so that he could lift up her head and knot it at the back of her neck. Maggie spat and gnashed her teeth and made angry gargling noises, but Darragh had tied it so tight that she couldn't loosen it.

Maggie had already lost her slippers, but while Kevan pinned her legs down, Murtagh reached underneath the hem of her baggy ginger sweater and took hold of the waistband of her black stretch leggings. She made even more gargling sounds as he tugged them down, centimetre by centimetre, and then rolled them right off, baring her thin white legs and a dark brown triangle of pubic hair.

Now Darragh pulled up her sweater, with Billy and Alroy helping him to wrestle her arms out of her sleeves. Darragh lifted up her head again by gripping her hair and then he dragged her sweater right off and slung it across the room.

Davy came up to the couch, leaning over Maggie with a smile that was almost beatific. She was naked now except for a black nylon bra, and he raised one hand as if he were a priest giving her a blessing. She glared up at him with glittering hatred, chewing at the tie-back between her teeth. In response, he smiled at her even more broadly, and leaned even closer, almost close enough to kiss her, so that he could reach with both hands behind her back to slide open the fastening of her bra.

After a few moments' jiggling he managed to take her bra right off. He held it up triumphantly and showed it around, as if it were a grey mullet that he had tickled out of the River Lee, and then he dropped it on to the floor.

'Well, you're *small*, wee doll, but perfectly formed,' he said, looking down at her breasts. 'What do you think, Billy?'

'I prefer my diddies a sight bigger than that, Davy, but beggars can't be choosers like, can they?'

'Go on, then, give her what we came for.'

Billy gave Maggie's right wrist to Darragh to hold. Then he went behind the couch, unbuckled his belt and dropped his jeans. He came back around the end of the couch wearing only his brown check shirt and mismatched socks, one calf-length and one short. His penis was only half-erect, and he was rubbing it furiously, but when Murtagh and Kevan forced Maggie's legs even wider apart, so that the lips of her vulva opened up, he stiffened immediately, until his penis stuck up between his shirttails like a long thin prong with a purple fig on the end of it. He unbuttoned his shirt from the bottom upwards and climbed on to the couch, kneeling between Maggie's skinny thighs.

Davy was now standing on the other side of the room with his back turned. The rain had reached the boreen outside and it was freckling the window panes. He had expected Maggie to struggle even more violently when Billy climbed on top of her, but all he could hear was Billy huffing and puffing and the monotonous squelching of the couch springs.

Liam was watching, but he stayed by the door.

Maggie had closed her eyes again and she lay floppy and unresponsive. She knew what these men were going to do to her, and she knew that she wasn't strong enough to resist them, so she had decided to let them get on with it and try and think of Niall and some of the happy hours they had enjoyed together. Niall had been a considerate lover, good in bed. He had been physically strong, and urgent, and he had hurt her occasionally, but she had enjoyed that, and he had always made sure that she was satisfied.

Billy kept on plunging and plunging, but as he reached his vinegar strokes he took himself out of her and gave himself a last quick rub so that his semen splattered all over her pubic hair.

'Dowcha, boy!' said Alroy, which was what hurling supporters shouted when the ball was slammed into the back of the net.

Billy climbed off and it was Alroy's turn next. He took off his leather jacket and T-shirt and jeans, although like Billy he left his socks on. Big-bellied and hairy and tattooed, with a penis that was short and stumpy and crimson, he clambered on to the couch and managed to push himself between Maggie's legs. Standing by the window, looking out, Davy guessed it was him because of his repetitive grunting and the much louder scrunching of the couch springs.

Alroy climaxed after only two or three minutes, grunting and snorting and repeatedly breathing *'feck, feck, feck'*. He was so exhausted by his efforts that Billy had to give him a hand to lift himself off the couch.

Next, Darragh took off his jacket and trousers and hung them over the back of one of the armchairs before he stepped out of his purple-spotted boxer shorts. He took his time, penetrating Maggie with an odd in-and-out motion, with a little quiver of his tightly squeezed buttocks every time he pushed himself into her. Maggie remained completely motionless. She might just as well have been a dead body as a live woman.

Kevan stripped himself completely naked and struck a bodybuilder's pose with his biceps bulging before he climbed on top of Maggie. He had a bramble-bush of gingery pubic hair and his erect penis was enormous, so that he had to stretch apart Maggie's vulva with his black-nailed fingers before he could force it in. When he started pumping at her, her hips were jounced up and down, even though she was trying to lie completely still.

Murtagh was last, but he didn't get on top of her. Instead, he stood beside the couch, unzipped his trousers, and took out his penis. He masturbated with quick, punchy, piston-like movements and when he was nearing his climax he moved even closer to the couch and shot sperm all over Maggie's cheeks and looped it across the bridge of her nose.

He tucked himself away and as he did so he grinned and said, 'You see that in all them porn videos, don't you, but my Breda would cut my bollocks off with a pair of pinking shears if I tried it on her.'

'Right, are you all finished?' asked Davy, turning around. 'What about you, Liam?'

Liam lifted his sling and shook his head. 'Don't want to bust my stitches, Davy.'

Billy and Alroy and Kevan let go of their hold on Maggie's arms and legs. She still didn't move or open her eyes, but Murtagh said, 'Don't worry, she's breathing all right. We haven't fucked her to death.'

Davy went over to the couch. He stood silent for a moment and then he said, 'You listen to me, wee doll. I know you can hear me. Don't you ever suggest to nobody ever again that it was me who shot Niall, especially the shades. You'll get more of the same if you do, but this was just a warning like, do you know what I mean? Next time it's going to be much, much worse. You'll get things pushed up you front and back that'll give you bad dreams for the rest of your life.'

He left the room, and the rest of the men followed him, all except for Liam.

Liam stood there looking at her and then he went across and picked up her sweater. He draped it over her middle and he was about to loosen the tie-back gag when he heard Davy calling out, '*Liam? Where the feck are you?*'

'I'm sorry,' he whispered to Maggie. 'I'm so, so sorry.'

'Liam!'

195

Twenty-one

Katie came into the conference room and walked over to the long table where Assistant Commissioner Magorian and Chief Superintendent MacCostagáin were already seated. Beside them sat Father Eoin Whooley, white-haired and solemn, his head bowed, and Billy Kelleher, the Fianna Fáil TD for Cork North Central.

On a separate table at the side of the room stood a row of framed black-and-white photographs of all the sixteen dancers who had died in the Toirneach Damhsa fire, and beside each photograph their relatives had placed a lighted candle in their memory. The faces in the photographs were fresh and young and elated. When Katie had seen them in the flesh, most of them had been ghoulishly charred and unrecognizable.

She had never seen the room so crowded, but she had never heard it so hushed. Usually there was a low hubbub of conversation, reporters answering calls on their mobile phones, and Fionnuala Sweeney from RTÉ tapping at her microphone to test it. This afternoon the gathering of bereaved families and media and local councillors and uniformed gardaí sat grim-faced, with their arms folded or their hands in their laps as if they were seated in church.

Katie herself had changed into the black collarless Max Mara jacket and the black skirt she always kept hanging in the wardrobe in her office for funerals and solemn occasions like this.

Once she had sat down, Frank Magorian stood up and cleared his throat.

'Father Whooley, Deputy Kelleher, ladies and gentlemen, you have been asked to come here today not only to commemorate

196

the lives of all those young people who so tragically died in the fire at the Toirneah Damhsa dance studio, but hopefully to help us bring to justice those responsible for their deaths. First of all, though, may I ask you all to stand and for Father Whooley to say a prayer to commend their souls to the Lord, and to ask for strength and succour for their families in this terrible time of loss.'

Everybody rose to their feet. When the shuffling and coughing had died down, Father Whooley crossed himself and said, 'Lord God, source and destiny of our lives, in Your loving providence You gave us the dancers of Toirneach Damhsa to grow in wisdom, age, and grace. Now You have called them to Yourself. We grieve over the loss of ones so young and struggle to understand Your purpose. Draw them to Yourself and give them full stature in Christ. May they stand with all the angels and saints, who know Your love and praise Your saving will. Amen.'

Once everybody had sat down again, Frank Magorian said, 'As you know, we've been making repeated appeals through the media for information that might lead us to identify the arsonist or arsonists who started this fire. This case is under the personal supervision of Detective Superintendent Maguire and her team of very experienced detectives, and I'm pleased to be able to report that we've already made considerable progress. One of our most important findings is that the fire was started with a highly sophisticated accelerant, so the arsonist must have had some very advanced understanding of chemistry.'

Dan Keane of the *Examiner* put up his hand and said, 'Excuse me asking, but if that's the case, what exactly was the point in going after Dara Coughlan?'

'Oh . . . you mean the fellow who murdered Detective Robert Dooley and then jumped out of the window?'

'That's your man.'

'We went after him because he had a record as a serial arsonist. But we'll be having a separate media conference about him and Detective Dooley after the autopsy – probably tomorrow or the day after.'

'But Coughlan was nothing but a petrol-slosher, wasn't he? I doubt if he could understand how to make a decent cup of tea, let alone advanced chemistry.'

'You'll have to ask Detective Superintendent Maguire about that. I'm sure she has a perfectly sound explanation. All I can tell you today is that she's coming very much closer to narrowing down the culprit for the Toirneach Damhsa fire. You're fully aware that she was promoted to detective superintendent because of her outstanding ability to close some of the most complex cases that we've ever had to deal with. Her skill is not letting her down in the solving of this case, either.'

Katie drew her microphone nearer and said, 'To be fair, sir, we still have a considerable number of suspects to interview before I can make anything like a conclusive announcement.'

'Oh, come on, Detective Superintendent Maguire, there's no need for you to be modest,' said Frank Magorian. 'From the way you've been talking to me, I reckon you'll have this case cracked by the end of the week. Gentlemen and ladies of the press – I think you can confidently say in your news reports that DS Maguire is within a hair's breadth of making an arrest.'

Katie immediately covered her microphone with her hand and beckoned Frank Magorian to lean over so that she could speak to him in confidence.

'*What in the name of Jesus did you say that for?*' she hissed. 'You know that we're still no nearer to lifting anybody now than we were at the very beginning.'

'I don't understand,' said Frank Magorian, talking to Katie but smiling at the audience with his best George Clooney look. 'I'm only trying to give the impression that you're right on top of this case, even if you aren't.'

'So what do you think they're going to say when I *don't* make an arrest by the end of the week?'

Frank Magorian continued to smile and nod at the audience as if Katie were telling him something reassuring. 'Then you'll just have to make sure that you do, won't you? Anybody would be better than nobody. You could always let them go later for lack of evidence. It would buy you some time at least.'

'I don't work like that, sir. I'm a Garda officer, not a politician.'

'Don't give me that, Katie. You're a superintendent. At your level you have to be a politician even more than a police officer. If you can't stand the heat, then stay out of hell.'

Katie was about to answer him when Frank Magorian stood up straight again and addressed the audience. 'Sorry about that. Detective Superintendent Maguire was just bringing me up to speed. Now perhaps she can bring *you* up to speed, too. DS Maguire?'

Katie stood up. The relatives of the dead dancers were sitting in the front row, right in front of her, some of them dabbing at their eyes with handkerchiefs, all of them looking washed-out and bewildered and distraught. At one end of the row she recognized Tadhg Brennan, the young musician who had been married to the Toirneach Damhsa dance instructor, Nicholas O'Grady – a blond young man with a wispy blond moustache and a wispy blond beard. Tears were rolling down his cheeks and he was making no attempt to wipe them away.

Katie said, 'First of all I want to give all of the relatives of the dancers who died my deepest personal sympathy and to pass on to you the condolences of every officer here in Anglesea Street. Father Whooley was right: sometimes it is very difficult for us to understand God's purpose, especially when such energetic and creative young people are taken away from us before they have had the chance to blossom.

'We've now completed almost all of our interviews with the relatives of those who died. I know how painful those interviews must have been, but they were necessary in order for us to make sure that none of your sons or daughters had been threatened by anybody for any reason.

'As Assistant Commissioner Magorian has just told you, we know from our forensic examinations that the fire was started by pyrophoric chemicals – that is, chemicals that can self-combust after a certain period of time, and very explosively if they are suddenly fed with oxygen. In fact, two fires were started – one on the staircase that led up to the studio and a second in the attic – so that even if they had survived the first blast, the dancers had little or no means of escape.'

'So you think you're close to making an arrest,' said Fionnuala Sweeney, as her cameraman zoomed in on Katie's face. 'Can we take that to mean that you have a reasonable notion of what the arsonist's motive was?'

'I can't answer that question at the moment,' said Katie.

'Oh. Is that because you don't want to alert the arsonist that you know who he is, or because you don't actually know yet what his motive was?'

'I'm sorry. I'm not a position to tell you that.'

Kenny Mulroney from Cork 96FM put up his hand and said, 'It's kind of been going around that this may have had something do with next Saturday's step-dancing *feis* at the Opera House.'

'Oh, yes?' said Katie. 'And where exactly has this "kind of been going around"?'

'Oh, you know like. Wherever two people get together to have a scoop or two.'

'And what's the suggestion?'

'Well, it may be something and nothing, but what they're saying is that Toirneach Damhsa were tipped to win the championship but another group of dancers was out to make sure that they didn't. Maybe these other dancers didn't intend to hurt nobody, let alone kill them, but now they're too scared to come out and say that it was an accident.'

'Of course I'm making enquiries into the possibility that a rival dance troupe may have been wholly or partly responsible,' Katie told him. 'I don't think that many people realize how fierce the competition is between some of those dancers. If the rumour *is* right, though – and I'm not saying if it is or it isn't – then I agree with you that the arsonist probably didn't intend that anybody should get hurt.'

'You mean they started a fire just to put their studio out of action but it went totally out of their control?' asked Dan Keane.

'Possibly. The chemicals used were very unpredictable. But I'm making no further comment about motive.'

Assistant Commissioner Magorian stood up again and laid his hand on Katie's shoulder. In front of the media, though, she couldn't twist herself away without making it obvious how unwelcome this was. She couldn't even stand the smell of his aftershave. But she remembered how she looked in newspaper photographs, and on TV, and so she lifted her chin a little so that she would appear calm and determined. If Nóirín O'Sullivan could look like that, so could she.

Frank Magorian said, 'DS Maguire still has a few loose ends to tie up, everybody, so I think we've given away enough information for the time being. Like I said, though, expect her to have this case all signed, sealed and delivered before you go to Mass on Sunday.'

Katie said, 'I'll be able to tell you more about Detective Dooley tomorrow, when I've had the chance to talk to his parents.'

'And what about the Niall Gleeson shooting, up at Gurra?' asked Kenny Mulroney.

'Still making enquiries,' said Katie, trying hard not to sound snappy.

Kenny Mulroney shrugged and turned away to talk to the girl sitting next to him, and the RTÉ TV camera turned away, too. Without looking up at him, Katie took hold of Frank Magorian's wrist and lifted his hand off her shoulder. When she did turn around, she was smiling politely but her green eyes were almost crackling with coldness.

* * *

As Katie was walking quickly back to her office, Bill Phinner caught up with her.

'That Magorian is counting his arsonists before they're lifted, isn't he?'

'Hmph,' said Katie, without slowing down.

'You're walking a bit fast for me there,' said Bill Phinner, skipping to catch up with her. 'I had another attack of the gout last night.'

'I usually walk much faster than this when I'm on my own.'

'Jesus! Thank God I'm never with you when you're on your own!'

Katie reached her office. 'Was there something you wanted to tell me, Bill?'

'There was, yes. We had the comparison macroscope fixed this morning and we've examined the bullet that we found in Niall Gleeson's car, as well as the bullet fragments from Ronan Barrett's skull. We still haven't found the bullet that was used to kill Saoirse MacAuliffe. It probably went right through the floor of the attic and into one of the rooms underneath.'

'But? Well? What's the result?' Katie asked him. Frank Magorian had left her with very little patience. The more he treated her as if she was suffering from PMT, the more she felt that she was.

'Both bullets were fired from the same gun.'

'What? Serious?'

'No question about it. There was enough scoring left on the fragments to make a one hundred per cent match.'

Katie went into her office and sat down behind her desk. Moirin came in and hovered in the background with a file of letters for her to sign. Bill Phinner just stood there, waiting for what she was going to say next.

Katie thought for a moment and then looked up at him. 'This means we could be looking for one offender, rather than two. But who would have a score to settle with Bobby Quilty's right-hand man *and* with two of the Toirneach Damhsa dancers? I mean, what possible connection could there be?'

'There may not necessarily *be* a connection, ma'am – apart from the likelihood that the same offender shot all three of them. Lookit, I gave my garage down the banks last week for not having my car ready on time, and later on the same day I complained to the waitress in Panda Mama because she knocked my Coca-Cola into my lap. I was sore vexed by the both of them, but there was no connection.'

'All right, Bill. I have you. Thanks for the update on the bullets. I'm just anxious to get this all wrapped up as soon as we can, do you know, but we seem to have more suspects than we know what to do with.'

Bill Phinner said, 'I heard what Frank Magorian said about you clearing this up by Sunday. I wouldn't worry about it, though. We haven't finished all the forensics yet, nowhere near. We're still trying to work out how long a delay there would have been before the chemicals self-ignited. I mean, that should tell us pretty accurately when they were planted and then you can see if anybody was caught on CCTV leaving the area within that time frame.'

'It would be a good idea if you mentioned that to Magorian yourself. You know, just in passing.'

'I will, I know what he's up to. I've seen that kind of thing happen before, when I was in Dublin. Praise your colleagues up to the skies, that's what you do, so that when they can't match up to it everybody thinks they're a failure. Don't you let it concern you, ma'am. I'll back you up to the hilt if it comes to it.'

Katie, very quietly, so that Bill Phinner could hardly hear her, said, 'Thanks a million, Bill.'

Twenty-two

Detective O'Donovan came in to tell Katie that he had contacted Steven Joyce, Danny Coffey's former partner at Toirneach Damhsa.

'I asked him if he could come in to the station early tomorrow morning for an interview and he said he would if he had to. The only trouble is, he would have to cancel a rehearsal that he's arranged and what with the *feis* so close his dancers need all the practice they can get – so could he come in first thing tomorrow afternoon?'

'Where does he rehearse?'

'I don't know, but I can ask him.'

'Okay, grand. Find out where it is and then we'll go along and talk to him there. Danny Coffey gave me the impression that he's fierce demanding, do you know what I mean? It'll be interesting to see him in action.'

She checked the clock on her desk. 'Okay, see what you can arrange. I've a couple of calls to make now – Robert Dooley's parents and then CUH.'

'I'll text you so,' said Detective O'Donovan. 'And – you know – give my best to the Dooleys. I don't know if Robert ever told you, but his older brother Paul was run over and killed by a drunken driver when he was only fifteen years old, which was the main reason why he decided to join the Garda. He said he had a personal motto, which was a little different from the official Garda motto. *Don't ever let the bastards get away with it.*'

204

* * *

The sky had been as grey as ash all day and as Katie drove to Togher, where the Dooleys lived, it started to rain, hard and cold, so that it hammered on the roof of her Focus and she had to switch on her windscreen wipers to full speed.

On the passenger seat beside her lay a bouquet of long white lilies that Moirin had bought for her that morning at Best of Buds, with a black-edged note of condolence – *Chaill muid ní hamháin ina laoch, ach cara* – We have lost not only a hero, but a friend.

Usually she played music when she was driving, but not this afternoon. She always felt personally responsible when one of her detectives was hurt or killed on duty, and as time went by her sense of responsibility seemed to have deepened so that now she felt not only responsible but guilty. She was fully aware that Robert Dooley had known the risks of his job, like every other garda, but that didn't make her feel any less remorseful.

She had begun to suspect that she had been affected more than she first realized by John being kidnapped by Bobby Quilty, and his amputations and subsequent death, and by the injuries that Kyna had suffered while she had tried to protect her. She just hoped that after her confession God had forgiven her, even if she hadn't yet forgiven herself.

Soon after her promotion to inspector her father had said to her, 'You can only be kind in this job by being hard, Katie. If you're soft-hearted, believe me, that's when people get hurt.'

She had taken his advice to heart, because he was talking from his own experience as a Garda inspector, but now she wondered if she had taken it too far. She had been hard, for sure, but people had still got hurt.

She parked outside the Dooleys' terrace house on Deanrock Avenue, opposite Clashduv Park recreation ground, where two teenage boys in anoraks were hanging from the crossbar of one of the goalposts and swinging themselves from side to side like pendulums. Seven or eight cars were already parked in front of the terrace and a small group of men was gathered on the pavement in raincoats and windcheaters, smoking in the rain. Katie put up the pointed hood of her own black parka and hurried to the front door, which was half-open. She knocked and then stepped inside.

Mr and Mrs Dooley were sitting on the couch in the living room, surrounded by at least a dozen of their friends and relatives. The glass coffee table in front of them was cluttered with teacups and mugs and two plates of shortbread biscuits. A single large candle was burning in the centre of the mantelpiece, with black-edged cards of condolence crowded on either side.

Euan Dooley was a short, round-shouldered man with grizzled grey hair and a worn-out look about him, as if he had been working hard all of his life and couldn't understand why all that hard work had brought him nothing but this small terrace house without even two living sons to inherit it when died. Agnes Dooley looked much more like Robert – slim and quite pretty, with an oval face that reminded Katie of pictures of the Virgin Mary, except that her dyed-black hair and jet-black cardigan and jet-black dress made her look even paler than she actually was.

Euan stood up as Katie came in. 'Superintendent Maguire,' he said. He was clenching both of his fists and he suddenly let out a noise that was halfway between a sob and a snort.

'It's all right, Mr Dooley, you're grand altogether,' said Katie. 'Please sit down.'

She handed the lilies to Agnes Dooley and said, 'These are from everybody at Anglesea Street. You have no idea how much we're going to miss Robert.'

'Let me take your coat,' said one of the male relatives, while another stood up and pushed a dining chair forward so that Katie could sit down.

'Would you care for a cup of tea?' asked Agnes Dooley. Katie smiled and said yes. She didn't really want one, but she knew that the Dooleys would feel embarrassed and upset if they hadn't offered her one or if she hadn't accepted it. Their nerves were all very raw at the moment.

'I've been in touch with the funeral home,' Katie told them. 'Also with Phoenix Park. The vigil is going to be held on Friday evening in the Holy Trinity, because of the number of people who are expected to attend, and then Robert will be given a state funeral the morning after, at eleven. Bishop John Buckley himself will conduct the requiem mass, and the Tánaiste and the Garda Commissioner will both be coming down from Dublin.'

'A send-off like that, he deserves it,' said Euan Dooley.

'He never deserved to die,' said Agnes Dooley, clasping her husband's hand. 'I would rather have him back alive than all the pomp and ceremony you could ever drum up.'

With that, she turned and stared at Katie with her eyes filled with tears, shaking her head from side to side as if to say, *No, no, no, why didn't you come here to tell me that he isn't dead after all?*

One of Agnes Dooley's sisters brought Katie a cup of milky tea and said, 'Help yourself to a biscuit. They're home-baked.'

Katie took a finger of shortbread and broke it in half, although she felt as if her mouth would dry up if she tried to eat it.

They talked for a while about Robert's career and how he had always wanted to be a detective. Agnes Dooley told Katie that another boy at his bunscoil had once been stealing sweets from a little girl's coat pocket in the cloakroom, so Robert had substituted the sweets for small pebbles and the culprit had broken one of his front teeth trying to eat one.

'Always looking out for other people was Robert. He'll even be doing that from heaven, you mark my words.'

Katie managed to eat her shortbread and drink most of her cup of tea, even though it was tepid and she usually never took milk and sugar. Eventually, she told the Dooleys that she would have to leave and stood up and shook the hands of everybody there.

'I want to tell you all that Robert was one of the finest young officers who ever joined my team at Anglesea Street,' she told them. 'He did us proud.'

Agnes Dooley showed her to the front door. It was growing dark now, and still raining, although it was only wetting now instead of lashing.

'Thanks a million for coming,' said Agnes Dooley, wrapping her cardigan tightly around herself, as if she could feel the chill of death blowing in. 'There was something I wanted to say to you, but you probably know already, and I didn't want to mention it in front of himself.'

'Is it something to do with Robert?'

'It is, yes. He dropped in for a shower and a bite to eat before he went out to talk to that terrible feller who murdered him.'

She glanced over her shoulder to make sure that her husband hadn't followed her out into the hallway, and that nobody else could overhear her.

'Go on,' Katie coaxed her.

'While he was here, his friend Kenny MacCarty called by. They were talking in the kitchen while Robert was eating his supper, and I was in and out all the time, so I didn't catch everything that Kenny was saying like. But I *did* hear him tell Robert that he'd been at the Roundy last week and he'd seen Danny Coffey from the Toirneach Damhsa along with his dance instructor, Nicholas O'Grady.'

'You know them – Coffey and O'Grady?'

'I do, of course. My next-door neighbour's little girl Megan used to dance with Toirneach Damhsa and I went to see her performing two or three times, that's how I know them. When she was fifteen, though, Megan put on a fierce amount of weight, poor girl. She almost crashed through the floor when she was practising her hard-shoe dancing and so they had to let her go. Then of course Robert was working on the case and so he told me all about it. Well, not everything. He never said much about his work, but he did say that Nicholas O'Grady was one of the ones who got burned and that you'd brought in Danny Coffey for questioning.'

'So what about Coffey and O'Grady at the Roundy?' The Roundy was a pub on the corner of Grand Parade and Castle

Street, named for its semicircular frontage. It catered for every kind of customer but it was a popular gay nightspot, too, with tapas and live music.

'Kenny saw Danny Coffey and Nicholas O'Grady dancing together – and, well, they was kissing. Almost eating each other alive without mayo, that's what he said. So when he read about the fire in the *Echo* a few days later, and he saw that Nicholas O'Grady was married, he thought "that's kind of strange like" – even though O'Grady was married to another feller rather than a woman and maybe the same rules don't apply when two fellers get married.'

'Well, thanks a million for the information, Agnes,' said Katie. 'Robert didn't tell me about his friend seeing Coffey and O'Grady together. He didn't mention it to any of his fellow officers, either, as far as I know, and there's nothing in his notes about it. I expect he wanted to look into it a bit further first.'

'But, that's not the whole of it,' said Agnes Dooley, leaning closer.

At that moment, Euan Dooley called out, 'Put a bush in the gap, Aggie, for the love of God! We're all freezing in here!'

Agnes Dooley closed the door and put it on the latch. Then she said, in a very low and confidential voice, 'While Danny Coffey and Nicholas O'Grady were sitting there hand in hand like a couple of lovebirds, another feller comes storming in and pulls Danny Coffey up on to his feet and starts to shove him around and shout at him, really effing and blinding. Two of the barmen come out from behind the bar and they grab hold of this feller and throw him out in the street.'

'Did Robert's friend know who this was?'

'Not by name, no. But he said he was tallish and the way he was speaking sounded like he came from Belfast, or Derry maybe.'

'And that's it?' asked Katie. 'That's all Robert's friend told him?'

Agnes Dooley nodded.

'So why don't you want your husband to hear any of this?'

'Because Kenny was more than just a friend like, do you know what I mean? Robert liked girls, but he could never quite make up his mind. After our Malcolm was taken away from us, Robert was his father's bar of gold and I think he would have had a heart attack if he had known that Robert had a soft spot for fellers as well as women.'

'Okay, I have you,' said Katie, and laid a comforting hand on Agnes Dooley's shoulder. Robert Dooley had been a smart and fashionable dresser, with brushed-up hair and skinny trousers, and he had always smelled of Boss aftershave, but he had made no secret of his attraction to Detective Padragain Scanlan, who was one of the prettiest female officers at Anglesea Street, and Katie had never guessed that he might be bisexual. It surprised her because she usually had a keen nose for sexual orientation.

'I'll need to send somebody to have a word with this Kenny,' she said. 'Do you have his address?'

'He lives in Ballyphehane somewhere, not too far up the road from the Tory Top Bar, I think. That's where him and Robert would meet each other most of the time. I don't know exactly which house, though.'

'That's all right,' said Katie. 'I expect his phone number or his address is on Robert's mobile. Thanks again for being so honest with me. I don't know how important this might be, this scuffle in the Roundy, but you never know. I'll see you at the vigil on Friday evening.'

'I haven't let him down, have I, by telling you that?' asked Agnes Dooley.

'Not at all. You might even have done the opposite, Agnes, and helped him to solve his last case.'

* * *

Adeen was sitting up in bed watching *Dig In Diner* on television when Katie arrived, with the sound turned very low. She was wearing pink pyjamas with stars on them and tightly holding a doll with crinkly platinum hair.

Katie shifted the chair closer to the side of the bed and gave Adeen the packet of Haribo sweets she had bought on the way to the hospital.

'Ask the nurse before you eat them,' she smiled. 'I wouldn't know how much sugar you're allowed.'

Adeen gave her the faintest of smiles, but didn't say anything.

Katie said, 'You're looking miles better today, Adeen, do you know that? You've some roses in your cheeks. You should be able to leave here soon and we'll find you some nice people to stay with.'

Still Adeen didn't speak, but she continued to stare at Katie as if she wanted to.

'That's a beautiful doll you have there,' said Katie. 'I used to have a doll like that. She could shut her eyes, so when it was bedtime I used to lie her down and sing to her and pretend that she was going to sleep.'

She reached out and stroked the doll's long blonde hair. Then, very softly, she began to sing, '*At the auld Lammas Fair girl . . . were you ever there . . . at the auld Lammas Fair in Ballycastle-o . . . Did you treat your Mary Ann . . . to some dulse and yellowman . . . at the auld Lammas Fair in Ballycastle-o?*'

Adeen, without any warning, began to cry. Her mouth turned down in misery and her eyes filled with tears. Katie pushed back her chair and sat on the bed next to her and put her arm around her. Underneath her pink pyjamas, her bony shoulders were shaking with grief.

'I'm sorry, I'm sorry,' said Katie. 'Did that upset you?'

'My mam used to sing it,' sobbed Adeen. 'My mam used to sing it when she was putting me to bed.'

Katie held her closer and stroked her hair. 'I'm pure sorry, Adeen. I didn't meant to make you cry. Where's your mam now?'

'She died and she's in heaven.'

Katie tugged a tissue from the box on the bedside table and gave it to Adeen so that she could wipe her eyes and blow her nose.

'Well, we'll have to think of another song for your doll now, won't we? One that doesn't make you feel sad.'

Adeen nodded. 'I sing her the birdeen song.'

'Yes, I know it. "*The birdeens sing a fluting song, they sing to*

211

thee the whole day long. Wee fairies dance o'er hill and dale, for very love of thee." Is that the one?'

'Yes,' said Adeen, and gave her doll a kiss on the forehead. She seemed to have forgotten that she was supposed to be mute.

'Where did she come from, your doll?' Katie asked her.

'Corinne gave her me, this morning. She's magic.'

Katie was sure now from Adeen's accent that she had been brought up in Ulster, not too far from Belfast by the sound of it. And by 'Corinne' she guessed she meant Corinne Daley from Tusla, the child protection agency, who would be finding foster parents for Adeen once she had been discharged from hospital.

'So, have you given her a name yet?'

Adeen nodded. 'Her name's Bindy. That's the same as my last dolly that got broke.'

'Bindy. That's a pretty name. But, tell me, how did your last doll get broken?'

Adeen turned away, towards the television where Muireann and Digger the Gardener were laughing with Cornsuela the corncob, and Katie thought for a moment that she didn't want to talk about it. After a moment, though, she said, 'She got stampit on.'

Her tone of voice was quite different when she said that, oddly high-pitched, as if she were trying to make Katie believe that it was Bindy the doll who was speaking, and not her. Katie had come across that before, when questioning other children, especially the victims of sexual abuse. They would pretend that it was their teddy bears talking, or their Lego men, or even their gloves, so that they would be detached from the trauma they were trying to describe.

'Oh,' said Katie. '*Stamped* on – that's desperate. Who stamped on her?'

Again, a moment's pause. Then, in the same high voice, 'My brother did.'

'That was mean of him. Why did he do that?'

'He said she gave him the heebie-jeebies.'

'She gave him the heebie-jeebies? But she was only a doll.'

'Yes, but she was one of thon dollies that look like a real baby

212

and our mam died when she was having a baby and he saw the baby and he said it reminded him of her.'

'Well, I'm very sorry to hear that. How about the baby? Did the baby die, too?'

Adeen nodded, still without looking round. 'I didn't see her, but my brother did.'

'What's your brother's name?'

'I can't tell you. He'll be raging if he finds out I've told you.'

'He won't find out, sweetheart. Nobody's going to tell him. I don't even know where he is. Was that him who came to see you and left you some flowers?'

Adeen nodded again.

'He wrote "Zippo" on his card,' said Katie. 'What did he mean by that?'

'Zip your lips. Don't say nothing to nobody.'

'You can talk to me.'

'I'm ascared to. I shouldn't have told you nothing.'

'You can tell me your name at least. We're friends now, aren't we? I can't keep on calling you "Adeen".'

Adeen turned to face Katie but she didn't answer. She simply stared at her and fiddled with her plaited green wristband.

'All right,' said Katie, smiling at her. 'You don't have to tell me if you're frightened. But if I knew how to get in touch with your brother I could talk to him and make sure that he doesn't get angry with you.'

Adeen still didn't answer and continued to tug and twist at her wristband.

'That's a very quare wristband you have there,' said Katie. 'Where did that come from?'

'It was Bindy's,' said Adeen.

'Poor Bindy who got stamped on?'

Adeen whispered, 'Yes.'

'But you really can't tell me your real name? Nobody else will know, only me.'

Adeen shook her head.

'All right, then, never mind for now,' said Katie. She knew there was no point in persisting with her questions, even though she urgently wanted to find out Adeen's real name and where she came from. It was even more critical for her to know why she had been in the attic when the Toirneach Damhsa studio had been set ablaze, and what she might have seen while she was there. But at least Adeen was talking to her now, and seemed to have confidence in her, and that was a start. She had also picked up two clues that could prove to be critical – that Adeen's wristband had once belonged to her doll, and that her doll had been so life-like that her brother had destroyed it.

There was also the possibility that if her brother had been disturbed to that extent by a doll, he could be mentally unbalanced and given to irrational acts of violence. Adeen certainly seemed to be very frightened of him.

Before Katie left the hospital she texted Detective Scanlan. She told her to search online for any maker of life-like dolls in Northern Ireland, and in particular any life-like dolls that wore woven green wristbands with gilt clasps.

Detective Scanlan texted back: *If I find one can I buy one on expenses? I always wanted a doll like that.*

Twenty-three

Liam didn't come into the Templegate until well past ten o'clock, and when he did he looked washed-out and distracted. Neither of his usual drinking companions had turned up, Murtagh or Billy, so he came up to the bar where Kyna was serving and perched himself on one of the stools.

In the pool room Sorcha was playing her guitar and singing 'The Dying Rebel' to a small crowd of twenty or thirty drinkers, although from the sound of their chatter and intermittent laughter they weren't paying her too much attention.

'The last I met was a dying rebel . . . kneeling o'er I heard him sigh . . . God bless my home in dear Cork City . . . God bless the cause for which I die . . .'

Kyna was pouring a pint of Guinness for an elderly man with wild grey hair sprouting out of his ears and a grey moustache that was yellow in the middle from years of smoking.

'Jesus, Liam, you look beat out,' she told him.

'I am, yeah,' said Liam. 'My hand's still throbbing like you wouldn't believe and we just had a get-together at Davy's house which went on for ever like. Sure like, I know I asked you if you'd come down to the Bodega tonight, but to be honest with you I don't think I have it in me. It's been one hell of a desperate day.'

Kyna took the elderly man's money and then poured Liam a pint of Murphy's. 'Do you want to tell me about it?' she asked him.

'No, I can't like. I don't want Davy stabbing my other hand.'

'Oh, so it's business.'

'You could call it that. I thought Davy was real sound like, do you know what I mean? But I'm beginning to think that he's some kind of headbanger. Like, Bobby always frightened the shite out of me but at least with Bobby you knew where you were. With Bobby it was flogging fags and only making out that we were IRA to scare off the other gangs like. With Davy, though, I don't know. He's deadly serious about all that political stuff . . . he's always banging on about the border and the cause and Christ knows what.'

He suddenly stopped and said, 'I shouldn't be telling you this. If Davy heard me he'd cut my mickey off.'

'Oh, stop.'

'No, Roisin, I mean it. He threatened to do it before. He followed me into the jacks and took out his knife and said that if I wasn't one hundred and ten per cent behind him he'd slice it clean off and flush it down the bog. Oh, and he meant it all right. I still have the mark where he cut me.'

Kyna glanced up at the mahogany clock above the bar. 'Listen,' she said, 'I'll be knocking off at eleven. We don't have to go clubbing. Why don't we go down to the town but just have a quiet drink together, somewhere like the Woodford?'

'Sure like, that'd be grand,' said Liam. 'I'd like that.'

He stayed at the bar to drink his pint and Kyna gave him a packet of chilli peanuts on the house. It was almost eleven when she heard a smattering of applause from the pool room and a few seconds later Sorcha appeared. This evening she was wearing a tight grey T-shirt and black skinny jeans and a pair of sparkly sandals with bells on.

'What would you like?' asked Kyna, as she came and sat on a bar stool next to Liam, with her sandals jingling.

Sorcha looked at her with those large onyx eyes and said, 'Guess.'

'To drink, I mean.'

'All right. I'll have a rum and Coke.'

'How did it go?' asked Kyna, pouring Bacardi into a tall glass and spooning ice into it.

'Oh . . . fair to Midleton. I don't think this crowd are much into Wolfe Tone songs. I think they'd probably prefer it if I sang "The Black Velvet Band" or some other old Dubliners shite.'

Kyna passed Sorcha her drink and as she did so Sorcha reached out and took hold of the bangles around her wrist, so that she couldn't take her hand away. 'What time do you finish?' she asked her.

'Eleven,' said Kyna.

'But she's coming out for a scoop with me like,' Liam chipped in.

Sorcha didn't look at him but continued to hold Kyna's bangles and stare unblinking into her eyes. 'You're not serious? With *him*?'

Kyna would have done anything to turn to Liam and tell him to forget about this evening and maybe they would go out some other time. It wasn't only Sorcha's face and full-breasted figure that attracted her, there was something in her look that told her they could be amazing together, both as friends and as lovers. It was a look she saw only rarely. She had seen it in Katie's eyes, too, but Katie was her commanding officer and so the problems of starting a relationship were almost insurmountable. She wouldn't have that particular problem with Sorcha, although there might be others, considering that her name wasn't really Roisin MacColgan, and that she wasn't really a barmaid but a detective sergeant in the Garda, and that she was here to find out who might have shot Niall Gleeson, and why.

'Maybe tomorrow?' she suggested.

'I won't be here tomorrow,' said Sorcha. 'I'm playing at Sin é till late. And the day after at the White Horse in Ballincollig. And who knows who I might meet there?'

'I'm sorry, Sorcha, no. I can't tonight,' Kyna told her. 'I simply can't.'

Sorcha shrugged and let go of Kyna's hand. 'Your loss,' she said. 'Thanks for the drink anyway.'

With that, she took her Bacardi and Coke and slid off her bar stool and made her way back to the pool room. After a few minutes Kyna could see her talking to a pretty young red-haired woman and they were both smiling and laughing. She felt like coming out from behind the bar and stalking over to her and saying, *Stop it, will you! It's you and me, we were the ones who were supposed to be together!*

Liam raised his glass and said, 'She's some lasher and no mistake, her. Kind of scary, though.'

Scary? thought Kyna. *If you knew who I really am,* then *you could talk about scary.*

* * *

They took a Hailo taxi down to the city centre. The Woodford was a stone-fronted Georgian building on Paul Street, with flower baskets hanging outside. Kyna had chosen to go there because there was less likelihood of them being seen by Davy or one of his cronies from Gurranabraher.

It was a big old-fashioned pub, with green-painted wooden panelling and brick walls and long red velvet curtains. By the time they arrived it was crowded and noisy, but they managed to find a small table for two next to the bar, with a lighted candle on it. Liam ordered another pint of Murphy's while Kyna asked for a Prosecco. She didn't usually drink on duty, but she wanted to make Liam feel that he was impressing her. They had to lean their heads close to each other to make themselves heard over the shouting and the laughter and the background music.

'Don't you have a girlfriend, Liam?' Kyna asked him.

'I did, up until a month ago, Moira, but we broke up. We was sort of living together, on and off, but I was out so much that she wanted a cat to keep her company. The trouble is cats make me sneeze and anyway who wants to be treading barefoot in a litter tray when you go to the kitchen in the middle of the night to fetch yourself a glass of water?'

'Well, not me, and that's for sure,' said Kyna.

'Besides that, Roisin, you're about a million times prettier than Moira. You are, girl, I don't mind telling you. You're a stunner.'

'You're not bad-looking yourself, Liam. And you're not stupid, either. I don't know what you're doing mixing with that Davy and those other fellows.'

'What? It's the grade, that's all. Well, mostly. And it means I get no bother from none of the scummers down my street, nor nobody else for that matter, because they know who I'm in with.'

'But what's this trouble you've been having with Davy? Why did he stab you in the hand like that?'

Liam took a swallow of his drink, wiped his mouth with the back of his bandaged hand, and looked around the pub as if he were making sure that nobody could overhear him.

'Like I told you, I thought he was sound. Between you and me, he was even going to get me a gun. Yeah, really. But it's like he's not so much interested in the fag trade any more. He's forever saying that we're at war with the Brits. For some reason he got it into his head that I'd been telling you about some of our private business and that's why he had forty thousand fecking canaries and stabbed me.'

'So what's this private business that he didn't want you to tell me about?'

Liam stuck out his lower lip and shook his head. 'He'd fecking kill me if he knew that I'd told you.'

'So why do you stay with him?'

'Because he'd fecking kill me if I didn't.'

'Do you think he might have shot Niall?'

'No – no, I don't think so. I mean, he was depending on Niall for selling the fags after Bobby went. And he always said that he liked him.'

'You said you had a get-together this afternoon. What was that all about?'

Liam didn't answer at first, but then he finished his pint and looked at his empty glass and said, 'I can't tell you, Roisin. But I will tell you one thing. What Davy's planning to do, it fecking scares me. I don't want to be spending the rest of my life in Portlaoise prison.'

219

'Are you sure you don't want to tell me? Maybe you'll feel better if you do.'

'No. I can't. It's like some kind of fecking nightmare. He always says it every time we meet like that: Zippo. Keep your bake tight shut and don't tell nobody nothing.'

'All right,' said Kyna. 'Let's talk about something else. Are you hungry at all?'

'I'm starving, actually. I've had nothing at all to eat since an apple I had for breakfast. I could eat the hind leg off the Lamb of God, to be honest with you.'

'What do you feel like? We could have something here. They do a fantastic burger, or we could share a plate of their tapas.'

Liam looked around and then he said, 'I don't know, Roisin. It's getting fierce crowded. Why don't we take a Burger King back to my place? I've a couple of bottles of white wine in the fridge that Moira bought before she walked out on me.'

'All right, then, why not?' said Kyna. She smiled at him and reached across the table to squeeze his hand as if she couldn't think of anything she would rather do. They stood up and shrugged on their jackets and elbowed their way out of the Woodford, walking hand in hand to Patrick's Street. Liam kept throwing surreptitious looks at Kyna and she could tell how proud he was to be out with her, and that he was growing increasingly excited. A passing gaggle of teenage boys gave her a connie burdle, a wolf-whistle, and that clearly pleased him even more.

While they were waiting in the queue in Burger King, behind a very drunk man with urine-soaked jeans who kept swaying from side to side, Kyna rang for a taxi. By the time their order was ready, the taxi had drawn up outside. As they climbed in, Kyna was going to apologize to the driver for the smell of their takeaway food, but he smelled so strongly himself of stale cigarettes and fenugreek that she decided he probably wouldn't notice.

'Sixty-nine St Anne's Road, Gurra,' said Liam. As they pulled away from the kerb he shifted himself nearer to Kyna and put his arm around her, with his thickly bandaged right hand resting on her shoulder. In response, she rested her hand on his thigh so that she could feel his bony leg through his jeans.

She had realized when she was only twelve years old that she was attracted to girls rather than boys, and she had never kissed a boy, not romantically. In the back of this taxi with Liam, she suddenly began to feel breathless and panicky. He leaned across and kissed her on the cheek, and when she turned towards him he kissed her hard on the mouth. His lips were dry and when he pushed the tip of his tongue into her mouth she could taste stout and cigarettes and cheese and onion crisps.

She kissed him back. She knew she had to. She closed her eyes and tried to imagine that she was kissing Katie, but Katie's skin was soft and her lips were always inviting and moist and glossy with lipstick. She didn't have prickly stubble and pimples and jumbled-up teeth like Liam, nor wiry hair that was thick with dandruff.

She opened her eyes and saw that the taxi driver was staring at them in his rear-view mirror. Liam leaned over again, but this time she quickly turned her face away so that his nose bumped against her right ear. It was bad enough kissing him, let alone having somebody watching her do it. She had no doubt at all, though, that he was only going to grow more passionate. Why else had he invited her back to his flat?

The house where he lived was halfway up St Anne's Road, in the middle of a grey pebble-dashed terrace. Liam paid off the driver with a handful of loose change, leaving Kyna to climb out of the taxi with the Burger King bag. Then he led her up a steep flight of concrete steps to the front door.

'The landlady's in,' he said, nodding towards the living-room window. The dark brown curtains were drawn, but they could see that a television was flickering inside. 'Mrs Devlin, fecking old wagon. She stays up till all hours, so we'll have to keep the noise down. No screaming.'

Holy Mary, Mother of God, you'll be lucky, thought Kyna. *The only screaming I'll be doing is screaming to get away from you.*

Inside the narrow hallway it smelled of boiled cabbage and overheated electric plugs. Liam pressed the light switch and climbed ahead of Kyna up the red-carpeted stairs.

He showed her first into his pale blue-painted kitchen, which was so small that she had to shuffle out on to the landing again while he opened the fridge door. He lifted out a bottle of Tesco white wine and then reached up to the cupboard to bring down two plates and two cloudy-looking wine glasses. Kyna handed him the Burger King bag so that he could take their food out: a double bacon cheeseburger for him and a veggie wrap for her.

'By the way,' he said, as they carried their plates and glasses into his bed-sitting room at the front of the house, 'that door there, that's the bathroom. Just in case you need to drain the spuds like, you know.'

His bed-sitting room was dominated by a sagging green couch which could fold down into a double bed, as well as a large flat-screen television and two mismatched armchairs: one orange, and one oatmeal with a scattering of grey stains on the seat cushion. Behind the television there was a built-in plywood wardrobe and under the window a shelf heaped with dog-eared *Men's Health* magazines and CDs and crumpled Mars bar wrappers and half-squeezed tubes of spot cream and a hairbrush clogged with hair.

On the wall over the couch Liam had pinned a large tattered poster from Bruce Springsteen's concert in Cork in July 2013.

'Here, take a seat,' he said, and he and Kyna sat side by side on the couch. Immediately he started to wolf down his bacon and cheeseburger, his mouth so full that he could barely speak to her. Kyna nibbled at the edges of her veggie wrap and sipped at her wine and looked around the room. She hadn't felt so trapped since she had gone undercover to work for Bobby Quilty and he had attempted to rape her. She could have simply stood up and left, but that would jeopardize all the work she had put into this investigation so far, and she would never find out what it was that Davy had told Liam to keep Zippo about.

222

'Wow, you hounded that,' she said, when Liam had finished his burger.

'I told you I was starving,' he said. 'You haven't eaten much of yours, though.'

'I wasn't as hungry as I thought.'

Liam wiped his mouth with his bandaged hand. He set his plate down on the floor and took away Kyna's plate, too, and set it down on top of it.

'C'm'ere,' he said and took her in his arms and pecked her twice, three times, on the lips. Before he tried to kiss her too deeply, though, he sat back for a moment and used the tip of his tongue to worry out the last few crumbs of burger meat stuck between his teeth.

'Liam—' she said. She was beginning to think that she may not be able to go through with this, even if it was critical.

But Liam said, 'Jesus, you don't know what you do to me, girl,' and kissed her more and more aggressively, his stubble rasping against her lips. Then he started to feel her breasts through her thin grey woollen dress and slide his good left hand up between her thighs. He was starting to pant as if he had run all the way here from Patrick's Street.

'Let's have this dress off of you,' he said, taking hold of the hem and trying to pull it upwards. But Kyna snatched at the hem and gripped it tight to stop him lifting it any further, and pressed her knees together.

'What?' he said, half-smiling. 'What's wrong?'

'It's not you,' she said.

'Then *what*?'

'I'm in my flowers, that's all.'

'What? You're never! Oh, Jesus, you're codding me!'

'No, Liam. I'm sorry. There's nothing I can do about the phases of the moon.'

Liam took hold of her hand and pressed it between his thighs so that she could feel how stiff he was. 'Do you see what you've done to me, and now you're saying that you're bullfighting? I don't fecking believe it!'

'It's true, Liam. I think you're a wonderful, wonderful feller, you know? But I can't show you just how much you turn me on . . . not tonight, anyway.'

She kissed him, and stroked his hair, and smiled at him as if he were a disappointed child that she hadn't been able to take to the circus.

'I'm busting here, girl,' said Liam. 'If I'd known you couldn't do nothing – Jesus – couldn't you give us a blowjob?'

'Liam—'

But Liam was already unbuckling his belt and tugging open the buttons of his jeans. He levered his erection out of his shorts and held it between finger and thumb and jiggled it up and down. Kyna didn't even want to look at it, but he said, 'There – there's the proof of how I feel about you, Roisin. The solid, hard proof. Stand up in a court of law, that would.'

Kyna glanced down and saw his swollen purple glans with the foreskin rolled back. She felt her gorge rising and prayed that she wouldn't bring up the mixed bean salad she had eaten for lunch. Liam laid his bandaged hand on her shoulder and pulled her even nearer towards him.

'You're something special you are, Roisin,' he told her. 'I feel like you and me were meant for each other, do you know what I mean like?'

That decided her. He might make her feel nauseous, but if he believed that fate had brought them together, and trusted her, there was a good chance that he would confide in her about Davy Dorgan and what he was up to.

She bent her head down and closed her eyes and then she took him into her mouth. She felt like gagging, but as she licked him, he let out a whinny, like a tinker's horse, and ran the fingers of his left hand into her short blonde hair so that he could pull her head down even further.

She tried to imagine that she was dreaming this and that she couldn't taste him or feel him or smell him. She sucked at him hard, bobbing her head rhythmically up and down, and probing the cleft in his glans with the tip of her tongue. The sooner it was over, she thought, the better. With every suck he groaned and snorted and whinnied some more and said, 'Holy Saint Peter, Roisin! Holy Saint Peter!'

It took only a few minutes before, without warning, he shuddered. At the same time he gripped the roots of her hair even harder, so that she couldn't twist her head away. Her mouth was flooded with warm slime, and then almost immediately he began to subside, so that he felt like a fat slippery worm.

'Holy Saint Peter, Roisin, you're fantastic. You're fecking fantastic.'

At last he let go of her hair and Kyna sat up straight, spitting as discreetly as she could into her hand. 'I need to pee,' she mumbled and immediately stood up, grabbed her purse, and headed for the toilet. Once inside she knelt on the floor and lifted the lid of the lavatory and vomited. Up came half-digested beans and Prosecco and even the remains of the fruit muesli she had eaten for breakfast.

She kept on vomiting, again and again, until her stomach hurt and all she could do was retch. While she was still kneeling there, Liam knocked on the door and said, 'Are you okay in there, Roisin? How about another glass of wine?'

'I'm grand altogether, thanks, Liam,' she said. 'I'll be with you in a second.'

She flushed the toilet and then washed her hands and scooped a handful of water into her mouth, gargled, and spat it out. She looked at herself in the small toothpaste-spattered mirror over the basin and thought: *Dear Mary, Mother of God, I am never doing that again – ever – no matter how desperate I am for information.*

Her gold eye make-up was messed up, but once she had dabbed it with toilet paper and applied some more lip colour she went back to the bed-sitting room. Liam was sprawled on the couch with a satisfied beam on his face, smoking a cigarette. She was relieved to see that he had put himself away and buttoned up his jeans.

'Ara musha, it's my fantastic girl Roisin,' he greeted her. 'After *that*, do you know, I almost feel like asking you to marry me!'

225

She sat down next to him and he put his arm around her, blowing smoke out of the opposite corner of his mouth so that it wouldn't go directly into her face.

'Oh, come on,' she said, giving him a quick kiss on his spotty cheek. 'I hardly know enough about you yet to do a line, let alone marry you.'

* * *

Using all of the interrogation techniques she had been taught at Garda College, Kyna led Liam step by step through his childhood, through the beatings he had suffered from his alcoholic father, through all the jobs in garages he had lost because he was always hungover and late for work. She discussed in detail all of his relationships with girls, and how every one of them had let him down. It had never been his fault, although he had to confess that he did have a temper, especially if he'd been drinking, or taking molly, or just felt humpy.

'I don't think nobody's ever appreciated you for who you are,' said Kyna, snuggling up closer to him and stroking the back of his hand with her fingertip.

'Well, that's right, they haven't. They always look at me and for some reason they think that I'm nothing but a wank job like, do you know what I mean?'

'Even Davy doesn't realize what you have going for you, does he? But you'd think that out of everybody he'd see that you're one of the smartest fellers he's got. Stabbing you like that . . . that was diabolical.'

'I don't know, I think he did it because he needs me the most and he wanted to make sure that I was never going to grass on him.'

'But you never would, would you? Even if it meant you going to prison, like you said.'

Liam took out another cigarette and lit it. 'No, of course not. But it still doesn't mean that I'm happy out. I mean like, this thing he's planning. It's totally scary.'

'If you think it's scary, Liam, then you shouldn't get yourself involved,' said Kyna. She tapped her forehead and added, 'You're not a wank job. You've got it all up here like, believe me – as well as down there.'

She paused for a moment, flapping away the smoke that he had just breathed out, but then she said, 'Mind you, I have no notion of what it is, this "thing" that Davy's planning, so I can't really tell you if you should get yourself involved in it or not. It *seems* scary all right, but come on, maybe it's not as scary as you think it is.'

'Mother of Jesus, Roisin. He's planning on shooting that British defence feller when he comes to the Opera House to watch the dancing. If *that's* not fecking scary, I don't know what the feck is.'

'What are you talking about? What British defence feller?'

'I don't know. Some British feller who's coming to Cork to talk to the navy like. He's been invited to watch the dancing *feis* and that's when he's going to be shot.'

'But Davy doesn't expect you to shoot him, does he?'

'No, of course not. Jesus, I've never fired a gun in my life – well, not with nobody standing in the way like. He's getting three fellers he knows down from the North.'

'So what do you have to do?'

'I shouldn't be telling you any of this. If Davy could hear me now, I tell you, he'd fecking murder me.'

'I'm only the barmaid, Liam. Who do you think I'm going to tell? And besides, we're getting close, aren't we, me and you? I don't want to see nothing bad happening to you, never.'

'All the same, I should keep Zippo, like Davy says. I don't want you getting into trouble, too.'

Kyna sat back. 'Have it your way. I was only trying to give you some female advice.'

Liam shrugged, and smoked, and shrugged again, and jiggled his feet, but he said nothing more. At last Kyna looked at her watch and said, 'I need to be going, Liam. I've an early start tomorrow.'

'Why don't you stay here?'

Kyna shook her head. 'Thanks for the invitation, but I only have the one Tampax with me and I want to get home and have a shower like. Besides, I need to change my dress. This one smells like a pub.'

She rang for a taxi and when it arrived outside she gave Liam a quick goodnight kiss and left him at the front door. He waved as she was driven down to the end of St Anne's Road.

Once the taxi had reached the junction with McSwiney's Villas, though, she said to the driver, 'Would you stop here for a moment, please? I have to make a call.'

She took out her iPhone and rang Katie's personal number. The phone rang and rang before Katie eventually answered, sounding sleepy and blurred.

'Kyna? What is it?'

'Are you at home, ma'am?'

'I am, yes.'

'I need to talk to you now. Like *now*. And I think I need somebody's shoulder to cry on, too.'

Katie said something that she couldn't quite catch, almost as if she were talking to somebody else.

'I didn't get that,' said Kyna.

'No, you're all right so. Come on over. I'll see you when you get here.'

Twenty-four

After he had left the Quayside Snooker Club to go home, Bernie Dennehy's nine-year-old Golf had died on him. Every time he turned the key, the starter motor groaned like a sow in labour, and then it had given up altogether as the battery had finally gone flat. He didn't have Road Rescue membership, so he had left the car in the yard behind the club.

His friend Alby Healy had offered to run him home, but as they were driving through the city centre Alby suggested they stop off at the old Vicarstown Inn on North Main Street for a couple of scoops. Bernie had been glad of an excuse not to go home to Maggie until later. Since Niall had been murdered she had been alternately scratchy and depressed, and nothing he had done or said to her had been right. He was hoping she would be asleep by the time he got back.

He and Alby sat with their pints on the leatherette seats at the front of the pub, their faces mottled red and green by the street lights shining in through the stained-glass windows.

'Do you know the pure tragedy of it, boy?' said Bernie, with a Guinness foam moustache. 'The tragedy of it is, I still love her, do you know? I love her with all of my heart. But I was never enough for her, not in any way at all.'

'You need to have more faith in yourself, Bernie, that's your trouble,' said Alby. 'She must have some fondness for you or she wouldn't stay with you, would she? All right, she's been acting thwarted, but the trick is for you to ignore it. Whatever she says to you, smile and be sweet. Buy her a bunch of roses every now and then and buy yourself some of them Via-Gahra pills.'

'Ach, I don't know,' said Bernie. 'She locks the bathroom door these days so I never even get to see her in the nip.'

'I never understood locks on bathroom doors,' said Alby. 'It's not as if somebody's going to come rushing in and steal your shite, is it?'

Eventually, after three pints, they left the pub and drove the rest of the way up to Fair Green and Nash's Boreen. No lights were showing in Bernie's house, so he clapped Alby on the shoulder and said, 'I won't invite you in for another. If I wake her up she'll give me the seven shows of Cork, believe me. But thanks for running me over, boy. And thanks for the words of advice. I'll buy her some flowers tomorrow and maybe she'll start being a shade more accommodating, if you know what I mean.'

Alby drove off and Bernie went across to his front door, jabbing at the keyhole several times before he managed to fit in the key and unlock it. He was surprised to find the whole house was in total darkness. That was unusual, because whenever he came home late Maggie would at least leave the small table lamp on for him in the living room – mostly because she didn't want him stumbling around and waking her up.

Bernie closed the front door and groped his way towards the kitchen. With any luck there would be some of that shepherd's pie that Maggie had cooked yesterday left in the fridge. Their microwave was banjaxed but he was so hungry he didn't even mind eating it cold.

Halfway along the hallway he bumped into something heavy and soft, which swayed when he pushed it. He reached out to feel what it was and to his horror he felt a dress, and a hip. He took two off-balance steps backwards and slapped frantically at the wall to find the light switch next to the living-room door.

When he found it and switched on the overhead light he saw what he had bumped into. It was Maggie, hanging from the banisters, her head tilted to one side. Her eyes were bloodshot but they were wide open and staring at him, and her tongue was sticking out. Her face was a pale shade of lavender, and she was wearing the purple dress she had bought for their pearl wedding anniversary, as if she had chosen it to match.

Bernie couldn't speak. He clambered up the stairs on all fours and tried to untie the cord that Maggie had fastened around her neck. It was a length of nylon washing line which she had tied in a double knot, but her weight had tightened it so much that it was impossible for him to unpick, especially with his bitten-down nails.

He bumped back down the stairs and pushed his way into the kitchen, switching on the light and dragging out the drawer with all the cutlery in it. It fell right out and dropped on to the floor, so that knives and forks and spoons clattered everywhere. He picked up the small sharp paring knife that Maggie always used for potatoes and staggered back out again and up the stairs.

He reached through the banisters with his left hand to hold the collar of Maggie's dress while he sawed frantically through the washing line. As soon as the washing line parted, though, her dress ripped all the way to the top of her sleeve and Bernie found her much too heavy to hold on to. She dropped on to the hallway carpet with a thump, flinging up one arm as she did so.

Clumsily, he barged back downstairs and knelt down next to her. He could hardly breathe and he wished to God that he wasn't so drunk.

'Maggie?' he said and lifted up her right hand. She was cool, but not yet cold, but he couldn't feel a pulse and from the way her blood-filled eyes were staring at the radiator he knew she was dead.

He started to cry, making a whining noise like a puppy. He didn't know what to do. He could call for an ambulance, but what would be the point of that, now she had passed away? She was still warm, so she couldn't have been dead for very long. If he hadn't stopped for those drinks with Alby maybe he could have caught her before she hanged herself.

He bent over her and whispered, 'Maggie? Maggie? Dear Jesus, Maggie, I love you. I'm so, so sorry.'

A terrible thought came to him. He had promised to buy her flowers tomorrow and now he knew that he would, for sure, but only to lay on her coffin.

After three or four long minutes he stood up. He would have to ring somebody. The guards, maybe, or a funeral home. He simply couldn't think straight. He couldn't leave Maggie the way she was. She had always been such a stickler for looking dignified and here she was with her crimson eyes wide open and her tongue protruding and her dress torn, her arms and legs all jumbled up in the hallway.

He bent over and put his arms around her and tried to lift her, but he was too drunk and he simply didn't have the strength. In the end, he took hold of her ankles and dragged her along the carpet into the living room. The hem of her dress rode up and he saw that her thighs were blotchy with blue and red bruises and finger marks.

Panting with effort, he managed to sit her up with her back against the couch and then heave her up on to it. He pulled down her dress and crossed her hands over her breasts. Then, with shaking fingertips, he closed her eyelids, although her left eyelid refused to close completely.

Retracting her tongue was more difficult, but he pulled down her jaw until it made a cracking noise and then her tongue slowly folded up and slid back into her mouth.

He stood beside her, still unsure what to do next. Maybe he should ring Father Tomás from the Church of the Ascension. Father Tomás would know how to handle a person's death. Jesus, he must have given the last rites often enough. Father Tomás could also advise him on whether he ought to call for the guards or not, and what to say to them if he did. At the moment he was reluctant to ring them because they knew all about the financial arrangement he had made with Niall Gleeson to keep Maggie satisfied. Their suspicion that he had shot Niall might be confirmed and they might suspect that he had killed Maggie, too, in a jealous rage.

He took out his mobile phone and was about to ring Father Tomás when he saw an envelope propped up on the mantelpiece, next to the silver-framed photograph of himself and Maggie on their wedding day. He went over and saw that it was addressed in Maggie's handwriting to *Mo Coinín Beag Daor – My Dear Little Rabbit* – which was the nickname she had given him when they first met, because he was always hopping around and could never sit still.

He started to weep again as he took the envelope off the mantelpiece and blindly tore it open. Through his tears he looked back at Maggie lying on the couch with her left eye half-open, as if she were keeping a sneaky watch on him.

Inside the envelope he found her wedding ring folded inside a letter. He sat down in one of the armchairs to read it, holding her wedding ring tightly in the palm of his hand.

> *Dearest Bernie,*
>
> *I was wide from the very start that Niall was paying you but I knew too that you did it because you did not want to lose me. I was pure selfish I know but I needed the lovemaking and what you did showed me how much you cherished me.*
>
> *I was sure that it was Davy Dorgan who murdered Niall and I was going to tell the guards but somehow Davy found out about it and he fetched some of his gang round here Murtagh and Billy and Kevan and Alroy among them and Liam too but Liam never touched me.*
>
> *What those demons did to me I am not about to tell you Bernie because I do not want you to be thinking of it inside of your head. All I can say is that I would never be able to let another man touch me ever again for the mortal shame of it. I can see no other way for me but to repent for all of my selfishness and my sins by giving my soul to Jesus and praying that he forgives me.*
>
> *Please forgive me too mo coinín beag daor. We will meet again in heaven if God is willing.*
>
> *Maggie.*

Bernie read her letter twice. Then he smeared the tears away from his eyes with his fingers and stood up, carefully setting down her letter with her wedding ring on top of it on the small side table under the lamp.

He went to the cupboard under the stairs and reached behind the upright vacuum cleaner so that he could take out the 12-gauge Fenian shotgun that was propped against the shelves at the back. There was a box of cartridges there, too, and he took those through to the kitchen table and opened them up. He loaded both of the shotgun's over-and-under barrels and crammed the remaining cartridges into the pockets of his anorak.

He stood thinking for a moment and then he laid the shotgun down on the kitchen table and went back into the living room. First he pushed Maggie's wedding ring on to his left-hand little finger, then he tore up her letter into pieces as small as confetti. He carried the pieces into the downstairs lavatory, dropped them into the toilet bowl, and flushed them away.

If by any chance he didn't come back tonight, he didn't want anybody to know why she had committed suicide. She had suffered enough humiliation because of what he had done.

Before he left the house, he stood in front of the mirror in the hallway. He felt as if his insides had turned into molten lava, churning and bubbling with rage and revenge, and yet he had never seen himself look so placid.

He crossed himself and said, 'For what I am about to do, O Lord, please forgive me, and if You can't find it in Your heart to forgive me, at least forgive Maggie and take her into Your arms and give her the comfort which I never could. Amen.'

With that, he opened the front door and stepped out into the night.

* * *

It took him over half an hour to walk down to Mount Nebo Avenue, down Bantry Park Road and Knockfree Avenue. A soft rain was falling so that the street lights looked like jinny-joes, the dandelion puffs that Cork children blow away and ask them to bring them back some chocolate.

He made no attempt to hide his shotgun. The streets were deserted and even though two taxis passed him by he didn't care if their drivers saw what he was carrying and reported him to the police. By the time the guards caught up with him he would have done what he had set out to do.

He reached the end-of-terrace house at the lower end of Mount Nebo Avenue where the Dorgans lived. He hadn't known the number but Davy's Mercedes was parked on the pavement outside. The house was painted mushroom-grey, with half a wagon wheel underneath the living-room window and fancy net curtains. Every window was in darkness, although an outside security light automatically clicked on as he walked up to the front door.

He rang the doorbell, keeping his finger pressed on the button for nearly half a minute. Behind the flowery red curtains in the front bedroom window a light was eventually switched on, and he could hear voices. He rang the bell again, intermittently, and then he banged on the door and shouted out, 'Davy Dorgan! Davy Dorgan! Come on out, you murdering whore's melt! Come on, Davy, come and get what's coming to you!'

In the bedroom windows of several neighbouring houses more lights were switched on and Bernie could see blinds being raised and curtains drawn back and people peering out.

'Come on out like a man, Davy Dorgan, you cancery bastard!' The light in the front bedroom window was switched off again, but when he looked up, Bernie thought that he could see the curtains parted and somebody looking out. He stepped away from the front door, cocked his shotgun and raised it to his shoulder.

He waited, but the house remained in darkness and nobody opened the front door. Maybe he shouldn't have called out for Davy Dorgan and just waited until somebody came to see who was ringing and knocking at this time of night. If he had done that, though, he wouldn't have known which member of the family was opening the door and he might have shot the wrong person.

'Davy Dorgan!' he shouted out again. 'Come on out, Davy Dorgan, you narrow back, or are you too fecking jibber?'

A light was switched on behind the front door and he pointed his shotgun at the house numbers – 23 – because they were at about chest level and that would mean he would shoot Davy Dorgan straight in the heart. His own heart was beating hard, but he took a deep breath and held it to keep his aim steady.

The door was suddenly opened, but only two or three centimetres. Bernie tightened his trigger-finger, ready to shoot, but at that moment Davy Dorgan appeared from behind the wheelie bins at the side of the house, wearing a black towelling bathrobe. He was holding an automatic pistol in both hands and without hesitation he fired at Bernie twice.

The first shot hit Bernie in the right shoulder. His black nylon jacket was ripped up and a fan of blood sprayed across the side of his face. He staggered and dropped on to one knee on the concrete path, but he managed to keep his grip on his shotgun and twist himself around so that he could fire back.

As he tried to aim at Davy Dorgan, though, the second shot hit him in the chin, so that his lips burst apart in a wild tangle of bloody shreds and his teeth exploded out of his mouth like white shrapnel. He tilted backwards and sideways, but he squeezed the trigger of his shotgun as he fell and there was a deafening boom that echoed all the way up the street.

A few seconds passed. Then the front door was cautiously opened wider and Davy's white-haired uncle Christy put his head around it.

'Davy?' he said. 'Davy, are you okay, boy?'

Bernie was lying on his back now, with his arms wide apart and one leg bent under him. He was gurgling in his throat and blowing blood bubbles out of the mess that was all that was left of his mouth. But underneath the living-room window Davy was also lying down, grey-faced and shuddering. His bathrobe had been ripped away from his white left thigh and his skin was freckled with shotgun pellets.

Uncle Christy came out of the house in his maroon-striped pyjamas, looking up and down the street to make sure that Bernie had been alone and there were no other gunmen waiting.

Bernie's nineteen-year-old cousin Declan came out, too, wearing a Spiderman T-shirt and flappy red shorts. Doors were opening all the way up the street and more bedroom lights were being switched on. Davy's uncle picked up Bernie's shotgun, broke it open to eject both the spent and the live cartridges, and then laid it back on the path.

'Declan,' he said, 'tell your ma to ring for an ambulance right away. Make sure they know that there's two fellers shot so they need to make a bust.'

Then, stiffly, he eased himself down on to the paving slabs next to Davy and laid his hand on his forehead. 'It's all right, Davy. You're not hurt too bad. That was self-defence that was. I'll testify to that for you.'

'Fecking Bernie Dennehy,' Davy whispered. 'That's who it is. Fecking Bernie Dennehy. Holy Mother of God, this hurts.'

'It's only a few pellets, boy. The docs will get those out for you.'

'Is he dead?' asked Davy. 'I can't see him from here.'

Davy's uncle turned around to look at Bernie. He was still gurgling and bubbling, although he was whistling now, too, as if he couldn't breathe properly.

'No, he's still with us. I can tell you something, though. He won't be singing "The Fields of Athenry" any time soon.'

'Take my gun, Christy. Give it a good wipe and then squeeze it into his hand to put his prints on it. Then give it back to me.'

'What's the point of that, then?'

Davy winced with pain, squeezing his eyes tight shut. After a few seconds, though, he managed to croak, 'Bernie shot me with his shotgun, so he did, but I knocked it out of his hand.'

'Oh yeah? Then what?'

'It was then that he pulled out the pistol on me, but I grabbed that away from him. I told him to cool his jets, but he picked up his shotgun again, so I had no choice but to use his own pistol against him. Self-defence, like you said.'

'That's some fecking story, Davy. You should have been a writer.'

Davy didn't answer that. All he knew was that the shades would run tests on the bullets they would take out of Bernie so it was essential that they were led to believe the pistol was his.

He laid his head back on the concrete and stared up at the sky. The drizzle had stopped and a milky moon was just visible behind the clouds. His leg felt as if he had been bitten by a shark – not that he had ever been anywhere in the world where sharks might have bitten him. Larne and Cork, they were the limits of his travels, although he had once visited a cousin in Coleraine.

'Don't get any of that mixed up, Christy. You saw it all for yourself.'

'Don't you worry, boy. Even if the pigs beat me I won't say any different. Us Dorgans always stuck together till the death.'

'Oh, thanks. You've made me feel better already.'

Twenty-five

Kyna reached Katie's house at Carragh View a few minutes after midnight. Katie was expecting her, so she had switched on the light in the porch. As she was paying the taxi driver the front door opened and Katie appeared, with Barney excitedly trying to push his way past her.

'Come along in,' said Katie. 'Holy Mother of God, what's happened to you? You look like you've been pulled through a hedge backwards!'

Of course, Katie knew that Kyna had been dressing herself up so that she would look the part of a Gurranabraher barmaid, but she wasn't prepared for seeing her with her hair messed up and her face so white and her mascara streaked from crying. Without any regard for the protocol they had established between them in the station, she opened her arms and hugged her tight. Kyna clung on to her for almost half a minute and Katie could feel her trembling and her shoulders shaking underneath her jacket. Barney circled around and around them, snuffling and tail-waggling.

'I'm sorry,' said Kyna at last, sniffing and wiping her eyes with the back of her hand. 'I was going to be so brave about it. I'd rather he'd have shot me, to be honest with you.'

'Who? Why? Look, come inside and sit down. Can I fetch you anything to drink maybe?'

Kyna followed Katie into the living room. To her surprise, Conor was sitting in one of the armchairs, wearing a mustard-coloured cable-knit sweater and a pair of black jeans, although his feet were bare.

'Oh, I'm so sorry, ma'am. I didn't realize you had company. I could have just texted you.'

Conor stood up and smiled and said, 'Hallo, Kyna. It's not a bother at all. Here, sit yourself down and make yourself comfortable. Work always comes first with Katie, I know that. She's always made it clear that I'll be playing second fiddle to half the criminals in Cork.'

Kyna sat down on the sofa and Katie passed her a box of tissues so that she could dab at her messy make-up.

'Conor came over to brief me about the dog-fight tomorrow,' Katie told her. 'Inspector Carroll has promised me half a dozen officers from Tipperary Town to back up the ISPCA inspectors in case they find themselves threatened, but Frank Magorian won't sanction a full-scale operation and Denis MacCostagáin can't approve it, either. We just haven't the budget.

'So – ' she shrugged, 'all we can hope to do is try to keep the cruelty to a minimum and take as much video footage as we can as evidence in case the ISPCA want to prosecute McManus privately.'

She sat down next to Kyna and took hold of her hands between hers. 'Anyway, that's enough of that. What on earth is the story with you?'

Kyna gave her a wobbly smile. 'I think I'll have that drink now, if you don't mind. A whiskey would be perfect.'

Katie got up and went over to the drinks table. She poured her a large measure of Midleton Barry Crockett Legacy, which usually cost €140 a bottle but had been given to her as a gift by Cork County Council.

'Erm . . . if there's any more of that going, I wouldn't exactly say no to a glass myself,' said Conor, raising one eyebrow.

Before she swallowed it, Kyna swilled her whiskey between her teeth as if it were mouthwash. Then she said, 'I'm sorry, ma'am. Is it all right if I talk to you alone?'

Conor stood up again and raised his glass. 'No bother at all, Kyna, like I said. I've a rake of emails to catch up on in any case. *Slainté!*'

He went through to the spare bedroom, which Katie still called the Nursery, and closed the door. Katie sat down beside Kyna again and said, 'What is it? What's happened?'

Haltingly, Kyna explained how she had gone out for a drink with Liam, and how she had pretended to find him attractive so that he would tell her what Davy Dorgan was up to. Katie listened without interrupting her. She could tell that even kissing Liam on the lips had made her feel sick.

'Davy Dorgan is a total fanatic when it comes to the cause, not like Bobby Quilty used to be,' said Kyna. 'Liam says that when the British defence secretary comes to Cork on Saturday he's arranging for three republican hit men to come down from Ulster and shoot him while he's attending the dancing *feis* at the Opera House.'

'You're *codding* me, aren't you? He must be stone-hatchet mad! Doesn't he have any idea what the security's going to be like?'

'Sure, he must know. I don't think he's stupid. But from what Liam was saying, I got the feeling that he's planning to set up some kind of diversion and he's expecting Liam to help him do it. The trouble was, Liam started to get windy that Dorgan would find out that he'd been talking to me, so he never got around to telling me what the diversion was actually going to be. I don't know. I can't say I totally blame him like. The reason Dorgan stabbed him in the hand was to warn him to keep his bake shut. Keep Zippo, that's what he said.'

'Dorgan said that? "Zippo"?'

'Yes, he did. Why?'

'That was exactly what Adeen's visitor wrote on the card that came with the flowers he fetched her.'

'Well, it could have been Dorgan, but I've heard other people use it.'

Katie took Kyna in her arms and hugged her again. 'I don't know what to say to you,' she said, sitting back and stroking Kyna's fringe. 'It seems like every time I assign you a case to investigate, you end up getting hurt. You didn't have to do what you did. I don't think I could have done it myself. I would have understood if you'd refused and just walked out on him.'

Kyna said, 'I know. But how do you think I would have felt if that politician had got shot and I'd found out later that I could have saved his life?'

'Well, what I'll do now is set up twenty-four-hour surveillance on Dorgan,' Katie told her. 'Then, first thing in the morning, I'll have DI Mulliken get in touch with Superintendent Mitchell in Belfast and ask him to contact the SRR. There's a chance they'll have some background details about Dorgan and his contacts in Ulster and they can give us some notion of who these hit men might be.'

'Sure, good idea,' said Kyna. 'If anybody knows who they are, the SRR will.'

It was officially denied that there was any SRR presence in the province, but Katie knew that a small active unit was still based at Thiepval Barracks in Lisburn, County Antrim. They were a detachment from the Special Reconnaissance Regiment of the British Army and they had taken over covert operations against Irish terrorists after the Good Friday Agreement and the subsequent disbanding of 14 Intelligence Company, usually known as 'The Det'.

Like The Det, today's SRR operatives kept constant tabs on dissidents with some of the most sophisticated listening and recording techniques available, and they had occasionally taken lethal steps to prevent the kind of assassination attempt that Davy Dorgan was planning. Mostly, their victims simply disappeared, or were made to look as if they were casualties of a gangland shooting, like the Kinahan–Hutch feud in Dublin.

If Davy Dorgan had even tenuous links to a republican splinter group in Ulster, the SRR would almost certainly have information about him. Detective Ó Doibhilin said that all you needed to do was hum a couple of verses of 'The Bold Fenian Men' while you were sitting on the toilet in the morning and the SRR would have you logged on their database as a potential terrorist.

'So what are you going to do now?' Katie asked Kyna. She had finished her whiskey but she was still pale and shaky.

'Call a taxi and go home so. Try to get some sleep. Try not to have nightmares about Liam. God, that was so mank. I can still taste him now. Like bleach-flavoured yogurt.' She stuck out her tongue and pretended to spit.

'You can stay here if you like,' said Katie. 'Have a shower and borrow one of my nighties. Come on, you're in no fit state to be going home alone. You don't mind sharing a bed, do you? I don't snore, or at least nobody's ever complained about it.'

Kyna nodded towards the Nursery door. 'What about—?'

'Conor? He'll be grand altogether. I'll admit that we've been seeing each other, but he's right in the middle of divorcing his wife and we've agreed to take things easy between us until everything's settled.'

'Is it serious, you and him?'

'I'm not one hundred per cent certain. It could be. Barney adores him. He has such a way with dogs. You'd think they were telepathic, the two of them.'

'Well, I'm so glad you've found somebody. I'm hoping that I have, too. There was a singer called Sorcha at the Templegate and there's only one word for her – *munya*.'

They talked a little longer and then Katie sent Kyna off to the bathroom to have a shower. She went into the bedroom to lay out a long white cotton nightdress for her, with small blue forget-me-nots on it, and then she went to the Nursery to see Conor. He was sitting up in bed, still in his sweater and jeans, tapping on his Apple notepad.

She went up and kissed him and then rested her hand on his shoulder. 'Would you mind sleeping in here tonight? Kyna's totally stressed out and she badly needs some comforting.'

'Well, I *was* hoping for another cuddle with you, to be honest.' Conor smiled. 'But that's okay. She's in a state all right, isn't she? What happened to her?'

'I'll tell you in the morning. Right now I don't even want to think about it. I'm sorry.'

Conor closed his notepad. 'I'd best be getting some sleep then. I had another email earlier from that ISPCA inspector, Derek O'Donnell. He's almost certain now that the dog-fight's scheduled to start at three o'clock in the afternoon just where we thought it was, by Cappamurra Bridge.'

'I've been having some thoughts about it,' said Katie. 'Even if we can't raise the manpower to arrest all of the dog-fighters who show up there, we can at least lift Guzz Eye McManus. He's the ringleader, after all.'

'McManus? Are you serious? That'll be taking your life into your hands. Apart from the fact that he has some of the most expensive lawyers in the country.'

'I can try at least, even if I can't get a conviction. We have to start breaking up these dog-fighting gangs somehow. We'll get ourselves a heap of publicity if nothing else, and maybe we can get some questions asked in the Dáil.'

'So who's going to lift McManus if you can't get Frank Magorian or your chief superintendent to back you up? The Tipp guards won't do it, will they? They've already said that they're only going to show up to keep the peace and take videos.'

'I'll do it myself,' said Katie. 'I'll take Markey and O'Mara with me. They're both hardy.'

Conor smiled again and slowly shook his head. 'You're a mad scone, you are, Katie Maguire. No wonder I love you so much.'

Katie kissed him again and said, 'I'll see you for breakfast. Sleep well.'

* * *

Kyna was already lying with her head on the pillow when Katie came to bed. By now it was 1.35 a.m. and it had started to rain harder outside, but Katie found the sound of it quite soothing. She snuggled under the duvet and put her arm around Kyna and kissed her on the forehead.

'I hope this isn't your side of the bed,' said Kyna.

'I don't care what side I sleep on. It's been a while since I slept with anybody else. How are you feeling?'

'Slightly langered, to tell you the truth. My stomach's empty and that whiskey went straight to my head.'

They held each other very close. In their different ways, they both needed the love they felt for each other. They knew that it would be impossible for them ever to be partners, not without abandoning their careers and their commitment to the Garda. But just for tonight they were sharing a warmth and affection and physical attraction that needed no words, and for which no words could ever be found – no words that anybody else would understand, anyway.

Kyna felt Katie's breast through her nightgown and lightly rubbed her nipple with her thumb so that it stiffened, but that was all. They kissed, touching and teasing the tips of each other's tongues, and then Katie said, 'Goodnight, sweetheart. *Aisling sona* – happy dreams.'

* * *

They were woken at eleven minutes past five by the phone ringing. Katie turned herself over and picked it up and said, '*What?*' Then, 'Jesus, what time is it?'

It was still dark and it was still raining outside, even harder. Kyna lifted her head from the pillow but said nothing. Whoever was calling, she knew that Katie wouldn't want them to hear her voice in the background.

'DS Begley, ma'am. Sorry to ring you so early.'

'That's okay, Sean. I was having a nightmare anyway. What's the story?'

'There's been a shooting up at Gurra, right outside the Dorgan house. Bernie Dennehy and Davy Dorgan have both been wounded. Dennehy's injuries look like they could be life-threatening, but Dorgan's only been hit superficially in the leg with shotgun pellets. They've both been carted off to the Wilton Hilton.'

Katie switched on her bedside lamp. 'Oh, Christ Almighty.

This Davy Dorgan's turning out to be some kind of a jinx. Is that where you are now? Gurra?'

'I am, yes. Mount Nebo Avenue, with Ó Doibhilin and Buckley, and about twenty uniforms. The technicians should be here soon, too.'

'So do you have any idea what happened?'

'We've talked to Dorgan's uncle, Christy Dorgan. He's the only one who claims to have seen it all, but I wouldn't like to say how reliable he is. He's a close relative, after all, and not only that, he's been pulled in himself a few times for this and that – mainly for cheating old folks by climbing up on their roofs and banging around and pretending that he's fixing their tiles for them, two hundred yoyos a time.'

'So what did he have to say for himself?'

'Well, according to him, Dennehy came around to the house with a shotgun, shouting and cursing, and when Davy Dorgan opened the front door he shot him, but he only hit him in the leg. He dropped his shotgun and pulled out a pistol but Dorgan snatched it away from him and so he picked up his shotgun again. That's when Dorgan fired back at him and hit him once in the shoulder and once in the mouth. His face is in a fierce mess, I can tell you. Imagine a dish of lamb's liver with broken teeth scattered in it.'

'Jesus. I see. So Dorgan's going to be pleading self-defence.'

'You have it exactly. Those were his uncle Christy's very words.'

'What about the media?' Katie asked him.

'Only that fat young fellow from the *Echo* so far. But I expect they'll all be showing up before too long. Meanwhile we're going house to house, interviewing all the neighbours. So far, though, none of them saw nothing. In other words, they're all scared to say anything just in case it's different from what Christy Dorgan's been telling us.'

'Thanks, Sean. Give me an hour and I'll be there at the station. Don't say anything to any of the media. I mean *nothing*. We have some extra complications with Davy Dorgan, to say the least. I'll tell you about them when I get in. I'm assuming we've posted an officer to keep an eye on him while he's in the hospital?'

'Four, in fact, all armed, from the RSU. Two for him, and two for Bernie Dennehy. We don't want any more Dorgans nipping in to casualty and finishing the job, do we?'

'Good man yourself,' said Katie. 'And if and when either of them get discharged from the hospital, make sure we keep a tail on them both, okay?'

'Already sorted, ma'am. I'll see you after so.'

Katie climbed out of bed. 'It seems like Bernie Dennehy and your good friend Davy Dorgan have been having a bit of a gunfight,' she said. She went across to her wardrobe to pick out what clothes she was going to wear, and as she did so she told Kyna about the shooting on Mount Nebo Avenue.

'I'll come with you,' said Kyna and climbed out of bed, too. She crossed her arms and tugged off her nightie and when Katie saw her naked she had the briefest pang of regret that they had done nothing last night but kiss and then fall asleep.

'Here,' she said and tossed Kyna a pair of clean white briefs out of her knicker drawer. Then she went into the kitchen to put on the kettle for coffee. She felt as if a silent storm was blowing through her mind, tossing up dust and dead leaves. How could she be so much in love with Conor and yet find Kyna so attractive?

Maybe it was stress, she thought. She had the Toirneach Damhsa fire to deal with, as well as Davy Dorgan and Guzz Eye McManus and twenty or thirty ongoing cases of theft and prostitution and drug-dealing and assault, and on top of that she had Frank Magorian putting pressure on her to come up with immediate results.

As the kettle boiled, Conor came into the kitchen wearing only his pale blue boxer shorts.

'You're off to work already?' he asked her, looking up at the kitchen clock. He put his arms around her waist and kissed her.

'Something's come up,' she said, stroking the dark hair on his chest.

'Pity it's not me,' he grinned.

She kissed him back and said, 'It won't always be like this, Con.'

'You mean people are going to stop committing crimes and let us have some time together?'

'Yes,' she said. Then, 'No, of course not. But one day I won't care any more.'

Conor gently lifted her chin and looked into her sea-green eyes.

'And when will that be?' he asked her. 'When we're both old and grey?'

Twenty-six

They were crossing over the Glashaboy River on their way into the city when Katie's iPhone rang. Above them the low grey clouds were gradually beginning to grow lighter, but over to the south-west they could see charcoal-coloured clouds which meant that more heavy rain was impending.

'Yes, Sean?' said Katie. It was Detective Sergeant Begley again. 'I'll be with you in less than ten minutes so.'

'I've just heard from Ó Doibhilin at the hospital, ma'am. Bernie Dennehy passed away about half an hour ago. The doctors said that some bullet fragments had penetrated his brain, along with twenty or thirty bits of his molars. He never regained consciousness, so we've had no statement out of him.'

'What about Dorgan?'

'Dorgan's had the pellets taken out of him and they should be discharging him by lunchtime. I've interviewed him under caution, but his story is the same as his uncle's. No surprise there like. Both guns have gone to the lab for fingerprinting and DNA and ballistics, and we may have some results from them later in the day with any luck.'

'Thanks, Sean.'

She turned to Kyna and said, 'This is getting more and more bamboozling by the minute. Why do you think Bernie Dennehy wanted to shoot Davy Dorgan? I can understand why he might have wanted to do away with Niall Gleeson, although he swore blind that it wasn't him. But why Dorgan?'

Kyna pulled a face. 'Who knows? From what Liam was saying

249

it seems like half of Cork would be dancing in the streets if Dorgan was disposed of.'

'Well, we'll have to go and see Dennehy's wife and tell her the tragic news. Maybe she'll have some idea what his motive was. I'll send Michael Ó Doibhilin around. He's always brilliant with grieving widows. He may sound like he has a *tocht* in his throat, but he always asks the sharpest questions.'

As they turned into the station car park at Anglesea Street, Kyna said, 'I'll go home and change now, if that's okay. I think I ought to show up at the Templegate this evening as per normal. I don't want Liam thinking that I've gone off him, because I may be able to get him to tell me more about this hit that Dorgan's setting up.'

'Kyna – you don't have to get intimate with him again. I mean it.'

'I swear to you, ma'am – hell will have to freeze over,' said Kyna.

They sat in the car and looked at each other for a moment. They didn't have to say anything. Katie squeezed Kyna's hand and then they both climbed out.

* * *

Detective Sergeant Begley was waiting for Katie in her office. While she sat at her desk and sipped a hot cappuccino he showed her the video that had been taken at the scene of the shooting outside the Dorgan house. This included footage of Davy Dorgan's pellet-spattered leg and Bernie Dennehy's blown-apart face.

'*Urrghh* – thank God I haven't had my breakfast yet,' said Katie. 'Is Dorgan still in hospital?'

'No – he's back home now, but we've taken his passport and we're keeping him under discreet surveillance,' said Detective Sergeant Begley. 'He won't be going anywhere at all without us knowing about it.'

'Well, just listen to this,' said Katie, and quickly briefed him about the information on Davy Dorgan that Kyna had given her.

'Serious?' said Detective Sergeant Begley. 'He's planning to assassinate Ian Bowthorpe? Lord lantern of Jesus, he must be out of his mind. How's he going to manage that? The security guards at the Opera House that evening will almost outnumber the dancers!'

'I don't know for sure,' Katie told him. 'He may have been codding. From what Ni Nuallán says about him, he's either a very cute hoor or else he's a raving psychopath. Or maybe he's a combination of both. That Liam sounds like some kind of a browl, too. It could all be fantasy, but I'm going to ask DI Mulliken to check with the PSNI anyway, and the PSNI can check with the SRR.'

They were still talking when Detective O'Donovan came in, the shoulders of his grey jacket spotted with raindrops.

'Christ on a bike, it's rotten out there. And it's going to get worse before it gets better.'

'How's it coming on?' Katie asked him. 'What time have you fixed to interview Steven Joyce?'

'Ten o'clock. His studio's halfway up John Redmond Street, so it isn't far. But I haven't been making too much progress otherwise.'

'With that tri-ethly-what's-it's-name, you mean?'

'That's right. My friend Barry Brady up at the barracks says there's been none missing from the armoury, and neither of those plastics companies in Bishopstown or Little Island have lost any either. Both of them said they keep a fierce tight check on it because it's so flammable. They've both had accidental fires with it. Three years ago at Cork Plastic Mouldings nearly half the whole factory burned down.'

'All right, Patrick. Keep trying. I'll be holding a briefing this afternoon to bring us all up to date and maybe we can come up with some new notions about where it might have come from. I really think that's going to be the key to finding out who started that fire.'

After Detective Sergeant Begley and Detective O'Donovan had left, Katie finished her coffee and then went along the corridor to see Detective Inspector Mulliken. On her way there, though, she heard feet hurrying up behind her and when she turned around she saw Detective Scanlan running to catch her up.

'I just went into your office to talk to you but you weren't there,' Detective Scanlan panted. 'You'll never guess – I've found out where Adeen's wristband came from. More than that, I think I've found out what her real name is and who bought her doll for her.'

'You have?' said Katie. 'That's the best news I've had all morning. Look – I'm on my way to see DI Mulliken. Come with me . . . this could be pure useful to him, too.'

As they walked the rest of the way along the corridor Detective Scanlan held up a sheet of paper that she had printed out from her computer. It was headed *Little Angels* and it carried six colour photographs of babies, two of them with their eyes closed, apparently sleeping, others smiling, one of them sucking a dummy.

'Reborn babies,' said Detective Scanlan. 'They're a huge business all over the world, but especially in Northern Ireland for some reason. These ones are made by an artist in Dungannon, Mary Fitzsimmons. I mean, they're horribly lifelike, aren't they?'

They reached Detective Inspector Mulliken's office and Katie knocked at his open door. Detective Inspector Mulliken was sitting at his desk, holding up a shaving mirror and trying to comb his thinning hair over.

'You've caught me in the act,' he said mournfully, dropping his comb and mirror into a drawer. 'Maybe I should admit defeat and go to the Baldy Barber and have it all shaved off.'

'Oh, come on, Tony, they do some grand men's wigs these days,' Katie told him. 'Try the Cork Hair Clinic on Oliver Plunkett Street. You could come in tomorrow looking like Gabriel Byrne. But anyway, I have something much more important for you to be worrying about. Go on, Padragain – finish what you were telling me.'

Detective Scanlan held up the pictures of the *Little Angels* so that Detective Inspector Mulliken could see it.

'So?' he said. 'What exactly do these babies have to do with the grass and the goose on the side of a mountain?'

'They're not real babies, sir. They're all dolls.'

'*Serious?*' said Detective Inspector Mulliken, leaning forward to peer at them more closely.

'Serious. They're made out of silicone mainly, and the dummy only stays in your one's mouth there because it's magnetic. Reborn babies, they call them.'

'So who buys them?'

'Collectors, of course, but a fair number are bought by women who have never been able to have babies, or they've lost one. For consolation, I'd say. Maybe they've had a hysterectomy, or they've never had a partner, or maybe they've miscarried, or the baby was stillborn, or died when it was only a few weeks old.'

Katie made no comment, but it was impossible for her not to think about her own little Seamus, lying still and cold in his cot in the Nursery. He had looked just like one of these reborn babies, with his eyes closed and his lips pouting, and she gave an involuntary shiver.

'Anyway, you can order these dolls with any clothing or accessories that take your fancy,' Detective Scanlan went on. 'You can have bonnets and coats and teddy bears, even baby buggies and cribs. In this case, though, I was only looking for a green woven wristband because that's what Adeen's wearing and she told DS Maguire that it came off of her doll.

'Out of all the reborn dolls on offer from different artists, Mary Fitzsimmons was the only one to offer a woven wristband – there, you can see one on this doll here – and it's identical to Adeen's, except that it's pink. In the past year she's had only the one order for a green one, last October the twelfth.'

She turned over the paper and checked what she had written on the back. 'It was ordered online by Mrs Jean McCabe, of Victoria Road, in Larne, County Antrim, who paid for it, but it was to be delivered to Miss Cissy Jepson of Old Glenarm Road, which is just around the corner from Victoria Road, with a card to wish her a happy eighth birthday.'

'Jepson,' said Katie, narrowing her eyes. 'That name rings kind of a bell somehow.'

'Oh yes?' asked Detective Inspector Mulliken. 'What manner of a bell?'

'I don't know . . . I'm not sure yet,' Katie told him. 'But listen, Padragain, why don't you contact this Mrs McCabe and send her a picture of Adeen? See if she recognizes her. And while you're at it, send her a picture of Davy Dorgan, too. I expect DS Begley will have taken a picture of him at the hospital when he questioned him. If not, you can take a screenshot from the video that we took after the shooting this morning up at Mount Nebo Avenue. Just don't show her his wounded leg.

'I'll be out for a couple of hours,' she added. 'If you get a firm identification on either or both of them, tell DI Mulliken here as soon as you can. And well done yourself for tracking down that wristband. Good work.'

'I will of course, ma'am,' said Detective Scanlan. 'And thank you.'

When she had gone, Katie told Detective Inspector Mulliken about Davy Dorgan's intention to murder the British defence secretary, Ian Bowthorpe. He listened with his mouth open in disbelief.

'At the Opera House? Your man must be half a bubble off true. Mind you, that'll be the only time Bowthorpe's going to be seen in public. The rest of the time he'll either be at Haulbowline, in the navy base, or else he'll be speeding around in a bulletproof car with motorcycle outriders. Still . . . I'd say that he's dreaming, this Dorgan. Either that, or it's nothing more than big words to impress this so-called Authentic IRA of his.'

'I have to agree with you mostly,' said Katie. 'The trouble is, we still have to take him seriously, even if we think he's cracked as the crows. Can you ring your friend Superintendent Mitchell in Belfast and see if he can contact the SRR? If there's any buzz going around about Davy Dorgan setting up an attempt on Bowthorpe's life, they're the most likely ones to have picked it up.'

'I'll do that, sure. But I have to tell you that they're not finding it so easy these days to keep tabs on the dissidents, not like they used to. The younger ones especially, they've wised up to all the technamalogical tricks like. A lot of it they get taught in school, of course. But now they can tell if somebody's hacking their computer, or listening in to their mobile phone calls, or if a tracker's been stuck to their car. The Invisible Republican Army, that's what they've taken to calling themselves.'

'See what you can come up with, anyway,' said Katie. 'I have the feeling that at last we're beginning to pull our boots up out of the bog. Maybe Frank Magorian was righter than he knew and we *will* have this investigation all wrapped up by Sunday Mass.'

Twenty-seven

Katie parked at a bus stop because John Redmond Street was so crowded on both sides with residents' cars. As she and Detective O'Donovan climbed out of her Focus they could hear fiddle and accordion music and the machine-gun rattling of hard step-dancing shoes, even down here in the street.

Detective O'Donovan looked up at the first floor of the cement-rendered building.

'Holy Saint Joseph,' he said. 'They're really going at it. Sounds like my brother's boat-repair workshop down at Kinsale.'

They went through a stone archway and climbed up the concrete steps to the first floor. On the door that led to the Laethanta na Rince dance studio a handwritten sign had been pinned up, *Quiet Rehearsal in Progress*. The music was so loud now and the sound of dance shoes so thunderous that Detective O'Donovan had to shout for Katie to hear him.

'That's a barefaced lie! Jesus!'

They opened the door and went inside. Sixteen girls in short pink skirts and black tights were practising their céili dancing, leaping and clicking and stamping in a slow triple jig.

Their dance teacher and manager, Steven Joyce, was standing at the side of the studio, clapping his hands in time to the music. He was a small man, with gingery-brown hair that was cut in a high fade with a hard parting, shaved up the sides but long and swept back at the top. He had a neat gingery-brown beard and watery blue eyes, and he put Katie in mind of a self-portrait by

Van Gogh, except that he was wearing a tight green cashmere sweater and skinny beige jeans.

She could now see why the hard-shoe dancing sounded so loud. The floor of the studio was covered with at least thirty wooden doors which had been unhinged and laid down side by side on top of the parquet. The dancers were leaping from door to door and then rattling their fibreglass-tipped shoes on the panels.

Steven Joyce caught sight of Katie and Detective O'Donovan and raised one hand to acknowledge their arrival. He crossed over to the sound system and switched off the jig, then he clapped his hands and called out, 'Five minutes rest, girls! But then it's the "Three Tunes" so, and I want to see perfect roly-polys! Not like the last time, when most of you looked like you were winding wool!'

He stepped over the doors and came up to Katie and said, 'I was expecting you yesterday, to be honest with you, or even the day before.'

Close up, he was only three or four inches taller than Katie, and he smelled strongly of L'Eau Froide, which was a cool unisex fragrance.

'We had a heap of background investigation to go through first, Mr Joyce,' said Katie. 'There's no point in asking people questions unless you know what you're supposed to be asking them about.'

'Sure like, I can understand that. Have you spoken to Danny Coffey yet? I'm sure Danny's been pure complimentary – not.'

'What's with the doors on the floor?' asked Detective O'Donovan, deliberately changing the subject so that Katie wouldn't have to answer either yes or no.

'Oh the doors! The doors are what make Laethanta na Rince so unique, yet totally traditional. Your hard-shoe step-dancing doesn't go back as far as some people think – only to the early eighteenth century. Most country cottages had only the rough dirt floors in those days, and they weren't at all suitable for dancing because they were covered at best with reeds and the pigs would come in and out and do their business.'

'That doesn't sound too savoury,' said Katie.

'Well, the wives used to scatter mint leaves on the floor so that when they walked around they'd crush them with their feet and make the place smell a little better. But when it came to dancing they would unscrew their doors and lay them flat to make a stage. Sometimes they'd coat the door with butter to make it easier for them to dance on it wearing their hobnailed boots.'

'I'll have to remember that next time I go to Havana Browns,' said Detective O'Donovan. 'Take a tub of Kerrygold with me and smear it on the soles of my shoes.'

Steven Joyce was plainly very serious about his dancing and he ignored that comment.

'It's dancing on doors that originally gave the hard-shoe jigs their resonance and their rhythms,' he continued, 'and of course, as you probably know, those cottages were fierce cramped for space, especially if you'd invited a whole crowd of friends and neighbours to watch you dancing, so you couldn't wave your arms around. Hence we dance with our arms held close down by our sides.'

'And, what? When you compete in a *feis*, do you take these doors with you?'

'We do, most of the time, and that's what's given us our great reputation. You have to leap and treble and stamp very precise when you're dancing on a door, I can tell you. You could easy trip on a transom and twist your ankle.'

'You and Danny Coffey used to be very close friends, I gather,' said Katie.

'We were, yes, when we first started Toirneach Damhsa.'

'He says you wanted more than your fair share of the profits and that's why the two of you parted company.'

'Is that what he said? Well, I suppose that's half of the truth. The way I saw it, I was doing all the creative work, all the choreography – me and Nicholas O'Grady between us, anyway – while Danny was doing a bit of driving and fetching the sandwiches and sitting on his arse.'

'All right. So what's the other half of the truth?'

Steven Joyce looked around to see if his dancers were listening to their conversation. They were standing and sitting around, chatting and drinking bottles of water, and didn't appear to be interested in what he was saying, but all the same he said, 'Let's go out on to the balcony.'

He opened up a pair of French windows and they stepped outside. From here they could see over the wet slate rooftops to the city below them, and the three tall spires of St Fin Barre's cathedral.

'If you want to know the absolute truth, it was Nicholas who split us up, more than the money.'

'Go on,' said Katie. After her interview with Danny Coffey, she had a strong feeling that she knew already what he was going to say.

'I'd known Nicholas for years. We were both taught to dance by Peggy McTeggart at the UCC School of Music and Theatre – may the Lord bless her memory, dear Pegs. I always thought that Nicholas and me would stay together for the rest of our lives.'

'You were partners?' asked Katie. 'Sorry to ask such an obvious question, but I want to be clear about it.'

Steven Joyce nodded. 'We didn't live together because Nicholas always said that he needed space in his life, but I think you could say that we were as close as two human beings can be.'

He hesitated for a moment and looked away, his mouth working with emotion. 'I always knew that he enjoyed flirting with other men. I tried not to think about it, although I warned him again and again about the dangers of HIV. He hurt me with all his flings, but I said to myself that he's a free agent and who am I to control his life for him? But then Danny Coffey came into our lives, fresh after leaving Michael Flatley, and we formed Toirneach Damhsa together.'

'And Nicholas had another of his flings, with Danny Coffey?'

'I found out about it only by accident. I went back to the studio one evening to pick up some messages that I'd forgotten and caught them in the changing room. I could never understand it. I mean, you've *seen* Danny Coffey, haven't you, for the love of God! He's not exactly an Adonis, is he? More like a middle-aged salesman from Kelly's Carpets. And he doesn't have the sweetest temperament, either. Just about everything gives him ire.'

'So what happened? You and Nicholas broke up and Nicholas stayed with Danny?'

'It was more complicated than that. Like I say, it was partly to do with the money and partly to do with the bookings that Danny wanted to set up. I told him he wasn't giving the dancers enough time to rest and train in between gigs, but he always had his eye on the profits rather than anything else.

'But – yes – whatever it was that Nicholas found so attractive about Danny, he stayed with him, rather than me. Of course, he found young Tadhg Brennan after a few months and they moved in together and got married. I was invited to the wedding, but I didn't go. I was still too sore about losing him to Danny.'

'Sore enough to take your revenge on the both of them?' asked Katie.

'Holy Jesus! I was still odd about it, but I never would have done anything like burn down that studio! I *knew* most of those poor young dancers. I trained them myself, right from when they were still at school, some of them.'

'Where were you exactly, when the studio was set on fire?' asked Detective O'Donovan.

'I was in Mallow as a matter of fact, having lunch at Peppers at the White Deer with Shelagh Murtry from the Centre Stage dance and drama school. I wanted to see if they had any young dancers who might be interested in joining us. I have the receipt to prove it.'

'You *were* there, yes,' said Detective O'Donovan. 'We've checked already. But of course you could have paid somebody to set the fire for you.'

'Oh, get out of that garden! I have a temper all right, but only when my dancers are out of step! I'm not saying I don't feel bitter about Danny and Nicholas – I am, or at least I used to be – but I've always been the kind of fellow who looks to the future. I picked myself up and started Laethanta na Rince, didn't I, even though I didn't have a pot to piss in nor a window to throw it out of?'

'All the same, you have to admit you had motive enough,' said Katie. 'We're still not clear if the arsonist realized that so many people would lose their lives. Did you know Ronan Barrett or Saoirse MacAuliffe?'

'Who? No. Neither of those names means nothing at all.'

'So you didn't train them, either of them, and they never danced for you?'

'No.'

'All right – one last question for now – if you didn't have anything to do with setting that fire, can you think of anybody who might have done?'

Steven Joyce stared at her. 'You really want me to answer that?'

'Yes, I do. That's why I asked you.'

'Well, if you want my honest truthful deep-down thoughts about it, I reckon it was Danny himself.'

'Do you seriously mean that?'

'I've heard rumours that Toirneach Damhsa haven't been doing too well financially. Danny owes a rake of back tax to the Revenue Commissioners and he's recently lost three of his best dancers – two of them because they left Cork to get married and one with a slipped disc. Like you say, he might not have meant to hurt anybody and it all went wrong. But the insurance would have set him straight, for sure.'

Katie said, 'Fair play, Steven, we'll look into it.'

She didn't tell him that she had already detailed Detective Ó Doibhilin to check how much Danny Coffey could expect from his insurers for the loss of the dance studio and the lives of the dance troupe themselves.

'You won't be telling Danny that I accused of him of it, though, will you?' said Steven Joyce, suddenly anxious. 'He'll fecking kill me to death if you do.'

* * *

When Katie returned with Detective O'Donovan to Anglesea Street she found Conor waiting for her in her office, talking to Moirin.

261

'We need to be setting off soon,' he told her. 'The traffic's bad on the M8 past Fermoy, so they say, because of the roadworks.'

'Give me ten minutes,' she told him. 'Moirin – would you call Markey and O'Mara and make sure they're all geared up and ready to leave for Tipp?'

She sorted quickly through the files that had been left on her desk and checked her emails and texts. She quickly answered a query from the clerk of the Circuit Criminal Court about the bill of indictment for a Somali drug-dealer named Ismail Tima Khatarta. As she was typing, Detective Scanlan came in, looking pleased with herself.

'Result!' she said.

Detective O'Donovan was about to leave, but Katie said, 'Stall it a second, Patrick. You might want to hear this.'

'I've managed to get through to Mrs McCabe at last,' said Detective Scanlan. 'She works in the Cancer Research charity shop in Larne in the mornings, which is why I couldn't get through to her earlier – but that's where she first met Cissy Jepson. Cissy came in looking for a doll to buy, but she didn't have enough money, even though the doll she wanted was only three pounds. Mrs McCabe promised to keep the doll aside for her until she had saved up.

'Cissy started coming into the shop regularly and talking to her. It seemed like she had no friends at all and was very lonely. Mrs McCabe said she met her once walking along Main Street with a young man, and said hello to her, but Cissy didn't answer and she got the impression that she didn't want the young man to know that they knew each other. The next time she came into the shop, though, she explained that the young man was her older brother.'

'You sent Mrs McCabe those pictures of Adeen and Davy Dorgan?'

'I did of course, and she recognized them instantly. No hesitation whatsoever. Cissy Jepson is Adeen and the young man with her was Davy Dorgan, although it seems certain that he was calling himself

Jepson, too. Mrs McCabe took Cissy home one day because it was lashing and she didn't have her own umbrella and she saw a card by the doorbell with the name *D. Jepson* on it.'

'Jepson,' said Katie. 'Now it makes sense. Or I think it does, anyway. I'm probably crediting Davy Dorgan with much more intelligence than he deserves. But Anne Jepson was the mother of Sir Roger Casement.'

'You've lost me there,' said Detective Scanlan. 'Why would Dorgan call himself after Sir Roger Casement's mother?'

'I expect he wanted an alias so that the PSNI and the SRR couldn't track him down. But maybe he wanted an alias that summed up who he was. I mean, I'm really guessing here, and it doesn't really matter one way or another now that we're sure who he is, but Sir Roger Casement was a fervent nationalist, wasn't he, and he tried to ship in German guns to fight the British and get Ireland united. That's why they stripped him of his knighthood and hanged him.'

'That's an interesting theory all right,' said Conor. 'It sounds like one of those theories that either cracks a case wide open or leads you up a blind alley. I've come up with a few like that myself when I've been trying to find a lost dog. Usually I end up chasing my own tail, instead of the dog's.'

'Well, we'll see,' said Katie. 'But what makes me suspect that it could be true is that Sir Roger Casement was found out to be gay, and so, as we know, is Davy Dorgan. It could be that Dorgan identifies with him and that's why he chose the name Jepson.'

Detective O'Donovan frowned and said, 'I don't want to sound like I'm politically incorrect here or nothing, but you may have hit on something there, ma'am. Danny Coffey's gay, and so are Steven Joyce and the late cremated Nicholas O'Grady. Don't ask me what it all points to, because I couldn't tell you, but it's worth taking on board.'

'I think we need to tie up some loose ends,' said Katie. 'See if you can locate Nicholas O'Grady's husband – what was his name, Brennan? And that Saoirse's fiancé. I know that both of them are very unlikely suspects, but I'm beginning to feel like this investigation is a wasps' nest. I can hear some fierce buzzing inside of it all right, but we need to give it a few hard knocks to break it apart and let the wasps out.'

'I'm allergic to wasps,' said Detective O'Donovan. 'One sting and I go into prophylactic shock.'

'You may die but at least you won't get pregnant,' said Conor.

Katie couldn't help smiling, but Detective O'Donovan had no idea what he meant and shook his head. 'I'll go after that Brennan character first, ma'am. I'll text you as soon as I've set it up.'

'Good man yourself,' said Katie and turned to Conor. 'Let's go, shall we? I can't wait to lift that monster McManus.'

Twenty-eight

They were delayed for over twenty minutes by resurfacing works on the M8 so that it was nearly a quarter to three by the time they arrived at the Dundrum House Hotel and Golf Club. Katie had arranged to rendezvous there with the ISPCA inspectors and the officers from Tipperary Town. She decided not to meet at the Garda station because there was a chance they might have been seen by somebody passing the end of St Michael's Road on their way to the dog-fight.

Katie stepped down from the marked Toyota Land Cruiser in which she and Conor and Detectives Markey and O'Mara had driven up from Cork, and Inspector Carroll came across the driveway to greet her.

He was a solidly built man, Inspector Carroll, shaven-headed under his uniform cap, and Katie could sense a kind of inner tension in him. He looked as if he could have been a useful amateur boxer when he was younger. His nose was bent to the left and had obviously been broken, and he had a glassy look in his eyes which made her think that he wore contact lenses.

He had brought seven uniformed gardaí with him in a marked van and a patrol car, as well as an unmarked black BMW. Katie introduced him to Conor and Detectives Markey and O'Mara, but after she had done that he stood close to her with his face turned away as if he were simply admiring the view and spoke quietly so that they couldn't overhear what he was saying.

'To be honest with you, ma'am, this is a pure farce, isn't it? If this dog-fight turns out to be as big a show as we suspect it is, we shouldn't have eleven officers here. We should have a hundred and eleven, and a helicopter to chase after any guttie who tries to do a legger over the fields. Not to mention a fleet of buses to take all of them into custody.'

'Well, I agree,' Katie shrugged. 'But . . .'

Inspector Carroll looked around the hotel grounds. The hotel building itself was a fine three-storey eighteenth-century mansion, surrounded by a golf course and immaculately mown lawns. Thirty kilometres to the south rose the Galtee Mountains, although they looked pale green behind the afternoon mist, as if they were seen in a dream.

'This place is massive,' said Katie.

'Oh, it's fantastic,' Inspector Carroll agreed. 'I stayed here once and had a wonderful lunch in the restaurant. For all the good we'll be able to do today, I'm almost tempted to say let's forget about the dog-fight and play a leisurely round of golf instead, and then treat ourselves to dinner.'

'Get thee behind me, Satan,' said Katie. 'We may not achieve very much today, I'll grant you, but at least we're showing these dog-fighters that we're not turning a totally blind eye to what they're doing.'

'As if they'll give a monkey's.'

'Well, I know,' said Katie. 'Frank Magorian's right about this, I have to admit, even though he and I disagree about almost everything else. If the rank-and-file gardaí keep threatening to strike because of their pay, and we can't afford to keep rural Garda stations open for lack of money, how can we justify spending X thousands of euros trying to stamp out dog-fighting?'

Three out of the seven ISPCA inspectors who covered the whole country had arrived to monitor the dog-fight – two men and a woman. One of them came over to Katie and held out his hand. He was a young, good-looking man with a black hipster beard and a wide toothy grin. He was wearing an official ISPCA cap and a navy-blue waterproof jacket with studded epaulettes, but also skinny jeans and brown Dubarry boots.

'Peter O'Dwyer, South Tipperary ISPCA,' he said. 'You must be Detective Superintendent Maguire.'

'Good to meet you,' said Katie. 'To be honest, I think you have some fierce bottle facing up to McManus and all the rest of his scum.'

Conor stepped forward and shook Peter O'Dwyer's hand. 'How's it cutting, Peter? I haven't seen you since I came up here looking for those four stolen Shar Peis, remember?'

'Janey Mack! Conor Ó Máille the famous pet detective, how about that? What's the story, Conor?'

'I'm still finding missing pets for a living, Peter, but at the moment I've been roped in by Detective Superintendent Maguire here to help her to break up this dog-fighting racket.'

Peter O'Dwyer turned to Katie and said, 'I want you to know how much we appreciate your support, ma'am, we truly do. This year we've been called to more and more dog-fights than ever, and the sheer bloody cruelty we've seen – that's been getting worser every day.'

'I thought the Animal Health and Welfare Act might have made a difference,' said Katie.

'Not at all. We've managed to stop fights in Sligo and Offaly and Leitrim and Laois, but it's been like whack-a-mole – except I shouldn't say that, should I, being an ISPCA inspector? Every time we get one dog-fighter into court, another two spring up, and we haven't been clocking up nearly as many successful prosecutions as we should be.'

'Well, I'm afraid we have to be realistic,' Katie told him. 'We're not looking to make any mass arrests here today. We don't have the manpower, to begin with. But we do want the dog-fighters to realize that they're under Garda observation and that if they commit any extreme acts of cruelty we'll have the video evidence. We could use that to support a possible arrest at a later date, or to give you the evidence to take out a private prosecution yourselves.'

She touched Inspector Carroll's arm and added, 'I will say one thing to you, though, Inspector. We know that McManus organized this dog-fight himself, to celebrate his fiftieth birthday. If I see or hear any clear evidence of that, I intend to lift him personally. I'm going to need your help and cooperation if it comes to taking him in. I know we won't be able to hold him for long, but at least we can show these scumbags that we have the power to arrest the so-called Lord of the Dog-fighting Rings and that we're not at all scared to do it.'

'Lifting him is one thing,' said Inspector Carroll. 'Getting an indictment in court, that's another story altogether. Technically, a court could give him a twenty-five-thousand-euro fine and six months in jail, as well as a lifetime ban from ever owning any kind of an animal ever again. Even a hamster. But . . . you know.'

'Not a hope in hell,' said Conor, shaking his head.

'Even a five-hundred-euro fine would do,' said Katie. 'A successful prosecution would attract a whole lot of attention in the media, wouldn't it, especially if it was the notorious Guzz Eye McManus? It might even make some would-be dog-fighters think twice about it.'

'You know exactly how I feel about it, ma'am,' said Inspector Carroll. 'Dog-fighting sickens me down to my stomach and if I had the authority to do it, and the budget, I'd go after every dog-fighter everywhere and have them locked up and treated exactly like the dogs they've been training.'

'The last dog-fight we stopped was two months ago, in Westmeath,' said Peter O'Dwyer. 'The dogs who lost their fights – those that were still alive, that is – they had clips connected to car batteries attached to their ears and then they were thrown into a big zinc bath full of water.'

'You're not serious.'

'I wish to God I wasn't. I never saw dogs scrabbling and screeching like that in my life, and all the crowd were standing around laughing their heads off. It's not just individual acts of cruelty we're trying to change here, it's a whole social mentality, do you know what I mean?'

'Let's do our best anyway,' said Katie. She checked her watch and then she said to Inspector Carroll, 'Zero hour.'

* * *

They drove fast, even though the roads between Dundrum and Goolds Cross were so narrow and overgrown. One of the two patrol cars from Tipperary Town headed up the convoy, followed by Inspector Carroll in his BMW and then Katie and Conor and the two Cork detectives in their Toyota, with the ISPCA inspectors close behind them and the second Tipperary patrol car riding shotgun.

They soon came across the first vehicles parked along the roadside and then they began to slow down. Cappamurra Bridge was the name given to a network of roads that criss-crossed the fields here and every one of them was lined nose-to-tail with Mercedes and camper vans and Range Rovers and even builders' lorries with scaffolding stacked on them.

'If we could call up enough tow trucks, we could give all of them a ticket for obstruction and tow them away,' said Detective Markey.

'Sure like,' said Detective O'Mara. 'But if my grandpa wore a mini-skirt and lipstick, I still couldn't call him granny.'

Eventually they reached an open five-bar gate which led to a long muddy track with high hawthorn hedges on either side. They turned into the gate and drove along the track at a crawl because fifty or sixty men were walking in front of them. Several of them had dogs on leads, pit bulls and boxers and mastiffs, and almost all of the dogs were muzzled.

Usually, the driver of the patrol car at the front would have bipped his horn so that the walkers would stand aside and let them through, but as soon as they heard them coming some of the men turned around and glared at the Garda vehicles with such hostility that it was almost laughable, and two or three of them openly gave them the finger, so he contented himself with creeping behind them at their own pace.

As Katie's Toyota passed him by, a tattooed man shouted close to her window, '*I smell bacon!*'

'Didn't I tell you?' said Conor. 'You can always count on a heartfelt welcome when you come to a dog-fight.'

The muddy track widened out into a rough grassy field, which was already crowded. Most of the crowd were men, although Katie could see a few young Pavee women with skimpy tops and gold hoop earrings, two of them pushing babies in buggies. There were children skipping around, too, laughing and throwing apple cores at each other. Katie knew why the children had been brought here – to act as bookies' runners when money began to change hands. The dog-fighters used them because they were too young to be arrested and to give evidence to the gardaí.

'Great way to bring up your kids, don't you think?' said Conor. 'Fetch them to watch some starving dogs ripping each other's tripes out, and tell them it's hilarious.'

Katie said, 'Look – over there! There's McManus.'

In the centre of the field a circular dog-fighting ring had been built out of bales of hay, three bales high. A small group of hard-looking men were gathered at one side of it, two of them holding the collars of white Staffordshire bull terriers, which were snapping and twisting themselves from side to side in a struggle to get free from their owners and attack each other.

Guzz Eye McManus was standing in the middle of this group, smoking a cigar. He was short and fat and totally bald, although this afternoon he was wearing a black peaked cap. As well as being bald he had no eyebrows, and thick rubbery lips, so that he looked like Buddha's evil twin. He was wearing a grey sheepskin coat with the collar turned up and black tracksuit bottoms that would have been baggy on a man whose legs weren't swollen like two giant drisheen. He had tiny feet, though, like a child's, and was wearing white Nike runners which were probably no bigger than size four.

Katie could see McManus staring at their procession of vehicles as they came slowly jouncing into the field and drew up alongside the trees that bordered it on the south-eastern side. Although he was still thirty metres away, and it was always difficult to read his expression because one of his eyes looked off to the right while the other looked at ninety degrees to the left, she could tell that he was both disbelieving and furious. He took his cigar out of his mouth and said something, and whatever it was made even the hard-chaw men around him back away.

Katie and Conor stepped down from the Land Cruiser while Inspector Carroll and his Tipperary gardaí climbed out of their cars, although they stayed where they were, under the trees, to set up their video cameras.

'I don't think His Guzzship is exactly overwhelmed to see us,' said Conor.

'Well, it's his party, after all,' said Katie. 'Let's go over and wish him many happy returns, shall we?'

'I'll say one thing for you, Katie. You have some nerve.'

'He's a fat raging old man, that's all. Come on.'

She walked across the grass towards the dog-fighting ring, with Conor beside her and Detectives Markey and O'Mara close behind. Most of the crowd in the field were staring at them now and she heard some whistles and shouts of 'Feck off, razzers! You're not wanted here! Get away with yourselves! Go and feck a cow!'

As Katie and Conor approached, McManus took his cigar out of his mouth, blew out a stream of smoke, and folded his arms across his chest.

'Well, hit me on the arse with a banjo,' he said. 'Redmond the dog-breeder and his scrubber Sinéad. Except that you're not really a genuine scrubber, are you, Sinéad, you're a banner. And as for you, Redmond, I don't know what you are, except that you're a fecking treacherous piece of shite.'

'Happy birthday, Mr McManus,' said Katie.

'I don't want no birthday greetings from the likes of you,' said McManus. 'That's worse than a curse. Now, this is private land and this is a private party and you're not welcome, so why don't you and your friends just fecking do one.'

'I'm Detective Superintendent Kathleen Maguire from Cork and this is Conor Ó Máille, a licensed private animal detective who has been helping me in my enquiries.'

271

'I don't care if you're the Virgin Mary from the wrong end of the bathtub and your pal here is Judas the fecking Iscariot. I'm breaking no laws here, so just get the hell out of my face.'

'Mr McManus – dog-fighting is an offence under section fifteen of the Animal Health and Welfare Act and anyone who holds a dog-fight can be fined and possibly sent to prison.'

'Do you see dogs fighting here? Come on, show me one single dog fighting! This is just a birthday party and if a few people have brought their pet pooches with them, where's the harm in that?'

'Mr McManus, I didn't come up the River Lee in a bubble. Pet pooches? Don't make me laugh. All of these dogs are quite clearly fighting dogs and I have reliable information that you have been arranging a fight with fifty dogs to celebrate your fiftieth birthday.'

'Who was it told you that? Tell me who it was and I'll give him a fecking pruning, I can tell you!'

'Mr McManus, it's not only an offence actually to hold a dog-fight, it's an offence to arrange or promote or advertise a dog-fight, and it's also an offence for anyone to allow their land or premises to be used for the purposes of dog-fighting. On top of that, any betting on dog-fighting is also against the law.'

McManus puffed at his cigar two or three times and then spat out a fragment of leaf. 'I'm not telling you again, Detective Superintendent Whatever-the-feck-your-fecking-name-is, there's no dog-fighting going on here and I recommend that you toddle off before we have to assist you to toddle off, if you get my meaning. Go on. Up the yard with you.'

While he and Katie had been talking, the men around McManus had shifted in closer and were glaring with undisguised menace at Katie and Conor and the two detectives. The owners of the two white Staffies repeatedly yanked at their leads so that the dogs were jerked up and back, almost choking, foaming at the mouth and snarling at Katie and Conor as if they couldn't wait to rush up and attack them.

Katie looked around the field and saw that the rest of the crowd were beginning to gather around them, too, with more vicious-looking dogs. There were several pit bulls, as well as boxers and mastiffs and a huge Rhodesian ridgeback. The mood of the crowd was so threatening that she could almost feel it in the air, like a storm approaching.

One of the men beside McManus came limping close up to Katie. He had bristly grey hair and a diagonal scar on his left cheek and was wearing silver earrings in both ears. His faded denim jacket was embellished with studs and chains and skull brooches.

'C'm'ere to me, girl,' he said, hoarsely, 'The Guzz is asking you polite-like to leave, so my advice to you and the rest of these razzers is to do what he asks and go. This is his birthday party, got it, and it took him weeks of time and trouble to fix up the dog-fight to end all dog-fights, but there's nobody going to get hurt except you if you stay here.'

Katie looked up at him. His eyes were jaundiced and he smelled strongly of drink.

'Did McManus tell you to say that?' she asked him.

'I'm telling you myself, girl. So do us all a favour and fecking feck off.'

Katie turned to Detectives Markey and O'Mara. 'Did you catch that, you two?'

'We did so,' said Detective Markey, giving her the thumbs up.

Katie walked back to Inspector Carroll who was still waiting with his officers beside their cars.

'How's it going?' asked Inspector Carroll.

'McManus is denying that there's going to be any dog-fight here today, but his skanky henchman has just openly admitted that there is, and that McManus arranged it. Both of my detectives heard him say so and I've recorded him on my lapel mic, as well as McManus making threats against us.'

'So what are you aiming to do now?'

'I think we need to be out the gap now as quick as we can because this crowd is starting to get ugly and I don't want anyone hurt. But I intend to arrest McManus and he's coming with us. They won't carry on this dog-fighting without him. It's supposed to be his birthday celebration, after all.'

Inspector Carroll looked at the gathering crowd with his eyes narrowed.

'You thought this out beforehand, didn't you, ma'am?'

'What? Killing two birds with one arrest? It was one of the options I was thinking about, I have to admit. Under the circumstances, though, I don't think we have any alternative.'

'It's health and safety I'm bothered about, ma'am. I don't know. There's over a hundred and fifty here, I'd say, and they don't look like they'd hesitate to assault a garda or turn a patrol car over. And I'm speaking from bitter experience.'

'I'm arresting McManus,' Katie told him. 'If your officers can, please come with me.'

'I'm afraid I'm going to have to question the wisdom of this, ma'am,' said Inspector Carroll. 'You know how I feel, but given the situation I think the wisest course of action is for us to withdraw and leave the ISPCA inspectors to record what they can and file a report.'

Katie closed her eyes for a moment to restrain herself. She could hear dogs yapping and people shouting and amplified music playing. Then she opened her eyes and said, 'I'm arresting McManus, Kenny, and you and your officers are going to assist me. If you have any doubts about it, that's an order. You can make a complaint to the Ombudsman after, if you feel that you have to.'

Inspector Carroll looked grim, but he didn't answer back and he beckoned to his seven burly uniformed gardaí in their yellow high-viz jackets. Once they were gathered around him, he said, 'Detective Superintendent Maguire has decided that she has sufficient cause to bring in McManus. You'll escort her while she does so and do what's necessary to ensure her safety. We'll take McManus directly to St Michael's Road and hold him there.'

Peter O'Dwyer said, 'What about us?'

'To be honest with you, Peter, I recommend that you leave, too,' said Katie. 'If I'm right, there'll be no dog-fighting here once we take McManus away, but I think the punters are going to be more than a little thick about it.'

'These people don't scare us. Neither do their dogs. Especially not their dogs.'

'All the same. Go.'

With the Tipperary gardaí flanking her on either side, as well as Detectives Markey and O'Mara, Katie walked back to Guzz Eye McManus. He was counting out fifty-euro notes into the hand of a man with slicked-back grey hair and a green bow tie and a ginger three-piece suit.

She went right up to him and laid her hand on his shoulder. 'Mr McManus, I'm arresting you for setting up a dog-fight, contrary to section fifteen of the Animal Health and Welfare Act 2014, and in particular to paragraphs one, two and four of that section. Would you come along with me, please?'

Guzz Eye McManus ignored her and carried on counting out the money.

'There,' he said, 'four hundred and fifty on Henchy's mutt.'

'Mr McManus, you're under arrest,' said Katie even louder.

'Will you ever feck off and stop bothering me,' McManus retorted. 'Dermot, what are the odds on that Presa Canario? Holy Jesus, that's a killer dog and a half!'

Katie stepped back and nodded to the gardaí. They pushed their way past the men surrounding McManus, took hold of his arms and wrenched them behind his back so that he dropped his cigar and his mobile phone into the grass.

'*What in the name of all the Christian saints do you bastards think you're doing?*' he screamed at them. The gardaí said nothing, but clicked a pair of handcuffs on him. Then they pushed him as quickly as they could towards the Garda van, humping him up bodily every time his knees gave way.

'Let him go!' screamed a woman in the crowd, and then another woman screeched out, 'Let him be, you sons of bitches! It's his birthday!' and yet another woman shouted, 'You won't be laughing when he takes a bite out of your arse!'

McManus twisted his head around and roared at Katie with his face almost maroon with anger, '*You're going to regret this, you fecking witch! You're going to regret this for the rest of your life! Sean! Michael! Gearoid! Don't just fecking stand there!'*

The hard core of men who had been surrounding McManus started to jog forward, with their two dogs wheezing and straining at their leads. The boozy man in the denim jacket stumbled up to Katie and tried to snatch her arm, but she ducked sideways out of his reach and raised both of her hands in the *bajiquan* style that her martial arts instructor had taught her.

'Don't you even think about it,' she warned him.

He staggered in the clumpy grass and tried to snatch her again, but this time she crouched down, whirling her arms, and gave him a short explosive *fa jin* punch in the chest. He dropped backwards without a sound and lay on the ground staring at the sky, stunned.

Now both of the men with Staffies let them off their leads. The two dogs came running towards Katie and Conor as fast as bullets.

Katie began to run towards the Toyota, but Conor took three or four quick steps backwards, almost as if he were dancing, and then stopped and stuck two fingers in his mouth and whistled. At first the whistle was low-pitched, but then it rose to a high piercing trill, and he kept it up for nearly a quarter of a minute.

The two Staffies froze, panting, with their tongues hanging out. They both seemed totally bewildered, as if they had forgotten who or what they were supposed to be chasing after, and had even forgotten that they were dogs.

One of their owners shouted, 'Whitey! Whitey! What in the name of God's got into you, you stupid fecking plonker? *Kill*, do you hear me? *Kill!'*

The dog called Whitey looked around, but when he did so Conor began to whistle again and this time his whistling was so shrill that Katie could hardly hear it. Immediately the two Staffies both made strange creaking noises in their throats and settled down in the grass with their heads resting on their paws. Katie could see that Conor's whistling was having an effect on the other dogs in the crowd, too, almost all of which had pricked up their ears and appeared to be mesmerized.

Still bellowing and cursing, Guzz Eye McManus had now been shut up in the Garda van and the Tipperary gardaí were climbing back into their patrol cars. Inspector Carroll remained standing by his BMW, waiting to make sure that Katie was safe, while Detective Markey took hold of her elbow and hurried her towards the Toyota. Detective O'Mara stayed close behind her to shield her in case the crowd started throwing stones or beer bottles.

Conor caught up with her and said, 'Let's get the giodar on, shall we? Those two mutts aren't going to stay hypnotized for very long.'

Katie was about to climb into the Land Cruiser when she heard a low roar of discontentment from the crowd. It sounded like the beginnings of an avalanche, or an ebb tide sliding over pebbles. It had obviously just got through to them that the Garda convoy was actually leaving, and that they were taking Guzz Eye McManus with them, and because of that there would be no celebratory dog-fight.

'Come on, ma'am,' Detective O'Mara urged her, holding the door open for her.

But Katie turned around and saw that the crowd was surging towards them and some of them had broken into a run. She had witnessed what had happened last year when there had been a riot outside the Cork County Council offices because of water charges. Two Garda patrol cars had been seriously damaged, with smashed windows, and a third had been set on fire. Five gardaí had needed hospital treatment and one sergeant had been burned so badly that he had been forced to retire.

Inspector Carroll clearly shared Katie's concern because he stepped forward to face the crowd with two gardaí close beside him and held up both of his hands.

'Let's all calm down now!' he shouted. 'We want no trouble and nobody hurt! McManus has been lawfully arrested and he'll be treated fairly, I can promise you that! Don't make it necessary for me to arrest anybody else!'

'Let the Guzz go, you bastards!' yelled one of the men at the front of the crowd. 'If you don't let him go, we're coming over there to get him out!'

'We're not letting him go!' Inspector Carroll shouted back at him. 'You know as well as I do that dog-fighting is illegal! I'm asking you all peacefully to leave this field and take your children and your dogs with you! Like I say, McManus will be treated with the greatest of respect and he will probably be released on station bail by this evening!'

'Fecking let him out, you manky razzer!' screeched one young woman. 'This is a free country, right? If a few dogs want to have a play together, it's no fecking business of yours!'

An empty Tanora bottle came flying out of the crowd and hit the Garda van with a loud clonk. Then another bottle, and another, and three or four wooden pallets.

'Calm down now, settle Ballyduff!' Inspector Carroll called out. 'We're catching all of this on our video cameras, all right, so anybody who causes a breach of the peace is liable to be identified and charged! So break it up, do you hear me? Break it up and leave quietly!'

Twenty-nine

More bottles were tossed and one of them struck Inspector Carroll on the shoulder. The gardaí who had already climbed into their patrol cars now piled out again and the two gardaí beside Inspector Carroll drew out their ASP extendable batons.

Katie went over to Inspector Carroll. 'It looks like I've badly misjudged this,' she admitted. 'I thought that once we'd lifted McManus the rest of them would call it a day.'

A Murphy's bottle bounced on the ground next to her and knocked her on the ankle.

'Let the Guzz go!' the crowd began to chant. 'Let the Guzz go!'

Now an uprooted fence post landed next to her, still wound around with barbed wire. This was followed by more bottles and then a triangular lump of concrete. Five or six young men ran up to the Garda van and tried to pull open its doors. When they found that the doors were locked, they began to pummel on the van's side panels and rock it from side to side.

'I'm calling for backup,' said Inspector Carroll. 'There's no way these gowls are going to calm down. And I think we'll have to let McManus go.'

The crowd had almost completely encircled them now and although they were still keeping a cautious distance they continued to chant 'Let the Guzz go! Let the Guzz go! Stinking razzer bastards, let the Guzz go!' Although it was only mid-afternoon, Katie could see that some of them were very drunk and eager for a fight. She knew that it would only take one bold character to run up and start attacking them and the rest of the crowd would follow. She and Conor and the gardaí could be very badly beaten, or even killed.

Inspector Carroll raised his hands again and shouted out, 'All right! Listen up, will you! We're letting McManus go! Do you hear me? For the sake of keeping the peace, we're letting him go!'

At that moment, though, quite unexpectedly, the two white Staffies came tearing out from between the legs of the crowd, heading straight towards him with their teeth bared and barking so harshly that they sounded as if they were screaming. They had snapped out of the trance that Conor's whistling had induced and now they seemed even more aggressive than before.

Katie didn't have time to think of alternatives. Both dogs would have been trained from birth to be killers – not only killers of other dogs, but of any animal or person that they were ordered to attack. If they didn't, their owners would punish them with hours of agony – beating and burning and whipping – and that was what made them so relentless.

The Staffies were almost within leaping distance when Katie reached under her jacket and tugged out her Smith & Wesson Airweight revolver. She aimed it with both hands and fired. The first dog she hit when it was still in mid-air and half of its face burst open in a spray of blood and bone splinters. It rolled and pirouetted like an Olympic diver and then dropped with a heavy thud into the grass, its legs shuddering with shock.

She half-turned and shot the second Staffie twice, once in the chest and then point-blank between the eyes. It flopped over sideways, its lip curling as if it were smiling sardonically. The entry wound in its head was round and neat, like a third eye, but the back of its skull had been blown off and its brains were plastered all the way down to its tail.

The crowd fell utterly silent. The only sound now was the amplified music on the other side of the field, playing 'Dicey Reilly'. The young men stopped thumping on the sides of the Garda van and retreated. Two or three people in the crowd dropped bottles on to the ground, deterred from throwing them.

Katie raised her revolver so that the muzzle pointed skywards, but kept it raised.

'Time we left now, Inspector,' she said, doing her best to keep her voice steady.

Inspector Carroll nodded to the gardaí around him and they collapsed their ASP batons and returned to their patrol cars. Conor and Detectives Markey and O'Mara climbed back into the Land Cruiser.

Katie was the last to climb aboard. She stood facing the crowd with the two bloodied white Staffies lying dead at her feet, and even though the crowd stared back at her as if they were willing her to drop down dead beside the dogs, none of them made a move towards her, and they all stayed silent.

You need to stay composed, Kathleen. But you also need to look grim – as if you'll shoot anyone without hesitation if they try to attack you or set a dog on you.

She was sorely tempted to tell the crowd what she thought of them for showing up to a dog-fight like this, and that the Staffies had at least met a quick and painless death, rather than being ripped to pieces in the ring. However, she decided it was prudent to say nothing. She didn't want to risk breaking the spell.

She took her seat in the Land Cruiser and slammed the door, but she lowered her window and kept her revolver in full view as they turned around and followed the van and the other cars out of the field. They bounced back along the track to Cappamurra Bridge and then turned south towards Dundrum. As soon as they reached the R661, which led straight into Tipperary, the patrol cars put on their flashing lights and sirens and drove as fast as they could, occasionally touching 90 kph.

'Well, I made a hames of that all right,' she said to Conor.

Conor frowned and cupped around his ear. 'What?'

'I said I made a bags of that. Thank the Lord none of the media showed up.'

'Oh, right! Sorry – I'm still deaf from those gunshots. I wish I'd known you were so determined to arrest McManus.'

'I thought, well – he's the ringleader, after all.'

'Katie – I know how sick he makes you feel, but you under-estimated how popular he is and how much power he has. He's always handing out money to help sick people and giving sweets to the kids. Last Christmas he gave five and a half thousand euros to Saint Vincent de Paul. Even the tax commissioners leave him alone.'

'We've scooped him now, though,' said Katie.

'Sure, yes, but he'll be out again in five minutes flat. You know that as well as I do. In one way, though, I'm not too sorry – not from my point of view, anyhow, as a pet detective.'

'What do you mean?'

'Let's put it like this: at least he's the devil I know. When somebody's pedigree Pomeranian disappears, the Guzz is the first person I go to, to see if he knows who's hobbled it. He's like the clearing house for stolen dogs – either for fighting, if they're suitable, or for ransom, if they're not, or for selling on for breeding. Nine times out of ten he'll be able to find it for me.'

Katie shook her head. 'Just because he makes life easier for you, Conor, that's no excuse. That's like me saying that I should let the Callahan and Creasey gangs carry on shooting each other because at least they're saving me from having to arrest them for drug-smuggling and they're harming nobody else.'

Detective Markey turned around from the front passenger seat and said, 'You can't be after blaming yourself, ma'am. A dog-fight on that scale – Jesus, we should have been able to set up a major operation to lift everybody there. If it had been my decision, I wouldn't have hesitated for a moment to collar McManus. And you're a fantastic shot. Hitting that dog when it was right in the middle of jumping – that was amazing.'

'You're not angling for promotion by any chance, are you, Nick?' asked Detective O'Mara.

* * *

Katie and Inspector Carroll entered the interview room together. Guzz Eye McManus was sitting at the table with Sergeant

Kehoe. In the far corner, with his arms folded, sat another uniformed garda, at least six foot five inches tall, with a blue-shaven Neanderthal chin. He looked quite capable of picking up McManus like a big fat wheezy baby, putting him over his knee, and spanking him with a wooden spoon.

Katie sat down opposite McManus and laced her fingers together. 'Mr McManus, you've been formally charged now with three offences under the Animal Health and Welfare Act. Inspector Carroll will be forwarding the paperwork to the Tipperary South state solicitor first thing tomorrow morning. Have you anything to say for yourself at this stage?'

'I have, yes,' said McManus, fixing Katie with his left eye and slowly stroking the septum of his nose with the ball of his thumb as if it were some kind of mafia-style gesture. '*Póg mo thóin.*'

'I see. "Kiss my arse." Is that all?'

McManus nodded.

'Very well, then,' said Katie, standing up. 'If that's everything, I'll be seeing you in court.'

McManus closed his eyes for a moment, and let out a dismissive *pfff!*

* * *

On the steps outside the Garda station, Conor and Detectives Markey and O'Mara were comparing notes with the ISPCA inspectors before they left for Cork. Inspector Carroll took Katie aside.

'What happened today at the dog-fight . . . who knows for sure like . . . but there could be some repercussions. It depends if the dog owners make a complaint, although I doubt if they will.'

'I'm aware of that, Inspector, but I believe I can justify everything I did.'

'All the same, if the Ombudsman starts looking into it, I'd like you to know that you'll have my support, one hundred per cent. In my opinion it was far too risky, arresting McManus, but you went ahead with it anyway. I'm not going to pretend that I didn't disagree with you, but it's too late now. If nothing else, he'll be given a hefty fine, or at least have to drop some money into the court poor box.'

Katie shrugged. 'That won't exactly make his guzzy eyes water, will it? But it would be something, I suppose.'

'As for the dogs you shot, ma'am . . . there's plenty of evidence that they were a lethal threat to all of us. If you hadn't hit that first dog when you did, it could well have torn my throat out.'

Katie gave him the faintest smile. 'Thank you for everything, Inspector. Don't worry. We'll catch those scummers one day. I only hope that when they die and go to hell all of the dogs they've ever tortured and killed are waiting for them, and that they're starving.'

Thirty

Detective Ó Doibhilin rang the doorbell for the second time but there was still no answer. He turned to Garda Bryony Leary and said, 'Wherever she's got herself to, it doesn't seem like she's here. I reckon we'll have to come back later.'

Garda Leary was plump and pale, with a brunette bun and a beauty spot, and a businesslike air about her. She nodded towards the house next door. 'I noticed the curtain twitching like. Maybe her neighbour knows where she is.'

Detective Ó Doibhilin leaned back from the porch so that he could see next door's living-room window and was just in time to see the curtain hurriedly tugged back.

'Come on,' he said, and they walked around and knocked at the door. The door knocker was in the shape of a gnome, or a leprechaun, with a leering grin on its face. He knocked again and this time the door was opened up and an elderly woman in a flowery apron and nylon curlers appeared.

'Yes? What are you after? I don't buy nothing on the doorstep.'

Detective Ó Doibhilin showed her his ID card. 'I don't mean to disturb you, ma'am, but would you have any notion where Mrs Dennehy is from next door?'

'Maggie Dennehy is it you're looking for?'

'That's right. Would you know where she is and what time she might be coming back?'

The elderly woman said, 'She's not gone out.'

'You're sure about that? We've been ringing at her doorbell and there's no reply so.'

285

'She's not gone out, I can assure you of that. Her husband Bernie, now *he's* out. He came in last night and then he went out again and he's not back yet so God alone knows where he's gone gowling off to.'

'She couldn't have nipped out without you seeing her maybe? Just to get the messages or something like that?'

The elderly woman shook her head emphatically. 'If I don't see her, I can always hear her banging her front door twice, because it gets stuck when the weather's damp, and then I know for sure that she's gone. I haven't seen or heard her since all those fellers came around to see her.'

'What fellers was that?' asked Garda Leary.

'I never saw any of them before, but there was five of them I'd say, maybe six. They came in and they was in there for maybe a half an hour or more and then they all left. Two cars they came in, a silvery one and a blacky one.'

'Would you reck them again if you saw them?'

'Oh, yes. I'm fierce terrible when it comes to the names but I have a great memory for the faces all right.'

'But you think Maggie Dennehy could still be at home but she's just not answering?' asked Garda Leary.

'She hasn't gone and if she hasn't gone she's still there,' the elderly woman told her.

As they walked back around to the Dennehy house Detective Ó Doibihiln said, 'That old wan should have been a detective, do you know what I mean? She has the real gileage for it.'

They went back up to the green front door and Detective Ó Doibhilin pressed the doorbell again. There was still no answer, so he took out the leatherette wallet he carried in his inside coat pocket and opened it up. Inside was a selection of pin lock jigglers – skeleton keys for cylinder locks. He peered at the door to identify the type of lock and then prodded at it with one jiggler after another until it suddenly clicked open.

'You're some genius,' said Garda Leary.

'My father worked for the Lock Doctor, that's all. I was brought up unlocking locks that I shouldn't have been, like the drawer in my brother's desk with his girlie mags in it.'

Detective Ó Doibhilin opened the door wide and called out, 'Mrs Dennehy? Mrs Dennehy? It's the police here, Mrs Dennehy! We just need to have a word with you, that's all!'

When there was still no answer he stepped into the hallway and Garda Leary followed him.

'Mrs Dennehy?'

He stopped, and sniffed, and then he said, 'Oh, no. Please don't tell me. Can you smell what I smell?'

They went into the living room. The curtains were drawn, so the room was gloomy, but there was sufficient light for them to be able to see Maggie Dennehy lying on the couch.

'Just open the curtains a little way,' said Detective Ó Doibhilin. 'Put on your gloves.'

Garda Leary snapped on a pair of black latex gloves and then went over to pull back the curtains. The brown smells of human faeces and early decomposition were not yet overwhelming, but they pervaded the whole room and Detective Ó Doibhilin couldn't help taking them in with every breath. After he had put on his forensic gloves, he tugged out his handkerchief and pressed it over his nose and his mouth.

He approached Maggie Dennehy and stared down at her. Then, very cautiously, he tried to lift up one of the hands that was crossed saint-like over her breasts. It was totally stiff. She was still in full rigor, so he guessed that she had died less than twenty-four hours ago. One eyelid was fully closed and the other creepily half-open, but both her eyeballs had now sunk deep into her head, and her face was a pale lavender colour. Her hands were lavender, too, and her fingernails were white. All of the blood had drained out of them and would now be pooled in the lowest extremities of her body.

Her neck was puffy, but he could clearly see that there was a deep purplish groove around her throat where the washing line had cut into it.

'Right, girl, let's get out of here,' said Detective Ó Doibhilin, muffled behind his handkerchief. Garda Leary was keeping her mouth tight shut and did nothing but nod.

Once outside again, they took two or three breaths of fresh air. Then Detective Ó Doibhilin called Detective Sergeant Begley.

'What's the story, Michael?' Detective Sergeant Begley asked him, briskly. He sounded as if he were hurrying along one of the station's corridors. 'How's it coming on with that Dennehy woman?'

'She's not being too cooperative, sir. In fact, we've found her deceased. Within the last day or so, I'd say, judging by the state of her.'

'Christ on a bike. Serious? All right. I'll give Superintendent Pearse the heads-up and I'll send you some backup, whoever's available, and the Technical Bureau, too. DS Maguire is up in Tipp this afternoon, chasing after those dog-fighters, but I'll text her as well.'

'Her nosy old neighbour told us there were five or six fellows around here yesterday, in two different vehicles,' said Detective Ó Doibhilin. 'She said they stayed here for thirty minutes maybe. Then Bernie Dennehy came home but he went out again after, and of course she hasn't seen him since, although I didn't tell her that he was dead, too.'

'What was the cause of death there, Michael? Any ideas?'

'I'd say strangulation of one sort or another. I suppose it could have been suicide, but she's lying on the sofa in the sitting room so if she'd hung herself somebody would have had to cut her down and carry her there.'

'Okay, Michael. I'll come up there myself and take a look. Jesus. This gets more and more complimicated by the minute.'

* * *

Katie's iPhone pinged as they were driving past Watergrasshill, less than twenty-five minutes away from the Cork City outskirts.

'Mother of God,' she told Detectives Markey and O'Mara. 'It's from Ó Doibhilin. He went to question Mrs Dennehy about

Bernie Dennehy being shot and he's found her dead. He says she looks like she's been hanged or garrotted.'

'Jesus. Does he know how long she's been there?' asked Detective O'Mara.

'She's still in rigor so it couldn't have happened much later than yesterday afternoon sometime.'

'What do you reckon, ma'am? Do you think maybe Dennehy killed her himself? They had this strange kind of arrangement, didn't they, what with him selling her off to Niall Gleeson for sex? Maybe he'd just had enough of it and killed them both.'

'But in that case, why did he go after Davy Dorgan?' asked Detective Markey.

'Well, we still don't know what his motive was,' said Katie. 'That was the whole reason why Ó Doibhilin went to talk to Mrs Dennehy. We'll be interviewing Dorgan about the shooting tomorrow morning in any case. Maybe Dennehy just flipped and wanted to take his revenge on everybody who'd ever thwarted him, like. It does happen. Remember that history teacher from the Pres last year – the one who stabbed his wife and his daughter and then came into school and tried to stab the boys in his class?'

'Oh, I remember him all right. Meaney his name was. That was one way of teaching his pupils a lesson they'd never forget in a hurry. Almost cut the nose off of one of them.'

Katie prodded out Detective Sergeant Begley's number. As she did so Conor leaned close and said, 'You'll be tied up tonight, then?'

'I will, yes, Conor. I'll be staying at the station most likely. What's the time? We're supposed to be interviewing the fiancé of that girl Saoirse at eight . . . that poor girl who was shot and then burned in the attic.'

'Fair play,' said Conor. 'But I'll be back at Gabriel guest house if you need to get in touch.'

In front of Detectives Markey and O'Mara he said this in a very flat, disinterested voice. He didn't want them to realize that if she found enough time when she was finished at Anglesea Street, he was inviting her to come back to the guest house.

'I'll call you if I need to,' she told him. At the same time, though, out of sight of her detectives, she grasped his hand.

Detective Sergeant Begley answered her call. 'We're here now at Nash's Boreen,' he told her. 'Inspector O'Rourke has come along with me just to make a general assessment and I have O'Brien and Buckley with me, too. Bill Phinner and his team turned up about ten minutes ago and they're starting to take pictures.'

'I'll be calling the deputy state pathologist as soon as I get in,' Katie told him. 'As soon as the forensics are all completed at the scene I want Mrs Dennehy's body taken to CUH for an urgent post-mortem. We need to know how she died, and the sooner the better.'

Katie sat back, thinking, while the lights of Cork City gradually came closer. She wished in a way that she hadn't tried to intervene in the dog-fighting that afternoon, especially since she had ended up shooting those two Staffordshire bull terriers. She felt so strongly about the cruelty that was inflicted on the fighting dogs, though, and about the misery that was caused to so many families because their dogs were stolen for fighting or breeding, or to extort a ransom out of them. What if that ever happened to Barney?

'I'll have to file a report about today,' she told Conor. 'What happened at the dog-fight, I mean.'

'If I were you, I'd make it short and snappy and straight to the point,' said Conor.

'Snappy? That's a good word to describe it.'

'What I'm saying is, none of those knackers are going to make a complaint against you. What are they going to say? "We were holding a massive fifty-dog fight like, and this detective superintendent came in and messed it up for us"? I don't think so.'

Thirty-one

Shortly after she arrived at Anglesea Street and switched on the lights in her office Inspector O'Rourke returned from Nash's Boreen.

'The press are all up there,' he said. 'I gave them a simple statement to the effect that Mrs Dennehy had been found deceased and that we're looking into the circumstances. They asked, of course, if it had any connection to Bernie Dennehy's death and the shooting of Davy Dorgan, but all I told them was that our investigation was still in its preliminary stages.'

Katie gave him a wry smile and shook her head. 'Good man yourself, Francis. Thank God I'm not some poor *Echo* reporter trying to wheedle a story out of *you*.'

'But, well . . . it very much looks as if Ó Doibhilin's first guess was spot-on,' Inspector O'Rourke told her. 'There's the cut-off remnants of a washing line dangling from the banisters. It's tied with some fierce tight knots, like it's had a heavy weight hanging from it, and the marks on Mrs Dennehy's neck correspond with the pattern of the cord.'

'So you think that she could have committed suicide?'

'It looks that way. Unless she was hung by those five or six feens that her neighbour saw and Bernie cut her down when he came home. Maybe that would have given him the motive for going after Dorgan.'

'Oh, stop,' Katie told him. 'I think we've done quite enough speculating. Dr Kelley's still in Cork so I've left a message for her and I'm hoping she'll be able to start her post-mortem early

291

tomorrow. What we desperately need is some tangible evidence.'

God must have had overheard her because at that very moment there was a rap at her door and Detective Inspector Mulliken came in, looking tired, with his Fota Golf Club tie askew, but holding up a torn-off sheet of notepaper as if he had won a few hundred euros on the lottery.

'Not interrupting, am I, ma'am?' he asked her. 'I've just come off the phone with Simon Mitchell in Belfast. I told him about that tip-off that Detective Sergeant Ni Nuallán picked up and he contacted the SRR immediately. He couldn't admit it in so many words, because they no longer have an official presence in the province. In some mysterious way, though, he managed to come up with a whole rake of background information about Davy Dorgan.'

'That's a result, Tony,' said Katie. 'What did he tell you?'

'Let's see,' said Detective Inspector Mulliken, reading from his notes. 'Davy Dorgan is the second son of Bryan Dorgan, who was the second-in-command of the IRA in Larne during the Troubles. Bryan Dorgan's other three sons all left Antrim and didn't want anything to do with the dissident republican movement, but Davy was different. When he was growing up on the Seacourt estate he was constantly harassed and attacked by UDA thugs.

'It seems like he was beaten up several times because of his homosexuality as much as his republican sympathies. When he was sixteen he was attacked by ten young men who cracked his skull with a flashlight and almost killed him. After that incident his behaviour became increasingly aggressive and disturbed, and he was arrested several times for attacking members of the Larne UDA. He was suspected to have stabbed and killed one of them at an eleventh-night bonfire, but it could never be proved.'

'Well, all this psychotic behaviour seems to fit,' said Katie. 'Were you given any information about his younger sister?'

'Yes . . . the Dorgans had a daughter Cecilia five years after their youngest son, Warren, was born. Mrs Dorgan fell pregnant one more time after that, at the age of forty-three, but both she and the baby died during a difficult childbirth at the Antrim Area Hospital.'

Katie thought about Adeen telling her why her brother had 'stampit' on her doll, Bindy – Adeen, or Cissy rather, now that she knew her real name.

'The Christmas after Mrs Dorgan's death there was a devastating fire in Curwen's Stores in Larne High Street,' Detective Inspector Mulliken went on. 'Seven people were trapped in the blaze and three of them died. The Curwens are a Protestant family so it was immediately suspected that the fire had been started by republicans. It was unusual, this fire, in that it was started more or less simultaneously in various departments of the store, and it was explosive.

'The PSNI forensics team discovered that it had been started by TPA – triethylaluminium thickened with polyisobutylene and diluted with n-hexane so it didn't burst into flame until the n-hexane evaporated. There – I managed to say all of that without spitting on you! But it was exactly the same compound that was used to set the Toirneach Damhsa dance studio alight. Exactly. Even down to the one per cent polyisobutylene.'

'Did they find out who started that fire at Curwen's?' asked Katie.

'They did, yes. The non-existent intelligence service who aren't officially in the province had a squealer and this squealer pointed the finger at Bryan and Davy Dorgan and two other IRA shitehawks. The PSNI went to pick them up but they'd gone – Bryan and Davy and his young sister, too. Bryan went to the UK and died in Liverpool of lung cancer eighteen months ago, but they never knew what became of Davy and his sister – not until you found out that they were living under the name of Jepson.'

Katie stood up and went to the window. It was dark outside now and raindrops were sparkling on the glass. She felt worn down – not only because of everything she had done today, but because of the constant warring she had to deal with between Catholics and Protestants, drug-dealers and pimps and people-smugglers and racketeers and frauds. Apart from that, there was all the internal politicking of An Garda Síochána she had to untangle. And Conor, too, expecting her to be passionate and attentive and give her every spare moment of her time.

She felt like throwing up her hands and shouting *Stop! Stop talking to me, stop expecting so much from me! Let me have just one day on my own, doing absolutely nothing at all but taking Barney for a walk on the beach, and then lying on my couch with a warm crochet blanket snuggled around me, sipping tea and eating barmbrack and listening to Claudie Mackula playing the flute and the bodhran and singing 'Where Everything Ends and Everything Begins', because that's the way I feel at the moment!*

That's the way I feel.

She turned away from the window and asked, 'Did they find out where Bryan Dorgan got it from, this TPA?'

'It turns out that several plastics companies in Antrim use it for moulding, and a semiconductor company, too. The chemicals they used to burn down Curwen's were stolen by one of Dorgan's cronies from a firm in the Willowbank Business Park called Plastishape . . . and, here's the cruncher, Plastishape discovered that since their last inventory, three weeks ago, a whole heap more TPA has gone missing. For some reason they never reported it. Embarrassed, most likely.'

'I think we can guess where that ended up,' said Katie. 'Jesus – do they have no security at all, these Plasti-people? Anyway, what about Kyna's tip-off about Davy Dorgan's plan to shoot this British defence secretary? What intelligence did your friend find out about that?'

'Well, that's our most critical concern of all. Ian Bowthorpe's attending a dinner in Dublin this evening, but he'll be on his way here to Cork tomorrow afternoon. The information you got from DS Ni Nuallán, that looks as if it could very well be sound. Three of the IRA men who used to associate with the Dorgans were seen to leave their homes at about 1500 hours this afternoon and drive south. Two of them have reputations as hit men and one has a long track record as a bomb-maker, which is why the non-existent security service have been keeping a fairly constant eye on them. Their car is being tracked, even though they don't know it.'

'Where are they now?'

'Simon thought at first they might be heading for Dublin, but they've already gone past the Mad Cow and the last information he received was that they were parked outside Harte's Bar and Grill in Kildare.'

'Okay. I suppose even hit men have to eat. He'll keep up us to date with their progress?'

'Oh, sure, yes. Minute by minute. But the non-existent security service have already alerted the National Surveillance Unit and the NSU have had armed officers following these two ever since they crossed the border. They're reluctant to stop them yet because they want to see if they're heading for Cork, and if they are, who they're going to be linking up with.'

'Davy Dorgan, presumably. But the NSU are right not to stop them too soon. If we lift them now, we could allow Dorgan time to set up another attempt. Or, if he doesn't, we may never be able to prove that it was him who planned it – that's if it was.'

'Of course. And we want to rope in as many of these Authentic IRA as we can. There's a fair few faces up in Gurra that I'd like to be looking at through the bars of a cell.'

Katie said, 'That's good work, Tony. Keep me posted. Right now I want to go downstairs and see how O'Donovan and Scanlan are getting on. They're interviewing the fiancé of that girl who was shot in the Toirneach Damhsa attic. But it's looking almost certain, wouldn't you say, that Dorgan was behind it? The shooting, and the fire? All we have to do is find out who else was involved, if anybody, and then prove it.'

Detective Inspector Mulliken folded up his sheet of notepaper. 'I hope I'm not wrong, ma'am, but I'm beginning to get a sense that things are joining up like. It's what I call my jigsaw feeling. Suddenly you see a piece of sky that fits, and then a piece of tree, and before you know it you have half a garden.'

* * *

Douglas Cleary was crying. He was sitting at an angle in his chair in the interview room, with one hand pressed over his mouth, and tears were trickling down his cheeks and over his fingers. Just as Katie came in, Detective Scanlan was passing him a box of paper tissues.

'Douglas here is still feeling very distressed about Saoirse,' said Detective Scanlan as Katie sat down beside her.

'Where's O'Donovan?' asked Katie.

'He went to fetch some paperwork that he's forgotten.'

Katie nodded. The paper in 'paperwork' was usually wrapped round tobacco and Detective O'Donovan had almost certainly nipped outside for quick faggawn. She didn't blame him. They had all been under enough stress since the dance studio fire and it was Detective Dooley's funeral tomorrow. Anglesea Street was not only fraught but still in mourning.

Douglas Cleary was a thin young man in a fashionably slim-fitting brown suit. He had a nose as sharp as the pointer on a sundial and a small Vandyke beard. Behind his hand he was quietly mewling and every now and then he would let out an agonized sob.

'I knew there was something wrong between us,' he wept. 'I don't know how I knew, but I did. Up until maybe a month ago Saoirse and me were that close, do you know what I mean? But then I don't know . . . I started to get the feeling that she had her mind on something else. Or some*body* else, as it turned out. But whatever – I would never have wished her dead. I would never have wished her dead, even if I had lost her.'

'Of course not,' said Detective Scanlan sympathetically, while he dragged out another tissue and blew his nose. 'But you must have been angry with her for cooling off you like that.'

'Angry? No, I wasn't angry. I was more like flummoxed. I didn't really understand what was going on with her. I rang her when I was in Manchester and said that we needed to have a bit of a talk together when I got back, but of course—'

Douglas Cleary started crying again, as painfully as a small boy.

Katie said, 'Did you know any of the dancers in Toirneach Damhsa?'

'Some of them I knew, but not too well. Saoirse's friend Catriona, and a fellow called Brendan.'

'Did you know Ronan Barrett, the fellow they found with Saoirse?'

'No. Well, I did by sight. I'd seen him in the dance studio, but I only recognized him when I saw his picture on the telly.'

'And you didn't suspect that he and Saoirse might have had something going on between them? Not that we know that for sure, Douglas. They were found in the attic together, but that doesn't necessarily mean that they were having any kind of relationship.'

Douglas Cleary took a deep breath to steady himself. 'Does anybody know for sure why they were up in the attic together and not downstairs dancing with the rest of them?'

'No, Douglas, we don't,' said Katie. 'At the moment we have only theories.'

'Did you know Nicholas O'Grady, the dance instructor?' asked Detective Scanlan.

Douglas Cleary nodded.

'What did you think of him?'

Douglas Cleary shrugged.

'What would be the first word you would to use to describe him to somebody who didn't know him?'

'I suppose, gay. Not that I'm prejudiced or nothing like that. If somebody wants to be gay, that's their business as far as I'm concerned. He was a bit one-two-three-*whoops*! though, wasn't he?'

'You mean flamboyant?'

'That's it. But Saoirse thought he was fantastic. Best dance teacher she'd ever had.'

'Did you ever meet Danny Coffey, the owner?'

'I bumped into him once or twice when I was picking up Saoirse after rehearsals.'

'And how would you describe him?'

'Okay, I'd say. Kind of humpy, but maybe I never met him on a good day like.'

'Gay?'

Douglas Cleary thought for a moment. 'I don't know. I remember thinking that it smelled like he'd emptied half a bottle of aftershave over himself, and he had this gold earring in his ear. But I know heaps of guys like that and they're not gay.'

'Did you ever see any spats between the two of them, Coffey and O'Grady?'

'I never saw them together for long enough. There's only one thing I remember and that was when one of the rehearsals was over and Coffey said to O'Grady, "So when's that husband of yours going to be showing up? I have to lock up now!" I mean that kind of took me aback, a feller having a husband. First time I'd ever heard anybody say that.'

'Did Saoirse ever mention any arguments between them?'

Douglas Cleary shook his head. 'Most of the time Saoirse talked about what kind of a wedding she wanted, and where we were going to go on honeymoon. Gran Canaria, that's what she kept talking about. That's until the last few weeks, anyway. Then she seemed like she was off in a world of her own.'

Katie said, 'How well do you know Davy Dorgan?'

'Who? I don't know of anybody by that name.'

'You're sure? How often do you drink at the Templegate Tavern?'

'I've never been there. Is that up in Gurra? My flat's on the corner of Watercourse Road, right next door to the Constellation. Why would I go up there?'

'And you've never met Davy Dorgan? Or Davy Jepson, maybe?'

'No. Don't know either of them.'

Detective Scanlan said, 'That's all for now, Douglas. We may need to speak to you again in the next few days, so don't be leaving the country, will you? I'm just going to call a technician to come up and take your fingerprints and a DNA sample. It's nothing to worry about, the DNA sample – you don't get pricked like a blood sample. It's just a swab in your mouth with a cotton bud.'

'Okay,' said Douglas Cleary. But as Katie stood up to leave he said, 'Why didn't she try to get out? That little girl got out, didn't she? Why didn't Saoirse try to get out?'

Katie said, 'There was a reason, Douglas. It'll all come out later, I promise you.'

'I just don't understand why she didn't try to get out.'

After they had left Douglas Cleary with one of Bill Phinner's technicians Katie and Detective Scanlan walked back to Katie's office.

'What's your opinion?' asked Katie.

'I don't think he had anything to do with it, to be fair. When he asked why his Saoirse hadn't tried to escape from the fire, that pretty much convinced me. If he'd known that she'd been shot, he wouldn't have been likely to ask that, even if he'd done it himself, or had some hit man do it for him.'

'I have to say I tend to agree with you. Either he's a pure good actor or else he's too wet to think of killing anybody.'

'By the way,' said Detective Scanlan, 'Robert's friend Kenny MacCarty rang this afternoon, when you were out. He'd heard from Mrs Dooley that we wanted to talk to him about Danny Coffey and Nicholas O'Grady shifting each other in the Roundy.'

'And?'

'He confirmed it almost exactly word for word the way Mrs Dooley told you. Including the fellow with the Belfast accent bursting in and attacking Danny Coffey, and the bartenders throwing him out. I emailed Kenny a picture of Davy Dorgan, on the chance that it might have been him. He took a look at it, but he said he couldn't be sure, because the place was black at the time and he only heard the scuffle rather than saw it.'

'Mother of God, it seems like this Davy Dorgan's everywhere,' said Katie. 'He's like foot-and-mouth disease.'

'Well, you know the cure for that, don't you, ma'am?' said Detective Scanlan. 'Shooting, and then burning.'

Thirty-two

Kyna was half an hour late in to work and when she arrived at the Templegate Tavern Davy Dorgan was already there. He was sitting at his usual table with his left leg thickly bandaged all the way up past his knee and covered in a white waterproof protector, and a pair of crutches was leaning against the wooden screen beside him.

Liam and Murtagh and Billy were sitting around him, as well as Kevan with his spotted dartboard face and Alroy, who was already so langered that he was having trouble pronouncing the simplest words.

Kyna had made a point of dressing much less provocatively this evening. She was wearing a simple black knee-length dress and black tights, and apart from her rings and earrings the only jewellery she was wearing was a necklace of shiny silver beads, almost as big as golf balls.

'How about fetching some refreshment over here?' Davy called out. 'Have pity on the poor disabled!'

'*Gobshite*,' muttered Patrick, the barman, under his breath, but Kyna came out from behind the bar and went across to ask Davy what he wanted to drink.

'My usual MiWadi, wee doll, and whatever these fellers want. What is it you're drinking, Alroy?'

'I'll be having Muff – Muff – Muffies, of coursh. Widda Padda shaysha.'

'Fetch him a pint of Murphy's with a Paddy's chaser, all right? Oh – and one more thing, wee doll, before you go.'

There was something in the tone of his voice that made Kyna's shoulders prickle. He looked up at her and he was smiling, but it was the deadliest smile she had ever seen on anybody's face, ever – like the snake in Disney's *Jungle Book*.

He knows, she thought. *He knows what Liam's told me.*

She glanced across at Liam, but as soon as she looked at him he turned away. *What a creep. He's only been after snitching on me. And to think I made myself craw sick to get that information out of him.*

'Come on, sir, I'm up the walls here,' she told Davy. 'What is it you want?'

Davy kept up that chilling, humourless smile. 'Sometimes young men get themselves persuaded to let out secrets that they shouldn't, did you know that?'

'I have no idea what you're talking about.'

'Oh, I believe you do. Now and again some manky floozie can cajole a young man into saying more than is good for his health, do you understand me now?'

'I'm sorry. I haven't a notion. Now, if you'll let me get on, I'll go and fetch your drinks for you.'

Davy suddenly lurched out to grab her wrist, but Kyna stepped back and with his bandaged leg he almost toppled off his chair.

'Don't you try to take the piss out of me, wee doll!' he hissed at her. 'I know what your game is! You're either a peeler or else you're the RIRA, spying for that Gerry Monaghan! So which is it?'

'You're cracked,' said Kyna. 'You need to take yourself off to St Stephen's, you do!'

Davy was about to say something else, but he restrained himself and sat back, although he lifted one finger and pointed at Kyna, as if to say, *Don't you worry, I'll have you. Make no mistake about it.*

Kyna went to fetch the drinks he had ordered. As she set them down on the table he said nothing, but he didn't take his eyes off her and he didn't blink. For her part, she didn't look at Liam once. She could guess why he had woken up this morning and thought that it would be safer if he confessed to Davy that he had told her too much. If Davy had found about his blabbing only after it was too late for him to change his plans, Liam would have ended up in the Lee, castrated and with his throat cut.

Kyna returned to the bar. 'I have to nip to the ladies' so,' she told Patrick. 'I won't be a minute.'

She went through the back of the bar but she didn't go the toilet. Instead, she took her short red coat off its peg and went straight out into the yard at the back, which was stacked with beer kegs and crates. The back gate was always locked, but she dragged over four beer crates, stacked them up, and then took off her high-heeled shoes and climbed up on to them. She balanced unsteadily on top of them for a moment, then dropped over into the alley behind the pub and started to run. She crossed diagonally over Cathedral Road and then down St Brigid's Road and McSwiney's Villas.

She didn't stop running until she had reached the white-painted frontage of another pub further down the hill, the Glenryan Tavern. Panting, she ducked into the entrance and pulled her iPhone out of her coat pocket. She glanced back up the road to make sure that nobody was following her and then she rang Katie.

'It's me, ma'am! I'm in the Glenryan Tavern, in Gurra!'

'What are you doing there?'

'It's that Liam. He's told Dorgan that I know about the hit on Ian Bowthorpe. Dorgan doesn't know for sure if I'm police or Óglaigh na hÉireann or some other IRA splinter group, but he made it clear that he's coming after me!'

Katie said, 'Where did you say you were again?'

'The Glenryan Tavern. It's down at the end of McSwiney's Villas.'

'I think I know it, yes. Look – I'll come and get you. Stay there, but keep well out of sight. You're sure you weren't followed when you left the Templegate?'

'I didn't see anybody. I said I was going to the ladies' and I was probably gone before Dorgan realized that I wasn't coming back.'

'All right. I'm only at the top of Summerhill at the moment so I won't be more than ten minutes.'

Two fat men in noisy waterproof jackets squeezed their way past Kyna in the doorway.

'Are you coming in, darling, or are you coming out?'

'Oh, sorry. I'm waiting for a friend.'

'How about a scoop while you're waiting? We promise we won't jump on you.'

'That's pure sweet of you boys, but I'm on a diet.'

'Sure like, darling, same as us two!' said one of them, grinning and slapping his stomach. 'We're on the well-known Guinness and chips and drisheen diet! Does wonders for the waistline!'

* * *

Katie arrived in her car exactly ten minutes later. She parked right outside the entrance to the Glenryan Tavern and leaned over to open the passenger door so that Kyna could run across the pavement and climb straight in. Then she sped off straight away, glancing in her mirror as she did so.

'Are you okay?' Katie asked her. 'Come on, fasten your seatbelt. I don't want you flying through the windscreen.'

'Shaken,' said Kyna. 'That Dorgan is a piece of work, isn't he? I never met a man before who made me shudder like him, not even Bobby Quilty. Jesus! The way Dorgan looks at you, you feel like he'd have no hesitation at all in slicing you wide open, and that he'd relish it, too.'

'You're best out of there now, anyway,' said Katie as they drove down Upper John Street towards the river. 'If Dorgan hadn't found out, it would have been a good idea for you to go in to work this evening, just in case he got suspicious about why you weren't there . . . but you're right, he's a total head-the-ball.'

'He'll be sure to be changing his plan now that he knows that I know,' said Kyna. 'Maybe with any luck he'll pull the plug on it and not try to shoot this Ian Bowthorpe after all.'

'His hit squad haven't turned round yet, Kyna. They've stopped in Kildare for the night at the house of a fellow called Tomas O'Bruadair who's known to the NSU as a dissident. They were tracking them by GPS when they first came over the border, but now they actually have a Ghost Team on them in case they try and swap cars. I last had a report about them an hour ago. They arrived at O'Bruadair's house at about half-past ten but there's been no sign of movement since.'

They started to drive along the river embankment. Kyna pressed one hand against her stomach and the other against her forehead.

'You're not feeling sick, are you?' Katie asked her. 'Do you want me to stop?'

Kyna shook her head. 'No – no thanks. I'm feeling the after-effects of Davy Dorgan, that's all. He genuinely scared me.'

'What do you want to do? Do you want me to drive you straight home? You can come back with me for a while if you like, but I'm staying overnight with Conor at the moment at the Gabriel guest house.'

'Oh come on, you don't want me intruding. Just take me home.'

'Look at the state of you la. You're white as a ghost. At least come and have a drink and settle yourself down.'

Kyna thought for a moment as they turned into MacCurtain Street. Then she said, 'All right. But only for a while. You're not my mother. You don't have to baby me.'

Katie patted Kyna's thigh and couldn't help laughing.

* * *

Conor was sitting in his midnight-blue dressing gown watching a TV programme about rhinoceros poachers when Katie and Kyna came in.

'Con . . . I hope you don't mind. Kyna's had a fair bit of a fright, to say the least. She's just come back for a drink and a chat to settle herself down.'

Conor switched off the television and said, 'Sure, that's absolutely fine. What happened, or shouldn't I ask?'

'Let's just say that she was threatened. You don't want to get yourself involved with the people she's been involved with. It's risky enough tangling with Guzz Eye McManus.'

'What would you like to drink, Kyna?' Conor asked her. 'I have some West Cork single malt if you'd like some . . . a glass or two of that is usually enough to make anyone feel mellow.'

Kyna took off her coat and sat down on the sofa and Katie sat next to her and held her hand.

'Whiskey . . . that sounds perfect,' said Kyna. 'I'm sorry if I'm interrupting your evening . . . I seem to be making a habit of it.'

'It's not a bother at all,' Conor told her. 'If you want to have a relationship with a detective superintendent you have to tolerate all kinds of interruptions – that's what I've learned, anyway. There's always somebody interrupting you by murdering somebody else while you're right in the middle of dinner together. If it's not that, there's some drug-dealer being stopped with ten kilograms of cocaine hidden in a chip van, just when you fancied going off for a walk on the beach.

'Besides,' he said, as he came over and handed her a large crystal tumbler of whiskey, 'I know that you and Katie have a special relationship. I'm not blind, or deaf.'

Katie looked up at him. She knew how sensitive he was, not only to Barney's feelings but to hers, but they hadn't talked about her affection for Kyna before now. She found it a considerable relief that she no longer had to pretend that she didn't find Kyna attractive.

Kyna must have felt the same way because she lifted her glass and said, '*Sláinte chugat!*' and smiled.

They talked about Davy Dorgan and the three Authentic IRA men who were on their way to Cork. They talked about Cissy Dorgan, too. She would be taken into care tomorrow by Tusla, so Katie intended to go and see her in hospital one more time before she went.

'We still need to know what she was doing in that attic,' said Katie. 'We also need to know if she saw what happened to Ronan Barrett and Saoirse MacAuliffe. The trouble is, she's absolutely terrified of her brother.'

'Holy Mary, she's not the only one,' said Kyna.

They also talked about Maggie Dennehy, and how she might have died. Dr Kelley had texted Katie to say that she would be able to carry out a post-mortem examination at about lunchtime tomorrow. After that, they told Kyna all about their raid on Guzz Eye McManus's fiftieth-birthday dog-fight.

'I never should have arrested him then and there,' said Katie. 'We should just have stayed back and observed and taken evidence. That's what Inspector Carroll advised me. McManus would have ignored us and carried on with the dog-fighting. He doesn't give a tinker's for the law, nor the ISPCA inspectors. Neither do any of the rest of those dog-fighters.

'I couldn't help myself, though. I'm too fond of dogs, that's my problem. When I saw all of those poor creatures there I couldn't allow them to tear each other to pieces. I know they're all dangerous, and most of them should probably be put down, but there's no need for them to suffer like that – especially when they're only suffering to line McManus's pocket.'

'Do you think you'll manage to get McManus up in front of a judge?' asked Kyna.

'I don't know. Hopefully. It depends on how determined Inspector Carroll is, and how devious McManus's lawyers turn out to be.'

Kyna reached across and stroked Katie's hair. 'Don't let it bother you. You did what you could and you saved a lot of dogs from being hurt.'

'Only for a while, though,' said Katie. 'McManus will probably hold those fights all over again.'

Conor poured them some more whiskey and now their conversation turned to Detective Dooley's funeral the next day. They were subdued for a while, but then they talked about the *feis* on Saturday, and about step-dancing, and both Katie and Kyna had stories to tell about their dance classes at school.

Katie said, 'Sister Bridget always told me that I looked like Bambi but I danced like a mule.'

'Oh, I was too springy, that was my problem,' said Kyna.

'"Anybody would think you were jumping up and down on a trampoline, Kyna!" that's what my dance teacher told me.'

* * *

They heard bells chiming in the distance and Katie said, 'My God, what time is it?'

'Two o'clock,' said Kyna, finishing the last of her glass of whiskey and standing up. 'I need to get home. I'll call for a Hailo.'

She staggered slightly as she reached for her coat. Conor held her elbow to steady her and Katie said, 'Lookit, why don't you stay? You're too fluttered to go home on your own. I'm sorry, it's our fault. We shouldn't have given you all that whiskey.'

'No, no, it's not your fault at all. It's my fault for drinking it. And anyway you've had just as much as me. Where's my phone? I'll call for a Hailo, don't worry.'

She found her iPhone in her coat pocket and sat down abruptly on the sofa again. She squinted at the screen and said, 'Hailo . . . where's the app for Hailo? I've lost it! Where is it?'

Conor looked at Katie and raised his eyebrows. 'It's okay with me,' he told her. 'That time back at your house, I was wondering if I ought to join you then. And look – the bed's plenty big enough.'

Katie knew that she herself was moderately drunk and that Conor's suggestion went against every moral and religious principle she had ever been taught – as well as the Garda code of conduct. When she had joined the Garda she had sworn in particular 'not to pursue any relationship that I know may create a conflict of interest, or any relationship with a person I come into contact with in the course of my work that might be an abuse of trust or power'.

But was her relationship with Kyna an abuse of trust or power? She might outrank Kyna, but emotionally and sexually Kyna was as powerful as she was. And she needed her now as much as she needed Conor, and Kyna needed her.

She also realized that Conor was as much aroused by the thought of them all going to bed together as she was.

307

Kyna was still fumbling with her phone, so Katie turned to her and gently took it away from her.

'Stay,' she said, and then leaned forward and kissed Kyna on the lips.

She sat back, and smiled, and then she kissed her again, and this time she parted her lips and licked the tip of her tongue. Kyna's eyes closed and Katie raised her hands and ran her fingers into her fine blonde hair. She tasted of whiskey, but she also tasted sweet and Katie felt that it was like kissing and caressing *Aes Sidh*, a fairy.

Katie reached around and tugged down the zip of her plain black dress, all the way down to her waist. She gave her three more quick kisses and then she stood up and helped Kyna on to her feet, too.

Kyna laughed, bright-eyed, and said, 'This is *insanity*, do you know that? We're all wrecked and this is insanity! But I love it!'

She kicked off her shoes and then let her dress drop to the floor and stepped out of it. Without her shoes she was only two inches taller than Katie. She almost lost her balance, but she held on to Katie's shoulders with both hands and kissed her again, and this time their kiss was deep and hungry and their tongues wrestled with each other.

Conor stood close behind Katie for a while, but then he went over to the bed, turned aside the dark red blanket and pulled the duvet open. Then he sat down, watching as Katie and Kyna continued to kiss and undress.

Kyna was wearing a black lacy bra and black tights, but no panties. Katie went around behind her to unfasten her bra and when it had fallen to the floor she reached around and cupped her small high breasts with both hands, rubbing and rolling her nipples. Kyna arched her head back and closed her eyes, and Katie kissed her hair and her ears and said, 'Look at you, you're lovely.'

She tugged Kyna's tights halfway down her thighs and then Kyna pulled them down the rest of the way herself. She had a little blonde plume of pubic hair and a tiny tattoo of a nightingale on the left side of her vulva. Katie reached down and stroked her hair and her lips with the tip of her ring finger.

'There's a song about The Songbird Tattoo, isn't there?' she said. '*I have a songbird, sweetheart... tattooed on my arm... it never sings, it never flies, but it reminds me of your charm...*'

'The Fenian Five sang it,' said Conor.

Now Kyna unbuttoned Katie's white blouse and unfastened her slim-fitting black trousers. When she took off Katie's bra she let her large rounded breasts fall into the palms of her hands as if she was receiving some unexpected gift. She caressed them and massaged them, looking into Katie's eyes, with her own eyes shining.

'You two can join me if you like,' said Conor. He reached across to the bedside table and switched off the main lights so that the bed was illuminated only by two pink-shaded lamps.

Katie sat down to take off her trousers and pop socks, and then her pink embroidered thong. When she stood up Kyna put her arms around her and held her close and kissed her again and again.

Naked, the two of them walked hand in hand over to the bed. Conor stood up and took off his dressing gown and now he was naked, too. With his brown beard and the cross of brown hair on his chest, Katie had thought when she first saw him undressed that he looked like Jesus or one of his disciples. He had beautiful hands and feet, with long fingers and long toes, the same kind of hands and feet that El Greco had painted in his crucifixion scenes.

His penis was so stiff that it was almost vertical and as Katie approached she took it in her hand like a thick crimson baton and rubbed it up and down, and kissed him. He shifted himself across to the other side so that Katie and Kyna could join him.

Kyna reached across Katie and tapped Conor's shoulder to get his attention.

'I just have to say one thing to you, Conor, I think you're a beautiful man. I do. In fact, I think you're perfect. If I was different, I'd say you were a pure sexy biscuit.'

'Well, thanks for the compliment,' smiled Conor. 'I think you're the beuorest beuor I've ever met, with the exception of Detective Superintendent Maguire.'

'Now then,' said Katie. 'I don't pull rank in bed.' She gave Conor a kiss and then she kissed Kyna.

'I'm not going to kiss you, Conor, that's all,' Kyna told him. 'I had to kiss that Liam and I swore to myself then that I was never going to kiss another man, not ever. Like, *yuck!*'

All three of them started to laugh, so hard that Katie could hardly catch her breath. They all knew that they were drunk, and that they shouldn't be in bed together, but all three of them felt so happy that they didn't care. They had all suffered so much stress that it was a huge release to think about nothing except their own physical pleasure and their love for each other.

Katie and Kyna started to kiss and fondle each other's breasts again. The lamplight was shining like spun copper in Katie's hair and fine gold in Kyna's, and their perfumes mingled together, Daisy Blush and Exclamation. Conor reached across for the jar of Nivea cream that Katie had left next to the lamp and unscrewed it one-handed. He scooped out a dollop with his fingertips and smeared it between the cheeks of Katie's bottom. Her vulva was already slippery, and so he mixed that juice in, too.

Holding his penis in his fist, he pressed it up against Katie's anus and then gradually pushed it in. Katie gave a little jump, because it hurt her when it first went in, but she knew that the secret was to push against him, rather than tighten her muscles inwards.

Slowly, grasping her hips in both hands, he forced himself deeper and deeper inside her until she could feel his pubic hair tickling the cheeks of her bottom and his balls between her thighs. Now she could rhythmically squeeze her rectum and anus, and the sensation of his huge rigid penis inside her grew more and more thrilling with every squeeze. She started to gasp and to push her hips even harder down on him, even though he couldn't be buried in her any further.

Conor held her shoulders now and gently tipped himself over on to his back, lifting Katie on top of him with his penis still inside her. She opened her thighs wide and reached down with both hands to part the smooth waxed lips of her vulva. Kyna knelt between Conor's legs, dipped her head down, and started to lick at Katie's clitoris.

'Oh God you're angels, both of you!' Katie panted. 'Oh God you're angels!'

Kyna licked quicker and quicker and occasionally darted her tongue into Katie's vagina. She licked her perineum, too, and around the tightly stretched ring of her anus, but she didn't lick Conor's wrinkled balls.

Even so, Conor suddenly climaxed. Katie was already on the very brink of a climax herself and the combination of Kyna's licking and Conor's convulsive shuddering was enough to make her world feel as if it were bursting apart. She had never been shaken by an orgasm like this before, ever. She almost blacked out, and she thought she would never stop quaking and shivering and her bottom would never stop flinching.

They lay there for minutes afterwards, sweating, not moving. Eventually Kyna fell back sideways and Katie slowly eased herself off Conor and lay beside her with her arms around her.

'Are you all right?' Katie asked Kyna. 'You didn't come, did you?'

Kyna gave her a dreamy smile. 'I'm more than all right, Katie. I'm in heaven. I can still taste the taste of you.'

Conor kissed Katie's neck and between her shoulder blades, which made her shiver.

'I never noticed those before. You have some freckles there, in the pattern of Sirius.'

'Sirius? What's that?'

'It's a star in the constellation of Canis Major, the Dog Star. I was thinking about calling my agency Sirius before I called it Sixth Scents. In the end, I thought that not too many Irish people would get the reference. But Sirius, Katie – that's the brightest star in the solar system. Like you.'

They continued to lie there, stroking and kissing each other occasionally, and the warmth and the sense of affection between them was unlike anything that Katie had ever experienced before.

She knew that a night like this might never happen again, and that she would have to think seriously about her professional relationship with Kyna. Right now, though, tomorrow's sun had not yet risen and she could forget about work-related problems until she had slept for a while and recovered from all that West Cork whiskey. They had drunk a whole bottle of it between them.

She stroked Kyna very gently between her legs, and sang, '*You never know what life will bring... what shadows and what pain... but my heart sings like a songbird... when you come home again...*'

Together they softly sang the chorus: '*I have a songbird, sweetheart... tattooed on my arm... it never sings, it never flies... but it reminds me of your charm...*'

Thirty-three

The sun was shining when Katie arrived at the hospital the next morning. She went through to the mortuary first, even though she knew that Dr Kelley would not have arrived yet. One of the morgue assistants was already there, though – a worried-looking young woman with very small spectacles and a surgical cap. Katie asked her if she could view Maggie Dennehy's body.

The assistant slid Maggie Dennehy out of the refrigerated drawer for her and lifted the green sheet that was covering her. Katie looked at her for a long time. Apart from the deep ligature groove around her neck, her body was dotted with small dark bruises, especially her thighs.

Rape, thought Katie. She had seen similar patterns on so many women's thighs before. An archipelago of suffering.

'Okay, thanks a million,' she said, and the morgue assistant covered up Maggie Dennehy's body and slid it back into the refrigerator.

When she went upstairs to see Cissy she found the garda outside her door eating a bacon sandwich. He hurriedly stood up and tried to hide it behind his back, but Katie waved her hand and said, 'You're grand altogether. Don't worry. I suffer from bacon sandwich blindness.'

Cissy was sitting in her chair with Bindy in her lap, watching SpongeBob SquarePants, although she had a very solemn expression on her face. She was wearing a brown corduroy dress with a cream Aran sweater underneath, and cream-coloured tights, and a brown duffel coat was lying on her bed, next to a small overnight bag.

313

She was all ready now for a representative from Tusla to come and collect her and take her to her foster home.

Katie went up to her and laid her hand on her shoulder.

'Cissy,' she said.

Cissy looked up at her and her eyes filled up with tears.

'Yes, I know what your real name is,' Katie told her. 'Don't be upset, please. There's no reason for you to be frightened. Now that you're nearly better some really nice people are going to take care of you.'

'My brother will throw such a rabie,' sobbed Cissy miserably.

'Don't you worry about your brother. You're going to have a new life now. A nice new house to live in, and a new school, and new friends. You can forget about all of the bad things that happened before. Those days are all over now.'

Katie sat down on the bed close to her and stroked her hair.

'It was Mrs McCabe who told us your name. She sounds like a nice woman all right.'

Cissy nodded. 'She is. She bought me Bindy for my birthday. Sometimes Davy didn't come home and I was locked out and so I used to go round to her house for my tea.'

'Well, the people who are going to be looking after you from now on are going to be just as nice as Mrs McCabe. And I'm going to keep in touch with you, too, just to make sure that you're happy. Look – I fetched you this.'

Katie opened her soft black leather shoulder bag and took out a box containing an iPhone. She opened it up and gave it to Cissy and said, 'I've charged it up already and before I go I'll set it all up for you. You don't have to worry about paying for it because it's registered to my account. Don't be afraid to use it whenever you want to, either. There's only one condition – you ring me at least once a week and tell me how you are. If ever there's anything wrong, or if you're worried or unhappy, all you have to do is call me and I'll sort it out for you.'

Cissy held the phone tightly and smiled through her tears. 'Thank you,' she whispered.

Katie waited for a moment, then she said, 'There are one or two questions I have to ask you, Cissy. I think you probably know what they are.'

Cissy stared at her and said nothing. Katie realized that it was probably futile to reassure her that she wouldn't allow her brother to come near her or threaten her, ever again. In spite of that, it was critical for her to find out what Cissy had been doing in the attic when fire broke out at the dance studio, and whether she had witnessed what had happened to Ronan Barrett and Saoirse MacAuliffe.

'When did you go up into the attic at Toirneach Damhsa?' Katie asked her. 'Were those two dancers up there already when you went up there? When you first saw them, were they still alive?'

Cissy lowered her eyes and still said nothing.

'If they were still alive when you first saw them, did you see who shot them? Or were they already dead when you got there? If they were already dead, why didn't you go downstairs and tell Nicholas O'Grady?'

Still Cissy said nothing.

'Cissy, sweetheart, it's fierce important that I find out how they died. Somebody killed them and then set fire to the dance studio so that all of those poor dancers were burned to death. We can't let them go unpunished. They might do it again to somebody else. They might do something much worse.'

Cissy turned her head away and stared at the television. SpongeBob had broken the spatula that he was using to grill burgers and was trying to give it CPR.

'Was there somebody else in the attic when you were there, Cissy? Did they see you, or maybe they didn't? If I showed you some pictures of different men, do you think you could at least nod if you saw one of them up in the attic?'

Katie took out photographs of Danny Coffey, Steven Joyce, Douglas Cleary and Tadhg Brennan. She held them up in front of Cissy one after the other, but she didn't respond to any of them. Either she had seen none of them in the attic, or else she was too frightened to say which one of them she recognized.

315

'Are you absolutely sure that none of them were up there?' Katie repeated.

Cissy turned away from the television to look at her, but her expression was unreadable and she still didn't speak.

Katie stood up and said, 'All right. I'll have to leave you now. I have a very sad funeral to go to. I'm not cross with you, Cissy. I know that you're too scared at the moment to describe what happened that day. I only hope that you can find a way to tell me . . . I mean, you could write it down, or maybe ring me, now that you have your mobile phone. Would either of those be easier?'

'I don't know,' said Cissy, so quietly that Katie could scarcely hear her over a cartoon explosion on the television.

Katie leaned over and gave her a hug. 'You'll be all right, darling, you wait and see. Just don't you forget to ring me.'

* * *

Detective Dooley's state funeral took place at noon, with a procession along Patrick's Street and Grand Parade by over three thousand uniformed gardaí from all over the country. The sun shone and the Garda band played the *Caoineadh* funeral march. The pavements all the way to the Holy Trinity Church on Father Mathew Quay were crowded with thousands of mourners, all watching in silence, bareheaded.

Neither the Dáil nor the Seanad were sitting today, out of respect, and the Oireachtas had cancelled all committee meetings.

Behind the hearse walked Garda Commissioner Nóirín O'Sullivan, accompanied by the Tánaiste, Frances Fitzgerald, the minister for justice, Joseph McNulty, and Assistant Commissioner Frank Magorian.

Katie was marching in her full blue dress uniform beside Chief Superintendent Denis MacCostagáin and Superintendent Michael Pearse, with her team of detectives marching behind her. The only member of her team missing was Kyna. Katie had told her not to join the parade because it would be televised from beginning to end and she didn't want to take the risk that Davy Dorgan might recognize her and realize that she was a Garda officer.

She felt that this funeral was completely unreal. It was such a bright day, with white clouds tumbling across the sky like burst pillows, and she found it impossible to imagine that the hearse they were following was carrying the badly burned body of young Robert Dooley.

His coffin was draped in the orange, white and green tricolour flag, with his Garda cap on top of it. It was carried into the church on the shoulders of his brothers and his fellow detectives.

Katie sat near the front of the church for the service, but for all of those thousands gathered outside large video screens had been erected so that they could follow the prayers and hymns. A solemn address was given by Father Hurley, who had been Detective Dooley's parish priest at St Finbarr's, and by Commissioner O'Sullivan.

'Too many hearts have been broken and lives shattered,' said Father Hurley. 'I say on this day from the depths of my heart, there is no place for violence in our society. Violence is wrong, always wrong.'

Commissioner O'Sullivan said, 'Let us not forget that Robert Dooley was not only a garda, he was a son and a brother, and a young man with a fine and fulfilling life ahead of him, so cruelly snatched away.'

Afterwards, Katie went outside and stood alone by the river for a few minutes, thinking about Detective Dooley. She almost expected him to appear beside her, grinning his mischievous grin and telling her that this state funeral had all been one of his elaborate practical jokes. *What did you think about that, then, ma'am? Everybody was doing the keen dog, weren't they? – even grumpy old MacCostagáin!*

Detective Sergeant Begley came over and said, 'Everything all right, ma'am?'

The band was playing the funeral march *Brón*. Katie nodded and followed Detective Sergeant Begley back to join the rest of her bereaved colleagues.

It was nearly 5 p.m. by the time she returned to her office. There had been a reception for the government ministers and senior officers at County Hall and Katie had been able to talk to Commissioner O'Sullivan about the progress she was making with the Toirneach Damhsa fire investigation. Because of Detective Dooley's death, the story had been prominent in the national newspapers.

'Frank Magorian seems to be very confident that you'll have it all wrapped up in the next few days,' Commissioner O'Sullivan had told her. 'I must say that he was pure complimentary about you, Detective Superintendent. It's good to hear that you're working so well together.'

Katie had thought of several stinging ways she could have answered that, but had decided that the wisest response was silence and a smile. Commissioner O'Sullivan had enough problems of her own.

Detective Inspector Mulliken came up to her office before she had even had the chance to change out of her uniform. He was still in uniform, too.

'We've just received an update from the Ghost Team, ma'am. The three AIRA fellows stayed all day at Tomas O'Bruadair's house, but they left about fifteen minutes ago, still in the same car. Now they're on their way south again, but they're going via Kilkenny and Callan rather than the M7. The detective sergeant in charge said that they've been trying to pick up phone signals from them, but no luck so far.'

'Where's Dorgan at the moment?'

'Still with the rest of his family on Mount Nebo Avenue. The only phone messages we've intercepted from that property have been one or two from his Uncle Christy ordering some spare tyres from O'Reilly's, and about five thousand from his niece Tasha gossiping with her school friends about somebody called Zayn, whoever that is.'

'Let's make sure we keep a fierce close eye on Dorgan,' said Katie. 'I'd love to lift him, but we don't have sufficient evidence against him yet. We've only the tip-off that Ni Nuallán got out of that Liam character and if we brought *him* to court to give evidence he'd only deny it. He'd be too scared not to.'

'No, don't worry, we won't be letting Dorgan out of our sight. And the NSU is keeping us in constant touch so we'll be able to join them in tracking these AIRA fellows as soon as they arrive in Cork. We have a full description of the vehicle. It's a Volvo V70 Cross Country T SE, safari yellow, with dummy Dublin plates.'

As Detective Inspector Mulliken left, Moirin came in. A manila folder of correspondence was tucked under her arm, leaving her hands free to carry a cappuccino and a beef and vegetable hand pie.

'Mother of God, you must be psychic,' said Katie. 'They had a buffet at the County Hall but I was too busy talking to all the bigwigs to eat anything.'

'It's not a bother,' said Moirin. 'I bought one for myself, too, and if you hadn't been hungry I could have easy eaten the both of them.'

While she ate her flaky-textured pie and drank her coffee, Katie caught up with her emails and her letters. She had three texts from Conor which made her smile. *Cant stop thinking about last night!!*, *Youre fantastic!!!* and *Love you DS Maguire!!!!* Each text was accompanied by an emoji of a different breed of dog.

Before she left the station she went along to see Chief Superintendent MacCostagáin. He was still wearing his uniform and in the light of his desk lamp he was hunched forward as if he were worn out. She had never seen his face look so lined and so old and his hair so grey.

'Are you out the gap now, Kathleen?' he asked her. His mouth sounded dry and he had to clear his throat.

'In a minute, sir, after I've had a word with Michael Pearse. Has Tony Mulliken been keeping you up to speed on this Ian Bowthorpe business?'

Chief Superintendent MacCostagáin nodded and then shook his head. 'They must be mad as a box of frogs, these Authentic IRA fellows. Do they genuinely think they're going to be able to get within a mile of the British defence secretary so they can take a pot-shot at him?'

'Well, the NSU Ghost Team could stop them and pick them up now,' said Katie. 'But if we let them join together with Davy Dorgan and all the rest of his crew, we should be able to jump on all of them for conspiracy, and Dorgan in particular for incitement.'

'You think it's worth the risk?'

'It's Dorgan I want. His late father was an out-and-out murdering terrorist in Larne, and he's even worse.'

Chief Superintendent MacCostagáin lifted his hand in acknowledgement. 'Carry on, then, Kathleen.'

Katie hesitated because she sensed that he wanted to say something else. 'Is that all, sir?' she asked him.

He looked up at her mournfully. 'It hurts, you know, doesn't it, when we lose one of our own? It doesn't matter what age they are, but Dooley was so young. What a send-off we gave him, though, didn't we? What a grand send-off! There's nobody puts on a state funeral like us! But I wish we never had to do it at all.'

'No, sir,' said Katie. 'Me too.'

She left him there, sitting at his desk, staring into space.

* * *

When she opened her front door her phone was ringing. She had to push her way past Barney, who was welcoming her home by running madly backwards and forwards up and down the corridor, and by the time she reached the phone in the living room the caller had rung off.

She rang back, wrestling off her coat at the same time. It was Corinne Daley, from Tusla.

'Oh hallo there! Detective Superintendent Maguire? So sorry to trouble you at home. I tried to ring you at the station but they told me you'd already left and I didn't want to ring you while you were driving.'

'No, it's not a bother. How's young Cissy going on? Does she like her new family?'

'That's why I'm calling you. I thought she was with you, at Anglesea Street.'

'*What?* What made you think that? Haven't you collected her yet? Don't tell me she's still at CUH.'

'No, she's not. I went to pick her up about eleven this morning. I was about a half an hour late because I'd had some trouble with one of our other children, little devil he is. When I got to the hospital, though, she'd gone, and so had your garda from outside her door. The receptionist on the front desk told me that two of your detectives had come to take her away because you needed to ask her some more questions.'

Katie felt cold. 'I sent no detectives to fetch her, Corinne. As far as I was concerned, it was Tusla who was going to be taking care of her.'

'Are you sure about that? The receptionist said that the detectives had shown her their ID and everything. And Adeen – I mean Cissy – she seemed to be quite happy to go with them. And of course your PA called me and said that you'd be fetching her around to our office here in Blackpool around teatime.'

'Oh, God. My PA never rang you, Corinne.'

'That's what I was starting to wonder when Cissy never showed up. You have me really worried now. Who do you think has her?'

Katie said, 'Corinne – this isn't your fault. There's only one person who would have gone to those lengths to take her and I believe I know who that is. I'll get in touch with the garda who was outside her room, and the hospital, too. They have CCTV inside and outside, twenty-four hours a day, and security guards on regular patrol around the corridors.'

'I'm so sorry, DS Maguire. I really honestly truly believed you were holding her today to try and find out more about her background like – you know, to make it easier for her foster parents to understand her needs. That's what your PA said. Or the woman who was making out that she was your PA, anyway.'

'Thanks, Corinne,' said Katie. 'I'll ring you back as soon as I have some news.'

Immediately she had put down the phone Katie called Detective Sergeant Begley. She knew he was on a late shift this evening and that he also had a close liaison with the acting chief security officer at the hospital.

'You think it was probably Davy Dorgan who took her?' asked Detective Sergeant Begley. 'Well, it couldn't have been himself personally, because he hasn't left the house today. But I'll check with the guard who was on duty outside the little girl's room and I'll see what the CCTV footage comes up with. If they took her off in a car, these fellows, that should have been recorded on CCTV, too, unless they parked it outside the hospital perimeter.'

'Let's see if we can identify who might have taken her first,' said Katie. 'There's something else, too – I gave her an iPhone to keep in touch with me. Hold on and I'll give you the number. So long as she hasn't switched it off or taken out the battery or thrown it away already, we might be able to track her with that. If we can't, then get back to me and I'll ask Superintendent Pearse to set up a full-scale search right away. I don't want to waste even a minute, Michael. Young Cissy knows things that she shouldn't know, and because of that she could be in danger of her life.'

'I have you, ma'am. Buckley and Markey are both here with me. We'll get on to this real quick. Will you be at home?'

'For the time being, yes. But I'll come back in if I'm needed.'

Katie hung up her coat and then went back into the living room, with Barney following her. She would have given anything for a very large vodka – partly because she was so stressed and partly to bury once and for all the West Cork whiskey hangover that had returned to haunt her from the night before. With Cissy missing, though, and those three Authentic IRA men coming ever closer to Cork, she knew that she would have to be satisfied with a can of Diet Coke.

She undressed and put on a nightshirt and a dressing gown, but she stayed in the living room watching the late-night movie, *Peggy Sue Got Married*. Barney settled down beside her with his chin on her knee, raising his eyes to look at her every now and then, as if he were making sure that she wasn't too upset.

At 1.37 a.m. her phone rang again. It was Kyna, and she sounded worried.

'I've taken a look through the CCTV from the hospital, ma'am. Those two who went to pick up Cissy – they were both Davy Dorgan's minions. One of them was Liam, and the other one was Murtagh. God alone knows how they were taken for detectives from Tusla, although Murtagh speaks quite posh, believe it or not.'

'That's the same Liam you—'

'Yes. Him. And it made me feel sick to my stomach just to see him, I can tell you. But I can see from the CCTV that the both of them had smartened themselves up a bit, you know, and they were showing ID cards.'

'You know as well as I do that you can buy fake Garda ID cards online. What about Cissy's iPhone? Have you been able to locate her with that?'

'No, not so far. Like you say, it might be switched off, or Dorgan might have found it and smashed it.'

'Maybe the NSU might be able to track it. They have those cell-site simulators, don't they, those Stingrays? What's the situation with those Authentic IRA?'

'We were sent another update about ten minutes ago. They've stopped again, this time at a house in Knockpogue Avenue, just opposite the Fairfield Tavern. The house belongs to another AIRA man, Joe Keenan.'

'Oh, Keenan. Yes, I remember him. One of Bobby Quilty's shamfeens. He specialized in breaking all your fingers if you irked Bobby Quilty, I seem to remember. Joe "Knucklecracker" Keenan.'

'What's the plan, then, ma'am?' asked Kyna. She sounded so serious that it was hard for Katie to believe that she was talking to the same young woman with whom she and Conor had been making love last night.

'Is Sean Begley still there with you?'

'He is, yes. He's right beside me now.'

'The first place you need to look for Cissy is the Dorgan house. If she's there, you can arrest Davy Dorgan for kidnap, even though

Cissy's his sister. If she isn't, tell him that we know now that she's his sister and that he needs to tell us where he's had her taken to. If he denies any knowledge, lift him anyway for obstructing our investigation.'

'If she's not there, she could be at Liam's, in St Anne's Road. Or Murtagh's, wherever he lives. I think it's up Wellington Road somewhere.'

'Kyna, just find her. It's desperate.'

Thirty-four

Katie quickly dressed in tight black jeans and a bottle-green polo-neck sweater. She checked that her revolver was loaded and fastened her holster on to her belt, then she shucked on her black waterproof jacket with the pointy hood.

Before she left she filled Barney's water bowl and shut him in the kitchen. In the morning she could ring Jenny Tierney and ask her to take him out for a walk and take care of him until she returned home.

'It's not that I don't love you, Barns,' she told him, tugging at his ears. 'But I have a frightened little girl to rescue and some very horrible scumbags to catch. I promise you I'll take you out to Marlogue Woods on Sunday afternoon to make up for shutting you up so much, and you can tear through the trees and up and down the beach to your heart's content.'

At this time of the morning traffic on the N8 into the city amounted to no more than five or six overnight delivery trucks, so Katie could drive for most of the way at over 90 kph and she reached the Lower Glanmire Road in less than fifteen minutes. As she was driving along Horgan's Quay, with the river glittering black beside her, her iPhone rang.

It was Detective Sergeant Begley. 'He's not here, ma'am.'

'Come here to me? Who's not where?'

'Davy Dorgan, ma'am. We've just raided the Dorgan house on Mount Nebo. He's not here and neither is his little sister.'

'How can he not be there? We've had the house under surveillance for the past twenty-four hours.'

325

'His car's still outside, but he's not inside. He must have slipped out somehow. Either out through the back yard, or disguised as his aunt. The last shift who were watching him say that some old one left the property around nine and she hasn't come back.'

'What about the two fellows who took Cissy from the hospital? Did you go to their houses, too?'

'Liam O'Breen and Murtagh McCourt, yes. The barman at the Templegate gave us their surnames and McCourt's address in Wellington Road. When we got there, though, neither O'Breen nor McCourt were at home. O'Breen's landlady hadn't seen or heard him since early yesterday morning, and the young woman who lives on the same landing as McCourt said she saw him go out at half-past seven and she hasn't seen him again since.'

'Right,' said Katie. 'I'll be in to the station in a couple of minutes or so. We need to set up a systematic full-scale search, starting with all known members of Dorgan's gang. We also need to check up on all the CCTV from the Wilton area around the time that Cissy was abducted. I'll have Mathew McElvey put out an urgent appeal to the media for anybody who might have seen her.'

She paused as she turned in to the Anglesea Street car park, but then she said, 'You don't think Dorgan might have gone up to this Joe Knucklecracker's house, do you, to meet up with his hit men?'

'That crossed my mind, too, ma'am, but the Ghost Team have had them under constant surveillance and there's been no sign of him.'

'Sean – *we* had him under constant surveillance ourselves and he gave us the slip. Are we sure that he hasn't managed to sneak in through the back yard or maybe go in through the front door dressed up as some Fair Hill brasser, or I don't know – a nun, even?'

'I should think the Ghost Team have had their eye on the back of the house as well as the front. They've assured me that nobody has been in or out since the three AIRA men arrived, not even a reverend mother or a local dirtbird.'

'Hmm,' said Katie. 'Now that Dorgan knows that Ni Nuallán is wise to his plan to shoot Bowthorpe, he's probably worked

326

out a completely different way of doing it. Ni Nuallán thought that he might call it off altogether, but I'm not so sure about that. Dorgan's fierce political by the sound of it and he doesn't care who he hurts to get what he wants. Maybe if he knew for sure that Ni Nuallán was a garda and that the ERU were on to him, he'd think twice, but I don't think he will. I've known villains like him before. They're dangerous enough even when they're not fighting for some cause. Remember Bobby Quilty.'

Katie locked her car and went into the station, still holding her phone to her ear.

'What's the craic, then?' asked Detective Sergeant Begley.

'I don't see that we have much of a choice. We've lost sight of Davy Dorgan, and we don't have any idea how he's changed his plan to shoot Ian Bowthorpe – or even *if* he's changed it – so we'll just have to stamp on this now. Maybe he still intends to take a shot at Bowthorpe at the Opera House this evening . . . maybe he's found some secret vantage point in the building where a sniper can get him in his sights. On the other hand, maybe he's thinking of shooting at him when he's visiting Haulbowline during the afternoon, or when he's going for dinner at the Hayfield Manor after the *feis*. Who knows?'

'Does that mean you're going to lift these Authentic fellows right now?'

'Like I say, Sean, I don't see what else we can do. I would have preferred to have caught Dorgan red-handed with them, him and all the rest of his crew, the whole netful of rotten fish, but I think we'll have to content ourselves with saving Ian Bowthorpe's life. We can track down Dorgan later. He can't escape for ever, and by that time with any luck we may have collected more admissible evidence against him.'

'I'll start setting up this search, ma'am,' said Detective Sergeant Begley. 'We have plenty of pictures of the little girl, don't we?'

'We do, sure . . . I'll have Scanlan make a selection and get some printed off. As for me, I'll have a word with the DS in charge of the Ghost Team and wake up Superintendent Pearse. I'd like to go in and scoop these characters before it gets light.'

'In that case, ma'am . . . let's see . . . you have exactly four hours and twenty-six minutes.'

* * *

Superintendent Pearse had been suffering from indigestion all night after a takeaway curry and hadn't been able to sleep so he wasn't at all disgruntled when Katie rang him to tell him that she was setting up a raid on Joe Keenan's house.

'I've had dealings with that gowl before. It'll be a pleasure and it'll take my mind off this fecking vindaloo. Is there a limit to the number of Alka-Seltzers you can take at any one time?'

'Well, I'd go easy, Michael. You don't want to be after needing a comfort break right in the middle of an armed raid.'

'So what time do you have in mind?'

'0530, if you can have your team up there by 0500. I'll contact DS Boyle from the Ghost Team right now to coordinate with him. He has six in his unit, all of them armed, of course.'

'Okay. I'm just trying to picture the location. Knockpogue Avenue, where it meets with Fairfield Avenue. I think four cars should just about cover it – eight officers altogether. I'll get on to Sergeant Mulroney right now.'

'Can you make sure we have an ambulance standing by, too? Just in case.'

Next, Katie called Detective Sergeant Boyle. He had a very husky voice, as if he were getting over a cold.

'We've seen no sign of life since about half-past midnight,' he told her. 'We've intercepted a fair number of mobile phone calls but none of those have been relevant to Ian Bowthorpe. Sure, it would have been ideal if we'd been able to take this Dorgan fellow and the rest of his gang in the one fell swoop. But – I agree with you, ma'am, it's best to be safe. You can imagine the diplomatic row if we allowed the British defence secretary to be shot while he was sitting in the Cork Opera House watching step-dancing. I mean, Holy Name of Jesus.'

328

'Superintendent Pearse will be in touch with you in a few minutes,' said Katie. 'I'll be coming up there myself, too. I want to see these AIRA fellows face to face – get some sense of who they are and what they're about.'

'In my experience, ma'am, they're nothing but a bunch of gougers. They wouldn't know a political cause if it gave them a toe up the hole, excuse my French.'

* * *

Detective Sergeant Begley returned to the station a few minutes later, along with Detective Ó Doibhilin. It was well past time for them to go off duty but they both volunteered to come up to Fair Hill with Katie.

'I know.' She smiled. 'It's only because you want the overtime. I don't even think that I can afford you – not now that every other garda has been given a pay rise.'

She didn't really need to go to see the AIRA men arrested, not in person. Superintendent Pearse's uniformed officers were more than capable of bringing them in, especially since they were accompanied by the heavily armed Ghost Team. She was conscious that Frank Magorian's criticisms of her might have some truth in them, that she did tend to interfere too much in day-to-day operations. But she had seen too many high-ranking Garda officers become detached from the reality of policing on the street, instead spending all their time on administration and attending policy meetings at Phoenix Park and going to Masonic dinners. Like her father, Katie didn't believe she could enforce the law effectively unless she knew the lawbreakers as intimately as she knew her fellow officers, and kept up to the minute with every new twist they devised to extort money, or sell drugs, or pimp girls, or steal anything at all – from old people's pensions to combine harvesters.

'I need to look them in their evil eyes,' her father always said. 'I need to get close enough to smell the stolen money in their wallets and the halitosis they get from telling so many lies.'

The sky was beginning to lighten as they drove up to Fair Hill
in their unmarked Toyota Prius. When they arrived at the corner
of Fairfield and Knockpogue Avenues everything appeared to be
quiet and there was no indication that a major Garda raid was
about to take place. They parked outside the closed-up frontage of
The Plaice 2B fish-and-chip shop, in the layby directly opposite Joe
Keenan's house, and Detective Sergeant Begley checked his watch.

'Red One in position,' he said, into his r/t mic.

'Roger that,' said Detective Sergeant Boyle's clogged-up voice.
And then, 'Roger,' said Sergeant Mulroney from Superintendent
Pearse's squad.

They sat and waited while the time ticked by and the sky
gradually grew paler and paler. Apart from a low bank of dark
clouds to the south-west it looked as if it might be a fine day.

Joe 'Knucklecracker' Keenan's house was at the left-hand end
of a terrace of three. It was pebble-dashed, painted salmon pink,
with a scarlet door. All its curtains were drawn, although the
living-room curtains were sagging in the middle where the hooks
had broken. Two cars were parked outside: a grey BMW and the
safari yellow Volvo estate in which the AIRA men had driven
down from the North.

'You'd have thought they would have chosen a vehicle that was
a little less conspicuous, wouldn't you?' said Detective Ó Doibhilin,
leaning over from the seat. 'It's a wonder they didn't come down
here in an ice-cream van like, with all the chimes going.'

At 5.30 exactly, Detective Sergeant Boyle coughed and shouted,
'Go-go-go!'

Two black Audi saloons came squealing around the corner
of Fairfield Avenue and stopped in front of Joe Keenan's house,
blocking the front driveway. As their doors opened and six men
in black jackets and black balaclavas scrambled out, two Garda
squad cars came around the corner and parked close behind them,
their blue lights flashing. Two more squad cars came speeding
down Knockpogue Avenue side by side and slithered to a stop
about thirty metres short of the house, blocking the road. Gardaí

in protective vests climbed out of all of the cars, but stood well back. They were there to prevent any suspects from trying to run away or anybody else from approaching. Katie climbed out, too, so that she could watch the raid from behind the Toyota.

She heard knocking on the front door, and shouting, '*Armed Garda! Armed Garda! Open up now!*' This was followed almost immediately by the banging of a battering-ram.

As the front door burst open, though, she heard shots from inside the hallway – three quick single shots and then a *brrrrrppp!* of sub-machine gun fire. Katie thought she could see one of the Ghost Team men pitch backwards into the front driveway, collapsing behind the BMW. The others ducked down and retreated from the front step. One of them reached around the side of the door and fired two automatic pistol shots into the house, but this was met with another *brrrrpp!* of sub-machine gun fire. Less than two metres behind Katie's head, two bullets smashed star-shaped holes in the front window of the fish-and-chip shop and another bullet hit the driver's door of the Toyota.

Katie didn't need to be told to crouch down. She pulled out her revolver, too, and held it high.

She could hear shouting and running feet, and then suddenly a prolonged crackling of shots. When it had subsided, she cautiously raised her head and saw that one of the upstairs windows in Joe Keenan's house had been opened and the barrel of a semi-automatic rifle was poking out from behind the curtains – an AK47 probably, or a Czech vz.52. The Ghost Team men were now kneeling down behind the low front walls of the house, and every time one of them tried to raise his head the AIRA man in the bedroom would take another shot and pink concrete shrapnel would spray in all directions.

Katie beckoned to Detective Sergeant Begley, who was crouching down behind the Toyota's front wheel.

'Tell DS Boyle to back off,' she said. 'And Sergeant Mulroney, too. Tell them to back off completely.'

'*What?*'

'One of our people's been shot there, Sean, by the looks of it, and who knows how long it's going to be before we can drag him away? He could be bleeding to death for all we know.'

'You're not serious. You want us to back off and let those scummers go free?'

'Listen, this is not the right time nor the right place for a siege situation. Who knows how many guns and how much ammunition those fellows have with them? They could well have explosives, too. If Dorgan's behind this, they could have some of that TPA stuff. There's neighbours living next door, and there's other people in that house besides those three.'

'Well, that's for sure. There's good old Joe Keenan, too, the Knucklecracker. If anything bad happens to him, then so much the better, that's all I can say. He got away with murder the last time we had him up in court – or manslaughter, anyway.'

'Sean, however much of a whore's melt he is, he's married, so his wife is probably in there. And take a sconce next to the garage.'

Detective Sergeant Begley looked across the street and saw what Katie was pointing at. Almost out of sight behind the BMW was a child's red-and-blue tricycle.

'And see there, too?' said Katie. 'That small bedroom window over the porch.' Now that the day was growing lighter the pattern on the curtains was visible – pale blue with circus elephants.

The shooting had stopped for the time being, but the Ghost Team men were still sheltering behind the front wall. Detective Sergeant Boyle waved to Detective Sergeant Begley and shouted, '*What's Plan B?*'

Detective Sergeant Begley turned to Katie. 'What *is* Plan B? We let them go and then what?'

'We follow them at a discreet distance until they're well away from any innocent bystanders. Then we stop them.'

'And supposing they manage to shake us off? They'd only have to be out of our sight for a second or two and they could abandon their car and we'd never see them again. Well, maybe not *never*. Not until they took a shot at our friend Ian Bowthorpe.'

'Sean – I don't want any more people hurt. I know what the textbook procedure is for a siege, but this is Davy Dorgan we're dealing with here and Davy Dorgan doesn't commit textbook offences. We back off, we let them get out of there, and *then* we go after them.'

'All right, ma'am, if that's the way you want to handle it.'

Detective Sergeant Begley called Detective Sergeant Boyle and Sergeant Mulroney on his r/t. He told them what Katie had ordered, and Katie could tell from the lengthy silence before he received a response from either of them that they were very reluctant to call their men off.

She heard Detective Sergeant Boyle's croaky voice saying, '*Serious?*' He pulled down his balaclava and frowned across the road at Katie with a deeply dubious expression on his face. Katie turned away. She felt that if she allowed this siege to go on any longer it would only escalate into a tragedy. If there was one lesson she thought that her male colleagues needed to learn, it was that sometimes there was greater strength in allowing themselves to appear to be weak.

Detective Sergeant Begley called in the ambulance that had been waiting in Close's Green, around the corner and out of the line of fire. It appeared within seconds, lights flashing, but silently.

Detective Sergeant Boyle ran over to it, his back hunched to make himself less of a target. He talked to the paramedics for a moment and then came back across the road waving a white pillowcase that he had taken from one of stretchers.

'Listen!' he shouted up to the bedroom window. 'We're leaving! We're letting you be! We don't want any more shooting here, do you hear me?'

He stood in full view in the driveway, still flapping the pillowcase from side to side. There was a lengthy pause and then the barrel of the automatic rifle was drawn inside and the bedroom window was closed. As soon as that happened four of the Ghost Team hurried across to the ambulance so that they could escort the two paramedics back to the narrow gap between the garden wall and the BMW where their wounded colleague was lying.

Katie came out from behind the Toyota and chivvied the rest of the uniformed gardaí back into their patrol cars. 'Crush, boys, quick – come on now,' she told them. 'But don't be going any further away than a couple of streets in each direction. Upper Fairhill to the west, Farranferris Green to the south, Fair Green to the north, and Rathpeacon Road to the east – that'll be far enough to take you out of sight, but not so far that you can't keep them in a box. The NSU boys here can follow them closer.'

Detective Sergeant Boyle came up to her, looking sour-faced.

'How's your man?' asked Katie.

'Flesh wound in the upper right arm and his chest badly bruised. But his vest saved his life, no doubt about that. One of those new PPSS vests, fantastic. You hardly know you're wearing them until somebody shoots you.'

'Thank God. That's a relief.'

Detective Sergeant Boyle looked up at the bedroom window and then at the doorway. The red front door was tilted at an angle on the floor, but there was nobody in sight in the hallway.

'Do you really think this is the right way to play this?' he said. 'This goes against all of our usual procedure, and all of my instincts, too.'

'I know it's fierce tempting to go charging in with all guns blazing when your blood's up,' said Katie. 'But think about it. These eejits have nowhere to go. What's the point in shooting them and risking the lives of anybody else in the house? There's at least one wain in there by the look of it.'

'Do you seriously think they're stupid enough to make a run for it?'

'I don't know. I hope they see the light and surrender.'

Detective Sergeant Boyle thought for a few moments and then he said, 'Okay. But what happens if they don't make a run for it, and don't surrender, and stay here in the house?'

'They're Ulstermen,' said Detective Sergeant Begley. 'If they decide to do that, we'll just wait outside here until they run out of tea.'

Although he was joking, it was a deadly serious joke, and they all knew what he meant. The AIRA men would either have to come out with their hands up or try and escape. Whatever they decided to do, there was no longer any chance that they would be able to carry out their intended mission and assassinate Ian Bowthorpe.

All four patrol cars drove off in different directions, with as much revving and screeching of tyres as possible, so that the AIRA men couldn't fail to hear that they had gone. Then the Ghost Team returned to their unmarked black Audis, noisily slamming their doors. Katie and Detective Sergeant Begley and Detective Ó Doibhilin followed Detective Sergeant Boyle's car. It went around the corner into Fairfield Avenue, but only about a hundred metres, and then it U-turned to face back towards Knockpogue Avenue. Detective Sergeant Begley pulled in close behind it.

They waited for another half-hour, but there was still no sign of the AIRA men leaving the house. Katie closed her eyes for a while. She was beginning to feel very tired, and hungry, too, and she would have given a month's salary for a cappuccino.

Detective Ó Doibhilin suddenly said, 'I hate to say this, ma'am, but my back teeth are floating.'

'Go on, then, go behind that wall over there,' said Katie.

Detective Ó Doibhilin climbed out of the car, hurried over to the wall by the bus stop, and stood there with his back turned while he urinated.

'Kids today,' said Detective Sergeant Begley. 'The first thing they trained us when I was at Templemore was how to hold it for twenty-four hours at a time, even if you were bursting.'

Katie said nothing. She wouldn't have minded going to the toilet herself and so she didn't want to think about it.

Detective Ó Doibhilin had zipped himself up and he was walking back to the car when Detective Sergeant Boyle's voice barked out over the r/t, *'They're away! They're going for it!'*

His Audi roared into life and pulled away from the kerb with its tyres shrieking. As it did so, the yellow Volvo estate came speeding out of Knockpogue Avenue, straight across Fairfield Avenue, and disappeared south towards the city centre.

The Audi slewed around the corner and went after it like a lion after a gazelle. Detective Ó Doibhilin scrambled back into their Toyota and before he had managed to slam his door shut Detective Sergeant Begley had started the engine and stamped on the accelerator pedal. None of them said a word as they skidded into Knockpogue Avenue and followed the Audi at over 80 kph, and Katie kept a tight grip on the door handle. Both sides of the road were lined with parked cars, which made it dangerously narrow at this speed, and their car hit a Range Rover's wing mirror with an explosive bang.

Flashing past Farranferris Green recreation ground they saw the Garda patrol car that had been waiting there, but it was clear that the Volvo had been driving far too fast for it to be stopped – not without risking a fatal collision. After they had gone by, though, the patrol car immediately lit up its flashing blue lights and came behind them.

'Why in the name of *God* don't they just pull over and call it a day?' exclaimed Detective Sergeant Begley as they rounded a mini-roundabout with their tyres screaming in chorus. But now the Volvo was speeding even faster, its suspension bouncing up and down as it plunged down Fair Hill.

Katie could see it colliding again and again with the cars parked by the sides of the road, with sparkling fragments of mirror flying in the air. It was obvious that the AIRA men were desperate, but it was equally obvious that they had no intention of stopping for anybody. She had come across this so many times before when suspects she was pursuing had lengthy criminal records. They would rather be shot dead trying to escape arrest than go back to spend another decade in prison.

As they neared the city centre and the River Lee the streets became narrower and steeper, but the yellow Volvo kept bounding and careering down between the shops and houses at the same reckless speed and Detective Sergeant Boyle's black Audi clung only three or four metres behind it. Katie could hear their suspension thumping and clonking as they hit the potholes in the tarmac.

Like some dramatic twist of fate, they reached the bottom of Shandon Street at Farren's Quay right beside the boarded-up shell of the Toirneach Damhsa dance studio. The Volvo's brakes smoked as it skidded to a halt. When it tried to turn left, though, it was suddenly confronted by a huge Guinness truck which trumpeted its horn like an outraged bull elephant.

Farren's Quay was one-way westwards and there was no room for the Volvo to manoeuvre its way past the truck even if it tried to drive over the pavement. The driver turned around in his seat and tried to reverse, but Detective Sergeant Boyle's Audi came around the corner and hit it just behind the nearside rear wheel, knocking it sideways.

The Ghost Team immediately opened up the rear doors of their car, but at the same time the passenger door of the Volvo opened up, too. An AIRA man in a black sweater and jeans raised a sub-machine gun and fired three quick bursts at the Audi, shattering its windscreen and one of its rear windows. The Ghost Team men dropped down to take cover behind their doors, and as they did so the sub-machine gunner slammed his door shut again and the Volvo backed up with its wheels spinning and rammed the Audi out of its way.

Detective Sergeant Begley was slowing right down as Farren's Quay came into sight and as soon as they heard the rattle of sub-machine gun fire he jammed his foot on the brake and reversed until they were shielded by the flower shop on the corner. Katie climbed out of the car, tugging her revolver out of its holster, and looked cautiously through the florist's windows to see what was happening.

The Volvo had backed into the railings at the corner of Griffith Bridge. It appeared to be jammed there because she could hear its tyres making an abrasive slithering sound and see clouds of black rubber smoke. The Ghost Team were taking advantage of that by shooting with their Heckler & Koch sub-machine guns into its radiator and front wheels. The cracking and popping and gunfire sounded like a firework display.

The passenger window of the Volvo came down and the AIRA man poked out his sub-machine gun to fire another burst. Bullets ricocheted in all directions, rattling across the pavement and hitting the façade of the funeral director's. Then the Volvo gunned its engine to screaming pitch, wrenching at the railings again and again. At last, with a metallic screech, it tore itself free and lurched forward, colliding with the Audi a second time. The Ghost Team men fired short concentrated bursts into its doors and boot and petrol tank. They avoided shooting directly into the windows – they were under orders not to kill the suspects unless they really had no alternative.

Katie was still shielded by the florist's windows when the Volvo's petrol tank exploded. There was a deep *whoomph* and a huge ball of orange flame rolled out of it, quickly turning into oily black smoke. Even around the corner she could feel the heat of it.

Almost at once, though, there was another explosion. This was ten times more forceful than the petrol tank blowing up. Katie felt as if a superheated wind had blasted over her. This time the flower shop windows were turned instantly to what looked like ice, and then dropped to the ground.

Two of the Ghost Team had been knocked on to their backs, but she couldn't take her eyes off the Volvo. It was burning like a giant white-hot stove. All she could see through the glare was the outlines of three men, two of them sitting in the front and one in the back, waving their arms almost comically, as if they were life-size marionettes.

In what must have been a last desperate attempt to save himself, the driver somehow managed to shift the Volvo into reverse and put his foot down. The burning car jolted backwards, mounting the pavement and forcing its way through the twisted railings with a scraping noise that put Katie's teeth on edge. It teetered right on the brink of the parapet for a few seconds and then dropped backwards into the river, landing with a deep double-slapping splash and a fierce hissing sound. Clouds of smoke and steam billowed up into the air, smelling of petrol and melting plastic.

Katie and Detective Sergeant Begley crossed quickly over to the bridge and looked down into the water. The tide was in, so the river was deep, but even the river hadn't extinguished the fire. The surface was boiling and bubbling furiously and underneath it they could see the incandescent green outline of the Volvo, still burning. Katie was sure she could even see the man who had been sitting in the passenger seat convulsively waving one arm out of the open window.

Detective Ó Doibhilin came up behind them and stared down at the weirdly luminous river and the car that was still ablaze beneath it.

'Now that – is – fecking – *impossible*,' he declared.

'No,' said Katie. 'That's TPA more than likely – the same stuff that was used to burn down the dance studio there. The petrol tank going up must have ignited it. It burns anywhere, TPA, even in a vacuum, or underwater, like magnesium.'

Detective Sergeant Begley was calling for the fire brigade and an ambulance. When he had put down his r/t, he came over and said, 'They'll be here in five minutes max, that's what they said. To be honest with you, I haven't a notion what the point is in calling for either of them. How can the fire brigade put out a fire underwater, and what can the paramedics do for three fellows after they've been incinerated and drownded, and probably shot a few times into the bargain?'

Thirty-five

Two hours later, Katie called an informal press briefing on the steps of the Garda station at Anglesea Street. It was sunny now, but a cold wind was blowing which made all their coats flap like washing on a line.

Fionnuala Sweeney from RTÉ's *Ireland AM* had been keen to use Farren's Quay with its twisted railings as a background, but Katie had ordered the north embankment of the River Lee to be cordoned off all the way westwards from John Redmond Street to the Shaky Bridge.

'All I can tell you at this stage is that there were three suspects in the vehicle whom we had been following for some time. They were thought to be in possession of firearms and explosives and that proved to be the case.'

'Do you know their identities?' asked Dan Keane from the *Examiner*.

'We believe we do, yes, but it would be premature of me to tell you who they were. I have to emphasize that what happened this morning was only one aspect of a much wider ongoing investigation.'

'And what wider investigation exactly is that, ma'am?'

'I'm not in a position to give you that information just yet.'

'So – these three suspects – were they affiliated with any gang or political organization? I mean, are we talking about crime here, DS Maguire, or terrorism?'

'Again, Dan, it could seriously compromise our enquiries if I were to tell you any more just at the moment.'

'There were two separate gunfights – one up at Fair Hill and one down here on Farren's Quay,' said Fionnuala Sweeney. 'I'm assuming they were connected.'

'No comment, I'm afraid.'

'Who was doing the shooting? Would it be right to say that armed gardaí from the Regional Support Unit were involved in both? Or were they detectives from the ERU?'

'I'm afraid I'm not at liberty to give you any more details about the operation, Fionnuala. I'll be making further statements in due course, but that's all for now.'

'What about the car that went into the river?' asked Dan Keane. 'I've talked to several witnesses and some of them said that it was still burning when it was under the water. How could that be?'

'No comment yet, I'm afraid.'

'But they said it was still alight, even though it was completely under the surface like.'

'No comment, Dan. For now, we've called in navy divers from Haulbowline to extricate the three bodies, and then the vehicle will be lifted up from the river bed by crane. When that's done, the Technical Bureau will be able to make a thorough forensic examination of both bodies and vehicle.'

'Is this investigation linked by any chance to the visit of the British defence secretary to Cork today?'

Katie gave one of her frigid smiles and said, 'That's all for now. Thank you for coming. Mathew McElvey will be in touch with you when and if there's any more.'

* * *

She went back up to her office. Moirin had arrived and brought her in a cappuccino. She took off her jacket and sat down on one of the couches under the window and eased off her ankle-boots.

'Mother of God, I'm beat out,' she said.

'I saw you on the news so,' said Moirin. 'That was something terrible by the sound of it, that car going into the river.'

341

'Not the happiest way to start the day,' said Katie. 'But I really need to get some sleep now, if only a couple of hours.'

'Can I fetch you something to eat?'

'No, later maybe, Moirin. I can scarce keep my eyes open.'

As soon as she had arrived at the station she had called Detective Inspector Mulliken to bring him up to date. Later this morning he would apply for a warrant to bring in Joe 'Knucklecracker' Keenan on possible charges of conspiracy. The Keenan house was already cordoned off, with four uniformed gardaí on duty outside to prevent anybody from entering or leaving.

Meanwhile, all across the city, the search for Davy and Cissy Dorgan had resumed. More than thirty officers were going house to house, to every known member of the Authentic IRA and Davy Dorgan's cigarette-smuggling gang, and following up any sightings reported by the public.

Neither Liam O'Breen nor Murtagh McCourt had returned home and neither of them had been seen since they had taken Cissy away from the hospital.

Katie had left it to Detective Sergeant Begley to give Chief Superintendent MacCostagáin a full rundown on the abortive siege at Knockpogue Avenue and the firefight at Farren's Quay. First she would need to have the identities of the three dead AIRA men confirmed, and find out from the burned-out wreckage of their car what weapons and explosives they had been carrying. Then she would hold a meeting to discuss what action they needed to take next. For this she wanted to bring in not only her own detectives but also the ERU detectives in charge of Ian Bowthorpe's security. With Davy Dorgan still at large she was concerned that he might be planning another assassination attempt, even though it was much less likely now that his three hit men from Ulster had been eliminated.

She lay on her couch and closed her eyes and fell asleep within minutes. She dreamed that she was walking through the woods with Barney, but that he kept disappearing. She called him and called him, but when he reappeared and ran up to her he looked different somehow, as if his red colour had lost its lustre and his eyes were bulging.

You're not Barney. You're another dog.

He ran off again and this time he didn't return. Katie struggled her way through the underbrush but it grew increasingly prickly and tangly, and after a while her coat was so snared with brambles that she was unable to move.

Where are you? I don't know where you are.

'I'm right here,' said a woman's voice.

Katie opened her eyes. Bending over in front of her with a smile on her face was Dr Mary Kelley, the assistant deputy state pathologist. Both of her thinly plucked eyebrows were raised in amusement.

'Oh, I'm sorry,' said Katie, sitting up. 'I went totally haboo then. I didn't get any sleep last night at all.'

'I'm so sorry to wake you, but I thought I'd come in to see you in person,' said Dr Kelley. 'I've completed my post-mortem examination of Mrs Dennehy and I'm on my way to catch the 12.20 to Dublin.'

'Oh. When will you be back? We'll be needing you again on Monday.'

'Sure, yes. I heard on the radio this morning that three deceased fellows were recovered from the river, but Dr Mulready will have to come down and deal with those. It's my anniversary and I'm having a few days off in Italy next week – Verona.'

Katie stood up and went over to her desk. Her cappuccino was still there but it was stone-cold now and the froth was flat. 'So . . . what's the story with Mrs Dennehy? It looked to me as if she'd been sexually assaulted.'

'Oh, you're spot on there,' said Dr Kelley. 'Sexually assaulted and not just by one assailant. Fortunately for us, she had *not* done what most women do when they're raped, which is to give themselves a thorough wash. It's almost as if she wanted to leave material evidence of what had been done to her.'

'So, how many assailants, would you say?'

'It's difficult to say exactly, but the acid phosphatase and Christmas tree tests definitely showed the fluid in Mrs Dennehy's vagina to be semen. We call it the Christmas tree test because of the dyes we use – picroindigocarmine stains the tails and necks of the sperm green, while nuclear red stains their heads scarlet.'

'Yes,' said Katie. She knew that, but she always thought it sounded unpleasantly flippant, considering why the test was usually carried out.

'Obviously the sperm cells had deteriorated considerably since she was raped, but they tend to survive longer inside the vagina,' Dr Kelley went on. 'Judging by the quantity, it was the semen of more than one man, possibly as many as three or four. Your average ejaculation is 3.5 ml and I found almost three times that. Some of it was ejaculated high up inside the vagina while I found some of it just inside the labia, and indeed some on the labia themselves, so it was possible to distinguish one sample from another.'

'Jesus. Poor woman.'

'There's another clear indication that there was more than one assailant, and that's the distinct difference in sperm count between different samples. Smoking and drinking can dramatically lower a man's sperm count, and at least one sample appeared to have oligosperma, or no sperm at all. It's even conceivable that there were more than four assailants and that some of them didn't ejaculate, which is why I also tested for prostate specific antigen. You have to be cautious with that, though, because it's also produced by the majority of women from glands around the urethra. It can even be present in breast milk.'

'You've sent the DNA tests to Bill Phinner?'

'Of course, yes. I brought them up here to the station with me and handed them over to him before I came up to see you.'

'Cause of death?'

'Asphyxia, by hanging with a ligature. It's up to the coroner to say if it was suicide or not, but I will simply remark that many suicides pad the ligature they hang themselves with so that it doesn't hurt so much.' She paused, and looked sad, and then she said, 'Maybe she wanted it to be painful. I've known that, too.'

'Thank you, Doctor.'

Dr Kelley handed over a pink plastic folder. 'There's my full report in there, as well as a DVD with all my photographs on it. Apart from all the bruises, she had no distinguishing marks on her body other than a small tattoo on her left shoulder.'

'Oh, yes? And what was that of?'

'A little bird. A nightingale it looked like.'

Katie found herself blushing as she took the envelope.

I have a songbird, sweetheart... tattooed on my arm...

* * *

She showered and changed into a dark green tweed suit, and Moirin brought her some fresh coffee and an egg sandwich.

She was still eating it when Frank Magorian came in to her office without knocking. He was wearing a black suit and a black tie, as if he had just come back from a funeral.

'Well, you made a real hames of that, I'd say,' he told her, walking right up to her desk and standing in front of her with his arms folded.

'Oh, good morning, sir,' said Katie, patting crumbs from her lips with her fingertips.

'I've had a stiff complaint this morning from Harcourt Street,' said Frank Magorian. 'They were more than slightly vexed by the way you handled that siege situation up at Fair Hill, overriding their team leader. And as for that firework display down by the river . . . what in the name of Saint Joan was that all about? My phone hasn't stopped ringing all morning.'

Katie took a steadying breath. 'Sir – I made a calculated decision to withdraw from the Keenan property because one ERU detective had already been shot and wounded and I didn't want to see any more casualties. There was a high risk to the other occupants of the house, and to the neighbours. There was so much gunfire that it would have been dangerous even to try to evacuate them.'

'And so you decided on a high-speed car chase down to the centre of the city, and one almighty fireball, from what I've been told about it? That was your less risky alternative, was it?'

Katie looked him directly in the eyes. 'It was very early in the morning and there were no pedestrians about. The fireball was caused by the highly explosive materials that the suspects were carrying in their own vehicle. The suspects themselves were the only fatalities. Considering they were firing at the NSU team with sub-machine guns, I would say that they rather brought it on themselves, wouldn't you?'

'I don't care for spectaculars,' said Frank Magorian. 'This is Cork, Katie, not the Wild West.'

Katie was about to retort that it was being upstaged by a woman that really annoyed him, but she said nothing. Detective Inspector Mulliken's request to the ERU to follow the three suspects would have gone through the Assistant Commissioner's office as a matter of protocol, and if the siege at Knockpogue Avenue had been successful Frank Magorian could have taken the credit for it.

Katie said, 'I'm holding a briefing about two-ish so that we can assess what further action we should be taking against Davy Dorgan and the rest of his gang. I'll notify you when I've fixed a time for it and you're more than welcome to come along.'

'I'll have to see. I'll be attending a lunch at the Maritime College with Commodore Tully and the Lord Mayor and the British defence secretary.'

'I do hope it's enjoyable, sir.' She was tempted to add, 'but don't come cribbing to me if you get a salmon bone stuck in your throat', but again she said nothing and simply smiled.

When she had finished her sandwich she went down to see Superintendent Pearse so that he could give her an update on the policing arrangements for that evening's step-dancing *feis* at the Opera House.

'We're expecting a capacity crowd, so that's a thousand,' said Superintendent Pearse. 'We'll have fifty officers stationed around Emmett Place and Lavitt's Quay, and another twenty inside the

Opera House itself, and of course this Ian Bowthorpe will have his five close protection officers.'

'It would ease my mind so much if we could track down Davy Dorgan before this evening,' said Katie. 'Still – all your officers have his picture, don't they, and pictures of his closest gang members?'

'They do, of course, and we conducted a thorough search of the building this morning, from the basement all the way up to the fly tower. We'll be searching it again immediately before the doors open, just to make sure nobody's left any suspicious packages lying around. There's also going to be a total ban on anybody going backstage apart from the dancers themselves and their managers.'

'That's grand, Michael, thank you.'

When she returned to her office she found that Kyna was there, sitting by the window. She was wearing a boxy grey jacket and a grey knee-length skirt and black high-shine lipstick. She stood up when Katie came in, but she didn't come across and kiss her because Moirin's door was open.

'What's the plan for this evening, ma'am?' she asked her.

'For you, Kyna, I think the most effective thing you could do would be to mingle with the audience at the *feis*,' said Katie. 'You've seen most of Dorgan's crew up at the Templegate, haven't you? If you reck any of them there, don't hesitate. Arrest them first and make excuses afterwards.'

Kyna nodded. She was silent for a moment, and then, without looking at Katie, she said, 'We need to talk, don't we?'

'Yes. Probably. But not now. Not today, in fact. Not till we've lifted Dorgan and I've found out what's become of little Cissy. I need you right now, Kyna. You know that collection of scummers better than any of us.'

She had started to tell her about the results of Dr Kelley's post-mortem on Maggie Dennehy when Bill Phinner appeared, holding up a clear plastic evidence bag as if it were a goldfish he had won at the fair. Katie could see that it contained the black Glock automatic pistol that gardaí had recovered from the shooting outside the Dorgan house.

'Can we stall it for a moment, Kyna?' she said. Then, 'Bill, what's the story? I hope you have some results for me there!'

'With any luck, ma'am,' he told her in his usual weary tone.

'I've just been telling DS Ni Nuallán here about the samples that Dr Kelley took from Mrs Dennehy. Gang-rape, no doubt about it.'

'We're testing those now,' said Bill Phinner. 'There's a fair old tangle of sperm there – a right whinge – but the DNA will tell us one from another.'

He laid the Glock down on Katie's desk. 'It's this gun that's interesting. It's a third-generation Glock 17C, manufactured in 1998. We've test-fired it and there's no question about it at all, it's the same weapon that was used to shoot Ronan Barrett in the dance studio attic and probably Saoirse MacAuliffe, too – and it's the same weapon that was used to shoot Niall Gleeson in his car. Apart from blowing the mouth off Bernie Dennehy, of course.'

'It was used to shoot *all* of them? So, have you been able to identify whose gun it is?'

'You can see how rough the chequering is on the frame grip, so it's almost impossible to lift a clear fingerprint off of it even with the Livescan. However, there are three very distinct fingerprints on the right-hand side and a thumbprint on the left. There's another fingerprint on the trigger and even though it's partially smudged it corresponds with one of the prints on the side.'

'And have you managed to make a match?'

'We have, yes. Davy Dorgan handled it, as he admitted that he did. The print on the trigger is his. But the other prints are Bernie Dennehy's. If the gun had belonged to Davy Dorgan, how did Bernie Dennehy's prints get on to it at all?'

'How many rounds are in the magazine?'

'Three, out of a possible eight. But here's another question that needs to be answered. The fingerprints on the rounds in the magazine match the fingerprints on the two spent casings we retrieved from the Dorgans' front garden, but none of them match Dorgan's or Dennehy's. Whoever loaded that gun, it wasn't either of them.'

'But whoever it was, don't we have their prints on Pulse?'

Bill Phinner shook his head.

'This is a right head-wreck,' said Katie. 'Somebody loaded that gun and somebody used it to shoot those two dancers. DI Mulliken was leaning towards Dorgan being the shooter because he would have been able to get hold of the chemicals that started that fire. On the other hand, Dennehy had a possible motive for shooting Gleeson because of the arrangement he had made for Gleeson to sleep with his wife. But if it was his gun, what possible motive could he have had for shooting the dancers? And what was the real reason he wanted to shoot Dorgan? And who loaded it?'

'And who gang-raped Maggie Dennehy?' asked Kyna.

Katie looked down at the gun on her desk. 'I think when we find that out, everything else may begin to slot into place. I hope so, anyway. DI Mulliken said that it was all coming together like a jigsaw, but if you ask me somebody just dropped the jigsaw on the floor and scattered all the pieces.'

'If we have the DNA records of any of the rapists, then I should be able to tell you later today who they were,' said Bill Phinner.

'Finding Dorgan and Cissy would be a good start, too,' said Katie. 'I'm praying that no harm has come to that little girl. If it meant saving his own skin, I wouldn't put it past Dorgan to sacrifice his own sister.'

Thirty-six

When Katie and Kyna arrived outside the shining glass frontage of the Opera House, Emmett Place was already crowded, although lines of people were beginning to file in slowly through the revolving door. Under their raincoats both of them wore evening dress. Katie was wearing the new maroon Roland Mouret dress she had bought in the sale last month at Brown Thomas, and Kyna a navy pencil dress that she had found in Cork Vintage Quarter.

Uniformed gardaí were positioned at each end of Emmett Place and all along the quay. At least half a dozen more were gathered in the foyer, ushering the guests into a walk-through metal detector and quickly frisking all those who made it beep. A black Labrador from the Dog Support Unit was sitting nearby, sniffing at everyone who passed by. In spite of the high level of security, the foyer was noisy with chatter and laughter, and the 'Banshee Reel' was playing from loudspeakers, which lifted the mood even more.

'I have to go up to the bar and make my presence known to the VIPs,' Katie told Kyna, as they left their coats in the cloakroom. She almost had to shout so that she could be heard over the hubbub.

'That's all right, ma'am,' said Kyna. 'I'll be after mingling now to see who I can see.'

She gave Katie's hand a quick, light squeeze and disappeared into the crowd.

Katie went upstairs to the Blue Angel bar, which was already packed with dignitaries in evening dress. Outside the high glass walls there was a sparkling view of the river. She could see that traffic was moving again along Camden Quay, although there

350

were orange flashing lights and barriers still around the corner of Griffith Bridge where the Volvo had crashed through the railings.

Ian Bowthorpe was standing at the far end of the bar, chatting to the Lord Mayor and two of the Cork TDs. Frank Magorian was there, too, looking large-headed and handsome and smooth, but Chief Superintendent MacCostagáin was wearing a dinner jacket that was far too tight for him, as if he hadn't worn it since he celebrated the millennium, and he looked hot and ill at ease.

Five well-built men were standing around Ian Bowthorpe, all in black tie, none of them smiling or talking. Their eyes were constantly scanning the guests in the bar, although Katie thought there was little danger of his being attacked by white-haired old Eibhlin O'Reilly from An Coimisiún Le Rinci Gaelacha, one of the Cork judges for the Commission of Irish Dance, who must have been at least eighty, or by the smart house manager, Feena McGrath, or any other of the specially invited guests.

Ian Bowthorpe himself was tall, almost as tall as Frank Magorian, but apart from a pot belly he was very slender, with a hooked nose and rounded shoulders, like a flamingo. His cheeks were two cherry-red spots and he had protuberant front teeth. Katie could pick out his distinctive English drawl from the opposite end of the bar.

When she had managed to struggle her way through the guests, Katie came up to him and Chief Superintendent MacCostagáin introduced her.

'I'd like you to meet Detective Superintendent Kathleen Maguire, one of our leading lights here in Cork,' he told him.

Ian Bowthorpe held out his hand. 'It's a great pleasure, Detective Superintendent. I've been very gratified to notice that women have been gradually taking more and more control of the Irish police force. They're so much more sensible, don't you think, women, and they don't let anybody get away with anything. At least, my wife doesn't!'

'Grand to meet you, too, sir,' said Katie.

351

'Perhaps you can answer one question that's always fascinated me.' Ian Bowthorpe smiled down at her. 'If you tell somebody here in Ireland that they're under arrest but they can only understand Irish, does it still count?'

Katie knew that he was being lighthearted, but she kept a serious expression on her face. 'Oh, yes, sir. I always say to every suspect, *An dtuigeann tú go mbeidh tú bheith i do chónaí ar aon rud ach arán agus uisce as seo amach?* That always makes it quite clear that they've been scooped.'

'I see,' said Ian Bowthorpe. 'That's answered that question, then.'

'I hope you enjoy the dancing, sir,' said Katie before he had a chance to ask her to translate what she had said. 'I think you'll find that we've some of the best step-dancers in the country here in Cork, even the very young ones.'

'Well, I'm really looking forward to it,' he told her. 'But what does—?'

Katie was already backing away and he lifted one hand as if to stop her leaving, but Feena McGrath pushed her way in between them and said, 'We really need to be taking our seats now, Mr Bowthorpe. The dancing will be after starting in a few minutes.'

As the Opera House managers and his close protection officers led him away, Ian Bowthorpe turned to Katie and gave her a hopeless shrug.

'Email me!' he called back.

'Don't tell me you've made a new friend of him, Kathleen?' asked Chief Superintendent MacCostagáin. 'That must be the quickest pick-up in history!'

Frank Magorian, on the other hand, gave her a testy look, as if he were disgusted at her for teasing a VIP guest.

Now it was time for everybody to be making their way into the high, semicircular auditorium. A twelve-piece band called the Quarry Yard Martyrs were already screeching and twanging and tootling as they tuned up fiddles and banjos and penny whistles and Uilleann pipes and bodhrans. Katie had chosen to sit in the dress circle on the left-hand side, which would give her a clear view of almost the entire Opera House. She had brought a compact pair of binoculars in her purse so that she could focus on individual members of the audience.

Detectives O'Donovan and Markey were there, too, on opposite sides of the stalls. She could see them in their seats already.

At last the house lights dimmed and the director of the *feis*, Kevin Moloney, came out on to the stage in a spangly green suit, his bald head shining.

'Folks – this is a very special *feis* we're holding here today. It's a qualifying *oireachtas* between fifteen different dance troupes, with the winners taking away the McGoldrick Trophy for the best step-dancers in the southern region. But it's also our way of entertaining Mr Ian Bowthorpe from the British government, who has come to Ireland, and Cork in particular, to show us that our two countries still have strong mutual interests after Brexit. Britain and Ireland have not always been the closest of friends, as we all know, especially down here in the Rebel County. But in music and dance this evening, we're celebrating what we share together, not what separates us.'

There was more applause, and whistling, and the band struck up with 'Garden of Daisies'. The curtains rose and on to the stage sprang the sixteen young girls from the Kilpatrick School of Dancing, their curly wigs bouncing, their tiaras and short red dresses glittering, their hard shoes hammering on the stage.

The stage lights were dazzling but the dancers had applied fake tan to their faces and knees so as not to look pallid.

Almost as soon as they had started dancing, Katie's iPhone vibrated. She saw that she had a call from Jenny Tierney, her next-door neighbour. She didn't answer it, but stood up and made her way along the line of seats to the entrance, apologizing to everybody who had to stand up to let her past.

When she came out on to the landing, she rang Jenny back. A garda who was standing by the railings couldn't take his eyes off her. He clearly knew who she was, but he had never seen her in evening dress before, with dangling crystal earrings.

Jenny Tierney was in tears. 'I couldn't think who to call first, Katie – yourself or the local guards. In the end I decided that you would know what to do for the best.'

'What's the matter, Jenny? What's wrong?'

'I was taking Barney out for his evening walk and we were down by Dock Cottages when this van pulled up alongside of us. Four fellows jumped out. One of them wrapped his arms around me so that there was nothing I could do to stop them. The others grabbed hold of Barney and shoved him in the back of the van. He was barking and struggling but they had a tight grip on his collar and couldn't pull himself free. Then it was *slam!* and the van doors were shut and they were away. It all happened so quick.'

Katie felt as if she were slowly being lowered into ice-cold water. She had to put one finger in her ear because the music was so loud and the audience were cheering and clapping in time.

'When did this happen, Jenny?'

'Not more than ten minutes ago. I tell you, I legged it all the way back to the house.'

'Did any of the men say anything?'

'Not a word, none of them. They just stopped, grabbed hold of Barney, and then they were gone.'

'You weren't hurt at all yourself?'

'No – not at all. Fierce shook up, I don't mind telling you. It put the heart crossways in me. But as soon as they'd snatched Barney away, the fellow let go of me.'

'Can you describe any of them, these fellows?'

'No. They were all pretty big, but they were all wearing them balumaclavas so you couldn't see their faces.'

'How about the van?'

'I'm not sure. I wouldn't know what make it was, but it was kind of a darky colour.'

'What – black? Or grey? Or navy blue, maybe?'

'I couldn't say for certain. The street light isn't all that clever along there.'

354

'Did you see a number plate?'

'I didn't, no. I couldn't be sure that it even had one.'

'All right, Jenny. I'm sorry you've had such a shock, but I'm glad you weren't injured. Can I ask you to do me a favour and ring Midleton Garda station? What's the time? I think Cobh will probably be closed by now. Tell them who I am and exactly what happened, and try to remember as many details about those men and their van as you can. I'm stuck here at the Cork Opera House at the moment, Jenny, and I simply can't leave, but I'll be back as soon as I can.'

'That poor devil Barney. He must be so frightened. Pray God those fellows do nothing to harm him. Why do you think they took him?'

'I don't know, Jenny. It could have been because of me – somebody wanting to take their revenge on me for some reason. Either that, or they took him simply because he's a fine-looking dog and they want to make some money out of him, for breeding or fighting or selling on – who knows?'

'Right you are, then, Katie, I'll ring the guards at Midleton directly. Is it okay if I call you back after?'

'Sure, Jenny. Any time.'

After Jenny had rung off, Katie stayed where she was for a while, with the garda still watching her. Inside the Opera House the music had changed now to 'King of the Fairies', but the whooping and stamping continued. She felt strangely light-headed and she desperately wished she was free to leave the Opera House right now and drive straight home to Cobh, even though she knew it would be pointless. Barney would either be dead by now or tens of kilometres away, depending on why he had been taken.

As conscientious as they were, she knew that the Midleton gardaí wouldn't regard this dog-napping as the crime of the century. Barney meant so much to her. John had given him to her after her first Irish setter, Sergeant, had been killed, and now John was gone, too. Not only that, Barney seemed to have such a special rapport with Conor, which made her think Conor was the right man for her. At the end of the day, though, he was only a dog, and one stolen dog couldn't justify the time and expense of a major investigation.

She gave the garda a rueful smile and went back into the auditorium.

Thirty-seven

During the interval, Kyna went to the bar and slowly circled around to see if she could recognize anybody there. She carried a glass of red wine in her hand so that she would look as if she were just another guest pushing her way back through the crowd to meet up with her friends. Almost all of the men smiled and winked at her as she breathed in to ease herself past them, and almost all of the women scowled. That secretly amused her, the way she felt about men.

She had been hoping to meet up with Katie, but Katie was on the opposite side of the bar by the window, busy talking to Assistant Commissioner Frank Magorian and Chief Superintendent MacCostagáin. The bar was too noisy and Kyna was too far away to hear what Katie was saying, but for some reason she looked worried. Chief Superintendent MacCostagáin had his hand on her shoulder as if he were reassuring her, and even Frank Magorian was looking concerned. Kyna would have to wait until later to find out what they were talking about, and even then Katie might not tell her. She was a detective superintendent, after all, and Kyna was only a detective sergeant, and there were plenty of policy matters and budgeting projections that she never discussed with her.

A bell rang. It was time now for the second half of the *feis*, and the audience started to file back into the auditorium. Kyna set down her wine glass on the bar and followed them into the stalls. Ian Bowthorpe and his close protection officers had not yet taken their places in the front row, although two of his detectives were standing on either side of their seats and one of them was talking into his throat mic.

The first performance of the second half was going to be a display by Laethanta na Rince, the dance troupe run by Steven Joyce. Because of that, the stagehands had used the interval to lay fifty oak doors flat on the stage, five across and ten down, almost completely covering it.

Again, the Quarry Yard Martyrs began to scrape at their instruments, and one of them tuned up by playing a few bars from the 'Lonesome Boatman' on the penny whistle, which was followed by spontaneous applause.

Ian Bowthorpe and his entourage hurried into the stalls and sat down just as the lights were dimming. The band struck up with 'Job of Journeywork' and Laethanta na Rince came dancing in from the wings to take up their formation on the stage. Their hard shoes thundered on the doors, far louder than the other dancers had sounded, and they were greeted with whistles and cheers.

Kyna didn't sit down. She walked slowly up the aisle at the side of the auditorium, carefully scanning the faces in one row after another. She saw Detectives O'Donovan and Markey sitting in the audience, and they saw her, but they deliberately didn't acknowledge each other.

She was beginning to think that when Katie had chased the AIRA men into the river she must have put an end to Davy Dorgan's plot to assassinate Ian Bowthorpe for good. Either that, or Dorgan had never really had a realistic plan to kill the defence secretary, and he had simply been boasting to his gang in the Templegate Tavern.

Some of the audience were up on their feet and cheering as Laethanta na Rince danced around in a circle, their shoes slamming harder and harder on the wooden doors and their steps becoming faster and increasingly complex. Kyna had reached the rear of the auditorium now, and she was turning around to watch them herself. As she did so, she looked out through the windows in the exit doors and glimpsed a stagehand hurrying past. She was startled to recognize him as Liam O'Breen.

All of the stagehands at the Opera House this evening were wearing identical T-shirts with *Oireachtas McGoldrick* printed on them in green lettering, but she never could have mistaken those curled-up ears and that mass of wavy brown hair.

She picked up the hem of her dress and half-ran and half-hobbled out into the foyer. She was just in time to see the door on the right-hand side of the foyer slowly closing, so she ran across to it and opened it. The lettering on it said STAFF ONLY, and it led along a plain whitewashed corridor to the back of the Opera House. She looked around. Three uniformed gardaí were standing by the entrance, chatting to the girl in the ticket office, with their Labrador sitting patiently beside them, but since everybody in the Opera House had been screened they weren't paying Kyna any attention. She could hear Liam's footsteps echoing along the corridor, so she tugged up her hem even higher and ran after him.

She caught up with him just as he was opening a wide metal door that led underneath the stage. The clattering of the dancers' hard shoes was deafening down here, combined as it was with the drum-like rumbling of the fifty oak doors and the fiddle and pipe music from the band.

'*Liam!*' Kyna screamed at him. '*Liam!*'

Liam looked round, shocked. He was swinging a large maroon duffel bag which looked as if it was stuffed full and very heavy.

'Roisin?' he shouted back at her. 'What the feck are you doing here?'

'I should be asking you the same question,' she said. She went right up to him and pushed herself in between him and the open doorway.

'Roisin—' he said. 'Get out of my fecking road, will you? Go on – feck away off!'

'My name's not Roisin, Liam, and I'm not a bar-girl.'

'I said get out of my fecking road, you slag. Otherwise I'll drop you, I swear it.'

'What's in the bag, Liam?'

Kyna seized the nylon cords of the duffel bag and tried to tug them away from him, but he swung his left arm and caught her on the side of the head, just underneath her right ear, knocking her sideways. She fell against the metal door frame and jarred her shoulder, but she still made another grab for the duffel bag. As she did so, the gold chain that was holding her own purse snapped and the purse dropped on to the floor.

'Would you feck off, Roisin, for the love of God, before I really hit you a box?'

'I told you, you gurrier, my name's not Roisin. I'm Detective Sergeant Ni Nuallán and you're under arrest!'

'You're fecking *who*?'

'I'm a detective, Liam, and you're lifted! So let go of the bag, will you, and come away out of here! That's unless you want to spend the rest of your twenties in Portlaoise!'

'*What!* You're taking the piss, aren't you? I don't fecking believe you!'

Again, Kyna tried to wrestle the bag away from him, but this time he punched her on the forehead and then again on the cheekbone and as she toppled backwards he kicked her on the hip. She tried to climb to her feet again, but he kicked her on the shin and then the kneecap. She rolled over, but then he lifted his foot and stamped hard on the small of her back.

He said nothing else, but went in through the metal door and slammed it after him. Kyna lay on the concrete floor for a few moments, panting with pain. She managed to climb to her feet at last and try to open the door but Liam had locked or bolted it from the inside. Leaning against the wall, she looked around for her purse because her iPhone was in it, but realized that during the scuffle it must have been kicked inside.

She limped her way back along the corridor as fast as she could, one hand held against her lower spine because it hurt so much. As soon as she came out into the foyer she shouted out to the gardaí standing by the entrance, 'Clear the building! Get everybody out as fast as you can! There could be a bomb!'

Two of them stared at her in bewilderment because they didn't recognize her in her navy-blue evening dress, but the third was a sergeant she had met during her last firearms refresher course and he acted immediately.

'Fire alarm!' he shouted to the girl from the ticket office. To the two gardaí next to him, he snapped, 'Haverty – into the stalls! Fagan – get up to the circle! Get inside there double-quick, but make sure there's no panic!'

He unclipped the mic from his lapel and put out a call to the ERU detectives who were protecting Ian Bowthorpe, and also to the gardaí stationed outside. As the alarm started to shrill, Kyna went over to him and shouted in his ear, 'We need to clear the stage urgently! The bomb could be right underneath it! The suspect has a duffel bag and he's wearing a McGoldrick T-shirt!'

The sergeant gave her the thumbs up and spoke again into his mic. Kyna waited until he had finished and then quickly gave him a detailed description of Liam and told him where she had last seen him. Seven gardaí had come barging in through the Opera House doors, three of them armed, and the sergeant directed them to the door that led to the back of the stage.

While he was doing that, Kyna headed for the stairs that led up to the dress circle. She needed to make sure that Katie was safe.

* * *

Katie stood up as soon as the fire alarm sounded, but the band didn't immediately stop playing and the dancers carried on dancing on the doors.

'Fire!' she shouted. 'Everybody out – *quick*! But stay calm!'

The band kept on playing and the dancers kept on dancing, though when Katie looked down she could see that Ian Bowthorpe's close protection officers were hurriedly pulling him out of the front-row seats in the stalls and Frank Magorian was helping the Lord Mayor to stand up, too.

Members of the audience were beginning to get to their feet, looking around in confusion. There was no smoke and no flames, and Katie knew that the public would almost always ignore a fire alarm unless they could actually see or smell some reason for them to evacuate. She would have to do some pushing and shoving and shouting to make them appreciate that this could be a genuine emergency.

Her iPhone rang and she was about to answer it when she was deafened by the loudest explosion she had ever heard in her life. She was thrown sideways over the row of seats behind her, on top of an elderly couple who had just begun to stand up, so that they tumbled to the floor, too. She hit her cheek hard against an armrest.

A fifteen-metre-wide hole had been blasted open in the centre of the stage, and the fifty oak doors had been shattered into tens of thousands of lethal splinters. Some were only two or three centimetres long, but scores of them were as long as spears and viciously sharp. A woolly cloud of dark grey smoke rolled out from under the stage and disappeared up inside the fly tower, and at the same time pulleys and wires dropped clanking down on to the carnage below.

Katie managed to climb to her feet, her ears singing. When she looked down to the stalls she saw that Ian Bowthorpe was lying in the left-hand aisle, flat on his face, with blood on his white shirt collar. Two of his close protection officers were lying a little nearer the stage and Katie could see that one of them had a metre-long shard of oak sticking out of the back of his neck.

Scores of members of the audience had been sprayed with fragments of wood and in spite of her deafness Katie could hear them screaming and crying. Many had been hit in the face and blinded, and their faces were bloody red masks. One of the TDs had been pinned to his seat by a two-metre javelin that had pierced his abdomen just below the breastbone. He was lifting his arms up and down like a small child trying to get out of a high chair and bubbles of blood were bursting from between his lips.

Although there were terrible injuries in the audience, the casualties on the stage were the most horrific. Almost all of the Laethanta na Rince dance troupe had been killed or seriously injured. Katie saw a girl no older than fifteen lying at the back of the stage, staring up at the ceiling. Both her arms had been blown off and her face was speckled all over with tiny sharp splinters. A young male dancer was perched right on the jagged edge of the hole that had been blown in the floorboards. He was gripping the broken boards to stop himself falling down into the darkness below, but his legs and pelvis had already disappeared and his intestines were hanging down from his waist in long pale loops, and were slowly beginning to unwind and slide out of sight.

Two girls must have been dancing close together when the explosion occurred, because it was impossible to tell which of them was which. Their legs were tangled together and they looked like a single four-legged girl with two heads, one of which looked as if it was screaming.

One of the broken doors was leaning upright at the side of the stage, its side panels blasted away, so that it looked like two crosses, one on top of the other. One of the male dancers was hanging from it with both arms extended, and he wore a crown of splinters.

The fire alarm kept shrilling and shrilling and the cacophony of screaming and shouting and moaning grew even louder, and Katie thought the scene inside the auditorium was like the performance of some opera about hell.

Although she was still badly shaken herself, she started to usher people out of the dress circle. She knew that she needed to get them out of the building as quickly as possible in case there was another explosive device planted somewhere in the auditorium to catch the first responders. It wasn't easy, though, because all of them were in a deep state of shock, some women were hysterical, and several had fainted.

As she was guiding them to the doors, Kyna appeared, grim-faced. She made her way down the aisle to Katie and briefly hugged her.

Then she said, 'Dorgan did it, I'm sure. He sent Liam in with a bag full of God knows what. I saw him downstairs and tried to stop him but he locked himself under the stage.'

'He blew himself up?' said Katie. 'You mean like a suicide bomber?'

Kyna pulled a face. 'I shouldn't think so. Liam probably thought that all he had to do was plant it and then get the hell out of there. But my guess is that when Dorgan heard the fire alarm he set it off remotely.'

Katie said, 'Let's clear these poor people out of here. We can worry about Dorgan later.'

After Davy Dorgan had disappeared from the house on Mount Nebo Avenue she had sent out an alert for gardaí to keep an eye open for him up at Cork airport and Kent railway station, and Ringaskiddy and Rosslare. If he had set off this bomb, though, he must still be in the country, and not too far away.

Kyna looked down at the massacre on the stage and the bloodied casualties lying around the stalls. 'I don't think I'm going to be able to sleep ever again,' she said. 'Not ever. Not after this.'

Thirty-eight

It was mid-morning before all the casualties were removed from the Opera House. Katie had set up a temporary office in Luigi Malone's restaurant on the opposite side of Emmett Place, and Bill Phinner's technicians had already erected a large blue tent outside the Crawford Art Gallery.

For several hours ambulances were lined all the way along Lavitt's Quay. Twenty-three people had been killed outright, most of them dancers from Laethanta na Rince and members of the audience who had been sitting in the front rows of the stalls. Ian Bowthorpe had suffered concussion and a deep cut on the back of his neck, and one of his close protection officers was in a critical condition with brain damage.

In all, there were nearly two hundred other injuries and at least fifteen people had suffered permanent hearing loss. Katie could still hear a persistent singing sound and she kept jiggling her fingertips in her ears to try and relieve it.

From her table at the front of the restaurant, Katie instructed Detectives O'Donovan and Markey to bring in as many known members of Davy Dorgan's gang for questioning as they could find. Each gang member should have his hands and clothing tested for traces of explosives, and a sample of his DNA taken, too.

She was talking on the phone to Dr Mulready, the pathologist, when an ordnance disposal technician from Collins Barracks came waddling into the restaurant, still wearing his yellowish blast-proof suit, although he had taken off his helmet.

'I've put in a call to Professor Cassidy to inform her how

many fatalities we have,' Katie was saying. 'Yes – she's promised to send down Dr Williams to assist you as soon as she can. And yes, I *do* understand that you'll be totally up the walls, Doctor, but this is the first time we've ever had to face a disaster on this scale. Like *ever*.'

The ordnance disposal technician came up to the table where Katie was sitting. 'I could murder a Coke if there's one going, ma'am. This suit's like a portable Turkish bath. Thirty-five pounds, it weighs, and that's without the helmet.'

Katie beckoned for the waitress and then she said, 'No sign of any other EDs?'

'No. None at all. We've carried out a thorough search with sniffer dogs under the stage and round the back of the building. That was a blast and a half, though. I reckon more than five pounds of C4. Here, look, this is your man.'

He took out his camera and passed it across so that Katie could see the pictures he had taken. At first she couldn't understand what she was looking at. Spread out across the floor was nothing but a pile of twisted red parcel string. It was only when the officer reached over and pointed out a blue running shoe that she realized that the pile of twisted red parcel string was Liam, blown inside out.

* * *

It was almost nine o'clock that evening before she returned to her office. The singing in her ears had subsided, but she still felt sick and didn't feel like eating anything. One of the waitresses at Luigi Malone's had brought her a vegetarian pizza and she had chewed one mouthful, but she hadn't been able to swallow it and discreetly spat it into her napkin.

She sat down and switched on her desk lamp. She sat there staring at the notes and paperwork in front of her, but she was unable to focus on them. Detective O'Donovan had left her a list of nine members of Davy Dorgan's gang that he and Detective Markey had been able to locate and bring in to the station, but a cursory glance at his report told her that all of them had refused to answer any questions.

She had been sitting there for almost ten minutes when her phone rang. She picked it up and said, 'DS Maguire.'

'Oh, you're back at last,' said a hoarse man's voice. 'This is about the fifty-eighth time I've tried to ring you today.'

'Have you seen the news?' Katie asked him. 'I was fierce tied up, to say the least.'

'The bomb at the Opera House. Oh, yes, I saw that all right. That was a shocker, wasn't it? Were you there? All them young dancers getting blown up. Desperate.'

'Is there something you wanted to talk to me about?' asked Katie.

'Well, there is, sure. It's about that dog of yours, as a matter of fact.'

'Barney? Do you have him? Who are you?'

'We do have him, yes. He's perfectly safe, though. Don't you be after worrying about that, Detective Super-duper Maguire.'

'Who are you?'

'If I told you that, it would kind of defeat the whole object now, wouldn't it? Because then you'd come after me and I wouldn't have the leverage any longer.'

'What leverage? What are you talking about?'

'Come on, now, think about it. Who did you collar lately, and who's on police bail waiting to have charges brung against him? Think "dogs" like.'

'You're calling for Guzz Eye McManus.'

'That's the very man. You have it.'

'So what you're telling me is that if I arrange for the charges against McManus to be dropped, you'll let me have Barney back.'

'Holy Christ on a donkey! No wonder you're a detective! You have it exactly! If you forget about the charges against the Guzz, your Barney will be returned to you safe and well and that'll be the end of it. We can let bygones be bygones and there'll be peace on earth and goodwill to all men and women and one or two dogs, too.'

Katie retched abruptly and had to press her hand over her mouth. *Not Barney. For the love of God, please don't let them hurt Barney.*

'Are you still there, Detective Super-duper?' the man asked her.

'Yes, I'm still here. I can't give you an answer right now, though. The paperwork will already have been passed to the DPP.'

'Ah sure, but that won't be any kind of a problem, will it? All you have to do is tell them you made a bit of a batoon and that the Guzz is innocent after all. Maybe a case of mistaken identity. Well, maybe not. Fierce difficult to mistake the Guzz for somebody else. But you'll think of some skit, I'm sure of it. You want your dog back, after all, don't you?'

Katie was shaking. It was all she could do not to scream at him and warn him that if he touched even one single hair of Barney's glossy red coat, she would find him, however long it took, and she would make him sorry that he had ever been born.

'How can I contact you?' she asked him.

'Don't try tracing this call because it won't get you anywhere at all, I can tell you that for starters. I'll ring you back tomorrow about two o'clock, how's that? That'll give you enough time to sort everything out, won't it?'

'Yes. Ring back about two. But in the meantime, please don't hurt Barney. Make sure you give him something to eat and drink and somewhere comfortable to sleep. If you do that, he won't give you any trouble at all, I promise you.'

'Not a bother, Detective Super-duper. You know us. We've years of experience when it comes to dealing with dogs.'

Katie was about to say something caustic to him – *I know what you've had years of experience doing to dogs, you sadistic gowl* – but he rang off.

At once she called down to Garda Greeley in communications and asked him to trace where the call had come from, even though she was in no doubt at all that her caller had been using a burner or a ghost phone. Then she rang Conor and told him what had happened. She had already rung him after the bomb had gone off to let him know that she was safe, but now she told him all about Barney being taken.

'Don't cry, Katie,' he told her. 'All you have to do is drop the charges against McManus.'

'I can't,' she sobbed, wiping her eyes with the sleeve of her dress. 'That would be giving in to blackmail, and think of all the other dogs he's going to go on hurting if we let him get away with it.'

'But you're talking about Barney.'

'Conor, I know, but if I drop the charges against McManus, Inspector Carroll will want to know why, and so will Frank Magorian, and I'll be guilty of professional misconduct.'

Conor was silent for a while. Then he said, 'I really don't know, then. I'll have to think about it. Let me see if any of my bent vet friends knows where they might have taken him.'

'Thank you,' said Katie. 'You can tell them there might be a reward in it for them.'

'I will,' he told her. Then, 'How are you now? I've been watching all about the bomb on the news.'

'Shattered, to be honest with you. I'll probably take a Nytol and see if I can get some sleep.'

'Katie—'

'Yes, Conor. I know you do. I'll talk to you again tomorrow, when I've got over the shock.'

* * *

Although she took two sleeping pills, she hardly slept at all that night. The strangest feeling was that she was alone and that there was no Barney sleeping in his basket in the kitchen. She climbed out of bed at 5.30 a.m. and made herself a strong mug of coffee and some plain buttered toast. She stood in the living room eating it and staring out at the rain, feeling empty.

She was back in the office by 7.15 a.m. She went over yesterday's paperwork again, but at the same time kept her television on so that she could watch the continuously running news stories about yesterday's bombing.

The whole country was in a state of shock. The Taoiseach had made a statement saying that it was the greatest tragedy in Ireland this century, and the Bishop of Cork and Ross was holding a Mass to pray for the souls of those who had been killed, as well as their bereaved relatives, and for the speedy recovery of the injured. Two more dancers had succumbed to their injuries and died during the night.

She had caught up on most of her texts and messages when Detective O'Donovan came in. His hair was still wet from the shower and he had sprayed himself a little too liberally with Lynx Iced Musk and Ginger.

'Ah, Patrick, how's it coming on?' asked Katie. 'I've been through the list of Dorgan's cronies you fetched in. It doesn't sound like they were particularly helpful.'

'Sure like, what did you expect? They may not have been involved in blowing up the Opera House, not themselves, but they were bound to have been doing something else illegal when it happened. We surprised one of them counting out eight thousand Bulgarian cigarettes in his kitchen, so we've charged him anyway. No, they all refused to answer any questions – as of course they're legally entitled.'

'But? You look pleased about something.'

Detective O'Donovan held up a clear vinyl folder. 'Bill Phinner gave me these DNA results about five minutes ago. Out of the nine members of Dorgan's gang we pulled in, four of them left traces of their bodily fluids inside Mrs Maggie Dennehy.'

'Serious? Now it's all starting to make sense again.'

'Not only that, there may be a fifth. Dr Kelley took a DNA sample of some traces of fluid on Mrs Dennehy's face and they appear to be a match with one of the gang. Bill Phinner has to test it again, though, because it was very degraded.'

'So it was Dorgan's gang after all who raped Dennehy's wife, like we kind of suspected,' said Katie. 'Maybe they murdered her, or maybe she committed suicide because she'd been raped. But whichever it was, if *that* wasn't Bernie Dennehy's motive to go looking for Dorgan with a gun, then I don't know what could have been.'

'Scanlan is going out to talk to some of Maggie Dennehy's friends and neighbours, to see if she confided in any of them about it. You never know.'

'Good thinking,' said Katie. 'And have her chat to her relations, too – sisters or brothers – especially sisters.'

They were still talking when Chief Superintendent Mac-Costagáin came in. Like almost everybody else in the station, he looked as if he hadn't slept well, and his tie was crooked.

'How's it going on, Kathleen?' he asked her.

'In some directions, sir, I think we're making some progress,' said Katie. 'If we could only track down Davy Dorgan, I believe we'd be close to having this all wrapped up.'

'I've just had Mathew McElvey on to me from the press office. It seems like the media are going to be making *snáth bán* of us later today. They're all asking how that bomber could have managed to fetch so much explosive into the Opera House in spite of all of our security. I mean, Jesus, Kathleen, we had metal detectors and sniffer dogs and more officers around that building than you could shake a stick at.'

'I know, sir, but we still don't know how he got the bomb into the building and we're still trying to find out,' said Katie. 'The bomber himself was a young fellow who was one of Davy Dorgan's crowd. In fact, he was the same young fellow who gave Detective Sergeant Ni Nuallán her information about those Authentic IRA men coming down from Larne.'

'Do you know how bad this makes us look, though?' asked Chief Superintendent MacCostagáin. 'Do you think any foreign government will trust us to protect their VIPs ever again?'

Katie said quietly, 'We'll find out how it was done, sir, believe me, and we'll never let it happen again.' She could tell by the tone of Chief Superintendent MacCostagáin's voice that he was only repeating what Frank Magorian had shouted at him.

'All right, then, fair play to you, Kathleen, but do everything you can to find out like yesterday. There's a rake of important people asking a rake of fierce awkward questions, not only the media. We've had Enda Kenny on the phone, too. Well, Frank Magorian has. How do you think it looks if we invite the British defence secretary to Ireland to discuss our mutual defence and he almost ends up getting blown to smithereens?'

Thirty-nine

Conor came in to the station to see her just before lunchtime.

'Are you sure I can't take you out for a bite to eat?' he asked.

'No thanks, Conor. I'm grand altogether. I have absolutely no appetite at all. If you'd seen those young dancers all in pieces.'

'And you're pretty sure now that it was this Davy Dorgan who was responsible?'

'There's some headers in some of the other IRA splinter groups, but I can't see any of them being mental enough to do this. The Opera House, that's our city's pride and joy. The best and biggest theatre in Ireland. And they didn't even manage to kill the fellow.'

Conor sat down by the window. In the grey light of a rainy morning, with his straight nose and his brown beard and his eyes as clear as Waterford crystal, Katie thought he looked like one of those romantic Irish poets, like Yeats or Kavanagh.

'I've called up a few disreputable people,' he said, picking at his thumbnail. 'I'm afraid they all gave me the same story. None of them knew offhand where Barney might have been taken, although one or two of them said they might be able to find out. The problem is that this is the Guzz we're talking about here and not one of them has the bottle to squeal on the Guzz.'

'Did you tell them there might be some cash in it for them?' .

He nodded. 'They still weren't interested. One of them said, "What good is money going to be to me in St Joseph's Cemetery, I'd like to know? There's no shops there." '

'So it looks like I have only two choices, doesn't it?' said Katie.

373

Conor stood up and came over and laid his hands on her shoulders. 'This is one decision I can't make for you, Katie. I know how much Barney means to you. I'm pure fond of him, too. But I can also understand the professional problem you're up against. If a detective superintendent drops charges against an offender just because her dog's been stolen . . . well, I can imagine what the *Irish Times* would make of it.'

'You really don't think you can find him?'

'I've still a few more contacts to try. Not very reliable ones, but I'll try them anyway. If I can't get any kind of a result by two o'clock when this fellow rings you, see if you can stall him. I have to say this to you, though – if I can't find him, then I don't think anybody can.'

'I know,' said Katie very quietly. 'Thanks for trying, anyway.'

* * *

She visited the Opera House again that morning. Emmett Place was cordoned off and there were still two fire engines parked outside, as well as three skip lorries which were being loaded with broken seats and shattered light fittings and splintered floorboards from the stage.

She walked down the aisle to the orchestra pit, where Bill Phinner was talking to Assistant Chief Fire Officer Matthew Whalen.

Matthew Whalen held out his hand as Katie approached and said, 'We meet again, Detective Superintendent, I'm sad to say, and far too soon.'

'We're fairly sure it was C4,' said Bill Phinner. 'DS Ni Nuallán said the bomber was carrying a duffel bag and a bag like that could have easy contained anything up to three kilos of explosive.'

'Three kilos could do this much damage?'

'Oh, easily,' said Matthew Whalen. 'C4 explodes at more than eight thousand metres a second and after the initial blast the force is all sucked back in again, so the human body doesn't stand much of a chance.'

Bill Phinner looked around and said, 'We've found shreds of Mylar plastic film almost everywhere, and that's usually used to seal each demolition block of C4. We've also carried out a quick preliminary test with thymol crystals and sulphuric acid. When you mix them with C4, they turn a rosy pink colour. Of course, we'll be taking more samples back to the lab for X-rays and thin-layer chromatography. But – C4, almost certainly.'

'I'm still wondering how the bomber got it in here,' said Katie. 'It's detectable, isn't it, C4, even before it's been exploded?'

'Generally, yes, because most of the C4 that Irish terrorist groups have been using comes from the States and American explosives are almost invariably mixed with a taggant, such as DMDNB, which makes them detectable to sniffer dogs. A sniffer dog can pick up the scent of DMDNB even if it's only 0.5 parts in a billion.'

Katie tried not to think of Barney when Matthew Whalen said that.

'So – even if it was sealed with this plastic and well wrapped up, it's unlikely that the bomb could have been brought in through our security screening?'

'We'll be able to tell you more when we've run our full range of tests,' said Bill Phinner. 'But, yes. Highly unlikely, I'd say, ma'am. Highly unlikely.'

* * *

By the time she returned to Anglesea Street three of the four suspects from the Maggie Dennehy rape case had been arrested and brought in to the station. Katie went downstairs to the interview rooms where they were being held waiting for their lawyers. She looked at each of them without introducing herself – Billy, Darragh, Kevan and Alroy – just because she wanted to see what kind of men they were.

They all looked back at her shiftily, but none of them spoke. She could hardly imagine anything worse than being sexually assaulted by those ugly, unkempt, unshaven men, every one of them reeking of stale alcohol and cigarettes and body odour.

Kyna met her in her office when she came back. Katie hadn't asked her to accompany her because the men would have recognized her as Roisin the bar-girl and she didn't want their lawyers pleading entrapment.

It was past two o'clock and the dog-napper had still not called back about Barney. Katie tried to put him out of her mind, but she couldn't help glancing at the clock on her desk every few minutes.

Kyna said, 'I went round to Liam's flat with O'Mara this morning and searched it. There was nothing there of any interest except for a few porn mags. Nothing to connect him with Davy Dorgan. He was scared stiff of Dorgan, but I still don't think he would have knowingly gone on a suicide mission.'

'I agree with you,' said Katie. 'They might be mental, the Authentic IRA, but they're not Isis.'

There was a long silence between them and then Kyna said, 'My mind's all jumbled up at the moment, ma'am. I'll stay here at Anglesea Street until this investigation's over, but then I think I'll probably be applying for a transfer to Dublin, like I was going to before.'

'Give yourself some time,' Katie told her. 'Like you say, we're all in a state of shock right now, so you don't want to be making any major decisions, not yet. I promise you I won't be putting any pressure on you myself, Kyna. You know how fond I am of you, don't you, but I'll never stop needing a man in my life, so the decision as to whether you go or stay has to be yours.'

Kyna's mouth puckered and she bent forward in her chair and clenched her fists and tears started to drip on to the folder she was holding.

'I love you, Katie,' she said miserably. 'I love you so much.'

Katie got up to hand her a tissue when her phone rang. She picked it up with her heart beating hard. 'DS Maguire.'

'It's me,' whispered a young girl's voice.

'Who?'

'It's me, Cissy.'

'Cissy! Where are you? Are you safe?'

There was such a long pause that Katie was afraid that she had rung off. At last, though, Cissy said, 'I'm with my brother.'

'You mean Davy?'

'Yes, Davy.'

'But where are you?'

'Pana.'

'You're in Patrick's Street? Where in Patrick's Street?'

'I don't know the number but it's upstairs.'

Katie covered the phone with her hand and said to Kyna, 'It's Cissy Dorgan. She's calling me on the mobile phone I gave her. She says she's with Davy somewhere on Patrick's Street.'

'I'll tell MacCostagáin and DI Mulliken,' said Kyna. She wiped her eyes, dropped her folder on Katie's desk, and hurried out.

'And call for an RSU unit, too!' Katie called after her. Then, 'Cissy, are you still there, sweetheart?'

'I am, yes.'

'Cissy, can you see out of the window at all?'

'I'll have to be careful. Davy's asleep.'

'Davy's actually there with you now?'

'Yes. So I mustn't wake him up. I kept this phone in my bag so he doesn't know I have it.'

'All right then, sweetheart, be very quiet, but try and tell me what you can see when you look out of the window.'

There was another long pause and some soft scuffling noises and then Cissy said, 'A shop called Mr Big Man.'

Katie knew exactly where that was – at the west end of St Patrick's Street just before it turned south into Grand Parade. As far as she could visualize it, the building on the opposite side of the street was next to Waterstone's bookshop, but empty and up for rental.

'Can you work out which floor you're on?' she asked Cissy.

'I don't know. I can't tell.'

'Look at the shop on the other side of the street. Can you see which floor you're on the same level as?'

'There's Mr Big Man and then there's another floor and then there's another the same as the one I'm on.'

'The second floor, then. Well done, Cissy. Good girl yourself. Listen – we'll be coming round to get you in just a few minutes. Whatever you do, don't say a word to Davy. Which room is he in? The front of the building or the back?'

'He's in the back,' Cissy whispered. 'He's sleeping on his mattress, with—'

'With who, Cissy?' Katie asked her, but Cissy didn't reply. 'Cissy, can you hear me? With who?'

There was only silence from the other end. Cissy's phone had been switched off, either by Cissy or by somebody else. Katie didn't dare to ring her back in case Davy was still asleep and the sound of her phone warbling woke him up.

She unlocked her desk drawer, took out her revolver, and pushed it into her holster. Then she lifted her raincoat off its peg and hurried breathlessly downstairs. Detective Inspector Mulliken was already waiting for her, along with Kyna and Detectives O'Donovan and Ó Doibhilin and Scanlan.

'I've alerted Superintendent Pearse,' said Detective Inspector Mulliken. 'There was already a foot patrol on Patrick's Street and he has them watching out for Dorgan.'

'Tell him he's on the second floor of the building that's to let, right opposite Mr Big Man. They'll need to keep an eye on the back of that building, too. I think there's an alleyway that comes out on to Paul Street.'

'We'll have three patrol cars backing us up, plus the RSU when they get here,' said Detective Inspector Mulliken as they went down in the lift to the car park.

'I don't know for sure if Dorgan is armed,' said Katie. 'On his past record, though, I'm not going to take any chances.'

'If it was him that set off that bomb,' said Detective Inspector Mulliken, 'you'd have thought he would have got himself as far away from Cork as possible, wouldn't you?'

'Hiding in plain sight,' said Katie. 'I've seen it plenty of times before. The last place they think we'd think of looking is under our noses. Do you remember that car thief – what was his name,

Hegarty – that fellow who rented a flat right next door to the Market Tavern across the road and used to walk past our front door every morning on his way to work? It was nearly six months before a sergeant bumped into him one day and recognized him.'

* * *

It was still raining hard when they reached St Patrick's Street and Katie had the pointed hood of her waterproof jacket turned up. She had kept her iPhone in her hand but she hadn't heard from Cissy again. She prayed that Davy hadn't discovered the phone she had given her. She might be his younger sister, but if he was capable of blowing up one of his own gang, who could guess what he might do to her if he thought she had been betraying him?

They parked around the corner in Grand Parade where Dorgan wouldn't be able to see them from his upstairs window. Two patrol cars parked out of sight in St Peter's and Paul's Place and a third parked right at the back of the block on Paul Street, in case Dorgan tried to escape that way.

Just as Katie and Detective Inspector Mulliken were approaching the front of the building she was told by Sergeant Croly that the Regional Support Unit had arrived and they, too, had parked in St Peter's and Paul's Place, with six armed gardaí. They came around the corner by the Bank of Ireland in their black uniforms and protective vests and helmets, two of them carrying sub-machine guns.

Before they forced open the front door, Katie put up her hand and said, 'C'm'ere – there's a young girl of nine years old in there, probably in the front room on the second floor. Take great care that she isn't hurt or distressed. The suspect, Davy Dorgan, may be in one of the back rooms. The last I was told about him he was asleep, possibly with somebody else, but of course he may be awake by now and I expect us breaking in will wake him anyway.'

The ground floor of the building had been a dress shop, so the upper two-thirds of the front door was glass. One of the RSU gardaí used a hand-held windscreen-cutter to remove it completely, which made no more than a purring sound. He lifted the panel right out and all he had to do then was reach inside and open the lock.

The armed gardaí ran quickly and quietly up the stairs to the second floor. It was there that Katie had told them to shout '*Armed gardaí!*' because she didn't want Davy Dorgan to start shooting and then claim afterwards that he had thought the RSU were criminals who were breaking in to rob him.

She drew her own revolver and followed Detectives O'Donovan and Ó Doibhilin upstairs, with Kyna and Detective Scanlan close behind.

Each flight of stairs was narrow and dark and smelled of damp and old linoleum. When she reached the second floor, panting, Katie found that two RSU gardaí had already entered the front room overlooking the street and were standing protectively over Cissy.

Cissy was sitting on a stained velvet cushion, dressed in a thick red overcoat with buttons like white chocolate drops, and Aran socks. Her face was filthy. Her hair had been chopped short and she was wearing a grubby white wool hat. She was tightly clutching the doll that she had christened Bindy.

As soon as she saw Katie she scrambled to her feet and ran over to her and hugged her.

'There, Cissy, I told you we'd come to get you, now didn't I?' said Katie. 'There now, shush, you don't have to cry! What a clever brave girl you were to ring me!'

She heard shouting from the back room and it was the unmistakeable Larne accent of Davy Dorgan.

'It was you, you frigger! It was you! Well, who else could it have been? I wouldn't trust you near a scabby dog, you!'

Katie crouched down and said to Cissy, 'I just have to see what's going on with Davy. Can you stay here with these two guards? They'll take care good care of you, I promise.'

Cissy clung on to her coat but Katie gently prised her hand free and said, 'I won't be long, sweetheart. But I have to make sure that everything's being done according to the rules. It's a bit like being a schoolteacher.'

Cissy reluctantly backed away and one of the RSU officers laid his black-gloved hand gently on her shoulder. At that moment, though, Kyna came up the stairs and into the room.

Katie said, 'Ah! Here, Cissy, this is my friend Kyna. She'll look after you. Kyna – this is Cissy, and this is Bindy.'

Kyna was about to say something to Cissy when they heard Davy Dorgan shouting, 'You know what's going to happen to me now because of you? I'm going to be stuck in the fecking slammer for the rest of my life! How much did they pay you, you shitehawk? Come on, how much did they pay you? Don't tell me they didn't! Otherwise how the feck did they know I was here?'

'It was never me!' screeched another man's voice. 'I swear to God, Davy, it was never me!'

'Lay your guns down on the floor, both of you!' demanded one of the gardaí. 'Lay your guns down and put your hands on top of your heads and back away to the wall!'

Katie left the front room and made her way cautiously along the landing. Three gardaí were standing in the doorway of the back room with their sub-machine guns raised. Because they were so tall and their protective black suits were so bulky Katie found it difficult at first to see what was happening inside the room, but then one of the gardaí went down on one knee and adopted a firing position. It was then that Davy Dorgan came into view, with his hair sticking up wildly, wearing nothing but a brown check shirt. He was holding an automatic pistol in each hand, pointing them stiffly at somebody else inside the room. She couldn't see who it was, but she could see a disembodied hand pointing another automatic pistol at almost point-blank range at Davy Dorgan.

'Fecking Mexican stand-off,' said one of the gardaí next to her. 'We have the two of them covered, but they have each other covered, too, for feck's sake!'

'I said, lay the guns down on the floor!' repeated the garda. 'Neither of you have any way of getting out of here, so you might as well stop behaving like a couple of eejits and come along with us quiet-like.'

For a long time nobody spoke and the only sound was the rustling of the gardaí's nylon jackets against the walls and the sprinkling of rain against the windows. Katie heard a creaking behind her and turned around to see Kyna leading Cissy out of the front room and down the staircase, treading very softly. She blew Cissy a kiss. *'See you after,'* she mouthed silently.

Suddenly, there were two deafening shots, which made her jump, one followed almost instantaneously by the other. Katie saw the top of Davy Dorgan's head flap open like the lid of a tea caddy and blood spray up to the ceiling. At the same time the gardaí opened fire with a short, rattling burst from their sub-machine guns. Katie heard two dull thumps, one after the other.

The back room was full of acrid grey smoke now and the gardaí were pushing their way in through the doorway, so she couldn't immediately see what had happened. She waited a moment on the landing until one of the gardaí beckoned her and said, 'All safe now, ma'am.'

She holstered her revolver and followed him into the back room, with Detectives O'Donovan and Ó Doibhilin close behind her. Detective Ó Doibhilin said, 'Holy shit, ma'am. Sorry – I mean, Christ on a camel.'

Lying sprawled on the floor, glassy-eyed, was Davy Dorgan. Lying with his head on Davy Dorgan's left shin, bony and pale-skinned and wearing nothing but a pair of white Calvin Klein underpants, was a young man with a wispy blond moustache and a wispy blond beard. There was a bullet hole in the right-hand side of his stomach, and another in his chest which must have hit him in the heart. Both men were smothered in blood.

'Tadhg Brennan,' said Katie. 'Nicholas O'Grady's husband. What in the name of God is *he* doing here?'

She was still staring down at his body when one of the RSU gardaí came in and said, 'Come and take a lamp at this, ma'am. I think this answers a whole rake of questions.'

She followed him into another back room that led off the landing. Its window was boarded up and it reeked of gun-oil and petrol and some other chemical smell. Along the wall behind the door there were stacks of amber-coloured C4 demolition packs, possibly a hundred of them. Along the opposite wall, on a long trestle table, at least thirty or forty AK47 assault rifles were arranged in lines, as well as a shoal of silvery automatic pistols with both eight-round and extended magazines.

It was what was lying at an angle right in the middle of the floor that caught Katie's attention the most, though. It was a large, six-engined drone, painted black, so that it looked like a massive spider.

'It's a DJI5900,' said the garda, smug that he knew exactly what it was. 'One of my cousins has the smaller version. He uses it to take photographs of people's houses from the air. This fellow, though – this can fly non-stop for nearly twenty minutes at a time and it can carry up to three kilos.'

'So what are you suggesting?' said Katie – but even as she was asking him she realized the implications of what she was looking at.

'Don't tell me,' she said. '*I* have you! Supposing you wanted to deliver three kilos of explosive to somebody in a building that had sniffer dogs and security guards posted at all of the doors—'

Detective O'Donovan had come in to the room now and was listening to what Katie was saying. 'That's it – rooftop to rooftop,' he added. 'Let's say from the top floor of Tesco's car park to the roof of the Opera House – *after* the Opera House has been searched top to bottom, and *after* everybody in the building has been screened. It would only be a few seconds' flight.'

'You're probably right,' said Katie, looking back towards the room where the two bodies were lying, with gun-smoke still eddying out of the doorway. 'But Dorgan's dead now. We may never know for sure.'

Detective O'Donovan shrugged and said, 'In this life, ma'am, c'mon – when do we ever know *anything* for sure?'

Forty

It was a week before the child psychologist at Tusla said that Katie could come and talk to Cissy – Katie, and only Katie. Cissy was still settling in with her new foster family in Douglas and she was not yet ready to meet any more strangers.

The Austin family lived in a neat four-bedroom detached house on Riverside, a quiet cul-de-sac overlooking the southern bank of the River Lee. Mr and Mrs Austin were both in their early forties and had two teenage girls of their own. Mr Austin was a rewards manager for Munster Insurance and spoke almost endlessly in a bland expressionless monotone. Mrs Austin sat close to him and nodded enthusiastically at everything he said, although she hardly said a word herself.

It was a bright grey morning, even if it was chilly, so Katie and Cissy went across the road to sit by the river and watch the ducks. A woman was walking a red Irish setter along the pathway and Katie felt a sharp pang for Barney. The dog-napper had never rung her back, even though he had promised he would, and she had to assume that she had lost Barney for ever. She could only hope that he had been taken for breeding – he was a pure pedigree after all. She prayed that they hadn't used him for bait for a dog-fight.

'Davy's funeral is on Wednesday,' she said. 'Cemetery Lodge, in Togher.'

Cissy was busy tying ribbons in Bindy's hair. 'I'm not going,' she said.

'Well, of course, you don't have to.'

'After what he did, I don't even want to say his name ever again. *Or* see it, *or* read it. Not even on a gravestone.'

Katie reached into her pocket and took out a paper bag of Oatfield Rosey Apples. She offered one to Cissy and Cissy took one, popping it into her mouth and clicking it around her teeth as she talked.

'You know that I'm going to have to ask you some questions, don't you, Cissy? The same questions I wanted to ask you before, except that you were too frightened of Davy to tell me.'

'Davy's not here any more. Davy's in hell.'

'You really think so?'

'After he killed all those dancers, of course he is. He's roasting and toasting.'

'Cissy – what happened in the attic at Toirneach Damhsa? Did you see Ronan and Saoirse up there?'

The red setter suddenly chased off after the ducks and Cissy pointed and laughed. Then she turned soberly to Katie and said, 'Yes.'

'But what were *you* doing up there?'

'Davy was always going to the dance studio. He used to go to the dance studio almost every day. Sometimes he took me with him because Auntie Abby was out and we'd go to McDonald's afterwards. I used to like it when they were practising because I could sit and watch the dancing. Nicholas promised that he'd teach me to dance, too. I liked Nicholas. Davy used to like Nicholas. He used to talk about Nicholas all the time, but something happened. I think they had an argument. It was something to do with Danny Coffey, but I don't know what. Davy kept on going there, but he and Nicholas were a bit funny with each other.'

'When you say "funny"?'

'I don't know. Sulky. But I think Nicholas was scared of Davy, so he didn't tell him he couldn't come to the studio any more.'

'So why was it that Davy visited the dance studio so often? I mean, what did he do when he was there?'

'He used to go up in the attic with Nicholas, and sometimes Tadhg would go with him, too, but then they had that argument.

He still went there, but after that it was mostly only Tadhg who went up into the attic with him.'

'Is that why you went up there, to find out what they were up to?'

Cissy nodded. Mrs Austin had taken her to have her chopped-off hair cut properly and it was very short now, but feathery at the back of her neck. In her green jacket and green tights she looked like an elf.

'So how did you get up there?' Katie asked her.

'Davy and Tadhg were carrying some boxes up from Davy's car into the attic. There wasn't going to be any dancing practice until later, so I told Davy I was bored and I was going to walk home. I often did that. But this time I waited until they had gone down to the car again and then I sneaked up into the attic and hid in this big wooden chest that was half-filled up with old papers and photographs and stuff.'

'Go on.'

'Davy and Tadhg came up with another box and this time they opened it. There was a gap under the lid of the chest I was in so that I could just see out.'

Cissy rattled what was left of her Rosey Apple in her mouth and licked her lips. Even with Davy and Tadhg dead, she seemed frightened to tell Katie what she had witnessed.

'And what was in the box, Cissy? Come on, you can tell me. Nobody else is ever going to know that you told me.'

'Guns. There was guns in it. You know those guns those guards had when you came to Pana and rescued me? They looked like those.'

'So Davy and Tadhg were using the attic to store guns?'

Again, Cissy nodded. But then she took out what was left of her boiled sweet, as if she couldn't eat a sweet and say what she was going to say next both at the same time.

When she did speak, she spoke in a very flat expressionless tone, almost like her foster father Mr Austin talking about rewards programmes.

'Davy picked up one of the guns and he pulled Tadhg by his shirt collar so that he was close up to him and pointed the gun at his head and said, "Kiss me." '

'And did Tadhg kiss him?'

'Yes.'

'Just a little kiss or a proper kiss? I'm sorry to have to ask you this, Cissy, but it's very important. Lots of young dancers have died and we have to know why.'

'A proper kiss. Like girls do with boys.'

'Then what happened?'

'Davy – Davy took down his trousers. He took down his trousers and he stuck his mickey out and pointed the gun at Tadhg and said, "Suck me." '

'I see. Was Tadhg scared, do you think?'

Cissy shook her head. She wasn't looking at Katie – she was looking across the river and Katie guessed that she was picturing in her mind what she had seen in the attic that day.

'Tadhg was laughing. They were both laughing. It was like they were playing a game.'

'And did Tadhg—?'

'Yes. And Davy kept saying harder! harder! or I'll blow your brains out!'

'How long did this go on for?'

'A long time. But then Ronan and Saoirse came up into the attic and saw them doing it.'

'So what did they say?'

'They just stared like—' and here Cissy widened her eyes and let her mouth drop open.

'And then what?'

'They started to turn around to go back downstairs, but Davy pointed the gun at them and shouted at them not to move and stay where they were. They put up their hands, but Ronan said that Davy shouldn't worry, they wouldn't be after telling anybody what they saw.'

'What did Davy say?'

'Davy said they'd better not because he'd make their life hell if they did. Ronan promised they wouldn't, and so did Saoirse. But then Nicholas was calling from downstairs and saying that he had to leave and would Davy come and move his car so that he could get out.'

'Go on,' Katie coaxed her. 'You're doing fantastic so far, Cissy. I'm pure proud of you, I can tell you.'

Cissy was clutching Bindy very tight now and stroking her hair over and over.

'Davy told Tadhg to open one of the boxes and take out a gun, and to open another box and take out some bullets and to load it.'

'What sort of a gun was it?'

'A little one.'

'You mean a pistol?'

'That's right. Davy wouldn't give him one of the big ones because he said he didn't know how to use it. He said to point it at Ronan and Saoirse and don't let them leave the attic until he got back from moving his car.'

'So Tadhg loaded the pistol and kept Ronan and Saoirse covered?'

'Yes. And Davy went downstairs. When he was gone, Ronan tried to tell Tadhg that they wouldn't say a word to Nicholas about catching him with Davy, but Tadhg started throwing a rabie. He said he didn't believe them for a moment and that his marriage to Nicholas was ruined now. He was talking real strange and babbly like one of those cartoons. Ronan said balm out will you, you're going to hurt one of us in a minute. He went up to him to take the gun away from him and it was then that Tadhg shot him. I nearly almost screamed but I bit my sleeve so I didn't.'

Cissy stopped for a moment. She was panting and needed to catch her breath. Then, before Katie could ask her to carry on, she said, 'Saoirse – she was crying "No! no! no!" and she ran over and knelt down beside Ronan. Tadhg pointed the gun right at her head and shot her, too.'

'What did Tadhg do then?'

'He just stood there and waited for Davy to come back up. When Davy saw that Tadhg had shot them, Ronan and Saoirse, he didn't go mad at all. He took the gun away from him, the pistol, but all he said was, "We need to get all of this stuff out of here now, before Nicholas gets back." He hardly even looked at the two of them lying there dead.'

'So they carried all the boxes of guns downstairs?'

'And some other boxes, too. I don't know what was in them. Then, when all the boxes were gone, Davy came back up on his own and he was fiddling around with something for ages although I couldn't see what he was doing. When he was gone, though, I could smell a funny smell.'

'Didn't you try to leave the attic, though, Cissy, once Davy and Tadhg had gone?'

'I was scared they were still downstairs. If they'd seen me coming down from the attic they would have known that I'd seen them. So I stayed there and waited. I heard the practice music starting, and the dancing, and then I heard some screaming, and then it was like the whole attic went *wooooff*—!' She flung her hands up to describe the TPA exploding.

Katie took hold of both of her hands and smiled at her.

'You've been wonderful, Cissy. You were the only person who saw what happened, but now you've told me all about it, I know for certain who killed Ronan and Saoirse and all of those poor dancers. I've recorded what you've said, so you won't have to say it all again, ever. I know it's going to stick in your mind for a long, long time to come, but try to think that it was only a very bad dream.'

The two of them sat by side, watching the ducks quarrelling close to the water's edge. After a while a soft fine rain began to fall and they stood up and walked back across to Cissy's new home, leaving the ghost of Adeen sitting by the river.

* * *

Katie went home at dusk and picked up Conor from the Gabriel guest house on the way. The soft rain was still falling, so that the landscape looked blurred.

Conor laid his hand on her thigh as she drove and said, 'You're quiet.'

'Yes. Sorry. It's not you. I'll tell you all about it when we get in. I've had a heap of stuff to take in today and I'm still kind of churning it over.'

'Oh well, there's nothing like a good churn, that's what I always say.'

She slapped his hand and said, 'Will you ever be serious, you?'

'I'm always serious. It's the rest of the world that's mad.'

Not long after they reached home, and Katie was looking into the fridge to see what they could eat for supper, her iPhone played 'Fear a' Bháta'.

'DS Maguire,' she said, taking out two thick gammon slices.

'It's me again, Detective Super-duper Maguire.'

'You told me you were going to ring a week ago.'

'I did, didn't I? But I changed my mind like, do you know what I mean? I thought, she's either going to drop the charges against the Guzz, or she's not. I'll leave it up to her, that's what I thought.'

'How's Barney?'

'Well, that's exactly my point, Detective Super-duper. If you wasn't prepared to drop the charges against the Guzz without any delay like, I thought, why should I hang about and give her more time to track me down?'

'So how is Barney? You haven't hurt him, have you?'

'Your Barney's a scrapper, I'll give him that.'

'Mother of God, if you've hurt him—'

'You're not going to drop the charges against the Guzz, are you, Detective Super-duper?'

Katie said nothing for a long time, but eventually she whispered, 'No. I'm not.'

'That's what I thought and so I acted according like. But don't worry. Your Barney will be returned to you before you can say, "Life's a bitch and then you die." '

He hung up and Katie was left standing in the middle of the kitchen holding her iPhone, feeling as if her whole world had suddenly come to a stop. In the corner of the kitchen was Barney's basket, and his blanket, and his bowl.

Conor came in and saw at once how stricken she was. He put his arms around her and said, 'It's Barney, isn't it? You've heard about Barney?'

She nodded, trying not to cry.

* * *

About twenty minutes later they heard a car pulling up outside the house with a scrunch of tyres. Katie stood up, but before she could go to the window to see who it was, it had driven away.

She went to the front door and opened it but Conor laid his hands on her shoulders and held her back.

'I'll go,' he told her.

He went out into the street and she could see him bending down. When he came back he was carrying Barney in his arms – Barney, with his red coat matted with mud and blood and thistles, his eyes half-closed and his tongue hanging out.

Katie turned away, biting her lip. She didn't want to remember him like this. She wanted to remember him running by the sea, with his ears flying, leaping in and out of the surf as if he was the happiest dog that had ever lived.